PENGUIN BOOKS

# THE LUCK OF THE BODKINS

P. G. Wodehouse was born in Guildford in 1881 and educated at Dulwich College. After working for the Hong Kong and Shanghai Bank for two years, he left to earn his living as a journalist and storywriter, writing the 'By the Way' column in the old *Globe*. He also contributed a series of school stories to a magazine for boys, the *Captain*, in one of which Psmith made his first appearance. Going to America before the First World War, he sold a serial to the *Saturday Evening Post*, and for the next twenty-five years almost all his books appeared first in this magazine. He was part author and writer of the lyrics of eighteen musical comedies including *Kissing Time*. He married in 1914 and in 1955 took American citizenship. He wrote over ninety books, and his work has won world-wide acclaim, having been translated into many languages. *The Times* hailed him as a 'comic genius recognized in his lifetime as a classic and an old master of farce'.

P. G. Wodehouse said, 'I believe there are two ways of writing novels. One is mine, making a sort of musical comedy without music and ignoring real life altogether; the other is going right deep down into life and not caring a damn . . .' He was created a Knight of the British Empire in the New Year's Honours List in 1975. In a BBC interview he said that he had no ambition left now that he had been knighted and there was a waxwork of him in Madame Tussaud's. He died on St Valentine's Day in 1975 at the age of ninety-three.

P. G. Wodehouse

# The Luck
# of the Bodkins

Penguin Books

PENGUIN BOOKS

Published by the Penguin Group
Penguin Books Ltd, 27 Wrights Lane, London W8 5TZ, England
Penguin Books USA Inc., 375 Hudson Street, New York, New York 10014, USA
Penguin Books Australia Ltd, Ringwood, Victoria, Australia
Penguin Books Canada Ltd, 10 Alcorn Avenue, Toronto, Ontario, Canada M4V 3B2
Penguin Books (NZ) Ltd, 182–190 Wairau Road, Auckland 10, New Zealand

Penguin Books Ltd, Registered Offices: Harmondsworth, Middlesex, England

First published 1935
Published in Penguin Books in 1954
Published in Penguin Books in the United States of America
by arrangement with Scott Meredith Literary Agency, Inc.
20 19 18 17 16

Printed in England by Clays Ltd, St Ives plc
Set in Times Roman

# Chapter 1

Into the face of the young man who sat on the terrace of the Hotel Magnifique at Cannes there had crept a look of furtive shame, the shifty, hangdog look which announces that an Englishman is about to talk French. One of the things which Gertrude Butterwick had impressed upon Monty Bodkin when he left for this holiday on the Riviera was that he must be sure to practise his French, and Gertrude's word was law. So now, though he knew that it was going to make his nose tickle, he said:

'Er, garçon.'

'M'sieur?'

'Er, garçon, esker-vous avez un spot de l'encre et une pièce de papier – note-papier, vous savez – et une enveloppe et une plume?'

'Ben, m'sieur.'

The strain was too great. Monty relapsed into his native tongue.

'I want to write a letter,' he said. And having, like all lovers, rather a tendency to share his romance with the world, he would probably have added 'to the sweetest girl on earth', had not the waiter already bounded off like a retriever, to return a few moments later with the fixings.

'V'là, sir! Zere you are, sir,' said the waiter. He was engaged to a girl in Paris who had told him that when on the Riviera he must be sure to practise his English. 'Eenk – pin – pipper – enveloppe – and a liddle bit of bloddin-pipper.'

'Oh, merci,' said Monty, well pleased at this efficiency. 'Thanks. Right ho.'

'Right ho, m'sieur,' said the waiter.

Left alone, Monty lost no time in spreading paper on the table, taking up the pen and dipping it in the ink. So far, so good. But now, as so often happened when he started to write to the girl he loved, there occurred a stage wait. He paused, wondering how to begin.

It always irked him, this unreadiness of his as a correspondent. He worshipped Gertrude Butterwick as no man had ever worshipped woman before. Closeted with her, his arm about her waist, her head nestling on his shoulder, he could speak of his love eloquently and well. But he always had the most extraordinary difficulty in starting getting the stuff down on paper. He envied fellows like Gertrude's cousin, Ambrose Tennyson. Ambrose was a novelist, and a letter like this would have been pie to him. Ambrose Tennyson would probably have covered his eight sheets and be licking the envelope now.

However, one thing was certain. Absolutely and without fail he must get something off by today's post. Apart from picture postcards, the last occasion on which he had written to Gertrude had been a full week before, when he had sent her that snapshot of himself in bathing costume on the Eden Rock. And girls, he knew, take these things to heart.

Chewing the pen and looking about him for inspiration, he decided to edge into the thing with a description of the scenery.

> 'Hotel Magnifique,
> 'Cannes,
> 'France, A.M.

'*My Darling Old Egg,*
'I'm writing this on the terrace outside the hotel.
It's a lovely day. The sea is blue –'

He stopped, perceiving that he had missed a trick. He tore up the paper and began again:

> 'Hotel Magnifique,
> 'Cannes,
> 'France, A.M.

'*My Precious Dream-Rabbit,*
'I'm writing this on the terrace outside the hotel. It's a lovely day, and how I wish you were with me, because I miss you all the time, and it's perfectly foul to think that when I get back you will have popped off to America and I shan't see you for ages. I'm dashed if I know how I shall stick it out.

6

'This terrace looks out on the esplanade. The Croisette they call it – I don't know why. Silly, but there it is. The sea is blue. The sand is yellow. One or two yachts are mucking about. There are a couple of islands over to the left, and over to the right some mountains.'

He stopped once more. This, he felt, was about as much as the scenery was good for in the way of entertainment value. Carry on in the same vein, and he might just as well send her the local guide-book. What was required now was a splash of human interest. That gossipy stuff that girls like. He looked about him again, and again received inspiration.

A fat man, accompanied by a slim girl, had just come out on to the terrace. He knew this fat man by sight and reputation, and he was a personality well worth a paragraph in anybody's letter. Ivor Llewellyn, President of the Superba-Llewellyn Motion Picture Corporation of Hollywood.

He resumed:

'There aren't many people about at this time of day, as most of the lads play tennis in the morning or go off to Antibes to bathe. On the skyline, however, has just appeared a bird you may have heard of – Ivor Llewellyn, the motion picture bloke.

'At least, if you haven't heard of him, you've seen lots of his pictures. That thing we went to see my last day in London was one of his, the thing called – well, I forget what it was called, but there were gangsters in it and Lotus Blossom was the girl who loved the young reporter.

'He's parked himself at a table not far away, and is talking to a female.'

Monty paused again. Re-reading what he had written, he found himself wondering if it was the goods, after all. Gossipy stuff was all very well, but was it quite wise to dig up the dead past like this? That mention of Lotus Blossom . . . on the occasion referred to, he recalled, his open admiration of Miss Blossom had caused Gertrude to look a trifle squiggle-eyed, and it had taken two cups of tea and a plate of fancy cakes at the Ritz to pull her round.

With a slight sigh, he wrote the thing again, keeping in the scenery but omitting the human interest. It then struck him that it would be a graceful act, and one likely to be much appreciated, if he featured her father for a moment. He did not like her father, considering him, indeed, a pig-headed old bohunkus, but there are times when it is polite to sink one's personal prejudices.

'As I sit here in this lovely sunshine, I find myself brooding a good deal on your dear old father. How is he? (Tell him I asked, will you?) I hope he has been having no more trouble with his –'

Monty sat back with a thoughtful frown. He had struck a snag. He wished now that he had left her dear old father alone. For the ailment from which Mr Butterwick suffered was that painful and annoying malady sciatica, and he hadn't the foggiest how to spell it.

## II

If Monty Bodkin had been, like his loved one's cousin Ambrose Tennyson, an artist in words, he would probably have supplemented his bald statement that Mr Ivor Llewellyn was talking to a female with the adjective 'earnestly', or even some such sentence as 'I should imagine upon matters of rather urgent importance, for the dullest eye could discern that the man is deeply moved.'

Nor, in writing thus, would he have erred. The motion picture magnate was, indeed, agitated in the extreme. As he sat there in conference with his wife's sister Mabel, his brow was furrowed, his eyes bulged, and each of his three chins seemed to compete with the others in activity of movement. As for his hands, so briskly did they weave and circle that he looked like a plump Boy Scout signalling items of interest to some colleague across the way.

Mr Llewellyn had never liked his wife's sister Mabel – he thought, though he would have been the first to admit it was a near thing, that he disliked her more than his wife's brother George – but never had she seemed so repulsive to him as now. He could not have gazed at her with a keener distaste if she had been a foreign star putting her terms up.

'What!' he cried.

There had been no premonition to soften the shock. When

8

on the previous day that telegram had come from Grayce, his wife, who was in Paris, informing him that her sister Mabel would be arriving in Cannes on the Blue Train this morning, he had been annoyed, it is true, and had grunted once or twice to show it, but he had had no sense of impending doom. After registering a sturdy resolve that he was darned if he would meet her at the station, he had virtually dismissed the matter from his mind. So unimportant did his wife's sister Mabel's movements seem to him.

Even when she had met him in the lobby of the hotel just now and had asked him to give her five minutes in some quiet spot on a matter of importance he had had no apprehensions, supposing merely that she was about to try to borrow money and that he was about to say he wouldn't give her any.

It was only when she hurled her bombshell, carelessly powdering her (to most people, though not to her brother-in-law) attractive nose the while, that the wretched man became conscious of his position.

'Listen, Ikey,' said Mabel Spence, for all the world as if she were talking about the weather or discussing the blue sea and yellow sand which had excited Monty Bodkin's admiration, 'we've got a job for you. Grayce has bought a peach of a pearl necklace in Paris, and she wants you, when you sail for home next week, to take it along and smuggle it through the Customs.'

'What!'

'You heard.'

Ivor Llewellyn's lower jaw moved slowly downward, as if seeking refuge in his chins. His eyebrows rose. The eyes beneath them widened and seemed to creep forward from their sockets. As President of the Superba-Llewellyn Motion Picture Corporation, he had many a talented and emotional artist on his pay-roll, but not one of them could have registered horror with such unmistakable precision.

'What, me?'

'Yes, you.'

'What, smuggle necklaces through the New York Customs?'

'Yes.'

It was at this point that Ivor Llewellyn had begun to behave like a Boy Scout. Nor can we fairly blame him. To each man is given his special fear. Some quail before income-tax assessors, others before traffic policemen. Ivor Llewellyn had always had a perfect horror of Customs inspectors. He shrank from the gaze of their fishy eyes. He quivered when they chewed gum at him. When they jerked silent thumbs at his cabin trunk he opened it as if there were a body inside.

'I won't do it! She's crazy.'

'Why?'

'Of course she's crazy. Doesn't Grayce know that every time an American woman buys jewellery in Paris the bandit who sells it to her notifies the Customs people back home so that they're waiting for her with their hatchets when she lands?'

'That's why she wants you to take it. They won't be looking out for you.'

'Pshaw! Of course they'll be looking out for me. So I'm to get caught smuggling, am I? I'm to go to jail, am I?'

Mabel Spence replaced her powder-puff.

'You won't go to jail. Not,' she said in the quietly offensive manner which had so often made Mr Llewellyn wish to hit her with a brick, 'for smuggling Grayce's necklace, that is. It's all going to be perfectly simple.'

'Oh, yeah?'

'Sure. Everything's arranged. Grayce has written to George. He will meet you on the dock.'

'That,' said Mr Llewellyn, 'will be great. That will just make my day.'

'As you come off the gang-plank, he will slap you on the back.'

Mr Llewellyn started.

'George will?'

'Yes.'

'Your brother George?'

'Yes.'

'He will if he wants a good poke in the nose,' said Mr Llewellyn.

Mabel Spence resumed her remarks, still with that rather trying resemblance in her manner to a nurse endeavouring to reason with a half-witted child.

10

'Don't be so silly, Ikey. Listen. When I bring the necklace on board at Cherbourg, I am going to sew it in your hat. When you go ashore at New York, that is the hat you will be wearing. When George slaps you on the back, it will fall off. George will stoop to pick it up, and his hat will fall off. Then he will give you his hat and take yours and walk off the dock. There's no risk at all.'

Many men's eyes would have sparkled brightly at the ingenuity of the scheme which this girl had outlined, but Ivor Llewellyn was a man whose eyes, even under the most favourable conditions, did not sparkle readily. They had been dull and glassy before she spoke, and they were dull and glassy now. If any expression did come into them, it was one of incredulous amazement.

'You mean to say you're planning to let your brother George get his hooks on a necklace that's worth – how much is it worth?'

'About fifty thousand dollars.'

'And George is to be let walk off the dock with a fifty thousand dollar necklace in his hat? George?' said Mr Llewellyn, as if wondering if he could have caught the name correctly. 'Why, I wouldn't trust your brother George alone with a kid's money-box.'

Mabel Spence had no illusions about her flesh and blood. She saw his point. A perfectly sound point. But she remained calm.

'George won't steal Grayce's necklace.'

'Why not?'

'He knows Grayce.'

Mr Llewellyn was compelled to recognize the force of her argument. His wife in her professional days had been one of the best-known panther-women on the silent screen. Nobody who had seen her in her famous rôle of Mimi, the female Apache in *When Paris Sleeps*, or who in private life had watched her dismissing a cook could pretend for an instant that she was a good person to steal pearl necklaces from.

'Grayce would skin him.'

A keen ear might have heard a wistful sigh proceed from Mr Llewellyn's lips. The idea of someone skinning his brother-in-law George touched a responsive chord in him. He had felt like that ever since his wife had compelled him to put the other on the Superba-Llewellyn pay-roll at a thousand dollars a week as a production expert.

'I guess you're right,' he said. 'But I don't like it. I don't like it, I tell you, darn it. It's too risky. How do you know something won't go wrong? These Customs people have their spies everywhere, and I'll probably find, when I step ashore with that necklace –'

He did not complete the sentence. He had got thus far when there was an apologetic cough from behind him, and a voice spoke:

'I say, excuse me, but do you happen to know how to spell "sciatica"?'


## III

It was not immediately that Monty Bodkin had decided to apply to Mr Llewellyn for aid in solving the problem that was vexing him. Possibly this was due to a nice social sense which made him shrink from forcing himself upon a stranger, possibly to the fact that some instinct told him that when you ask a motion-picture magnate to start spelling things you catch him on his weak spot. Be that as it may, he had first consulted his friend the waiter, and the waiter had proved a broken reed. Beginning by affecting not to believe that there was such a word, he had suddenly uttered a cry, struck his forehead and exclaimed:

'Ah! La sciatique!'

He had then gone on to make the following perfectly asinine speech:

'Comme ca, m'sieur. Like zis, boy. Wit' a ess, wit' a say, wit' a ee, wit' a arr, wit' a tay, wit' a ee, wit' a ku, wit' a uh, wit' a ay. V'là! Sciatique.'

Upon which, Monty, who was in no mood for this sort of thing, had very properly motioned him away with a gesture and gone off to get a second opinion.

His reception, on presenting his little difficulty to this new audience, occasioned him a certain surprise. It would not be

12

too much to say that he was taken aback. He had never been introduced to Mr Llewellyn, and he was aware that many people object to being addressed by strangers, but he could not help feeling a little astonished at the stare of horrified loathing with which the other greeted him as he turned. He had not seen anything like it since the day, years ago, when his Uncle Percy, who collected old china, had come into the drawing-room and found him balancing a Ming vase on his chin.

The female, fortunately, appeared calmer. Monty liked her looks. A small, neat brunette, with nice grey eyes.

'What,' she inquired, 'would that be, once again?'

'I want to spell "sciatica".'

'Well, go on,' said Mabel Spence indulgently.

'But I don't know how to.'

'I see. Well, unless the New Deal has changed it, it ought to be s-c-i-a-t-i-c-a.'

'Do you mind if I write that down?'

'I'd prefer it.'

'. . . -t-i-c-a. Right. Thanks,' said Monty warmly. 'Thanks awfully. I thought as much. That ass of a waiter was pulling my leg. All that rot about "with a ess, with a tay, with a arr", I mean to say. Even I knew there wasn't an "r" in it. Thanks. Thanks frightfully.'

'Not at all. Any other words you are interested in? I could do you "parallelogram" or "metempsychosis", if you wished, and Ikey here is a wizard at anything under two syllables. No? Just as you say.'

She watched him with a kindly eye as he crossed the terrace, then, turning to her brother-in-law, became aware that he was apparently in the throes of an emotional crisis. His eyes were bulging more than ever, and he had produced a handkerchief and was mopping his face with it.

'Something the matter?' she asked.

It was not immediately that Mr Llewellyn found speech. When he did, the speech he found was crisp and to the point.

'Listen!' he said hoarsely. 'It's off!'

'What's off?'

'That necklace. I'm not going to touch it.'

'Oh, Ikey, for goodness' sake!'

'That's all right, "Oh, Ikey, for goodness' sake." That guy heard what we were saying.'

'I don't think so.'

'I do.'

'Well, what of it?'

Mr Llewellyn snorted, but in an undertone, as if the shadow of Monty still brooded over him. He was much shaken.

'What of it? You forgotten what I told you about these Customs people having their spies everywhere? That bird's one of them.'

'Oh, be yourself.'

'That's a lot of use, saying "Be myself".'

'I admit it's an awful thing to ask you to be.'

'Think you're smart, don't you?' said Mr Llewellyn, piqued.

'I know I'm smart.'

'Not smart enough to understand the first thing about the way these Customs people work. A hotel like this is just the place where they would plant a spy.'

'Why?'

'Why? Because they know there would be certain to be some damn-fool woman coming along sooner or later shouting out at the top of her voice about smuggling necklaces.'

'You were the one who was shouting.'

'I was not.'

'Oh, well, let it go. What does it matter? That fellow wasn't a Customs spy.'

'I tell you he was.'

'He didn't look like one.'

'So you're so dumb you think a spy looks like a spy, are you? Why, darn it, the first thing he does is to see that he doesn't look like a spy. He sits up nights, studying. If that guy wasn't a spy, what was he doing listening in on us? Why was he there?'

'He wanted to know how to spell "sciatica".'

'Pshaw!'

'Must you say "Pshaw"?'

'Why wouldn't I say "Pshaw"?' demanded Mr Llewellyn, with an obvious sense of grievance. 'What on earth would a man – at twelve o'clock on a summer morning in the South of France – want to spell "sciatica" for? He saw we had seen him, and he had to say the first thing he could think of. Well, this lets me out. If Grayce imagines after this that I'm going to so much as look at that necklace of hers, she's got another guess coming. I wouldn't handle the thing for a million.'

He leaned back in his chair, breathing heavily. His sister-in-law eyed him with disfavour. Mabel Spence was by profession an osteopath with a large clientele among the stars of Beverly Hills, and this made her something of a purist in the matter of physical fitness.

'The trouble with you, Ikey,' she said, 'is that you're out of condition. You eat too much, and that makes you weigh too much, and that makes you nervous. I'd like to give you a treatment right now.'

Mr Llewellyn came out of his trance.

'You touch me!' he said warningly. 'That time I was weak enough to let Grayce talk me into letting you get your hands on me, you near broke my neck. Never you mind what I eat or what I don't eat ...'

'There isn't much you don't eat.'

'... Never you mind whether I want a treatment or whether I don't want a treatment. You listen to what I say. And that is that I'm out of this sequence altogether. I don't put a finger on that necklace.'

Mabel rose. There seemed to her little use in continuing the discussion.

'Well,' she said, 'use your own judgement. It's got nothing to do with me, one way or the other. Grayce told me to tell you, and I've told you. It's up to you. You know best how you stand with her. All I say is that I shall be joining the boat at Cherbourg with the thing, and Grayce is all in favour of your easing it through. The way she feels is that it would be sinful wasting money paying it over to the United States Government, because they've more than is good for them already and would only spend it. Still, please yourself.'

She moved away, and Ivor Llewellyn, with a pensive frown, for her words had contained much food for thought, put a cigar in his mouth and began to chew it.

Monty, meanwhile, ignorant of the storm which his innocent request had caused, was proceeding with his letter. He had got now to the part where he was telling Gertrude how much he loved her, and the stuff was beginning to flow a bit. So intent, indeed, had he become that the voice of the waiter at his elbow made him jump and spray ink.

He turned, annoyed.

'Well? Que est-il maintenant? Que voulez-vous?'

It was no idle desire for conversation that had brought the waiter to his side. He was holding a blue envelope.

'Ah,' said Monty, understanding. 'Une telegramme pour moi, eh? Tout droit. Donnez le ici.'

To open a French telegram is always a matter of some little time. It is stuck together in unexpected places. During the moments while his fingers were occupied, Monty chatted pleasantly to his companion about the weather, featuring *le soleil* and the beauty of *le ciel*. Gertrude, he felt, would have wished this. And so carefree was his manner while giving out his views on these phenomena that it came as all the more of a shock to the waiter when that awful cry sprang from his lips.

It was a cry of agony and amazement, the stricken yowl of a man who has been pierced to the heart. It caused the waiter to leap a foot. It made Mr Llewellyn bite his cigar in half. A drinker in the distant bar spilled his Martini.

And well might Montague Bodkin cry out in such a manner. For this telegram, this brief telegram, this curt, cold, casual telegram which had descended upon him out of a blue sky was from the girl he loved.

In fewer words than one would have believed possible and without giving any explanation whatsoever, Gertrude Butterwick had broken their engagement.

# Chapter 2

On a pleasant, sunny morning, about a week after the events
which the historian has just related, a saunterer through Waterloo Station in the city of London, would have noticed a certain
bustle and activity in progress on platform number eleven. The
boat train for the liner *Atlantic*, sailing from Southampton at
noon, was due to leave shortly after nine; and, the hour being
now eight-fifty, the platform was crowded with intending
voyagers and those who had come to see them off.

Ivor Llewellyn was there, talking to the reporters about
Ideals and the Future of the Screen. The members of the All
England Ladies' Hockey Team were there, saying good-bye
to friends and relations before embarking on their tour of the
United States. Ambrose Tennyson, the novelist, was there,
asking the bookstall clerk if he had anything by Ambrose
Tennyson. Porters were wheeling trucks; small boys with refreshment baskets were trying to persuade passengers that what
they needed at nine o'clock in the morning was a slab of milk
chocolate and a bath bun; a dog with a collecting-box attached
to its back was going the rounds in the hope of making a quick
touch in aid of the Railwaymen's Orphanage before it was too
late. The scene, in short, presented a gay and animated appearance.

In this, it differed substantially from the young man with
the dark circles under his eyes who was propping himself up
against a penny-in-the-slot machine. An undertaker, passing
at that moment, would have looked at this young man sharply,
scenting business. So would a buzzard. It would have seemed
incredible to them that life still animated that limp frame. The
Drones Club had given Reggie Tennyson a farewell party on
the previous night, and the effects still lingered.

That the vital spark, however, was not quite extinct was

proved an instant later. A clear, hearty feminine voice suddenly said: 'Why, hello, Reggie!' about eighteen inches from
his left ear, and a sharp spasm shook him from head to foot,
as if he had been struck by some blunt instrument. Opening
his eyes, which he had closed in order not to be obliged to
see Mr Llewellyn – who, even when you were at the peak of
your form, was no Taj Mahal – he gradually brought into
focus a fine, upstanding girl in heather-mixture tweed and
recognized in her his cousin, Gertrude Butterwick. Her charming face was rose-flushed, her hazel eyes shining. She was a
delightful picture of radiant health. It made him feel sick to
look at her.

'Well, Reggie, I do call this nice of you.'

'Eh?'

'Coming to see me off.'

A wounded, injured expression came into Reggie Tennyson's ashen face. He felt that his sanity had been impugned.
And not without reason. Few young men would care to have
it supposed that they had got up at half-past seven in the morning to say good-bye to their cousins.

'See you off?'

'Didn't you come to see me off?'

'Of course I didn't come to see you off. I didn't know you
were going anywhere. Where are you going, anyway?'

It was Gertrude's turn to look injured.

'Didn't you know I had been chosen for the England Hockey
Team? We're playing a series of matches in America.'

'Good God!' said Reggie, wincing. He was aware, of course,
that his cousin was addicted to these excesses, but it was not
pleasant to have to hear about them.

A sudden illumination came to Gertrude.

'Why, how silly of me. You're sailing, too, aren't you?'

'Well, would I be up at a ghastly hour like this, if I wasn't?'

'Of course, yes. The family are sending you off to Canada,
to work in an office. I remember hearing father talking about
it.'

'He,' said Reggie coldly, 'was the spearhead of the movement.'

'Well, it's about time. Work is what you want.'

18

'Work is not what I want. I hate the thought of it.'

'You needn't be so cross.'

'Yes, I need,' said Reggie. 'Crosser, if I could manage it. Work is what I want, forsooth! Of all the silly, drivelling, fat-headed remarks . . .'

'Don't be so rude.'

Reggie passed a careworn hand across his forehead.

'Sorry,' he said, for the Tennysons did not war upon women, 'I apologize. The fact is, I'm not quite myself this morning. I have rather a severe headache. I expect you've suffered in the same way yourself after a big binge. I overdid it last night in the society of a few club cronies, and this morning, as I say, I have rather a severe headache. It starts somewhere down at the ankles and gets worse all the way up. I say, have you noticed a rummy thing? I mean, how a really bad headache affects the eyes?'

'Yours look like boiled oysters.'

'It isn't how they look. It's what I see with them. I've been having – well, I wouldn't attempt to pronounce the word at a moment like this, but I dare say you know what I mean. Begins with "hal".'

'Hallucinations?'

'That's right. Seeing chaps who aren't there.'

'Don't drool, Reggie.'

'I'm not drooling. Just now I opened my eyes – why, one cannot say – and I saw my brother Ambrose. There was no possibility of error. I saw him plainly. Shook me a bit, I don't mind confessing. You don't thin' it's a sign that one of us is going to die, do you? If so, I hope it'll be Ambrose.'

Gertrude laughed. She had a nice, musical laugh. The fact that it sent Reggie tottering back against his penny-in-the-slot machine cannot be regarded as evidence to the contrary. A fly clearing its throat would have had a powerful effect on Reginald Tennyson this morning.

'You are a chump,' she said. 'Ambrose is here.'

'You aren't going to tell me,' said Reggie, stunned, 'that he's come to see me off?'

'Of course not. He's sailing himself.'

'*Sailing?*'

Gertrude regarded him with surprise.

'Of course. Haven't you heard?'

'Heard what?'

'Ambrose is off to Hollywood.'

'What!'

'Yes.'

It hurt Reggie to stare, but he did so.

'To Hollywood?'

'Yes.'

'But what about his job at the Admiralty?'

'He's given it up.'

'Given up his job – his nice, soft, cushy job bringing in a steady so much per and a pension at the end of the term of sentence – to go to Hollywood? Well, I'm –'

Words failed Reggie. He could but gurgle. The monstrous unfairness of it all robbed him of speech. For years now, the family, so prone to view him with concern, had been pointing at Ambrose with pride. To Ambrose and himself had been specifically allotted the rôles of the Good Brother and the Bad Brother – the Diligent Apprentice, so to speak, and the Idle Apprentice. 'If only you could be sensible and steady like Ambrose!' had been the family slogan. If he'd heard them say that once, he had heard them say it a hundred times. 'Sensible and steady, like Ambrose.' And all the while the man had been saving this up for them!

Then there came to him a more brotherly and creditable emotion – that of compassion for this poor ass who was heading straight for the soup. Speech returned to him like a tidal wave.

'He's cuckoo! The man's absolutely cuckoo. He hasn't a notion what he's letting himself in for. I know all about Hollywood. I saw a lot at one time of a girl who's in the pictures, and she told me what things were like there. The outsider hasn't a dog's chance. The place is simply congested with people trying to break in. Authors especially. They starve in their thousands. They're dying off like flies all the time. This girl said that if you make a noise like a mutton chop anywhere within a radius of ten miles of Hollywood Boulevard, authors come bounding out of every nook and cranny, howling like wolves.

My gosh, that poor boob has dished himself properly. Is it too late for him to ring up the Admiralty blokes and tell them that he was only kidding when he sent in that resignation?'

'But Ambrose isn't going there on the chance of finding work. He's got a contract.'

'What!'

'Certainly. You see that fat man standing over there, talking to the reporters. That's Mr Llewellyn, one of the big picture men. He's paying Ambrose fifteen hundred dollars a week to write scenarios for him.'

Reggie blinked.

'I must have fallen into a light doze,' he said. 'I dreamed,' he went on, smiling a little at the quaint conceit, 'that you told me somebody had offered Ambrose fifteen hundred dollars a week to write scenarios.'

'Yes, Mr Llewellyn did.'

'It's true?'

'Certainly. I believe the contract actually has to be signed in New York, but it's all settled.'

'Well, I'm dashed.'

A thoughtful look came into Reggie's face.

'Has he touched the stuff yet?'

'Not yet.'

'No advance payment? Nothing in the shape of a few hundred quid which he might feel like blueing at the moment?'

'No.'

'I see,' said Reggie, 'I see. And when does the balloon actually go up? When does he expect to connect?'

'Not till he gets to California, I suppose.'

'By which time I shall be in Canada. I see,' said Reggie, 'I see.'

He relapsed for a moment into gloom. But only for a moment. There was fine stuff in Reginald Tennyson. He was a man who could rejoice in the good fortune of others, even though he himself might not be in on the distribution. It may be, also, that the thought had crossed his mind that there is a good postal service between Canada and California and that much of his best work had been done with pen in hand.

'Well, this is wonderful,' he said. 'Good old Ambrose! I'll

tell you what I'll do. I'll give him a letter of introduction to that girl I was speaking of. She'll see that he has a pleasant ...'

His voice trailed away. He seemed to swallow with some difficulty. He was staring at something over his cousin's shoulder.

'Gertrude,' he said in a dry whisper.

'What's the matter?'

'I was right about those hal – what you said. That may have been Ambrose in the flesh all right that first time, but I've got them now beyond a doubt.'

'What do you mean?'

Reggie blinked three or four times in rapid succession. Then, convinced, he bent towards her and lowered his voice still further.

'I've just seen the astral body of a pal of mine who, I know for a fact, is at this moment in the South of France. A fellow named Monty Bodkin.'

'What!'

'Don't look now,' said Reggie, 'but the spectre is standing right behind you.'

A voice spoke.

'Gertrude!'

So hollow was this voice – so pale, so wan, so croaking – that it might well have proceeded from a disembodied spirit. It caused Gertrude Butterwick to turn sharply. Having turned, she subjected the speaker to a long, cold, hard stare. Then, not deigning to reply, she jerked a haughty shoulder and turned away again, her eyes stony, her chin tilted; and the wraith, having stood for a moment on one leg, smiling in a weak and propitiatory manner, seemed to recognize defeat. It slunk away and was lost in the crowd.

Reggie Tennyson had watched this drama with protruding eyes. He saw now that he had been mistaken in his hastily formed diagnosis. This was no unsubstantial creature of the imagination but his old friend Montague Bodkin in person. And Gertrude Butterwick had just given him the raspberry as completely as he, Reggie, in a fairly wide experience of raspberry-giving, had ever seen it administered. He could make nothing of all this. He was puzzled, perplexed, mystified, bewildered and at a loss, and gave expression to these emotions with a plaintive 'I say!'

Gertrude was breathing tensely.

'Well?'

'I say, what's all this?'

'What's all what?'

'That *was* Monty.'

'Yes.'

'He spoke to you.'

'I heard him.'

'But you didn't speak to him.'

'No.'

'Why not?'

'I have no wish to speak to Mr Bodkin.'

'Why not?'

'Oh, Reggie!'

Another facet of this many-sided mystery presented itself to the wondering young man. How the dickens, he was asking himself, did Gertrude and old Monty come to be in this position of giving and receiving the raspberry on station platforms? He had not supposed that they had so much as met one another.

'Do you know Monty, then?'

'I do.'

'I didn't know you did.'

'Well, I do. If it interests you, we used to be engaged.'

'Engaged?'

'Yes.'

'Engaged? I never heard about it.'

'Father would not allow it to be announced.'

'Why not?'

'He didn't wish it.'

'Why not?'

'Oh, Reggie!'

Reggie was gradually assembling his facts.

'Well, well! So you and Monty used to be engaged, eh?'

'Yes.'

'But you aren't engaged any longer?'

'No.'

'Why not?'

'Never mind.'

'Don't you like old Monty?'

'No.'

'Why not?'

'Oh, Reggie!'

'Everybody else likes him.'

'Indeed?'

'Certainly. He's a most sterling bloke.'

'I don't agree with you.'

'Why not?'

'Oh, Reggie, for goodness' sake!'

It seemed to Reginald Tennyson that the time had come to speak the word in season. His heart was bleeding for Monty Bodkin. Any ass could have spotted from his demeanour during the recent scene that the poor blighter was all churned up by what had occurred, and all this funny business, felt Reggie, had gone far enough. A pretty state of things, he meant to say, if girls were to be allowed to go about the place getting it up their noses and coming over all haughty towards excellent coves like Monty.

'It's no use saying "Oh, Reggie, for goodness' sake!"' he rejoined sternly. 'You can say "Oh, Reggie, for goodness' sake!" till you burst your corsets, but you won't get away from the fact that you are a foolish young pipsqueak and are making the floater of a lifetime. You girls are all alike. You go swanking round, giving the bird to honest men and thinking nobody's good enough for you, and in the end you get left flat on your – in the end you get left. One of these days you will wake up in the cold grey dawn kicking yourself because you were such a chump as to let Monty get away from you. What's the matter with Monty? Good-looking, amiable, kind to animals, wealthy to bursting point – you couldn't have a better bet. And, in the friendliest spirit, may I inquire who the dickens you think you are? Greta Garbo, or somebody? Don't you be a goat, young Gertrude. You take my advice and run after him and give him a nice big kiss and tell him you're sorry that you were such a mug and that it's all on again.'

An all-England centre-forward can be very terrible when

24

roused, and the levin flash in Gertrude Butterwick's handsome eyes seemed to suggest that Reginald Tennyson was about to be snubbed with a ferocity which in his enfeebled state could not but have the worst effects. That hard stare was back on her face. She looked at him as if he were a referee who had just penalized her for sticks in the game of the season.

Fortunately, before she could give utterance to her thoughts bells began to ring and whistles to blow, and the panic fear of being left behind by a departing train sank the hockey player in the woman. With a shrill and purely feminine squeak, Gertrude bounded off.

Reggie's pace, as became an invalid, was slower. So much slower that the train had already begun to move when he reached it, and he had only just time to leap in. When he had at length succeeded in reassembling his jolted faculties, he discovered that he was alone in a compartment with the one man he most desired to see – Monty Bodkin, to wit. The poor old buster was sitting hunched up in the opposite corner, looking licked to a custard.

Reggie could have wished for nothing better. In all London there was no young man more heartily devoted than he to pushing his nose into other people's business, and this opportunity of getting first-hand information about the other's shattered romance delighted him. His head was giving him considerable pain, and he had been hoping to employ the journey in catching up with his sleep a bit, but curiosity came before sleep.

'Ha!' he exclaimed. 'Monty, by Jove! Well met, i' faith!'

# Chapter 3

'Good Lord!' said Monty. 'What are you doing here, Reggie?'

Reggie Tennyson waved the question aside. In ordinary circumstances it was a keen pleasure to him to talk about himself, but he had no desire to do so now.

'I'm off to Canada,' he said. 'Never mind about that for the nonce. A full explanation will be supplied later. Monty, old boy, what's all this about you and my cousin Gertrude?'

Monty Bodkin's first reaction to the spectacle of Reggie Tennyson invading his privacy like a sack of coals, after the initial astonishment of seeing him there at all, had been a regret that he had not had the presence of mind to nip the whole thing in the bud by pushing him in the face and sending him out again. He had earmarked the next hour and a half for silent communion with his tortured soul, and did not relish the prospect of having to talk to even an old friend.

But at these words a powerful revulsion of feeling swept over him. His whole attention during the episode on the platform having been concentrated upon the girl he loved, he had not recognized the vague figure standing beyond her. Reason now told him that this must have been Reggie, and what he had just said suggested that Gertrude had been confiding in him. Reginald Tennyson had turned, in short, from an unwelcome intruder to a man who could give him inside information straight from the horse's mouth. He was too far in the depths to beam, but his drawn face relaxed and he offered his companion a gasper.

'Did she,' he asked eagerly, 'tell you about it?'

'Rather.'

'What did she say?'

'She said you had been engaged and it had been broken off.'

'Yes, but did she tell you why?'

'No. Why was it?'

'I don't know.'

'You don't know?'

'I haven't a notion.'

'But, dash it, if you had a row, you must know what it was about.'

'We didn't have a row.'

'You must have had.'

'We didn't, I tell you. The whole thing is inexplicable.'

'Is what?'

'Rummy.'

'Oh, rummy? Yes.'

'Shall I place the facts before you?'

'Do.'

'I will. You will find them,' said Monty, 'inexplicable.'

There was silence for a moment. Monty seemed to be wrestling with his soul. He clenched his fists, and his ears wiggled.

'The odd thing is,' said Reggie, 'that I didn't know you had ever met Gertrude.'

'I had,' said Monty. 'Otherwise, how could we have got engaged?'

'Something,' Reggie was forced to admit, 'in that. But why was it all kept so dark? Why is this the first I have heard of any bally engagement? Why wasn't the thing shoved in the *Morning Post* and generally blazoned over the metropolis like any other engagement?'

'That was because there were wheels within wheels.'

'How do you mean?'

'I will come to that. Let me begin at the beginning.'

'Skipping early childhood, of course?' said Reggie, a little anxiously. In his present delicate state of health, something a bit on the condensed side was what he was hoping for.

A dreamy look came into Monty Bodkin's eyes – dreamy and at the same time anguished. He was living once more in the dear, dead past, and a sorrow's crown of sorrow is remembering happier things.

'The first time I met Gertrude,' he began, 'was at a picnic on the river, down Streatley way. We found ourselves sitting next

27

to one another and from the very inception of our acquaintance we were, in the best and deepest sense of the words, like ham and eggs. I squashed a wasp for her, and from that moment never looked back. I sent her flowers a bit and called a bit and we lunched a bit and went out dancing a bit, and about two weeks later we became engaged. At least, sort of.'

'Sort of?'

'This is what I meant when I said there were wheels within wheels. It was her father who wouldn't let it be an ordinary straightforward engagement. Do you know her blasted father, by any chance – J. G. Butterwick, of Butterwick, Price & Mandelbaum, Export and Import Merchants? But of course you do,' said Monty, with a weary smile at the absurdity of the question. 'He's your uncle.'

Reggie nodded.

'He is my uncle. No good trying to hush that up at this time of day. But when you say know him – well, we don't mingle much. He doesn't approve of me.'

'He didn't approve of me, either.'

'And do you know what he's gone and done now, the old wart-hog? You asked me what I was doing on this train, and I told you I was on my way to Canada. You will scarcely credit this, but he has talked the family into shipping me off to Montreal to a foul office job. But don't let me get started talking about my own troubles,' said Reggie, realizing that he was interrupting a narrative of poignant interest. 'I want to hear all about you and Gertrude. You were saying that my blood-stained uncle John did not approve of you.'

'Exactly. He didn't actually call me a waster –'

'He did me. Frequently.'

'But his manner was sticky. He said that before giving his consent to the match he would like to know how I earned my living. I told him I didn't earn my living because a recent aunt had left me three hundred thousand quid in gilt-edged securities.'

'You had him there.'

'I thought so, too. But no. He simply looked puff-faced and said that he would never allow his daughter to marry a man who had no earning capacity.'

'I know those words. An earning capacity was what he was always beefing about me not having. He used to say: "Look at your brother Ambrose with his steady position at the Admiralty, and devoting his leisure time to writing novels which, while I have not read them myself ..." I say, talking of Ambrose, the most amazing thing has happened.'

'Shall I go on?' said Monty, a little coldly.

'Oh. rather,' said Reggie. 'Yes, do. Only I must tell you about Ambrose later. You'll be astounded.'

Monty was looking out at the flying landscape with a frown on his agreeable face. Thinking of J. G. Butterwick always made him frown. In his heart, he had always hoped that the other's sciatica would not yield to treatment.

'Where,' he asked, coming out of his dark thoughts, 'had I got to?'

'The earning capacity gag.'

'Ah, yes. He said he would never allow Gertrude to marry a man without an earning capacity, so all bets were off unless I proved myself, as he called it, by getting a job and holding it down for a year.'

'Barmy. I've often thought so. But surely Gertrude didn't stand for rot like that?'

'She did. Naturally my first step was to urge her to pack a suitcase and slide round the corner with me to the registrar's or Gretna Green or somewhere. But would she? No. Not a trace of the modern spirit did she exhibit. Said she loved me devotedly, but flatly refused to marry me until the aged parent had hoisted the All Right flag.'

'You don't mean that!'

'I do.'

'I didn't know there were girls like that nowadays.'

'Nor did I.'

'Sounds like something out of a three-volume novel.'

'Quite.'

Reggie pondered.

'It's an unpleasant thing to say about anyone,' he said, 'but the fact of the matter is, Gertrude's the soul of honour. I believe it comes from playing hockey. What did you do?'

'I got a job.'

'You?'

'Yes.'

'You couldn't have done.'

'I did. I worked it through my Uncle Gregory, who knew Lord Tilbury, who runs the Mammoth Publishing Company. He wangled me the assistant editorship of *Tiny Tots*, a journal for the Nursery and the Home. I got fired.'

'Of course. And then –?'

'Uncle Gregory got Lord Emsworth to take me on as his secretary at Blandings Castle. I got fired.'

'Naturally. And then –?'

'Well, then I took matters into my own hands. I ran into a fellow named Pilbeam, who owns a Private Inquiry Agency, and finding that he employed skilled assistants got him to make me one.'

Reggie stared..

'Private Inquiry Agency? Do you mean one of those detective things?'

'That's right.'

'You aren't telling me you're a ruddy sleuth?'

'That's right.'

'What, Maharajah's rubies and measuring bloodstains and all that sort of thing?'

'Well, as a matter of fact,' said Monty, becoming more specific, 'they don't give me a great deal to do. I'm simply down on the books as a skilled assistant. You see, what happened was that I told Pilbeam I would give him a thousand quid if he would take me on, and we did business on those lines.'

'But my uncle John doesn't know that?'

'No.'

'All he knows is that you have got a job and are holding it down?'

'Yes.'

Reggie was mystified.

'Well, if you ask me, it seems to me that that sounds extraordinarily like the happy ending. Whether a chap is, or is not, a mug to cough up a thousand pounds simply in order to marry my cousin Gertrude is a point into which we need not go. The price appears stiffish to me, but no doubt you look at it from another angle. What went wrong?'

Monty's twisted face betrayed the tortured soul.

'I don't know! That's what has got in amongst me so frightfully. I simply haven't a notion. I went off to Cannes for a bit of a holiday, feeling that everything was splendid and that I was sitting pretty. Nobody could have been matier than Gertrude when I left. She was all over me. And then one morning a telegram comes from her, breaking the engagement and giving no reasons.'

'No reasons?'

'Not one. Nothing. Simply the raspberry. It was inexplicable, I was stunned.'

'Naturally.'

'I came back at once by aeroplane, and called at her house. She wouldn't see me. I rang her up on the telephone, and drew nothing but a butler with adenoids. So, knowing that she was going to America with this hockey push, I thought the only thing to do was to go, too, and have it out with her on the voyage. There's evidently been some footling misunderstanding.'

'Could she have heard something about you?'

'There's nothing to hear.'

'You didn't by any chance, while at Cannes, whoop it up with those mysterious foreign adventuresses who haunt those parts? And somebody might have told her about it, I mean?'

'There weren't any foreign adventuresses. At least, I didn't see any. My life at Cannes was as blameless as dammit. I just bathed and played tennis most of the time.'

Reggie reflected. The thing did, as Monty had said, seem to have a touch of the inexplicable.

'Do you know what I think?' he said at length.

'What?'

'It looks to me as if she had just got fed up with you.'

'Eh?'

'Thought it all over, I mean, and decided that you aren't the type. Girls do, you know. They take just that one look too many at the photograph on the dressing-table and the scales fall from their eyes.'

'Oh, my gosh!'

'In which case, of course, pretty drastic measures are called for. The subject has to be given a good sharp jolt.'

'How do you mean, a jolt?'

'Oh, there are various ways. However, don't you worry. I'll handle this business for you. It's pretty obvious that that is what must have happened. She's gone off you. You've lost your glamour. But there's no need for you to get worked up about it. Everything will come right.'

'Do you really think so?'

'Definitely. I understand Gertrude. I've known her since she was so high. I'll tackle her. As a matter of fact, I was starting to just before the train went, and I think I had got her going. Once we're on board, I will go to her and give her the works.'

'It's awfully good of you.'

'Not at all. There isn't much,' said Reggie, regarding his friend with sincere, if bleary-eyed, affection, 'that I wouldn't do for an old pal like you, Monty.'

'Thanks, thanks.'

'And I don't imagine that you would hold back if you had a chance of doing me a good turn.'

'I should say not.'

'You would spring to the task.'

'Like a panther.'

'Exactly. Well leave everything to me. I'll have that glamour of yours functioning again before you know where you are. And now,' said Reggie, 'if you don't mind, I think I'll just close my eyes for a while. I was in bed this morning at five-fifty and it's left me a little drowsy. A spot of sleep may do my headache good.'

'Have you got a headache?'

'My dear chap,' said Reggie, 'last night the Drones gave me a farewell party with Catsmeat Potter-Pirbright in the chair. Need I say more?'

# Chapter 4

On a fine summer day, with the sun shining and the wavelets
sparkling and a clean, cool breeze blowing out of the west, there
are few things pleasanter than to travel from Southampton to
Cherbourg in an ocean liner. Always provided, that is to say,
that you have not got somebody like Monty Bodkin on
board.

If Monty Bodkin had resembled a spectre at Waterloo Station, still more did he resemble one during the few hours which
it took the R.M.S. *Atlantic* to pull out of Southampton Water
and cross the Channel. During those hours he shimmered un-
ceasingly, causing annoyance to all.

Patrons of the smoking-room choked over their beer as he
shimmered in through the doorway, gazed about him with haggard eyes, shimmered out again and then – sometimes only a
few minutes later – shimmered back and stood gazing once
more. Old ladies, knitting in the drawing-room, sensed his silent
approach and dropped stitches. Girls in deck-chairs started as
his shadow fell upon their books and, looking up, recoiled from
the stare of his snail-like eyes. There seemed to be no getting
away from him.

For Monty was looking for Gertrude Butterwick, and it was
his intention to explore every avenue. Only when the vessel
lay motionless outside Cherbourg harbour did he abate the
nuisance. By that time, his shoes had begun to hurt him, and
he went to his state-room to lie down on the bunk. This, he felt,
would enable him not only to take the weight off his feet but to
do some constructive thinking. And if ever a situation called
for constructive thinking, this did.

His feelings on opening the door and finding the bunk occupied by Reggie Tennyson were mixed. There was regret, for
his feet were now exceedingly painful and he wanted that bunk

himself; joy, because he presumed that the other would not be there unless he had come bearing news.

This, however, proved an erroneous theory. Reggie had no news. His eager 'Well?' produced merely the information that his friend had not so much as set eyes on Gertrude since arriving on board.

'I've looked everywhere for her,' said Reggie, anxious to remove any idea that he had been loafing on his errand of mercy, 'but she seems to have gone to earth in some secret dug-out.'

There was a pause. Then, just as Monty was about to suggest that if Reggie could spare the bunk he would be glad to have it, his attention was diverted by the sight of an alien suitcase on the floor.

'What's that?' he asked, surprised.

Reggie sat up. His manner betrayed a certain diffidence.

'Oh, that?' he said. 'I was wondering when you would notice it. That's mine.'

'Yours?'

'Yes. Monty,' said Reggie, speaking with some urgency, 'do you recollect what we were saying in the train?'

'About Gertrude?'

'Not about Gertrude. About you and me. About what extraordinarily good pals we had always been, so that if there ever happened to be a moment when one of us could do the square thing by the other he wouldn't hesitate. You said, if you remember, that if you had a chance of doing me a good turn you would spring to the task?'

'Of course.'

'Like a panther, if I recall?'

'Absolutely.'

'Right,' said Reggie. 'Well, now is your time. This is where you do your stuff. I've changed state-rooms with you.'

Monty stared. His intelligence was a little clouded from long meditation.

'Changed state-rooms?'

'Yes. I've had your things shifted down to mine.'

'What on earth for?'

'It had to be done, old boy. The fact of the matter is, a rather awkward situation has arisen.'

Reggie made himself comfortable amongst the pillows. Monty took off his shoes. The relief thus obtained put him in broad-minded mood. Twiddling his released toes, he told himself that Reggie would not have done this thing without some good reason. It remained only to elicit this reason.

'How do you mean, an awkward situation has arisen?'

'I will tell you. Before doing so, however, let us relax. Have you such a thing as a stinker?'

'Here you are.'

'And a match?'

'Here you are.'

'Thanks,' said Reggie. 'Well,' he proceeded, puffing, 'it is like this. You know Ambrose?'

'Your brother Ambrose?'

'My brother Ambrose.'

'Oh, yes, fairly well. We were up at Oxford together, and we see a certain amount of one another . . .'

'Did you know he was on board this ship?'

'Ambrose? But he's at the Admiralty.'

'No. He's not. That's the whole point. I was trying to tell you in the train, but you wouldn't listen. At this hour, as you say, Ambrose ought to be at the Admiralty, initialling memoranda in triplicate or dancing hornpipes, or whatever it is they do there, but in actual fact he is roaming the deck of this ocean-going ship in a pin-stripe flannel suit and a yachting cap. He has chucked the Admiralty and is going to Hollywood to write motion-picture scenarios.'

'You don't mean that?'

'And, what is more – this is the part that will test your credulity to the utmost – on a five years' contract at fifteen hundred dollars a week.'

'What!'

'I thought you would be surprised. Yes, that is what a bloke called Ivor Llewellyn is paying him – fifteen hundred dollars a week. Have you ever read any of Ambrose's bilge?'

'No.'

'Well, it's absolute drip. Not a corpse or a mysterious Chinaman in it from beginning to end. And this fellow Llewellyn is paying him fifteen hundred dollars a week! I tell you, Monty, it's – what's that word of yours?'

'Inexplicable?'

'That's the one. It's definitely inexplicable.'

No man in Reggie Tennyson's condition, already shaken from saying 'initialling memoranda in triplicate', can utter the words 'definitely inexplicable' without Nature taking its toll. A sharp twinge of pain contorted his face, and he lay for a moment with his hands pressed to his temples, trying to pull himself together.

'But what, you are about to ask,' he resumed, when the spasm had ceased, 'has the fact of Ambrose being on board got to do with my wanting to change state-rooms? I will tell you. I remember in the train, when you were talking about your engagement and why it had been kept dark, you used an extra-ordinarily neat phrase. You said – what was it? Ah, yes. You said that there were wheels within wheels. Wasn't that the expression?'

'That's right,' said Monty, who thought it good himself. 'Yes. Wheels within wheels.'

'Well, there are wheels within wheels here. As I said just now, a very awkward situation has arisen. Did I ever happen to mention to you a girl of the name of Lotus Blossom?'

'The film star?'

'The film star.'

'I've seen her on the screen, of course, but I don't remember you ever mentioning her.'

'Odd,' said Reggie. 'I suppose I must be one of these strong, silent chaps. Because we were once very close together. In fact, I don't mind telling you that I asked her to marry me.'

'Really?'

'Yes. One night when we were dining together at the Angry Cheese. I've never seen a girl laugh so much. It was shortly after that she put a piece of ice down my back. I mention these things,' explained Reggie, 'to show you that we were terrific pals. We went around everywhere together. This was when she was over in London a year ago, doing a picture for one of the English companies. Well, that's Reel One. You get the idea? Lottie and I were terrific pals.'

'Yes, I get that.'

'Right. We now come to Reel Two. I was up on deck just now, and someone suddenly caught me a ghastly slosh on the back, bringing me to within a short step of the tomb, and when the mists and blackness and whirling sparks had cleared away I found myself gazing upon my brother Ambrose. We fell into conversation, and, of course, I congratulated him on this Hollywood thing and then, out of sheer goodness of heart, I offered to give him a letter of introduction to Lottie Blossom. I knew she knew everybody in Hollywood and could get him invited to all the parties and what not, so I said I would give him a letter of introduction to her. Pretty brotherly, what?'

'Most.'

'So I thought, especially considering he'd just nearly knocked my spine through my waistcoat. But it was a bloomer of the worst description, old boy, and I'll tell you why. Noticing on his map, as I said these words, a broad smile and fancying it was one of those sceptical, I-bet-if-you-ever-met-the-girl-at-all-it-was-simply-in-a-crowd-and-she's-forgotten-your-very-name-by-now smiles – you know the sort of smiles chaps do smile when you tell them you know anybody celebrated – I rather extended myself on the subject of how thick Lottie and I had been. Looking back, I can see that I must have made the thing sound like something out of the home life of Antony and Cleopatra. "Dear old Lottie!" I remember saying. "What a pal! What a nib! You must meet dear old Lottie! She'll do anything for a brother of mine. How we two did use to whoop it up together, to be sure!" You know how one does.'

'Quite.'

'Old boy,' said Reggie solemnly, 'he's engaged to her!'

'What!'

'Absolutely. When I said he must meet her, he said he had met her, at Biarritz a couple of months ago, when he went down there on the occasion of the Admiralty blokes pushing him off for his annual vacation. And when I said: "Oh, how did you like her?" he replied that he liked her very much and that they were engaged to be married and what precisely had I meant by the expression "whoop it up". Dashed embarrassing, you'll admit.'

'Dashed.'

'Nor did the embarrassment in any way diminish with the passage of time,' said Reggie. 'Things grew stickier and stickier. "She comes aboard at Cherbourg," he said. "That," I said, rattled, but holding up as well as I could, "will be jolly." "For whom?" he said. "For you," I said. "Yes," he said. "What did you mean by 'whoop it up'?" "Does she know about this Hollywood job of yours?" I said. "She does," he said. "I'll bet she's pleased," I said. "No doubt," he said. "You have not yet explained what you meant by the expression 'whoop it up'." "Oh, nothing," I said. "Just that we were pretty pally at one time." "Oh?" he said. "Ah!" And there the matter rested. You see the situation? You get the general trend? The blighter is in nasty mood. He suspects. He views with concern. And Lottie comes aboard at Cherbourg.'

'We're at Cherbourg now.'

'Exactly. I imagine she is already with us. And we now come, old boy, to the very nub of the thing. Do you know what?'

'What?'

'I happened to take a look at the passenger list, and I'm blowed if I didn't find that her state-room was next door to mine! Well, you know what Ambrose is like. Already fairly near the boil and crammed to the gizzard with low suspicions, what was he going to say when he discovered that?'

'Ah!'

'That's it precisely – Ah! So there was only one thing to do. I had to change state-rooms with you. You follow? You grasp?'

'Yes.'

'And you don't mind?'

'Of course not.'

'I knew it,' said Reggie with emotion. 'I knew I could rely on you. Staunch to the eyebrows. I don't know how Ambrose strikes you, Monty, but from childhood up I have always found him a hard egg. As a boy, he had a habit, when stirred, of suddenly lashing out with a foot and catching me on the seat of the trousers, and from the way he was looking when I removed myself just now I don't believe the years have softened and mellowed him a damn' bit. Your decent behaviour regarding this switch of state-rooms has probably saved me a very nasty flesh wound. And don't think I shall forget it, either. You can rely on me to strain every nerve in re that young chump Gertrude. Be sure that I shall watch over your interests. Do nothing in that direction till you hear from me.'

'I was thinking of going to the library and writing her a letter.'

Reggie weighed this.

'Yes. I see no harm in that. Don't grovel, though.'

'I wasn't going to grovel,' said Monty indignantly. 'If you want to know, I was going to be bally bitter and dashed terse.'

'Such as —?'

'Well, to begin with, I thought of starting off "Gertrude". Like that. Not "Dear Gertrude" or "Darling Gertrude". Just "Gertrude".'

'Yes,' agreed Reggie. 'That'll make her think a bit.'

' "Gertrude," I was planning to write, "Your behaviour is inexplicable." '

'You couldn't do better,' said Reggie cordially. 'Go on up and smack into it now. I, personally, propose to take a short turn on deck. The last time I was there, till Ambrose bashed me between the shoulder-blades, the sea air seemed to be doing my headache good. That sensation of white-hot corkscrews through the eyeballs appeared to me to be easing up a trifle.'

# Chapter 5

While Monty Bodkin was making his way to the library, stern in his determination to write Gertrude Butterwick a letter which would bring the blush of shame to the cheek and the tear of remorse to the eye and, generally speaking, show her what was what, Mr Ivor Llewellyn stood leaning over the rail of the promenade deck, watching the approach of the tender which bore his sister-in-law Mabel.

None of the reporters who had listened at Waterloo Station to his views on the Screen Beautiful had suspected that they were interviewing a soul in torment, but such was the painful truth. Mr Llewellyn was not feeling merry and bright, and it would be giving a totally false impression to the public to say that he was. Even when dilating on the brightness of the Screen's future, he had been thinking how vastly it differed from his own.

For nights now he had tossed restlessly on his pillow, wincing at the thought of what lay before him. Sometimes he would try to foster a hope that Grayce, thinking things over, might have a little sense and decide to abandon her lawless project. Then the reflection that if Grayce showed sense it would be for the first time, sent him into the depths once more. Smugglers have always been pictured as rather dashing, jovial men. Ivor Llewellyn proved himself the exception to the rule.

The tender arrived. Its passengers disembarked. And Mr Llewellyn, detaching Mabel Spence from their ranks, drew her aside to a secluded portion of the deck. She eyed him in his agitation with that placid, amused pity which he so often caused her.

'You do fuss so, Ikey.'

'Fuss!'

'I suppose what's on your mind is that –'

'Sh!' hissed Mr Llewellyn, like a stage bandit.

Mabel Spence jerked an impatient chin.

'Oh, don't behave like a dying duck,' she said, for it was of this rather than of a bandit that her brother-in-law reminded her as he hissed and quivered. 'Everything's all right.'

'All right?' There was a strange, wild note of hope in the motion-picture magnate's voice. 'Haven't you brought it?'

'Of course I've brought it.'

'Doesn't Grayce want me to –?'

'Of course she does.'

'Then what,' demanded Mr Llewellyn, with pardonable heat, 'do you mean by saying it's all right?'

'All I meant was that it's going to be perfectly simple and easy. I wouldn't worry.'

'You wouldn't – no,' said Mr Llewellyn.

He removed his hat, and passed a handkerchief across his forehead.

'George –'

'Yes, I know,' said Mr Llewellyn, 'I know.'

In the faint hope that there might be some merit in that George scheme which had hitherto escaped him, he ran over it again in his mind. It brought him no comfort whatsoever.

'Listen,' he said. An urgent, tear-compelling note had now succeeded the note of hope in his voice. It was the same one he was wont to employ when trying to persuade the personnel of the studio to take a cut owing to the depression. 'Say, listen. Is Grayce so dead set on this thing?'

'She seems so.'

'You think she would be disappointed if I ...' He broke off, Walls have ears. '... If I didn't?' he concluded.

Mabel reflected. She was rather exact in the matter of speech. She liked the *mot juste*. 'Disappointed' in this case, did not seem to her to be it.

'Disappointed?' she said musingly. 'Well, you know what Grayce is like. When she wants a thing done, she wants it done. If you renig on this ... well, ask me, I think she'd get a divorce on the ground of inhuman mental cruelty.'

Mr Llewellyn shuddered. That word 'divorce' had always been a spectre, haunting him. His attitude towards his young and lovely wife ever since their marriage had been consistently that of a man hanging by his finger-tips to the edge of a precipice.

'But listen . . .'

'Where's the sense in telling me to listen? I'm not Grayce. If you want to get a line on how she feels, she gave me a letter to give you. It's in my bag. Here it is. She wrote it just after I got back to Paris and told her about what you said. About how you weren't going to touch the proposition. She said, "Oh, he won't, won't he?" – you know that way of Grayce's when she draws back her upper lip so that the teeth show, and sort of sinks her voice to a whisper –'

'Don't!' begged Mr Llewellyn. 'Yes, I know it.'

'Well that's how she acted when she sat down to write this letter. She said she was going to put the whole scheme in simple language so that you couldn't possibly go wrong on that hat trick, and after that she would use up the rest of the ink-well explaining what would happen if you didn't come through. It's all down there. You'd best read it.'

Mr Llewellyn took the bulky envelope from her and opened it. As he perused its contents by the light of the library window, his lower jaw drifted slowly from its moorings, so that by the time he had finished his second chin had become wedged into the one beneath it. It was plain that no calmer thoughts had intervened to cause his wife to soften the tenor of her remarks. She had written precisely as she had said she would write.

'Yes,' he murmured at length.

He tore the letter into small fragments and dropped them overboard.

'Yes,' he said again. ''Myes.'

'I guess,' he said, 'I'll go and mull this over.'

'Do. Give it a good think.'

'I will,' said Mr Llewellyn.

Pensively, he made his way to the library. It was empty except for a young man who sat with bowed head in one of the corners, his eyes fixed on a sheet of note-paper. Mr Llewellyn welcomed this solitude. Sitting down, he inserted a cigar in his mouth and gave himself up to thought.

That way of Grayce's . . .

She had drawn back her upper lip so that the teeth showed . . .

Yes, yes, how often he had seen her do that, and how often, seeing her, had he felt that unpleasant sinking feeling which he was experiencing now.

Could he ignore that look?

Gosh!

But the alternative?

Once more, Gosh!

The trouble was that, having other and more immediately urgent matters constantly occupying his mind, he knew so little of the pains and penalties attaching to this smuggling business . . .

At this moment, the purser came in and started to hurry across the room. Just the man Mr Llewellyn wanted.

'Hey,' he called. 'Got a minute?'

Pursers at the beginning of a voyage never really have a minute, but the speaker was a passenger of more than ordinary importance, so this one stopped.

'Something I can do for you, Mr Llewellyn?'

'Just like a word with you, if you're not too busy.'

'Certainly. Nothing wrong, I hope?'

Mr Llewellyn nearly laughed mirthlessly at this. It was as if somebody had asked the same question of a man on the rack.

'No, no. It's just that I'd like your advice about something. Seems to me you'd be the man to know. It's about smuggling stuff through the Customs. Not that I'm planning to do it myself, y'understand. No, sir! I'd be a swell chump to try that game, ha, ha!'

'Ha, ha,' echoed the purser dutifully, for he had been specially notified by the London office to do all that lay in his power to make the other's voyage pleasant.

'No, it simply struck me, mulling things over, that it ought to be one could get a good picture out of this smuggling racket, and I want to have the details right. Listen. What happens to a guy that's caught trying to ease stuff through the New York Customs?'

The purser chuckled.

'The answer to that, Mr Llewellyn, can be given in one word. Plenty!'

'Plenty?'

'Plenty,' said the purser, chuckling again. He had a very rich, jovial chuckle, not unlike the sound of whisky glug-glugging into a glass. It was a sound which Mr Llewellyn, as a rule, liked, but it froze him now with a nameless dread.

There was a pause.

'Well, what?' said Mr Llewellyn at length, in a thin voice.

The purser had become interested. He was a man who enjoyed instructing the ignorant. He forgot that he was busy.

'Well,' he said, 'suppose this fellow in your picture was caught trying to run through something pretty important like a pearl necklace . . . I beg your pardon?'

'Didn't speak,' mumbled Mr Llewellyn.

'I thought you said something.'

'No.'

'Oh? Well, where was I? Oh, yes. This fellow of yours, we'll say, is trying to run a pearl necklace through New York Customs and gets caught. He then finds himself up against a rather stiff situation. Smugglers can be sent to jail, of course, or the authorities may just confiscate the goods and impose a fine of anything up to their full value. Personally, if I may offer a suggestion, I would say, for the purposes of your story, make them confiscate the goods, impose the full fine and send the man to jail as well.'

Mr Llewellyn swallowed rather painfully.

'I'd rather keep it true to life.'

'Oh, that would be quite true to life,' the purser assured him encouragingly. 'It's frequently done. More often than not, I should say. Why I suggest it is that it would give you some prison scenes.'

'I don't like prison scenes,' said Mr Llewellyn.

'Highly effective,' argued the purser.

'I don't care,' said Mr Llewellyn. 'I don't like them.'

The purser seemed a little damped for the moment, but soon recovered his enthusiasm. He had always been much interested in the pictures, and he knew that a man in Mr Llewellyn's position would want to see all round a subject before deciding which angle was the best from which to approach it. Possibly, he felt, Mr Llewellyn, with that *flair* of his in matters of this kind, was not visualizing the thing as drama at all, but more as comedy. He put this to him.

'It's the funny side of it that appeals to you, perhaps? And I expect you're right. We all like a good laugh, don't we? Well,' said the purser, chuckling that fruity chuckle of his at the visions rising before his mental eye, 'there would certainly be lots of comedy in the scene where they searched the fellow. Especially if he was fat. You get some good fat man – the fatter he is the funnier he'll be – and I'll guarantee that at the Southampton Super-Bijou, at least, they laugh so much you'll be able to hear them over in Portsmouth.'

The ghoulish tastes of the patrons of the Super-Bijou Cinema at Southampton did not appear to be shared by Ivor Llewellyn. His face remained cold and stodgy. He said he did not see where that would be funny.

'You don't?'

'Nothing funny about it to me.'

'What, not when they took that fat man's clothes off and gave him an emetic?'

'An emetic?' Mr Llewellyn stared violently. 'Why?'

'To see if he was hiding anything else.'

'Would they do that?'

'Oh, yes. Almost routine.'

Mr Llewellyn gazed at him bleakly. He had disliked many continuity writers in his time, but none so much as he now disliked this purser. The unrestrained relish of the man in these revolting details seemed to him quite sickening.

'I never knew that before.'

'Oh, yes.'

'It's monstrous!' said Mr Llewellyn. 'In a civilized country!'

'Well, people ought not to go in for smuggling,' said the purser virtuously. 'You would think they would have enough sense to know it was hopeless, wouldn't you?'

'Is it hopeless?'

'Oh, quite. They have the most extraordinarily efficient spy system.'

Mr Llewellyn licked his lips.

'I was going to ask you about that. How do these spies of theirs operate?'

'Oh, they're everywhere. They loaf about London and Paris and all over the Continent ...'

'Places like Cannes?'

'Cannes more than anywhere, I should say, except London and Paris. You see, so many Americans nowadays like to take this new Southern route home, on one of the Italian boats. More sunshine, and it's a novelty. I should think you would find a Customs spy at any of the big hotels at Cannes. I know there's one at the Gigantic and another at the Magnifique –'

'The Magnifique!'

'That's the name of one of the hotels at Cannes,' explained the purser. 'I've no doubt each of the others has its man, too. It pays the United States Customs people to keep them there, because sooner or later they're sure to justify the expense. You see, people are so apt to talk injudiciously at foreign hotels, and they get overheard. They don't imagine there's anything wrong with the well-dressed young man who happened to brush against them in the bar while they were discussing how to get the stuff through, and when they meet the same fellow on board it never occurs to them that he's there for a reason. But he is, and they find it out when they land in New York.'

Mr Llewellyn cleared his throat.

'Ever – ever seen him? The Magnifique fellow?'

'Not myself. A friend of mine did. Tall, well-dressed, languid, good-looking young chap, my friend said he was, the last person you would ever suspect ... Good heavens!' said the purser, looking at his watch. 'Is that the time? I shall really have to run along. Well, I hope I have been able to be of some use to you, Mr Llewellyn. I would certainly have a Customs spy in this picture of yours, if I were you. Most picturesque profession, I have always thought. And now you will excuse me, won't you? I have a thousand things to attend to. Always the way till we clear Cherbourg.'

Mr Llewellyn excused him gladly. He had derived no pleasure whatever from his conversation. He fell into a reverie, his teeth grinding at the unlighted cigar that lay between them. And this reverie might have lasted indefinitely, had not something occurred to interrupt it.

A voice spoke behind him.

'I say,' it said, 'excuse me, but do you happen to know how to spell "inexplicable"?'

Mr Llewellyn's physique was such as to make it impossible for him, whatever the provocation, to turn like a flash, but he turned as much like a flash as was in the power of a man whose waistline had disappeared in the year 1912. And having done so he uttered a faint, mouselike squeak and sat goggling.

It was the sinister stranger of the terrace of the Hotel Magnifique at Cannes.

At this moment, the door opened and Gertrude Butterwick walked in.

# Chapter 6

Gertrude Butterwick had spent the early hours of the voyage closeted with Miss Passenger, the captain of the All England Ladies' Hockey Team, trying on hats. That was why Monty, for all his assiduity, had failed to find her. While he had been shimmering about the promenade deck, the boat deck, the drawing-room, the smoking-room, the library, the gymnasium and virtually everywhere else except the engine-rooms and the Captain's cabin, she was in Miss Passenger's state-room on Deck B, trying on, as we say, hats.

Miss Passenger had done herself well in the matter of hats, for it was her intention on this first visit of hers to the United States of North America to give the natives a treat. She had blue hats, pink hats, beige hats, green hats, straw hats, string hats, and felt hats, and Gertrude had tried them on, all of them, one by one. She found that the process helped to dull the pain that gnawed at her heart.

For, little as anybody would have suspected it who had seen her at Waterloo Station, there was a pain gnawing at her heart. Her pride made it impossible, after what had occurred, for her ever to consider the idea of marrying Monty, but that did not mean that she did not think of him with a wild, aching regret. Reggie Tennyson had been quite mistaken in supposing that she no longer found her former fiancé glamorous. His fatal spell still operated.

She was doing her best to shake it off, when the supply of hats gave out. Miss Passenger had stockings, too, but stockings are not quite the same thing. She excused herself, accordingly, and went on deck. And, happening to find herself outside the library, it occurred to her that she had better have a book. There might, she felt, be a wakeful night before her.

The position of affairs by the time she entered was as follows.

Mr Llewellyn and Monty had parted company. The motion-picture magnate remained hunched up in his chair, and Monty had returned to the corner from which he had come. A man in his state of mind is easily discouraged, and the complete failure of his attempt to get Mr Llewellyn to cooperate with him in the spelling of the word 'inexplicable' had caused him to abandon his letter for the time being. When Gertrude came in, he was staring before him, chewing the pen.

Gertrude did not see him. The library of the *Atlantic* is tastefully decorated with potted palms, and one of these interrupted her line of vision. She went to the shelves, found them locked, discovered that the attendant was not at his post, and crossed to the round table in the middle of the room and took up a magazine.

This enabled Monty to catch sight of her, with the result that scarcely had she settled herself in a chair by the window and begun to read when there was a sound of emotional breathing above her head, and, looking up, she beheld a pale, set face. The shock made her hiccough. Her magazine fell to the floor. This was the first intimation she had received that he was not still in London. She had never for a moment supposed that his presence at Waterloo had meant that he was catching the boat train.

'Ha!' said Monty.

Two things prevented Gertrude Butterwick from rising to her feet and sweeping out of the room. One was that the chair in which she sat was so deep that to extricate herself from it she would have had to employ a sort of Swedish exercise quite out of keeping with the solemnity of the moment. The other was that Monty, having said 'Ha!', had begun to gaze at her sternly and accusingly, like King Arthur at Queen Guinevere, and the colossal crust of this held her spellbound. That this man should behave as he had done with one hand and come gazing sternly and accusingly at her with the other made her proud spirit boil.

'At last!' said Monty.

'Go away!' said Gertrude.

'Not,' said Monty, with quiet dignity, 'till I have spoken.'

'I don't want to talk to you.'

Monty laughed like a squeaking slate pencil.

'Don't you worry. I'll do all the bally talking that's required,' he said – the very words, in all probability, with which King Arthur had opened his interview with Guinevere. Much brooding on his wrongs, taken in conjunction with the fact that his feet were still hurting him, had turned Monty Bodkin into something very different from the apologetic bleater who had stood on one leg in this girl's presence at Waterloo. He was cold and pop-eyed and ruthless.

'Gertrude,' he said, 'your behaviour is inexplicable.'

Gertrude gasped. Her eyes flashed amazement and indignation. All the woman in her rose to combat the monstrous charge.

'It isn't!'

'It is.'

'It is not.'

'It is. Quite inexplicable. Let me recapitulate the facts.'

'It's nothing –'

'Let me,' said Monty, waving a hand, 'recapitulate the facts.'

'It's nothing of the –'

'Lord love a duck!' cried Monty, with sharp rebuke. 'Will you or will you not let me recapitulate the facts? How the devil am I to recapitulate the facts if you keep interrupting all the time?'

The stoutest-hearted girl is apt to quail when she finds herself confronted by the authentic cave-man. Gertrude Butterwick did so now. Never, in all the months of their association, had Montague Bodkin spoken to her like that. She had not known that he could speak to her like that. And his words – and more than the words, the tone in which they were uttered – struck her as dumb as any Ivor Llewellyn asked to spell 'sciatica'. She felt as if she had been bitten in the leg by a rabbit.

Monty was shooting his cuffs masterfully. In his eyes there was no lovelight to soften resentment. Only that stern, accusing gleam.

'The facts,' he said, 'are these. We met. We clicked. I squashed a wasp for you at that picnic, and two weeks later you stated in set terms that you loved me. So far, so good. On that basis of understanding I buckled to and prepared to fulfil

50

the loony conditions laid down by your chump of a father as a preliminary to our union. It was a tough assignment, but I faced it without a tremor. That chap in the Old Testament – Jacob, or some such name – had nothing on me. I was willing, even anxious, to sweat myself to the bone to win you, because I loved you and you said you loved me. "Before you marry my daughter," said your blighted father, "get a job and hold it down for a year." So I got a job. I became assistant editor of *Tiny Tots*, a journal for the Nursery and the Home.'

He paused to take in breath, but so glittering was the eye with which he held her that she could not speak. The Games Mistress at school, who had taught her hockey, had had exactly that same hypnotic effect upon her.

His lungs refilled, Monty resumed.

'You know what followed. In writing the weekly letter of Uncle Woggly To His Chicks, I made an unfortunate bloomer, striking a note which met with the disapproval of Lord Tilbury, my boss, who fired me. And what happened then? Was I discouraged? Did I quail? No. Many chaps would have been discouraged to quailing point, but not me. The old Jacob spirit burned as strongly as ever. I spat on my hands and secured a secretarial appointment with Lord Emsworth at Blandings Castle.'

As he allowed his memory to dwell upon the vicissitudes which that visit to Blandings Castle had forced him to undergo, a bitter laugh escaped Monty Bodkin – not like a slate pencil this time, but so hyena-like in its timbre that Ivor Llewellyn, cowering in his chair, leaped and hit himself in the eye with his cigar. There had been, to Mr Llewellyn's mind, something utterly inhuman about that laugh. It was the laugh of a man who, catching somebody with the goods, would have no ruth or pity.

'After some days of incessant nerve strain, old Emsworth bunged me out. But did I give up? Did I throw in the towel? No! I did not throw in the towel. I ingratiated myself with that weird little blister Pilbeam and obtained a post at his Inquiry Agency. That post I still hold.'

He had never mentioned to Gertrude that he had paid Percy Pilbeam a thousand pounds to enrol him among his assistants,

51

and he did not mention it now. Girls are not interested in these technical details. They just like to get the broad idea.

'That post,' he repeated, 'I still hold, in spite of the laborious and uncongenial nature of its duties. I don't say Pilbeam keeps me on the go all the time, but on at least two occasions I have been given assignments which would have caused a weaker man to hand in his portfolio. One was when I had to stand outside a restaurant for two and a half hours in the rain. The other was when I was sent to a wedding reception in Wimbledon to guard the presents. Nobody who has not done it can have any conception what an ass a fellow feels, guarding wedding-presents. Still, I went through with it, I stuck it out. All this, I told myself, is bringing Gertrude nearer to me.'

Once more that hideous laugh rang through the room. It had slightly less of the hyena about it now and rather more of the soul in torment, but it was just as unpleasant for a man with a sensitive conscience to listen to, and Mr Llewellyn again shied like a startled horse.

'My left elbow it was bringing you nearer to me! I had hardly settled down at Cannes for a much needed holiday when bing, right in the eyeball, I get that telegram of yours, returning me to store! Yes,' said Monty, his voice quivering with self-pity, 'there I was, a mental and physical wreck after weeks and weeks of ceaseless toil, suddenly informed that my nomination had been scratched and that I had had all my trouble for nothing.'

Gertrude Butterwick stirred. She seemed about to speak. He waved her down.

'I can only suppose that while my back was turned some other man came along and stole you from me. Unless you have gone completely off your rocker, that, I presume, must be the explanation of your conduct. But let me tell you this. If you think you can play fast and loose with me, you are very much mistaken. Right off it. Nothing like it at all. I jolly well intend to have it out with this human snake who has wriggled his way into your affections, if necessary knocking his bally head off. I shall go to him, and I shall first warn him. Should this fail, I shall ...'

Gertrude found speech. She had shaken off the hypnotic

spell which he had been casting on her. Her face was working and her eyes blazed indignantly, so that Mr Llewellyn, watching her, suffered another moment of discomfort. She reminded him of Grayce, his wife, that time when he had suggested that her brother George might find some more suitable outlet for his talents than the post of Production Expert to the Superba-Llewellyn Corporation.

'You hickaprit!'

This was a new one to Monty.

'Hickaprit?'

'Hypocrite, I mean.'

'Oh, you do, do you?'

He stared at her, outraged.

'What on earth are you talking about?'

'You know what I'm talking about.'

'I don't know what you're talking about.'

'You do know what I'm talking about.'

'I certainly do not know what you're talking about. And it's my firm belief,' said Monty, 'that you don't know yourself. What do you mean – hypocrite? Where do you get that hypocrite stuff? Why hypocrite?'

Gertrude choked.

'Pretending that you loved me!'

'I do.'

'You do not.'

'I tell you I do. Gosh darn it, I ought to know whether I love you or not, oughtn't I?'

'Then who's Sue?'

'Who's Sue?'

'Who's Sue?'

'Who's *Sue*?'

'Yes. Who's Sue? Who's Sue? Who's Sue?'

Monty's manner softened. Something of tenderness came into it. Though she had treated him shamefully and had now begun to talk like a cuckoo clock, he loved this girl.

'Listen, old bird,' he said, and there was a touch of appeal in his voice, 'we could go on like this all night. It's like trying to say "She sells sea-shells by the seashore." What exactly is it that you are gibbering about? Tell me, and we'll get the whole thing straightened out. You keep saying "Who's Sue? Who's Sue?" and I don't know any ...' His voice trailed away. An anxious look had come into his eyes. 'You don't by any chance mean Sue Brown, do you?'

'I don't know what her beastly name is. All I know is that you went off to Cannes pretending to love me, and a week later you had this girl's name tattooed on your chest with a heart round it, and it's no use trying to deny it, because you sent me a photograph of yourself in bathing costume and I had it enlarged and there it was.'

There was a silence. The cave-man Bodkin had ceased to be, and in his place stood the Bodkin of Waterloo Station. Once more Monty was supporting himself on one leg, and that weak and anxious smile was back on his face.

He was blaming himself. It was not as if this was the first time that that heart-encircled 'Sue' had led to trouble. Only a few weeks before, at Blandings Castle, there had been all that difficult explanation to Ronnie Fish on the very same subject. Ronnie had asked awkward questions, and now Gertrude was asking awkward questions. With a good deal of fervour Monty Bodkin was telling himself that if by some miracle he got through this sticky spot successfully, he would obtain washing soda or pumice-stone or vitriol or whatever you used for the eradication of tattoo marks and be done with that 'Sue' for ever. And that went for the heart round it, too.

'Listen,' he said.

'I don't want to listen.'

'But you must listen, dash it. You're quite mistaken.'

'Mistaken!'

'I mean you're all wrong on a very important point. A vitally important point, I may say. You have fallen into the error of supposing that tattoo mark a recent growth. It's not. The matter is susceptible of a ready explanation. I had it done – like an ass – goodness knows why I ever thought of such a damn' silly thing – three years and more ago, before I had ever met you.'

'Oh?'

'Don't say "Oh?"' begged Monty gently. 'At least, say it if you like, of course, but not with that sort of nasty tinkle in the voice, as if you didn't believe a word I was telling you.'

'I don't believe a word you're telling me.'

'But it's true. Three years ago, when scarcely more than an unthinking boy, I was engaged to a girl named Sue Brown, and I suppose it seemed only civil to have her name tattooed on my chest with a heart round it. It hurt like the dickens and cost much more than you would expect. I'd scarcely had it done, when the betrothal conked out on me. After being engaged about a fortnight, we talked it over, decided that the shot wasn't on the board, parted with mutual expressions of esteem, and she went her way and I went mine. The episode was over.'

'Oh?'

'When you say "Oh?" – if you mean what I think you mean – you're quite wrong. I never saw her again, never so much as set my eyes on her, till about a month ago, when we met by pure accident at Blandings Castle . . .'

'Oh!'

'You say "Oh!" this time as if you were under the impression that upon our meeting once more things hotted up between us. Nothing could be farther from the truth. Any fleeting affection I may have felt for Sue Brown had long since gone phut, and the same on her side. I don't say I didn't still think she was a dashed good sort, but the boyish infatuation was no more. Only Love's embers remained. Well, dash it, when I tell you that she was crazy about Ronnie Fish and is now happily married to Ronnie Fish – well, I mean to say!'

'Oh!'

There was nothing in the familiar word this time to arouse the critical spirit in Monty Bodkin. This was not a sceptical 'Oh,' a sneering 'Oh,' one of those acid 'Oh's' which, emitted by the girl he loves, make a man feel as if he has stepped on a tintack. It had relief in it, and kindliness, and remorse. It spoke of misunderstandings cleared away, of grievances forgotten. In fact, it was scarcely an 'Oh' at all, properly speaking. More like an 'Oo!'

'Monty! Is that true?'

'Of course it's true. A line to Mrs R. O. Fish at Blandings Castle, Shropshire, to be forwarded if away, will enable you to check up on the facts and will reveal them to be as I have stated.'

55

The last traces of that frozen look, which is always so unpleasant in the eyes of those we love, had faded from Gertrude Butterwick's gaze. The thaw had set in, and those twin lakes of hazel were moist with unshed tears of self-reproach.

'Oh, Monty! What a fool I've been!'

'No, no.'

'I have. But you see what I was feeling, don't you?'

'Oh, rather.'

'I thought you were the sort of man who goes about making love to every girl he meets. And I simply wasn't going to stand it. You can't blame me, can you, for simply not being going to stand it?'

'Absolutely not. Very proper attitude.'

'I mean, if the man you're engaged to is a mere butterfly, much better to end it all.'

'Quite. A firm hand with the butterflies. The only way.'

'Even if it hurts frightfully.'

'Exactly.'

'And father always said you were that sort of man.'

'He did?' Monty gasped. 'The old son of a – sorry, forget what I was going to say.'

'Of course, I told him you weren't, but, you know, you are so awfully good-looking, Monty darling. I feel sometimes that every girl in the world must be after you. I suppose it's silly of me.'

'Dashed silly. Whatever gave you the idea that I was good-looking?'

'But you are.'

'I'm not.'

'Of course you are.'

'Oh, well, have it your own way,' said Monty, conceding the point. 'Never noticed it myself, I must confess. But, dash it, even if I were the World's Sweetheart, do you imagine I'd so much as glance at any other girl but you?'

'Wouldn't you?'

'Of course I wouldn't. Greta Garbo – Jean Harlow – Mae West – bring 'em on! I'll show them something.'

'Monty! My precious angel pet!'

'Gertrude! My outstanding old egg!'

'No, Monty, you mustn't. Not now. There's a fat man looking.'

Monty turned, and found her statement correct. 'Fat man'
was right, and 'looking' was right. There were few men fatter
than Mr Llewellyn, and few fat men had ever looked at anything more intently than he was now looking at them.

'Blast him!' he said. 'That's Ivor Llewellyn, the motion-picture chap.'

'I know. Jane Passenger sat next to him at lunch.'

Monty frowned discontentedly. He was craving for self-
expression. In this holy moment of reconciliation he yearned
to embrace the girl he loved, and he could not possibly do it
beneath the motion-picture magnate's saucer-eyed stare. The
thing above all others that the holy moment called for was
privacy and privacy in the presence of Ivor Llewellyn was out
of the question. There was only one of Mr Llewellyn, but
somehow he created the illusion of being a large and fashion-
able audience with opera-glasses.

Suddenly Monty brightened. He had seen the way.

'Wait!' he said, and hastened from the room.

'There!' he said, returning a few moments later.

Gertrude Butterwick uttered a squeal of rapture. On the
hockey field as ruthless and coldblooded a fighting machine
as ever whacked an opponent over the shins without a pang,
off it she was purely feminine, with all a woman's love for the
rare and the beautiful. And she had seldom seen anything rarer
or more beautiful than what Monty was holding out to her.

It was one of those objects which, not so common on land,
seem to break out in ships' barber-shops like a rash – a brown
plush Mickey Mouse with pink coral eyes. Monty had selected
it in preference to a yellow teddy bear, a maroon camel, and
a green papier-mâché bulldog whose head waggled when you
shook it. Something seemed to tell him that that was what
Gertrude would prefer.

Nor was he mistaken. She clasped it to her bosom with little
cries of ecstasy and mirth.

'Oh, Monty! For me?'

'Of course, ass. Who did you think it was for? I saw it in
the barber-shop this afternoon and spotted it as a winner right

away. The head screws off. You put chocolates and things in it.'

'Oh, Monty! It – Oh, hullo, Ambrose.'

The novelist had entered the room and was standing in the doorway, gazing about him as if looking for someone. He came over to where they sat.

'Hullo, Gertrude,' he said. His manner seemed distrait. 'Ah, Bodkin, I didn't know you were on board. Have you seen Reggie anywhere?'

'I haven't,' said Gertrude.

'I saw him just now,' said Monty. 'I think he's on deck somewhere.'

'Ah,' said Ambrose.

'Look what Monty's given me, Ambrose.'

The novelist accorded the mouse a cursory glance.

'Capital,' he said. 'Excellent. I'm looking for Reggie.'

'The head screws off.'

'Couldn't be better,' said Ambrose Tennyson absently. 'Excuse me – I must go and find Reggie.'

Gertrude was crooning over the mouse. She had just discovered that by one of those odd coincidences which make life piquant it was extraordinarily like Miss Passenger.

'It might be Jane,' she said. 'I've seen that expression on her face a hundred times when she was giving us a pep talk before a match. I'm going to take it straight down and show it to her.'

'Do,' said Monty. 'I should think she would be frightfully pleased. I, in the meantime, will, I think, step up to the bar and have a quick one. The emotional strain through which I have recently passed has left me sorely in need of refreshment.'

With a loving arm about her shoulders, he escorted Gertrude to the door. Ambrose, about to follow, was halted by a noise like a buffalo taking its foot out of a swamp, and perceived that his employer, Mr Llewellyn, wished to have speech with him. He went over with an inquiring cock of the eyebrow.

'Yes, Mr Llewellyn?'

Ivor Llewellyn was feeling a little better. Into the blackness of his depression and anguish there had shone during the last few minutes a gleam of light. A faint, sickly, anaemic hope was coming to life within him. Surely, he told himself, a spy in the pay of the New York Customs would not be on intimate terms with that nice, wholesome-looking girl. If a spy had a female friend, would she not be something perfumed and slinky, with a foreign accent and probably a dagger in her stocking? And when Ambrose entered and proved to know the fellow too, the hope really began to throw its chest out a bit. Mr Llewellyn had been rather impressed by Ambrose and could not bring himself to believe that he would hob-nob with spies.

'Say,' he said.

'Yes?'

'That young fellow that's just left. You seemed to know him.'

Oh, yes. I've known him some years. His name is Bodkin. We were at Oxford together. Excuse me –'

'You were?' said Mr Llewellyn, on the verge of beginning to wonder what he had been making so much fuss about.

'I was a year or two senior to him –'

'But he's a friend of yours?'

'Oh, yes.'

'I have an idea I ran into him at Cannes.'

'Oh, yes? Excuse me –'

'And I was wondering,' said Mr Llewellyn, 'if you happened to know what he is.'

'What he is?'

'What he does. What's his racket?'

Ambrose Tennyson's face cleared.

'Oh, I see what you mean. It's odd that you should have asked that, because it is certainly the last thing in the world anyone would take him for. But my cousin Gertrude assures me that it is true. He's a detective.'

'A detective!'

'That's right. A detective. Excuse me, won't you? I've got to run along and find my brother Reggie.'

# Chapter 7

For some minutes after his companion had left him Mr
Llewellyn sat where he was, once more congealed. Then a
drove of flappers invaded the library, accompanied by some
of the ship's junior officers, and he heaved himself up and
went out. He wished for solitude.

Ambrose Tennyson's words had struck that growing hope
of his with a bludgeon, so that it lay dead by the wayside. It
did not even quiver.

His emotions, as he dragged himself from the room and
made his way below, were almost exactly similar to those which
he had experienced one morning about a year ago when, his
doctor having recommended mild exercise, he had thrown a
medicine ball at a muscular friend on Malibu Beach, and the
muscular friend, throwing it back before he was ready for it,
had hit him in the solar plexus. On that occasion the world had
rocked about him, and it was rocking now.

He went down to his state-room, more as a wounded animal
seeks its lair than with any definite intention of doing anything
when he got there, and the first thing he saw when he entered
it was his wife's sister Mabel. Her sleeves were rolled up, and
she was bending over a chair in which sat a slender youth of
leaden complexion. She appeared to be giving him an osteo-
pathic treatment.

When a man who has come to a state-room to be alone with
his thoughts finds that his wife's sister, whom he has never
liked, has converted it during his absence into a clinic, his
feelings in the first shock of the discovery are apt to be too
deep for words. Mr Llewellyn's were. He stood gaping, and
Mabel Spence looked at him over her shoulder in the calm and,
as he considered, off-hand way which always annoyed him
so much. There was an English playwright with horn-rimmed

spectacles under contract at the Superba-Llewellyn who looked at him rather like that, and the fact had done much to give Ivor Llewellyn that dislike for English playwrights which was so prominent a feature of his spiritual make-up.

'Hello,' said Mabel. 'Come on in.'

Her patient hospitably backed up the invitation.

'Yes, come on in,' he said. 'I don't know who you are, sir, or what you're doing in a private state-room, but step right in.'

'I shan't be long. I'm just curing Mr Tennyson's headache.'

'Mr Tennyson junior's headache.'

'Mr Tennyson junior's headache.'

'Not to be confused,' proceeded the patient, 'with Mr Tennyson senior's headache, if he has one — which, I'm afraid, he hasn't. I don't know who you are, sir, or what you're doing in a private state-room, but I should like to tell you that this little girl here — you don't mind me calling you "this little girl here"?'

'Go right ahead.'

'This little girl here,' said Reggie, 'is an angel of mercy. You can search till you're blue in the face, but you'll never find a better description of her than that. It fits her like the paper on the wall. She met me on deck just now, gave me a keen glance, diagnosed my complaint in an instant, and brought me down here and started in on me. I shall have to look in the mirror later to make sure that my head is still attached to the parent body, but apart from an uneasy suspicion that I've come in half I'm feeling better.'

'Mr Tennyson —'

'Mr Tennyson junior.'

'Mr Tennyson junior had a hangover.'

'He had. And may you never have one like it, sir — I don't know who you are or what you're doing in a private state-room ...'

'This is my brother-in-law, Ivor Llewellyn.'

'Ah, the magic lantern chap,' said Reggie agreeably. 'How are you, Llewellyn? Pleased to meet you. I have heard of you from my brother Ambrose. He speaks very highly of you, Llewellyn, very highly.'

61

The motion-picture magnate was not mollified by the courteous tribute. He eyed the young man sourly.

'I want to talk to you, Mabel.'

'All right. Shoot.'

'In private.'

'Oh? Well, I shall be through in a moment.'

She wrought forcefully upon Reggie's neck for a while, eliciting from him a plaintive 'Ouch!'

'Baby!' she said reprovingly.

'It's all very well for you to say "Baby!"' said Reggie. 'You'll look silly if I come apart in your hands.'

'There. That ought to do. What's the verdict?'

Reggie allowed his head to revolve slowly for a moment. 'Say "Boo!"'

'Boo!'

'Louder.'

'Boo!'

'Now closer to the ear.'

'Boo!'

Reggie rose and drew a deep breath. There was an awed expression on his face.

'A miracle! That's all it is. Just a bally miracle. I feel a new man.'

'Good.'

'And I should like to say that I consider it a privilege to meet a family like yours. I never in my puff encountered such a sweetness-and-light-scattering bunch. You, Miss –'

'Spence is the name.'

'You, Miss Spence, bring corpses to life. You, Llewellyn, place real money for the first time within the grasp of my brother Ambrose. This acquaintanceship must not be allowed to end here. I must see more of you, Miss Spence, and of you, Llewellyn. Golly,' said Reggie, 'if anybody had told me half an hour ago that I should be capable of looking forward to dinner tonight like a starving tapeworm, I wouldn't have believed him. Good-bye, Miss Spence, and you, Llewellyn, or rather *au revoir*, and thanks, thanks, Miss Spence, and you, Llewellyn. Thank you a thousand times. What's your first name?'

'Mabel.'

'Right,' said Reggie.

The door closed. Mabel Spence smiled. Mr Llewellyn did not.

'Well,' said Mabel, 'that's today's good deed done. I don't know where that boy picked up his jag, but he had certainly gone after it with both hands. You wouldn't think, to see him now, that he's probably quite good-looking. I've always admired that slim, long-legged type.'

Mr Llewellyn was in no mood to give his attention to lectures on the personal appearance of Reggie Tennyson, and he had begun to indicate this by dancing about the state-room in a rather emotional manner, like a wounded duck.

'Say, listen! Will you listen!'

'Well go on. What?'

'Do you know who's on board this boat?'

'Well, I'm pretty clear about Tennyson senior and Tennyson junior, and I met Lotus Blossom on the tender, but outside of that –'

'Let me tell you who's on board this boat. That Cannes guy. The fellow on that hotel terrace at Cannes. The one who wanted to know how to spell "sciatica".'

'Nonsense.'

'Nonsense, eh?'

'You've got that bozo on the brain. You're imagining it.'

'Is that so? Well, get this. I was sitting in the library after I left you and he popped up from nowhere and breathed down the back of my neck. This time he wanted to know how to spell "inexplicable".'

'He did?'

'That's what he did.'

'Well, well, that boy's certainly attending to his education all right. He'll have quite a nice little vocabulary before he's through. Did you tell him?'

Mr Llewellyn danced another step or two.

'Of course I didn't tell him. How should I know how to spell "inexplicable"? And if I had of known, do you think I was in shape to tell anybody how to spell anything? I simply sat and stared at him and tried to catch up with my breath.'

'But why shouldn't he be going across? Lots of other people are. I can't see that his being on board is so exceptionally significant. And try,' said Mabel Spence, in passing, 'spelling those two when you're at leisure.'

'You can't, can't you?'

'I can't, no.'

'Well, try this one on your cottage piano,' said Mr Llewellyn urgently. 'Ambrose Tennyson came along and seemed to know the fellow, so I asked him what his racket was, and Tennyson said he was a detective.'

'A detective?'

'A detective. D – e – ... Detective,' said Mr Llewellyn.

This did impress Mabel. She bit her lip thoughtfully.

'Is that so?'

'I'm telling you.'

'You're sure it was the same man?'

'Of course I'm sure it was the same man.'

'Odd.'

'What's odd about it? I told you that morning at Cannes that he was one of these Customs spies, and if you don't believe me perhaps you'll believe the purser. The purser ought to know what he's talking about, oughtn't he? And the purser tells me that you can't throw a brick at any of those Cannes hotels without hitting one. He says they hang around, listening in on conversations, and sooner or later some dumb woman says something about smuggling something, and then they get busy. This guy's come aboard to keep an eye on me. That's what they do. The purser was telling me. Once they hit the trail, they never let go. So now what?' said Mr Llewellyn, collapsing on the bed and sitting there breathing stertorously.

Mabel Spence had never been a great admirer of her brother-in-law, but she was not without feminine pity. There were plenty of things she could have said, and would have liked to say, about Mr Llewellyn's blood pressure and his need for a rigid system of diet, but she left them unspoken. She pondered for a moment, turning a woman's practical eye on the problem. It was not long before her shrewd brain enabled her to point out the bright side.

'Don't worry,' she said.

The condition of Mr Llewellyn's nerves being what it was, she might have worded her remark more happily. The motion-picture magnate, already mauve, turned a royal purple.

'Don't worry? That's good.'

'There's nothing to worry about.'

'Nothing to worry about? That's a honey.'

'Well, there isn't. I thought at first that you were making a lot out of nothing, but if this man is a detective you're probably right about him having come on board because of what he heard us saying that day. Still, why get apoplexy? The whole thing's quite simple. He's probably like everybody else – ready to be fixed if you make the price right.'

Mr Llewellyn, who had been about to speak – taking the words 'quite simple' as his cue – gave a start. He seemed to swallow something, and a marked improvement became notice-able in his complexion. It faded back to mauve again.

'That's true.'

'Sure.'

'Yes. I guess that's about right, at that. He probably is.'

Her words had made him feel as if, after wandering through a morass, he had suddenly touched solid ground. When it came to fixing people, he knew where he stood.

Then the Soul's Awakening look which always comes into the eyes of motion-picture magnates when the question of fixing people arises slowly died away.

'But how's it to be done? I can't just walk up to him and ask for the tariff.'

'You don't have to.' There was scorn for the slower mascu-line intelligence in Mabel's voice. 'Did you take a good square look at him?'

'Did I take a good square look at him!' echoed Mr Llewellyn. 'For what seemed about an hour I did nothing else but. If he'd of had pimples I could have counted each in-dividual one.'

'Pimples are just what he hasn't got. That's the whole point. He's a darned good-looking fellow.'

'I didn't admire him.'

'Well, he is. Rather like Bob Montgomery. And I'll bet he knows it. I'll bet he's been wanting to break into pictures ever since he started shaving. I'll bet if you took him on one side and offered him a job at Llewellyn City, he'd jump at it. And then –'

'Then he couldn't dish the dirt to those Customs sharks!'

'Of course he couldn't. He wouldn't want to. Why, anyone in your position, with jobs in the pictures to give away, can fix anybody. This guy will drop the moment you start talking.'

''Myes,' said Mr Llewellyn.

The brightness had suddenly gone out of his voice. A pensive look was on his face. He was musing.

Unless absolutely compelled to do so, Ivor Llewellyn had no desire to add to the number of blood-sucking parasites already battening on his firm's pay-roll. Every Saturday morning he was paying out good money to his wife's brother George, his wife's Uncle Wilmot, his wife's cousin Egbert and his wife's cousin Egbert's sister Genevieve – who, much as he doubted her ability to read at all, was in the Reading Department of the Superba-Llewellyn at a cool three hundred and fifty dollars a week. If needs must, of course, he could add to these a Monty Bodkin at whatever fantastic salary that cold-hearted human bloodhound might see fit to demand, but he was wondering if needs really did must.

Then he saw that it was the only way. The old, sound principle of stopping the mouth of the man who knew was one which it was impossible to better. It had served him many a time before, and it must serve him again.

'I'll do it,' he said. 'Ambrose Tennyson is a friend of his. I'll have him put through the deal. That'll be better than if I approach him direct. More dignified. I think you're right. He'll drop.'

'Sure he will. Why wouldn't he? I don't suppose they pay these fellows much. A nice fat salary at Llewellyn City will look like the earth to him. I told you there was nothing to worry about.'

'You certainly did.'

'And wasn't I right?'

'You certainly were,' said Mr Llewellyn.

He gazed with positive benevolence at his sister-in-law, won-

dering how he could ever have got the idea that he did **not**
like her. For an instant he even went so far as to consider **the**
notion of kissing her.

Thinking better of this he reached for his case, produced **a**
cigar and began to chew it.

# Chapter 8

Monty Bodkin, having had his quick one, had not lingered on in the smoking-room, full though it was of pleasant fellows with whom in his mood of exalted happiness he would have found it agreeable to forgather. He had gone below to inspect the state-room, formerly the property of Reginald Tennyson, which was to be his home for the next five days. He was thus privileged to obtain his first view of Albert Eustace Pease-march, the bedroom steward assigned to that section of the C deck. This zealous man was not actually visible when he entered, being manifest only as a sound of heavy breathing from the bathroom, but a moment later he emerged and Monty was enabled to see him steadily and see him whole.

His immediate reaction on doing so was a feeling that, as far as his chances of getting a feast for the eye were concerned, he had come a little late. He should have caught Albert Pease-march a decade or so earlier, before the years had taken their toll. The steward was now a man in the middle forties, and time had robbed him of practically all his hair, giving him in niggardly exchange a pink pimple on the side of the nose. It had also removed from his figure that streamline effect. Nobody who had recently come from the presence of Ivor Llewellyn would have called him fat, but he was certainly overweight for a man of his height. He had a round, moon-like face, in which were set, like currants in a suet dumpling, two small brown eyes. And these eyes caused Monty, as he met them, to experience a slight diminution of the effervescing cheerfulness which he had brought with him into the room.

It was not that he minded Albert Peasemarch's eyes being small. Some of his best friends had small eyes. What damped him was the fact that in their expression he seemed to detect a certain disapproval, as if the other did not like his looks. And the thought of anyone not liking his looks, at a moment when he had just become reconciled to Gertrude Butterwick, cut Monty like a knife.

He resolved to address himself to the task of removing this disapproval, of making Albert Peasemarch all smiles, of showing Albert Peasemarch, in fine, that if by some unfortunate chance he, Monty, had happened to fall short in any way of his, Albert's, standard of physical beauty, the inner, essential Bodkin was well up to sample.

'Not strictly handsome in the classical style,' Albert would go back and tell his mates, though goodness knew he had no claim to set himself up as a critic, 'but a very pleasant young gentleman. Nothing stand-offish about him. No haughtiness. A most entertaining conversationalist' – or however bedroom stewards put it when they wanted to say 'entertaining conversationalist'.

With this end in view, he let loose a gay and ringing 'Good evening.'

'Good evening, sir,' said Albert Peasemarch coldly.

Monty's impression that the man disapproved of him deepened. The fellow's manner was unquestionably austere. It was his first ocean voyage, so he had no means of estimating from past experience what was the average mean or norm of geniality in stewards, but surely, he felt, he was entitled to expect more chumminess.

He took a line through butlers. If he had arrived on a visit at a country house and had found the butler as unresponsive as this, he would have had serious misgivings that the man must have overheard his host saying derogatory things about him at the dinner-table. He could not help feeling that in some way, for some reason, Albert Peasemarch was prejudiced against him.

Still, he had determined upon being an entertaining conversationalist, and an entertaining conversationalist he would be.

'Good evening,' he said again. 'You, I take it, reading from right to left, would be the steward of this state-room, what?'

'Of this and the adjoining ones, sir.'

'Bustling about, I perceive. Earning the weekly envelope with honest toil.'

'I have been arranging your effects, sir.'

'Good.'

'I have just laid out your razors, razor-strop, toothbrushes, toothpaste, mouth-wash, sponge, sponge-bag, and shaving-brush in the bathroom, sir.'

'Stout fellow. I mean,' said Monty, feeling that in the circumstances the phrase had a certain tactlessness and laid itself open to misconstruction, 'thanks.'

'Not at all, sir.'

There was a pause. The sunlight had not yet come into the steward's eyes. In fact, in the matter of sunniness, he seemed to have gone back a bit, if anything. However, Monty persevered.

'Lots of people on board.'

'Yes, sir.'

'And a lot more have come on here, I suppose?'

'Yes, sir.'

'Going to have a nice voyage, I shouldn't wonder.'

'Yes, sir.'

'If it keeps calm, of course.'

'Yes, sir.'

'Fine boat.'

'Yes, sir.'

'Pretty different from the old days, what? I mean, a ship like this would have made Columbus open his eyes a trifle.'

'Yes, sir,' said Albert Peasemarch, still with that same odd reserve.

Monty gave it up. He had shot his bolt. It was too dashed absurd, he considered, to stand here trying to suck up to a bally steward who declined to expand and be matey, when he might be out in God's air, taking Gertrude for a spin round the deck. Besides, he felt, for the Bodkins, though amiability itself if you met them half-way, had their pride, what the hell! If this chap didn't appreciate him, he meant to say, there were plenty who did. A little stiffly, he turned to the door, to be checked as his fingers touched the handle by a grave cough.

70

'Excuse me, sir.'

'Eh?'

'You shouldn't have done it, sir, you shouldn't, really.'

Monty was amazed to note that this Peasemarch was now regarding him with quiet reproach. The spectacle stunned him. To aloofness he had become inured, but why was Peasemarch reproachful?

'Eh?' he said again. There are some situations in which 'Eh?' is the only possible remark.

'I don't understand how you could have brought yourself to do such a thing, sir.'

'Such a thing as what?'

The steward made a rather dignified gesture, spoiling it at the last moment by scratching his left ear.

'I fear you may think it a liberty, me talking like this –'

'No, no.'

'Yes, sir,' insisted Albert Peasemarch, once more scratching his ear, which appeared to be irritating him. 'And technically it is a liberty. Until the ship docks in New York harbour our relations are those of master and man. In my dealings with any of the blokes in my sheds – any of the gentlemen who occupy the state-rooms under my charge, I always say to myself that for the duration of the voyage I am a vassal and he is – temporarily – my feudal overlord.'

'Golly!' said Monty, impressed. 'That's rather well put.'

'Thank you, sir.'

'Dashed well put, if you don't mind my saying so.'

'I had a good schooling, sir.'

'You weren't at Eton, by any chance?'

'No, sir.'

'Well, anyway, it was dashed well put. But I'm interrupting you.'

'Not at all, sir. I was merely saying that, our positions being those of feudal overlord and vassal, I shouldn't by rights be speaking to you like this. By rights I ought to just go to Jimmy the One –'

'To – ?'

'The chief steward, sir. The proper thing by rights would be to just go to the chief steward and report the matter and

71

leave him to deal with it. But I don't want to cause unpleasantness and get a young gentleman like you into trouble –'

'Eh?'

'– because I know very well that it was due to high spirits and nothing more. So I do hope you will not take offence, sir, where none is meant, when I say that you ought not to do that sort of thing. I am old enough to be your father ...'

Monty had been feeling that the essential thing to do was to institute a probing system of inquiry with a view to inducing this mystic steward to come out into the open and explain what on earth he was talking about. But this statement sidetracked him.

'Old enough to be my father?' he said, surprised. 'How old are you?'

'Forty-six, sir.'

'Well, dash it, then you couldn't be. I'm twenty-eight.'

'You look younger, sir.'

'It isn't a question of what I look. It's what I am. I'm twenty-eight. You'd have had to have married at – seventeen,' said Monty, relaxing the strained frown on his face and ceasing to twiddle his fingers.

'Men have got married at seventeen, sir.'

'Name one.'

'Ginger Perkins – redheaded feller in the stevedoring business down Fratton way,' said Albert Peasemarch rather surprisingly. 'So, you see, I was right when I said I could have been your father.'

'But you aren't.'

'No, sir.'

'We aren't related at all, so far as I know.'

'No, sir.'

'Well, carry on,' said Monty, 'but I may as well tell you frankly that you're making my head swim. You were saying something about something I ought not to have done.'

'Yes, sir. And I say it again. You ought not to have done it.'

'Done what?'

'Young blood may be young blood –'

'I don't see what else it could be.'

'But that doesn't excuse it, to my mind. Youth!' said Albert Peasemarch. 'It's the old, old story. See jew-ness savvay.'

'What are you babbling about?'

'I am not babbling, sir. I am alluding to the bathroom.'

'The bathroom?'

'What's in the bathroom, sir.'

'You mean my sponge-bag?'

'No, sir. I do not mean your sponge-bag. I mean what's on the wall.'

'My strop?'

'You know very well what I'm referring to, sir. All that writing in red paint. A lot of trouble and extra work that's going to cause, cleaning of it off, but I reckon you didn't think of that. Heedless, that's what youth is. Heedless. Never looks to the morrow.'

Monty was staring, bewildered. But for the fact that his articulation was so beautifully clear and his words so finely chosen – that 'see jew-ness savvay' gag – good stuff there – he would have said that this steward who stood before him was a steward who had had one over the eight.

'Red paint?' he said, at a loss.

He walked across to the bathroom and looked in. The next moment he had staggered back with a choking cry.

It was even as Albert Peasemarch had said. The writing was on the wall.

# Chapter 9

Owing to the bold and dashing hand in which this writing had been inscribed, a person seeing it for the first time, as Monty was doing, had a momentary illusion that there was more of it than was really the case. The wall seemed not so much a wall with writing on it as a mass of writing with a wall somewhere in the background. In actual fact, the complete opus, if one may so call it, consisted of two phrases, one over the mirror, the other to the left of it.

The first ran:

'Hi, baby!'

The second:

'Hello, there, sweetie!'

A calligraphy expert would probably have deduced that the author was of a warm-hearted, impulsive nature.

In the other historic case of writing on the wall, that which occurred during the celebrated Feast of Belshazzar, and, as Belshazzar said at the time, spoiled a good party, it will be remembered that what caused all the unpleasantness and upset the Babylonian monarch so much was the legend 'Mene, mene, tekel, upharsin.' It is odd to reflect that if somebody had written that on the wall of Monty's bathroom, he would not have turned a hair; while, conversely, knowing what those Babylonian monarchs were like, one can picture Belshazzar reading the present script and rather enjoying it. So strangely do tastes differ.

Monty was frankly appalled. About the words 'Hello, there, sweetie!' there is nothing intrinsically alarming, and the same may be said of 'Hi, baby!'. Yet, gazing at them now, he felt very much as Mr Llewellyn had felt on the occasion when his muscular friend had hit him in the solar plexus with the medicine ball. The bathroom swam about him, and for an instant he seemed to see two Albert Peasemarches, both shimmying.

Then his eyes returned to normal, and he fixed them on the steward with a wild surmise.

'Who's done this?'

'Come, come, sir.'

'You silly ass,' cried Monty, 'you don't think I did it, do you? What the dickens would I want to go doing a thing like that for? It's a girl's writing.'

It was this discovery that had caused so powerful an upheaval in Montague Bodkin, and who shall say that he had not reason to be perturbed? No engaged young man with his betrothed travelling on the same boat is pleased at finding his state-room richly decorated with loving messages in a girlish hand, but the engaged young man who likes it least is the one who has just squared himself in the matter of a female name tattooed on his chest with a heart round it. With a sickening sense of being in the toils, Monty perceived that there was a heart round the words 'Hi, baby!'.

The only bright aspect of the whole affair was that this revelation of the woman's hand seemed to have had an extraordinarily bracing effect on Albert Peasemarch. That minorprophet-like austerity of his had vanished, and he appeared genuinely amused and pleased.

'I see it all, sir. It's the young lady next door.'

'Eh?'

Albert Peasemarch chuckled fatly.

'A very larky young lady she is, sir. Just the sort to play this kind of game. Well, let me give you an instance, sir. Half an hour ago it may have been, the bell rang in her shed and I went in and there she was, reddening of her lips at the mirror with a red lipstick. "Good evening," she says. "Good evening, miss," I says. "Are you the steward?" she says. "Yes, miss," I says, "I am the steward. Is there anything I can do for you?" "Why, yes, steward," she says, "there is. Will you be so good as to open that little wickerwork basket on the floor there and reach me out my smelling-salts?" "Certainly, miss," I says. "Only too happy." And I go to the basket and I lift the lid and I pretty near do a somersault over backwards. And the young lady says: "Why, steward," she says, "what is it? Your manner is strange. Have you been having a couple?" And I says: "Are you aware, miss, that there is a living organism in that basket, a living organism that snaps at you when you raise the lid and would pretty near have took the top of my thumb off if I hadn't of looked slippy?" And she says: "Oh, yes, I forgot to tell you. That's my alligator." There in a nutshell, sir, you have the young lady next door.'

Albert Peasemarch paused for breath. Perceiving that his feudal overlord was not yet capable of speech, he resumed:

'It transpires that she is one of these motion-picture actresses and maintains the animal on the advice of her Press representative. Such, sir, is the young lady next door, and if you will forgive me once again taking a liberty and speaking quite frankly, I think you are making a mistake, sir, a very serious mistake.'

Monty was still in the rudimentary stages of pulling himself together. He closed and unclosed his eyes, and swallowed once or twice. Then, slowly, it penetrated to his consciousness that his companion had said that something would be a mistake.

'Mistake?'

'Yes, sir.'

'Who's made a mistake?'

'I said that you were making one, sir.'

'Me?'

'Yes, sir.'

'How?'

'You know what I mean, sir.'

'I don't.'

Albert Peasemarch seemed to stiffen.

'Very good, sir,' he said distantly. 'Just as you wish. If you would prefer me to be silent and keep my place, I will be silent and keep my place. Technically, you are right in wishing me to do so. But I was hoping that, considering that all this has, in a manner of speaking, brought us somewhat close together, if I may use the expression, you would have waived our relationship of overlord and vassal, of bloke – that is to say, passenger – and steward, and allowed me to speak frankly.'

Nothing in this speech contributed in any way to Monty's enlightenment, but it was plain that he had somehow managed to hurt the other's feelings. Albert Peasemarch's words might be cryptic, but not his face. He was looking respectfully pained.

'Oh, rather,' he said hastily, eager to staunch the wound. 'Of course. Certainly.'

'I may speak frankly?' said Albert Peasemarch, brightening.

'Quite. Quite.'

A kindly look came into the steward's eye, a look full of the indulgent affection natural in one who, if he had married Monty's mother at the age of seventeen – though in actual fact, as we have seen, he had not – might have been the young man's father.

'Thank you, sir. Then, sir, let me say once more that in my opinion you are making a very serious mistake. What I mean to say, in allowing your heart to become involved with a young lady, knock-out though she is to look at, so larky in disposition as the young lady next door.'

'Eh?'

'The young lady next door,' proceeded Albert Peasemarch, 'is an actress, sir – Miss Blossom her name is – and my old mother used to say to me "Keep away from actresses, Albert." And she was right, as I discovered for myself when, disregarding her warning, I took and fell in love with one that was playing small parts in the Portsmouth panto. It wasn't long before I realized that actresses and ordinary men like me moved in different spears and hadn't the same views on things, at all. No notion of punctuality she hadn't got, to start with. Many's the time I've waited three-quarters of an hour under the Town Hall clock, and had her walk up as cool as you please and say: "Oh, there you are, Face. Not late, am I?"'

He broke off, coughing. In order to give verisimilitude to his story, he had uttered the last nine words in a sardonic falsetto, and this had tried his vocal cords. Recovering from the paroxysm, he resumed:

'And it wasn't only her having no notion of punctuality. It was everything. I never knew where I was with her, sir, I tell you straight. Take the simple matter of sugar in her tea. If I put it in, she'd say: "Trying to ruin my figure, are you, or what is it?" and next time, when I didn't, it was, "Hoy! Come along with that ruddy sugar," and probably a derogatory epithet tacked on to it.'

He uttered a hard laugh, for these things rankle. Then, seeing that his companion had the air of a man who wished to speak, he went on rapidly:

'Temperament, they call it, I believe – the artistic temperament, and I soon saw that it and me didn't mix. It was the same thing all the time. Take her relations with her fellow artists, for instance. I would escort her to the stage door for the performance and she'd be talking of nothing but what a cat Maud or Gladys that she dressed with was, and I'd meet her after the performance and, merely wishing to make things comfortable for all concerned, I'd say: "I do hope, dear, that you haven't been annoyed tonight by that cat Maud or Gladys," and she'd draw herself up in a cold and haughty sort of manner and reply: "I'll thank you, if you don't mind, not to go calling my dearest friends cats," and then next afternoon I'd say: "How's your friend Maud or Gladys?" and she would answer: "I don't know what you mean 'friend'. I hate the sight of the woman." Very wearing it was, sir, and that's why I say to you, as one who's been through it, don't you have nothing to do with actresses, no matter how beautiful they may be. Cool off towards the young lady next door is my advice to you, sir, and you'll be happier for it in the end.'

Monty was breathing tensely. There had been a time when, actuated by the universal benevolence with which he had been overflowing, he had liked Albert Peasemarch. This state of things no longer existed.

'Thank you,' he said.

'Not at all, sir.'

'Thank you,' repeated Monty, '(a), steward, for telling me the story of your bally life –'

'Only too pleased, sir.'

'– and (b), steward, for giving me the benefit of your dashed valuable advice. In reply, steward, may I inform you that, so far from being enamoured of the young lady next door, I've never so much as met her. And it's no good,' said Monty, his voice rising, 'casting a meaning glance at that bathroom, because –'

Albert Peasemarch's face, as has been indicated, was an open book that all might read. In it now Monty read astonishment and incredulity.

'You've never *met* the young lady next door, sir?'

'Never.'

'Well, sir,' said Albert dubiously, 'I must apologize, then. I was misled. When my mate on the B deck told me you had persuaded his bloke to let you change state-rooms with him, and when I'd had a look at the young lady next door and seen what a scorcher she is as regards personal experience, and when I come in here and see loving messages all over the walls, I naturally assumed that your motive in changing state-rooms with your gentleman friend on B deck was so that you could be adjacent and contiguous to the young lady next door.'

Monty's breathing became more tense.

'I didn't change state-rooms with my gentleman friend on B deck. He changed with me.'

'It's the same thing, sir.'

'It's not at all the same thing.'

'And you've never met the young lady next door?'

'I've told you I've never met the young lady next door.'

The steward's face suddenly cleared. He looked like a man who has been poring over a clue in a crossword puzzle, at a loss to divine what 'large Australian bird' can possibly be, and in an unexpected flash has had it come to him. Just as such a man will quiver in every limb and cry 'Emu!', just as Archimedes on a well-known occasion quivered in every limb and cried 'Eureka!' – so now did Albert Peasemarch quiver in every limb and cry 'Coo!'

'Coo, sir!' cried Albert Peasemarch. 'I see it all now, sir. It was not love that made the young lady next door write that writing on the wall, but just larkiness. I told you how larky she was, didn't I, sir? I've known that to happen before. When I was a hunky-dunk on the *Laurentic*, the Dooser gave a party to some theatrical ladies we had with us –'

'Who the dickens is the Dooser?'

'The second steward, sir. Always known as the Dooser. Well, as I was saying, the Dooser gave this party and the proceedings continued to a late hour, and the Dooser, having to get his bit of sleep so he could be fresh for his duties next day, excused himself to the young ladies and went off and turned in with Scupperguts –'

'Who the devil's Scupperguts? I wish you'd talk English.'

'The head waiter, sir. Invariably termed Scupperguts. Well, sir, as I was saying, the Dooser dossed with Scupperguts, and when he got to his own room next morning he found that one of the young ladies had written a number of highly copperizing things on his wall with lipstick, and the way he carried on had to be seen to be believed, so I was informed by those who witnessed his emotion. You see, he was afraid that at any moment the Old Man might take it into his head to have a ship's inspection.'

'All dashed interesting –'

'Very, sir. I thought you'd think so. And he couldn't get it off, the Dooser couldn't this writing, because lipstick's undeliable.'

'Undeliable?'

'A scientific term, sir, meaning impossible to be got off without the proper chemicals and what not.'

'What!'

There was a sharp agony in Monty's voice which caused the steward to look quickly at him. He observed that the young man's knotted and combined locks had parted and that each particular hair now stood on end like quills upon the fretful porpentine.

'Sir?'

'Steward!'

'Yes, sir?'

'You don't think – do you think – you don't think that writing in there was done with lipstick?'

'I know it was done with lipstick, sir.'

'My sainted aunt!'

'Yes, sir. That's lipstick, that was.'

'Oh, golly!'

Albert Peasemarch could not quite follow this. He was

unable to fathom the reason for this, as it seemed to him, excessive perturbation. The Dooser, yes. The Dooser had had an official position to keep up. If the pitiless light of publicity had been thrown on the writing in the Dooser's cabin, the Old Man would have had more than a word or two to say. But Monty was a carefree passenger.

However, it was plain that the young man was taking the thing a good deal to heart, so Albert Peasemarch endeavoured to cheer him up by pointing out another aspect of the matter. He was a deep thinker in his off hours, and he proceeded to give Monty the benefit of his hard-won philosophy.

'The way to look at these things, sir, is to keep telling yourself that it's just Fate. Somehow, if you know a thing has been fated from the beginning of time, if I may use the expression, it doesn't seem so bad. I'm always telling my mates in the Glory Hole that, but you'd be surprised how they don't seem to see it. If you want to know what's wrong with the average steward on an ocean liner, sir, he don't have no breadth of vision. I wonder, sir,' said Albert Peasemarch, warming to his theme, 'if you have done much thinking along those lines – devoted your mind, I mean, to considering the inscrutable workings of Fate – or, as some call it, Destiny. Take this simple instance here before us now. What have we got? Lipstick. Very well. Whose lipstick? The young lady next door's. Right. Now, before the war ladies didn't use lipstick. It was the war that brought about lipstick. So, if there hadn't been a war, the young lady next door wouldn't have had a lipstick to write on your bathroom wall with.'

'Steward,' said Monty.

'Ah, but wait one moment, sir. We can go farther back than that. What caused the war? That bloke in Switzerland shooting the German Emperor. So if that bloke hadn't have shot the Emperor, there wouldn't have been no war, and there wouldn't have been no lipsticks, and the young lady next door wouldn't have had one to write on your bathroom wall with.'

'Steward,' said Monty.

'Just one instant, sir. We haven't finished even yet. We go back still farther. What caused the bloke in Switzerland? The fact that his father and mother happened to meet and get married. Probably they met at the pictures or somewhere. Very well. Now you just reason it out for yourself, sir. Suppose it had been raining that night and she had stayed at home. Suppose, just as he was putting on his boots, a couple of his pals had dropped in on him and taken him off to the pub to play darts. What follows? The bloke-who-shot-the-Emperor's father would never have met the bloke-who-shot-the-Emperor's mother, so there wouldn't have been any bloke to shoot the Emperor, so there wouldn't have been any war, so there wouldn't have been any lipsticks, so the young lady next door wouldn't have had one to write on your bathroom wall with.'

'Steward,' said Monty.

'Sir?'

'You may not know it,' said Monty, speaking with some difficulty, 'but you're trying me a little high.'

'I'm sure I'm very sorry to hear that, sir. I was merely pointing out the strange and wonderful workings –'

'I know.' Monty passed a hand across his forehead. 'But don't. Do you mind?'

'Not at all, sir.'

'I'm a little upset, steward.'

'You do seem a little upset, sir.'

'Yes. You see, I'm engaged to be married . . .'

'I hope you'll be very happy, sir.'

'So do I. But will I? That's the point. That's the question.'

'What's the question?' asked Reggie Tennyson, entering as he spoke.

# Chapter 10

The emotions which flooded Monty Bodkin's bosom as he beheld his old friend sauntering into the state-room were similar to, though more intense than, those which must have come to the beleaguered troops in Lucknow as they heard the swirl of the Highland pipes. He was just the man Monty wanted to see. You could have offered Montague Bodkin at that moment the cream of the world's wit and beauty and intellect, and he would have chosen Reggie Tennyson.

'Reggie!' he cried.

An awed expression came into the other's face.

'It's astounding,' he said. 'Positively miraculous. I come in here, into this small, enclosed space, and when I'm about six inches away from you you inflate your lungs and bellow "Reggie!" in my ear-hole at the top of your voice, and I don't so much as wince. And an hour ago, if a bird on a distant tree had tweet-tweeted in the most confidential of undertones, I'd have leaped straight out of my skin and cried like a child. And this change, old boy, was brought about purely and simply by a smallish girl attaching herself to my neck and twisting it into the shape of a corkscrew. Yes, it's a fact. With those slim hands she cured my headache in the space of –'

Monty was dancing much as Mr Llewellyn had danced before Mabel Spence.

'Never mind your headache!'

'I don't now. It's gone. As I tell you –'

'Reggie, we've got to change state-rooms!'

'What are you talking about?'

'About our changing state-rooms.'

'But we've changed state-rooms.'

'Change them again, I mean.'

'What, you shift up and me shift down?'

'Yes.'

'Thus placing me next door to Lottie Blossom?'

Reggie smiled a faint, sad smile, and shook his head.

'No, laddie,' he said. 'I'm sorry, but no. Not unless you give me definite assurance that my brother Ambrose has fallen overboard. You have no conception, Monty,' proceeded the younger of the Tennysons earnestly, 'you have literally no conception how Ambrose has warmed up since our last meeting. I take it he has seen the passenger list. At any rate, ever since I left you and went on deck for that breath of fresh air he has been following me about all over the ship, exuding hostility and menace. I lose him from time to time, but he always finds me again, and when he finds me he glares, breathing noisily through the nose. It would be courting a hideous doom for me to be such a mug as to change state-rooms. Why do you want to change, anyway? This is a nicer state-room altogether than the one I've got. No comparison. Softer bed, better furniture, two old English prints on the wall instead of one, prettier carpet, handsomer steward –'

'Thank you, sir,' said Albert Peasemarch.

'Don't dream of changing. You'll be as cosy in here as a worm in a chestnut. And this room has got a private bath –'

'Ha!'

'Eh?'

Monty's face twisted.

'You mentioned the word "bath". Go and take a look at it.'

'I've seen it.'

'See it again.'

Reggie raised his eyebrows.

'You're pretty mystic this p.m., Monty, and I fail to grasp the gist. Still, if it will please you – Golly!' he said opening the bathroom door and falling back a step.

'You see!'

'Who did that?'

'Your friend Lotus Blossom, with a lipstick.'

Reggie was unquestionably impressed. He looked at Monty as if he were seeing him with new eyes.

'I say,' he said reverently, 'you must have been making the pace in the most amazing way for her to let herself go like.

that! Lottie isn't a girl it's easy to get chummy with in a hurry. Full of reserve. It was weeks before she put that piece of ice down my back. I had no notion you were such a swift worker, old man. Why, you can't have known her more than about half an hour.'

'I don't know her! I've never met her.'

'Never met her?'

'No. I came in and found the wall as you see it. I suppose she meant that writing for you.'

Reggie considered this theory.

'I see what you mean. Yes, that might be so. Gosh, I'm glad I've moved!'

'You haven't moved.'

'Yes, I have.'

'Reggie!'

'I'm sorry, old boy, but that's final.'

'But, dash it, Reggie, listen. Think of my position, I'm engaged!'

'I'm sorry.'

'Engaged! Engaged to be married. And my fiancée liable at any moment to walk into that bathroom –'

'Well, really, sir!' said Albert Peasemarch.

The steward was looking his austerest. Twenty years of ocean travel had not weakened those high principles which he had imbibed in boyhood from a Victorian mother.

'Well, really, sir! A pure, sweet English girl ... Is the young lady English?'

'Of course she's English.'

'Very good, sir. Then, as I was saying,' said Albert Peasemarch with quiet rebuke, 'a pure, sweet English girl is hardly likely to come wandering in and out of a bachelor young gentleman's bathroom. She wouldn't dream of doing such a thing, not a pure, sweet English girl wouldn't. She would blush at the thought.'

'Exactly,' said Reggie. 'Well spoken, steward.'

'Thank you, sir.'

'A bull's eye, absolutely. He's right, Monty. I can't understand a decent-minded chap like you so much as entertaining such an idea. If you want to know, I'm a little shocked. How can you suppose that a girl of Gertrude's rigid propriety would ever contemplate the notion of coming in here for her morning tub? Really, Monty!'

It was the first faint glimmering of a silver lining that had come to brighten the cloud wrack of Monty's horizon. He definitely perked up.

'Why, of course!' he said.

'Why, of course!' said Reggie.

'Why, of course, sir!' said Albert Peasemarch.

'Why, of course!' said Monty. 'She wouldn't, would she?'

'Certainly not.'

'What a relief! You have thrown,' said Monty, regarding his vassal gratefully, 'a new light on the – what's your name, steward?'

'Peasemarch, sir. Albert Peasemarch.'

'You have thrown a new light on the situation, Albert Peasemarch. Thanks. For throwing a new light on the situation. All may not yet be lost.'

'No, sir.'

'Still, to be on she safe side, I wish you'd get a mop and have a pop at that writing.'

'It wouldn't be any use, sir. It's undeliable.'

'All the same, get a mop and pop.'

'Very good, sir. If you wish it.'

'Thanks, Peasemarch. Thank you, Albert.'

The steward withdrew. Monty threw himself down on the bed and sought to complete the calming of his agitated nerves with a cigarette. Reggie took a chair, tested it and sat down.

'Intelligent fellow, that,' said Monty.

'Oh, quite.'

'Taken a load off my mind.'

'I suppose so. Not,' said Reggie, 'that it would be such a bad thing if Gertrude did go into that bathroom.'

'Don't gibber, old man,' begged Monty. 'Not now.'

'I'm not gibbering. I've been thinking pretty closely about this business of you and Gertrude, Monty – pretty closely. I don't think you know much about feminine psychology, do you?'

'I don't even know what it is.'

'I thought as much. If you did, you would have seen for yourself what it was that made Gertrude break off your engagement. No,' said Reggie, holding up a hand, 'let me speak. I want to explain it all to you. I've got the whole thing taped out. Now, let us just run through the main facts of your association with Gertrude. You say you started off by squashing a wasp for her at a picnic. Excellent. You couldn't have begun better. It lent you glamour, and girls love glamour. You can gather that from the fact that about two days later she consented to marry you.'

'Two weeks.'

'Two days or two weeks – the actual period of time doesn't matter. The point is that you clicked with amazing rapidity. That shows that you must have had glamour. I shouldn't wonder if during those two weeks she didn't look on you as a king among men. Well, all right, then. Up to that point you were going like a breeze. You don't dispute that?'

'No.'

'You then, however, proceed to muck up the whole thing. You make a fatal move. You go and crawl to her father.'

'I didn't crawl.'

'I don't know what you call crawling, if what you did wasn't. Ask me, you simply grovelled. He started shooting off his head and laying down absurd conditions and you, instead of telling him to put a sock in it, agreed to them.'

'What else could I have done?'

'You could have been masterful and dominant. You could have gone to Gertrude and insisted on her marrying you at the nearest registrar's and, had she refused, biffed her in the eye. Instead of which, you took it all lying down, and what was the result? Phut went your glamour. Gertrude found herself saying: "This Bodkin bird, what about him, if you come right down to it? Good with the wasps, yes, but are wasps everything?" She felt that she had been deceived in you, that that wasp was just a flash in the pan. She said to herself: "If you want my candid opinion, I believe the chap's a wash-out." From that to giving you the raspberry was a short step. There you have the whole thing in a nutshell.'

Monty puffed at his cigarette with a quiet smile. He was enjoying this. If he had had a complaint against his friend in the past, it was that Reggie Tennyson was one of those fellows who always think they know everything. Sound egg though he was in other respects, you could not get away from the fact that it could be extremely irritating, that habit of his of telling you what to do or, if you had already done it, telling you you had done it wrong.

Reggie Tennyson was the sort of chap who, discovering that you went to Butters & Butters for your socks, would wonder that you didn't know that Mutters & Mutters were the only firm in London who supplied the sock perfect: and when, having rushed off to Mutters & Mutters and stocked up with socks, you then bought a shirt or two in addition, would say: 'Not shirts, old boy. Not Mutters & Mutters for shirts. Stutters & Stutters. The only place.'

A bit rasping it had been at times, and Monty welcomed this opportunity of putting him in his place for once. He finished his cigarette, and lit another with an air.

'So that's how it was, eh?'

'Just like that.'

'How do you know?'

'My dear chap!'

'Ever been wrong, Reggie?'

'Once, in the summer of 1930.'

'Well, you're wrong this time.'

'You think so?'

'I do think so.'

'What makes you think so?'

'The fact,' said Monty, triumphantly unmasking his batteries, 'that Gertrude and I have just had a complete reconciliation and that I found out that the trouble had been that, for reasons into which I need not go, she had got the idea into her head that I was a chap who went about making love to every girl I met.'

It was pleasant to him to note that he had in no way overestimated the magnitude of the wallop he had been waiting to deliver. There was nothing complacent about Reggie now. The shattering of his carefully reasoned theory had hit him hard. He was plainly taken aback. Indeed, he seemed to Monty to be overdoing the thing a bit. Just because a fellow had scored off you, there was no reason to look as rattled as all that. 'She – what was that you said?'

'She thought I was a sort of butterfly,' said Monty. 'And you know what butterflies are like. No solid qualities. Flitters and sippers. She thought I flitted and sipped.'

Reggie seemed to be finding some difficulty in speaking. He rose from his chair, paced the room, walked into the bathroom, turned on a tap, turned it off again and, from the sound, appeared to be beating a tattoo on a glass with one of Monty's toothbrushes.

'I say, Monty,' he said at length, his voice proceeding hollowly from the bathroom, 'I don't quite know how to break it to you, but I'm afraid I've made – with the best intentions – something of a bloomer.'

'Eh?'

'Yes,' proceeded the disembodied voice, 'I think one may fairly term it a bloomer. You see, I had the idea that the trouble between you and Gertrude was that she thought you a spineless piece of cheese. And when a girl thinks a man a spineless piece of cheese, there's only one way to make her get rid of the notion – viz., play up his popularity with the opposite sex – lead her to suppose that he is in reality a devil of a fellow, the sort of bloke it isn't safe to take your eye off for a second – in short, as you were saying just now, one of the butterflies and not the worst of them.'

Monty laughed. It was an amusing idea, and no doubt there was quite a good deal in it. Reggie had always been full of these whimsical theories.

'I see what you mean. Rather ingenious. Still, I'm glad you didn't tell Gertrude that about me.'

There was silence in the bathroom for a moment. Then Reggie's voice spoke, not unlike that of a remorseful ventriloquist.

'I think you're rather missing the point, old man. You haven't, if you don't mind my saying so, quite followed me. I did.'

'What!'

'That's exactly what I did tell her, and I can understand now why she seemed so thoughtful as I left. A sort of pensive look she had. You see, in my desire to spare no effort on your behalf, old boy, I'm afraid I rather spread myself. I pitched it quite fairly strong. As a matter of fact, what I actually told her was that she was totally mistaken in supposing you a spineless piece of cheese, because in reality you were the sort of chap who never had fewer than three girls on your hands at any given moment and were such a smooth performer that you could make each of them believe that she was the only female you had ever cared for in your life.'

Here the speaker let fall into the basin what seemed to be a bottle of mouth-wash. The resulting crash drowned all competing sounds, so that it was only when it had died away that Monty became aware that he was no longer in the state-room.

The young lady next door was in his midst.

# Chapter 11

In the first shock of actual personal encounter with this, as one might say, almost legendary figure, Monty Bodkin, the historian must admit, failed rather signally to live up to the dashing reputation with which his friend Reggie Tennyson had credited him. Nothing in his manner and deportment in any way suggested the modern Casanova: nor, unless the fact that he flitted may be said to have placed him in that class, could anyone have behaved less like a butterfly.

Flit he certainly did. The intrusion had come at a moment when he was already tottering on his base, and its effect was to send him flitting backward so abruptly that he nearly cracked his skull on the framed notice which hung on the wall explaining to those who preferred not to drown during the voyage the scientific method of putting on a lifebelt.

Nor must this be taken as evidence of any unusual lack of *savoir-faire* on his part. Most people who had seen Lotus Blossom only as a moving photograph were somewhat similarly affected when they met her in the flesh.

It was her hair that did it, principally. That and the fact that on the screen she seemed a wistful, pathetic little thing, while off it dynamic was more the word. In private life, Lottie Blossom tended to substitute for wistfulness and pathos a sort of 'Passed-For-Adults-Only' joviality which expressed itself outwardly in a brilliant and challenging smile, and inwardly and spiritually in her practice of keeping alligators in wickerwork baskets and asking unsuspecting strangers to lift the lid.

But principally, as we say, it was her hair that caused the eye of the beholder to swivel in its socket and his breath to come in irregular pants. Seeming on the screen to have merely a decent pallor, it revealed itself when she made a personal appearance a vivid and soul-shattering red. She looked as if she had been dipping her head in a sunset: and this, taken in conjunction with her large, shining eyes and the impression she gave, like so many of her sisters of the motion-picture art, of being supremely confident of herself, usually hit the stranger pretty hard. Monty, for one, felt as if he had just been run down by a motor-car with dazzling headlights.

He stood gaping silently, and Miss Blossom, perceiving that she had his attention, smiled that brilliant smile of hers and lost no time in opening the conversation.

'Dr Livingstone, I presume? But much changed. Or, if not,' she said, 'who?'

Monty could answer that. He may not have been mentally at his best, but he did remember his name.

'My name's Bodkin.'

'Mine's Blossom.'

'How do you do?'

'I'm fine, thanks,' said the lady agreeably. 'Yass'r, tol'able pert. What are you supposed to be doing in here?'

'Well –'

'Where's Ambrose?'

'Well –'

'This is his state-room, isn't it? Ambrose Tennyson.'

'Well, no.'

'Then the passenger list has gone haywire. Who does this bijou interior set belong to, then?'

'Well, me.'

'You?'

'Well, yes.'

She stared.

'You mean it isn't Ambrose's at all?'

'Well, no.'

Something appeared to be amusing Miss Blossom. She clung to the dressing-table for support, laughing heartily.

'Listen, boy,' she said, dabbing at her eyes as the paroxysm spent itself, 'I've got a surprise for you. Grab yourself a load of this. Do you ever take a bath? Because, if so –'

A strong shudder shook Monty.

'I've seen it.'

'You have?'

'Yes.'

'That stuff I wrote on the bathroom wall?'

'Yes.'

'Some fun, kid, ha? I did it with my lipstick.'

'I know. Undeliable.'

'Is it?' said Lottie Blossom, interested. 'I never knew that.'

'So Peasemarch, Albert, informs me.'

'Who's he?'

'The local steward.'

'Oh, that guy? He had a run in with my alligator.'

'He informed me of that, too.'

Lottie Blossom considered the matter in this new light.

'So that stuff's there for the duration, is it? Well, well. Every time you take a bath you'll think of me.'

'I shall,' said Monty sincerely.

'You don't seem pleased.'

'Well, the fact is –'

'All right. I understand. Well, I'm sorry.' said Miss Blossom handsomely. 'And a girl can't say more than that, can she? I did it in a moment of impulse. It was meant for old Pop Tennyson. I don't suppose you know him?'

'Yes. I know him.'

'How do you know him?'

'We were at Oxford together.'

'I see. What a man, yes?'

'Oh, quite.'

'He and I are engaged.'

'Yes.'

'And it seemed to me that, being engaged, I could hardly do less than – But listen. I don't follow this continuity at all. You being in here, I mean, and not Ambrose. On the passenger list it says as plain as anything "A. Tennyson".'

'R. Tennyson.'

'Sure, I know. But that's a misprint. It can't be R. Reggie Tennyson's not on board.'

'Yes, he is.'

'What!'

'Yes. In fact . . .'

Monty was looking at the bathroom door. It was now closed. But even so, he felt, Reggie must have heard their voices, and it surprised him that he had not long since come and joined the party.

The explanation was, in reality, simple. Reggie had certainly heard a female voice, but he had supposed it to be that of his cousin Gertrude. Reflecting on what he had told her, he imagined that it would not be long before she established communication with Monty. And he had no desire to meet Gertrude. There might, he foresaw, when they did meet, be some thoughtful explaining to do, and he wished to postpone the moment as long as possible.

What brought him out now – for an instant later the door of the bathroom opened and out he came – was the fact that Monty's announcement of his presence on board had caused Lottie Blossom to throw her head back and emit a piercing squeal of pleasure. She had always been devoted to Reggie, and the news delighted her. And as anybody who had once heard Lottie Blossom squeal was able ever afterwards to recognize the sound, Reggie came out, though in no spirit of joyous welcome. It was his purpose to urge his old friend to buzz off as quick as she knew how to, because with Ambrose prowling and prowling around like the troops of Midian there was no knowing when the jarring note might not be struck. The last thing Reggie desired was to be caught by Ambrose hob-nobbing with Lottie in a state-room, and not even the fact that Monty might be considered to be acting as a sort of chaperon made the prospect any more agreeable.

What ensued, therefore, was one of those unfortunate meetings where the two principals do not see eye to eye. Lottie Blossom was all ecstatic joy. Reggie looked like a member of the Black Hand trying to plot assassinations while hampered by a painful gumboil. His manner was dark, furtive and agitated.

'Reggie!'
'S'h!'
'Reg-GEE!'
'Shut up!'
Lottie Blossom bridled. Her feelings were wounded.

'Well, that's a nice thing to say to an old college chum! What do you mean by it? Aren't you glad to see me, you young spawn of a boll-weevil?'

'Of course. Rather. Quite. Only don't,' urged Reggie, looking nervously at the door, 'make such a dashed –'

'Whatever are you doing here?'

'I was having a word with Monty –'

'Chump! On this boat, I mean.'

'I'm sailing.'

'Why?'

'Pushed off.'

'Pushed off?'

'Yes. Driven out into the snow. Family.'

'What?'

Monty felt that a little explanation might help. His friend's staccato methods were not making the situation as clear to Miss Blossom as could have been desired.

'His family,' he said, 'are shoving him off to Canada. You're going into some office or other, aren't you, Reggie?'

'That's right,' said Reggie. His manner was distrait. He had sidled to the door and was evidently on the alert for prowling sounds without. 'The family have got me a job with some loathsome firm in Montreal.'

There was no question of Lottie Blossom not understanding now. The whole dreadful tragedy had been revealed to her in all its stark horror, and she was deeply affected.

'You mean they're making you *work*?'

'Yes.'

'Work? You?' A sort of divine pity radiated from the girl. 'Reggie, you poor, unfortunate child, come right here to mother!'

'No, no.'

'Come right here to mother and be comforted,' repeated Miss Blossom firmly. 'The idea of anyone being so brutal as to make you work! The all-in champion of the lilies of the field. The king of the toil-not-nor-spinners. I never heard of such a thing. Why, it's enough to send you into a nervous decline. Come *here*, Reggie.'

'I won't.'

'I want to kiss the place and make it well.'

'I dare say you do, but you bally well aren't going to. You don't understand the frightful trickiness of the position. Ambrose. . .'

'What about Ambrose?'

Having reached the door and got his fingers on the handle, Reggie felt a little easier.

'When I heard that Ambrose was going to Hollywood,' he explained, 'I offered to give him a letter to you. I didn't know then that you and he were engaged.'

'When did he tell you?'

'Almost immediately,' said Reggie in a pale voice, 'after I had told him how you and I used to whoop it up together.'

'You mean he's jealous?'

'He's as jealous as billy-o. Smear a bit of burnt cork on him, and he could step right on to any stage and play Othello without rehearsal. He's been following me all over the ship to see that I don't talk to you.'

Reggie quivered. He was remembering that brotherly eye which had bitten into him like an acid. Miss Blossom, on the other hand, seemed pleased and flattered.

'Dear old Ammie! He's been that way ever since the evening at Biarritz when I shyly murmured "Yes." Remind me to tell you some time what he did to a Spaniard there, just because ... but we're wandering from the point. A girl can kiss her future brother-in-law, can't she? Of course she can. Hoity-toity! What next! Kindly step this way, please.'

'Well, good-bye,' said Reggie.

There was nothing dilatory in the manner in which he turned the handle and slid out, and there was still less that was dilatory in the leap which Miss Blossom made in the direction of his vanishing form. Her intentions might have been those of a mother yearning to comfort, but the general effect was more that of a tigress bounding upon a lamb. The next moment, Monty was alone in the state-room, leaning limply against the wall. He was a good deal unnerved. All this sort of thing, he presumed, would have been the merest commonplace of every-day life in Hollywood, but to one who, like himself, was mixing for the first time in motion-picture circles it was rather breathtaking. He felt as if he had been plunged into the foaming maelstrom of a two-reel educational comic.

Dazedly, he listened to the noise of pursuit as it rolled along the corridor. What Reggie's emotions were he could only conjecture, but the lady herself was plainly in merry mood. He could hear her jolly laughter. He could, indeed, have heard it if he had been at the other end of the ship. Demure, even melancholy, on the screen, Lottie Blossom had a happy nature off it, and her lungs were good. When she laughed, she laughed.

Suddenly, however, there was a dramatic change. The laughter ceased abruptly, to be succeeded by a confused uproar, unmistakably sinister in its general trend. Voices made themselves heard. He recognized the clear soprano of Miss Blossom, the light baritone of Reggie, and competing with these a deeper note which brought back to him childhood memories of being taken to the Zoo to see the lions fed.

Then silence, and a few moments after that footsteps outside. Miss Blossom came in and sat down on the bed. Her face was flushed. She was breathing quickly. It was plain that she had been passing through some emotional experience.

'Did you hear all that?' she asked.

'I did,' said Monty.

'That,' said Miss Blossom, 'was Ambrose.'

Monty had divined as much, and he waited with no little interest for further details. It was not immediately that these came, for his companion was busy with her thoughts and a powder-puff. Presently, however, she spoke:

'He came on us round the corner.'

'Oh?'

'Yes. I had caught Reggie and was kissing him.'

'I see.'

'And I heard a noise like a tyre exploding, and there was Ambrose.'

'Ah.'

Miss Blossom gave her nose a final dab, and put away the puff.

'Ambrose took it rather big.'

'I fancied I heard him taking it quite fairly big.'

'He called me some most unpleasant names, and I'm going to

have a word with him about it later. Love's love,' said Miss Blossom with spirit, 'but I'm not proposing to let any bimbo come the man of chilled steel over me just because I happen to kiss an old friend. Would you?'

'Would I what?'

'I mean, wouldn't you?'

'Wouldn't I which?'

'Bawl Ambrose out for making such a boob of himself.'

'Oh, ah.'

'What do you mean, "Oh, ah"?'

Monty was not quite sure what he had meant, beyond wishing to convey in a general sort of way that he would prefer, if it could be avoided, not to become embroiled in what was so obviously a purely personal misunderstanding. Fortunately, before he was obliged to state and define, she continued:

'The trouble with writers is, they're all loopy. I remember the fellow who did the dialogue for *Shadows on the Wall* stopping rehearsal once to tell me that when I said "Oh!" on finding the corpse in the cabin-trunk I must let the word come slowly out in the shape of a pear. Well, I ask you! And Ambrose is loopier than that.'

'Yes?'

'Yes, sir. You should have seen him at Biarritz.'

'What did he do at Biarritz?'

'What didn't he do at Biarritz! Just because he pinched my leg.'

'Ambrose pinched your leg?'

'No, a Spaniard that I met at the Casino did, and by the time Ambrose had finished with him I guess he must have thought he'd been in a bull-fight. It wouldn't surprise me if he wasn't running yet. It's only two months ago.'

This revelation of the novelist's sterner side came as no surprise to Monty.

'Reggie tells me that Ambrose has always been a pretty hard egg.'

'Yes, and up to a point that's fine. A girl likes to feel she's going around with a fellow that she knows any moment he can sasshay up to Spaniards if they get fresh – and, mind you, Spaniards do get fresh – and ask them what the hell. But when he starts in behaving like King Kong purely because I was saying "Hello" to his young brother Reggie, that's not so good. I shall certainly have a word with Ambrose. I'm not standing for that sort of thing. Am I a serf?'

Monty said no, she was not a serf.

'You're just about right, too, I'm not a serf,' agreed Miss Blossom. 'No, sir!'

Women are subject to swift and sudden changes of mood. Up to this point, nobody could have been more firm and resolute than this injured girl. Her lips were tight, her eyes aglow. But now, abruptly, those lips began to quiver, those eyes to film over, and with acute discomfort Monty became aware that, her case stated, she was about to have a good cry.

'I say!' he said, concerned. 'I say!'

'Oomph,' whimpered Miss Blossom. 'Oomph.'

There are practically no good things to say to a girl who is moaning 'Oomph' in your state-room. The finest vocabulary will not serve a man here. It becomes a matter for the gentle pat and nothing but the gentle pat. You can administer it on the head, or you can administer it on the shoulder, but you must administer it somewhere. Monty selected the head, because it was nearest. Bowed in her hands, it offered a gleaming invitation.

'There, there,' he said.

She continued to moan. He continued to pat. And for some moments matters proceeded along these lines.

But there is one rather bad snare in this patting business, which should be pointed out for the benefit of those who may some day find themselves having to do it. Unless you are very careful, after a while you forget to take your hand off. You just stand there resting it on the subject's head, and that is apt to cause people who see you to purse their lips.

Gertrude Butterwick did. She came in just as Monty fell into this error. After patting for perhaps a minute and a quarter, he stood there in the attitude described. A sharp sound rather like a cat choking on a fishbone caused him to look round, and there in the doorway was Gertrude Butterwick pursing her lips.

# Chapter 12

It was a moment fraught with embarrassment, and Monty recognized it as such. His first action was to remove his hand from Miss Blossom's hair with a swiftness which he could scarcely have excelled had that hair been as red hot as it looked; his second to utter a careless laugh. Finding, however, that this was coming out more like a death-rattle than the jolly guffaw for which he had intended it, he switched it off in its early stages and a silence fell upon the state-room. He looked at Gertrude. Gertrude looked at him. Then she looked at Miss Blossom, then at him again. After that, she took the Mickey Mouse from under her arm and placed it on the settee. Her manner in doing this was that of one laying a wreath on the grave of an old friend.

Monty found speech.

'Oh, there you are!' he said.

'Yes,' said Gertrude. 'Here I am.'

'What a pity,' said Monty, moistening his lips slightly with the tip of the tongue, as if he were going to have his photograph taken, 'you didn't come earlier. You missed Reggie.'

'Oh?'

The way in which she spoke this favourite word of hers would not have commended itself to Miss Blossom's friend, the author of the dialogue of *Shadows on the Wall*. It did not come out slowly in the shape of a pear but with a rather horrifying abruptness, and Monty was compelled to moisten his lips again.

'Yes,' he said, 'you missed Reggie. He was here. He's only just left. And Ambrose. He was here. He's only just left. And the steward – he's only just left – he was here, too, a very pleasant, well-informed fellow of the name of Peasemarch,

And Ambrose. And Reggie. And this chap Peasemarch. We were quite a crowd.'

'Oh?'

'Yes. Quite a crowd we were. By the way, I don't think you know one another, do you? This is Miss Lotus Blossom, the film star.'

'Oh?'

'We saw her in that picture, you recall.'

'Yes. I remember,' said Gertrude, 'that you admired Miss Blossom very much.'

Lottie Blossom started like a war-horse at the sound of the bugle.

'What picture was that?'

'*Lovers in Brooklyn.*'

'You should have caught me in *Storm over Flatbush.*'

'Tell us all about *Storm over Flatbush,*' said Monty.

'I don't want to hear about *Storm over Flatbush,*' said Gertrude.

Embarrassment supervened once more. Its ugly shadow was still brooding over State-room C 25 when a large mop came in, followed by Albert Peasemarch.

'I've brought the mop, sir,' said Albert.

'Then take it away again.'

'I was under the impression that you desired a mop, sir.'

'Well, I don't.'

'Very good, sir,' said Albert Peasemarch stiffly. 'I was put to some considerable trouble to procure it, but if you now in-struct me to take it back again, very good.'

Ignoring Monty in a pointed manner, he turned to Lottie Blossom.

'Might I have a word with you, Miss?'

Lottie Blossom gazed at him wearily. She was not feeling *en rapport* with this man. It seemed to her that what the world wanted was fewer and better Peasemarches.

'You wouldn't,' she said, endeavouring to clothe this thought in speech, 'consider getting to hell out of here, would you, steward?'

'In one moment, miss, after I've had this word to which I allude. It's with ref. to that alligator of yours. Are you aware,

101

miss, that the reptile is navigating at the rate of knots along the corridor and may at any moment begin scaring the day lights out of nervous people and invalids?'

Lottie Blossom uttered a bereaved cry.

'Didn't you fasten the lid of its basket?'

'No, miss. In answer to your question, I did not fasten the lid of its basket. When a lady instructs me to open a wicker-work basket and I find inside a young alligator which if it had aimed half an inch more to the left would have took the top of my thumb off, I don't hang about fastening lids. It would be nearing the main companion-way by now, I fancy, and if you wish for my opinion, miss, I think it should be overtook and fetched by some responsible party.'

The prospect thus held out of getting rid of Miss Blossom enchanted Monty. It was not that he was actually looking forward to being left alone with Gertrude, but there could be no doubt that the situation would be greatly eased if that red hair was no longer there for the dear girl to stare at.

'He's quite right,' he said. 'You'd better get after it immediately. Mustn't have alligators roaming the ship, what? Might annoy Scupperguts, eh, Peasemarch?'

'The matter,' said Albert Peasemarch coldly, 'would scarcely fall within Scupperguts's province.'

'Well, the Dooser.'

'Nor into that of the Dooser. It would be more a case for Jimmy the One.'

'And we don't want to upset Jimmy the One, do we?' said Monty heartily. 'I should start now, if I were you.'

Lottie Blossom moved to the door, muttering strange Beverly Hills expletives beneath her breath.

'It's a wonder people wouldn't fasten lids,' she said querulously.

'You fail to appreciate my position, miss,' urged Albert Peasemarch, following her out. 'You don't, if I may venture to say so, quite seem able to understand my point of view. To have fastened that lid would have involved putting my hand a lot closer to the reptile's iron jaws than what I would have wished to put it. Use your intelligence, miss . . .'

His voice died away in the distance, reasoning closely, and

a gulp at his side told Monty that the committee of two, into which he and Gertrude had been formed, was about to go into session.

He braced himself to play the man. That things were looking a trifle glutinous, he could not deny. Bodkins, from the days of the great crusader, Sieur Pharamond de Bodkyn, had done their bit in England's rough island story, running risks of which their insurance companies would not have approved, but not a Bodkin on the list, he felt, had ever been in a tougher spot than that in which their twentieth-century representative now found himself. For what is a jab from a Paynim lance or a bullet through the leg at Fontenoy compared with the prospect of having one's life's happiness laid in ruins?

Gertrude's eyes were cold, her lips set. Her whole aspect was that of a girl who has been doing a lot of hard thinking about butterflies.

'Well?' she said.

Monty cleared his throat, and endeavoured with his tongue to correct a certain dryness of the mouth.

'That,' he said, 'was Miss Blossom.'

'Yes. You introduced us.'

'So I did. Yes. She's a bit disappointing, don't you think?'

'In what way?'

'Off the screen, I mean. Not so pretty as one would have expected.'

'You did not think her pretty?'

'No. No. By no means. Not at all. Quite the reverse.'

'Oh?' said Gertrude, employing in her utterance of the word that rising inflection which he liked least.

He applied first-aid treatment to his palate once more.

'You were doubtless surprised,' he said, 'to find her in here.'

'I was.'

'You wondered, no doubt, what she was doing?'

'I could see what she was doing. She was letting you stroke her head.'

'Quite, quite,' said Monty hastily. 'Or, rather, not quite. You don't get what I mean. I mean, you wondered, no doubt, what her motive was in coming in here. I will tell you. And I

103

wasn't stroking her head, I was patting it. Her motive in coming in here was to see Ambrose.'

'Ambrose?'

'Ambrose. Your cousin Ambrose. That was her motive in coming in here. To see him. She wanted to see Ambrose, you understand, and she thought this was his state-room.'

'Oh?'

'There was apparently some confusion in the passenger list.'

'Oh?'

'Yes. Some confusion.'

'And what has she got to do with Ambrose?'

'Why, they're engaged.'

'Engaged?'

'Yes. Didn't you know? I suppose they kept it dark – like us. Few people,' Monty reminded her, 'know of our engagement.'

'I'm not at all sure that there is an engagement for them to know of.'

'Gertrude!'

'I'm trying to make up my mind. I find you in here, stroking this woman's head –'

'Not stroking. Patting. Any man with a heart would have done it. She was in trouble, poor thing. She had just had a row with Ambrose. All through Reggie, the silly ass.'

'Reggie?'

Something seemed to go off in Monty's head like a spring. There was a ringing in his ears, and the state-room flickered about him. The sensation was entirely novel to him, but what had happened was that he had had an inspiration. It was as if the mention of Reggie's name had released a flood of light, illuminating the perilous path along which he had been timorously picking his way.

For the first time since she had come into the room, he found himself facing the situation with an uplifted heart. His voice, as he spoke, had a strange, new ring of confidence.

'Reggie,' he said primly, 'has been behaving very badly. I was just coming to look for you, to tell you about it. I want to talk to you about Reggie.'

'I came to talk to *you* about Reggie.'

104

'Did you? Have you heard, then? About him and Ambrose and Miss Blossom?'

'What do you mean?'

Monty's face took on an almost Peasemarchian expression of disapproval. He looked like an aunt.

'I think,' he said, even more primly than before, 'that you ought to have a word with Reggie. Or somebody ought. I mean to say, that sort of thing may be amusing from his point of view, but, as I told him, it's not quite playing the game. I hate these practical jokes. I can't see anything funny in them.'

'What *are* you talking about?'

'I'm talking about what Reggie's been doing. What he doesn't realize – mere thoughtlessness, of course, but what he doesn't realize –'

'But what has Reggie done?'

'I'm telling you. You know what he is – one of the biggest liars in London –'

'He isn't.'

'Pardon me, yes. And on top of that he's got this distorted sense of humour. So what happens? The silly ass goes to Miss Blossom and fills her up with a lot of rot about what a devil Ambrose is and how she's a mug if she trusts him an inch, and so on and so forth. A nice thing, what? I can tell you I was pretty terse with him. I didn't like it, and I let him see that I didn't like it. As I told him, jokes of that sort may so easily lead to trouble and unpleasantness. Well, take this case. Miss Blossom won't speak to him. To Ambrose, I mean. She took it all in, like a chump, and went off the deep end. You saw how she was crying just now.'

Gertrude seemed spellbound.

'Reggie did that?'

'Yes.'

'But – but why?'

'I'm telling you. Because he's got this distorted sense of humour. Anything for a laugh.'

'But where does the fun come in?'

'Don't ask me. But he tells me he often does it. Goes to girls, I mean, and kids them that the fellows they're engaged to are regular hell hounds. Just to see them jump.'

'But it seems so unlike Reggie.'

'I thought so, too. But there it is.'

'Why, he's a little fiend!'

'In human shape. Absolutely.'

'The little brute!'

'Yes.'

'Poor old Ambrose!'

'Yes.'

'I'll never speak to Reggie again.'

Gertrude's eyes blazed. Then suddenly the fire was quenched. A tear stole down her cheek.

'Monty,' she said remorsefully.

'Hullo?'

'No. I don't know how to tell you.'

'Tell me?'

A struggle seemed to take place inside Gertrude Butterwick.

'Yes, I will. I must. Monty, do you know why I came here?'

'To take me off to dinner? It'll be dinner-time soon, I suppose. Whose table are you at?'

'The captain's. But never mind that –'

'I'm at Jimmy the One's. What a nuisance we aren't together.'

'Yes. But never mind that. I want to tell you. I feel such a beast.'

'Eh?'

Gertrude gulped. Her eyes fell. The blush of shame was on her cheek.

'I came here to return the Mickey Mouse you gave me.'

'What!'

'I did. You'll hardly believe this, Monty –'

'Believe what?'

'This evening, Reggie came to me and told me about you exactly what you say he told Miss Blossom about Ambrose.'

Monty stared.

'He did?'

'Yes. He said that there was never a moment when you were not making love to three girls at a time –'

'Good heavens!'

106

'– and that you were so artful that you could persuade each of them that she was the only one you cared for.'

'Well, I'm dashed!'

Another gulp escaped Gertrude.

'And, oh, Monty darling, I believed him!'

There was a tense silence. Monty registered amazement, pain, incredulity, and indignation.

'Well, really!' he said.

'I know, I know!'

'Well, really,' said Monty, 'this beats everything. Upon my sacred Sam, I positively am dashed. I wouldn't have thought it of you, Gertrude. You have hurt me inexpressibly, old egg. How you could be such a mutton-headed little juggins –'

'I know, I know. But, you see, coming right on top of that tattoo thing on your chest –'

'I explained that. Explained it fully.'

'I know. Still, you can't blame me for thinking things.'

'Yes, I can. A pure, sweet English girl ought not to think things.'

'Well, anyway, I don't believe it any longer. I know you love me. You do, don't you?'

'Love you? Well, when you reflect that in order to win you I became assistant editor of *Tiny Tots*, a journal for the Nursery and the Home, and then secretary to old Emsworth – and what a soft snap *that* was! – and after that one of Percy Pilbeam's skilled birds, I should think you ought to be able to realize by this time that I love you. If you can't get that into your fat head –'

'It is fat, isn't it?' said Gertrude, with remorse.

'Pretty fat,' assented Monty sternly. 'Why, look at what happened just now. Would anybody but a fat-head have taken up the attitude you did when you found me in here with Miss Blossom? I don't mind telling you that I was not a little wounded by your manner. You shot a very nasty look at me.'

'It seemed so odd that you should be stroking her head.'

'Not stroking. Patting. And that only in the very lightest possible way. My motives were pure to the last drop. I thought I had made that clear. The girl was in trouble, and I patted her cupola in precisely the same spirit – no more, no less – as

107

that in which I would have patted a bull pup with stomach-ache.'

'Of course.'

'It's no pleasure to *me* to pat girls' heads.'

'No, no – I quite understand.'

Faintly from along the corridor there came the sound of a bugle blowing.

'Dinner!' said Monty, with a sigh of satisfaction. He felt he needed it.

He kissed Gertrude.

'Come along,' he said. 'Shake a leg, old egg. And afterwards we will walk on the boat deck and talk of this and that.'

'Yes, that will be lovely. Oh, Monty, I'm so glad you came on this boat. What fun we shall have.'

'Rather!'

'I wonder if there will be dancing in the evenings?'

'Sure to be. I'll find out from Albert Peasemarch.'

'Who's he?'

'The steward chap.'

'Oh, the steward. He seems rather a character.'

'Quite a character.'

'What was all that about the mop?'

Monty quivered. His eyes became a little glassy.

'Mop?'

'Why did he bring a mop?'

Monty moistened his lips.

'Did he bring a mop?'

'Yes, don't you remember?'

Monty pulled himself together.

'Of course, yes. So he did. But heaven knows why. I remember wondering at the time. Must have misunderstood something I said, I suppose. Half these stewards on liners are practically loonies. What on earth should I want a mop for? A mop, I mean! So damn silly. I say, do let's push along and collect that dinner.'

'All right. Where's my mouse?'

'Here it is.'

Gertrude regarded the Mickey Mouse with tender remorse.

'Just imagine, Monty! I brought this to give it back to you.

Because I thought everything was over between us.'

'Ha, ha!' laughed Monty jovially. 'Of all the cuckoo ideas!'

'I feel so ashamed of myself.'

'Quite all right, quite all right. All set now for the quick dash to the trough?'

'In one minute. I just want to bathe my eyes in your bathroom.'

Monty clutched at the door handle. He needed some strong support. Everything seemed to have gone black.

'No!' he cried, with extraordinary vehemence. 'You don't want to bathe any bally eyes.'

'Aren't they red?'

'Of course they're not. They look fine. They always look fine. You've got the most terrific eyes.'

'Do you think so?'

'Everybody thinks so. It's all over London. Like twin stars.'

It was the right note. There was no more talk of going into the bathroom. She allowed him to turn her round, to steer her through the door, to lead her out into the passage. They began to walk along it together. Her hand was in his, and she prattled at his side.

Monty did not prattle. He was vibrating gently, as a man will who has just escaped from a great peril. He felt faint and hollow.

Everything was fine. The luck of the Bodkins had held, and the danger was past. But it would be some little time before he rounded into mid-season form again.

As his crusading ancestor, the Sieur Pharamond de Bodkyn, to whom we have alluded, had put it, writing home to his wife and telling her how he had been unhorsed at the Battle of Joppa – 'Ytte was suche a dam near squeake as I never wante to have agayne in a month of Sundays. E'en now am I sweatinge atte every pore, and meseems I hardlie knowe if I stande on ye head or, ye heels.'

# Chapter 13

It was not until the third morning of the voyage that Mr Ivor Llewellyn proceeded to put into operation the scheme outlined by his sister-in-law Mabel Spence for drawing the fangs of the Customs spy whose dark shadow was blotting the sunshine from his life. To be exact, at fourteen minutes past ten on the third morning of the voyage.

Considering with what enthusiasm he had welcomed the idea when it had been proposed, this delay may strike the reader as strange. Brought up from childhood in the creed that the presidents of motion-picture corporations are men who think on their feet and do it now, he may be saying to himself that this is scarcely the old Llewellyn form and speculating as to the possibility of that great executive brain having lost its grip a bit. The matter is, however, as Monty Bodkin would have said, susceptible of a ready explanation. Just as he was about to get action, up sprang a terrific gale and took his mind off business.

For the first few hours after leaving Cherbourg nothing could have been calmer and serener than the ocean. The vessel purred through waters that seemed to be trying to compete in blueness and blandness with those of the Mediterranean. People played deck tennis, shuffleboard became rampant, and the heartiest of meals were consumed by one and all. In short, 'Youth on the prow and Pleasure at the helm' only faintly expresses the conditions on board.

And then, quite suddenly on the second morning, just as the first shy deck stewards were beginning to steal out with cups of soup and the fluting cry of the shuffleboard addicts was making itself heard in the drowsy stillness, the skies turned from blue to grey, the horizon became dark with unwholesome-looking clouds, and the wind, veering to the north, blew with a gradually increasing force till presently it was howling through the rigging with a shrill melancholy wail and causing the R.M.S. *Atlantic* to behave more like a Russian dancer than a respectable ship. Ivor Llewellyn, prone in his bunk and holding on to the woodwork, was able to count no fewer than five occasions when the vessel lowered Nijinsky's record for leaping in the air and twiddling the feet before descending.

For a whole day and part of the following night the *Atlantic* staggered on her way, buffeted by the hurricane – or, as the dull and unimaginative officer who wrote up the ship's log described it, the 'fresh north-easterly breeze'. Then the wind dropped, the sea grew smooth, and the third day of the voyage found the sun smiling through once more.

Among the first to greet it, if 'greet' is the right word to use of a man who, passionately fond of his sleep, is routed out of bed by the night-watchman at five o'clock in the morning, was Albert Peasemarch. Together with his forty-nine companions in the Glory Hole, he rose, dressed himself sketchily and, having partaken of bread and jam and tea, went to work on the alleyways of his section of the C deck. At eight-fifty a bell rang informing him that his presence was desired in Stateroom C 31. He went in and found Mr Llewellyn propped up among the pillows, looking pale and interesting.

'Good morning, sir,' said Albert Peasemarch, with that bright courtesy which stewards, no matter how early they may have risen, always contrive to put on like a garment. 'You wish for breakfast, sir? What may I bring you? Boiled eggs? Eggs and bacon? Bloaters? Haddock? Sausages? Curry? Many gentlemen like to start the day with curry.'

A shudder closely resembling those given by the R.M.S. *Atlantic* when shipping heavy seas shook Mr Llewellyn, and his eyes flickered as if he had received a blow. In the interval between the completion of his mopping and scrubbing and this summons from his feudal overlord, Albert Peasemarch had returned to the Glory Hole and made a more careful toilet, so that he was now his usual spruce and ingratiating self. Nevertheless, the seigneur of State-room C 31 gazed upon him with a sullen loathing. Watching Mr Llewellyn's face, you might have supposed that he was looking at his wife's brother

George, or even at his wife's cousin Egbert's sister Genevieve, who was employed in the Reading Department at three hundred and fifty dollars a week.

'Coffee!' he said, mastering his emotion.

'Coffee, sir? Yes, sir. And with the coffee, sir?'

'Just coffee.'

'Just coffee, sir? Very good, sir. Odd,' said Albert Pease-march, who had never been one of those men who are taciturn in the morning, 'how widely gentlemen's tastes vary with respect to the first meal of the day. A man in my position meets all sorts, as you can well imagine. I had a bloke in one of my sheds on the old *Laurentic* who liked nothing so much as a raw Spanish onion. And there was another who was always after me to try to get him a dozen oysters. Sir?'

'Get that coffee,' said Mr Llewellyn huskily.

'Very good, sir. Still feeling a little shaky, no doubt, after that capful of wind we ran into. I noticed that you kept to your bed yesterday, and I said to myself: "There's one bloke that's copped it. There's one gentleman," I said, "whose dining-room steward isn't going to be run off his feet." I may say that your absence excited remark, sir. There was a Mr Ambrose Tenny-son inquiring after you this morning. Also a Miss Passenger, a muscular young lady who, I understand, is the leader of this hockey troupe that's going to the States. Now, there's a thing we didn't see so much of when you and I were young, sir. You didn't find ladies racing down fields with mallets in their hands then. Well, sir, I mustn't stand here talking, must I? You're wanting your coffee. I forget what it was you said you desired with the –'

Mr Llewellyn's eyes bulged.

'COFFEE!' he said.

Albert Peasemarch's brain grasped the position. The gentleman wanted coffee. Not Spanish onions. Not oysters. Coffee.

'Coffee, sir – yes, sir. You shall have it in one moment, sir. I'll just draw the shade back from your port-hole, sir. You will find it a nice, sunny morning.'

He did so, rather in the manner of some important function-ary unveiling a statue, and a golden glow filled the state-room.

112

It effected a marked change for the better in Mr Llewellyn. Taken in conjunction with the fact that he was now relieved of Albert Peasemarch's society, it definitely eased the strain. Even now, you could not have described him as rollicking, but he certainly felt less like a corpse on a slab. He lay there, watching the sunlight and thinking, and it was not long before his thoughts began to drift in the direction of Monty Bodkin.

Hitherto, when he had thought of Monty, it had been with the uneasy alarm of a rabbit meditating on a weasel. The face of Monty, rising before his eyes, had given him a sort of sick feeling. But now, so pronounced was the optimism engendered by the improved weather conditions, it seemed to him that he had been allowing the man's menace to agitate him unnecessarily. Mabel, he felt, was perfectly right. One had simply to offer the fellow a contract with the Superba-Llewellyn and he would fall over himself in his eagerness to oblige. There had been times, notably while in conference with imported English playwrights, when Mr Llewellyn had regretted that he had ever become a motion-picture president, but he saw now that it was the ideal walk in life. A motion-picture president could fix anybody.

His coffee, arriving a few minutes later, completed the restoration of his sense of well-being. So much so that quarter of an hour after that he was ringing the bell again and ordering a mushroom omelette, and a quarter of an hour after that smoking a cigarette, and half an hour after that ringing the bell once more and commanding Albert Peasemarch to summon Ambrose Tennyson.

And presently Ambrose, having been located on the promenade deck, where he was walking up and down like Napoleon on the *Bellerophon*, was ushered into his presence, given his instructions and despatched to Monty's state-room, an accredited ambassador.

Monty, like Mr Llewellyn, had proved a ready victim to the recent storm. It was his first experience of the Western Ocean in one of its less attractive moods, and he had succumbed while the ship was still, as it were, just shuffling its feet before actually going into its dance. For the whole of the previous day he

113

had remained in bed, to awake this morning with a sense of having passed through the valley of the shadow and somehow scrambled safely to the other side, which at one time he had never expected to enjoy. He had not yet risen, but he had partaken of an excellent breakfast, and at the moment of Ambrose's arrival was chatting to Reggie, who had looked in to borrow cigarettes.

Ambrose's entry cast a certain constraint upon what had been a pleasant getting together of old friends. In Reggie's case, this was due to the fact that his brother's last words to him, spoken at the conclusion of that Lottie Blossom episode in the corridor, had been the statement that for two pins he would wring his neck, and there was no knowing, Reggie felt, whether on a well-equipped ship like this he might not, in the interval, have succeeded in obtaining those pins.

Monty, on his side, found the novelist's presence jarring upon him because the latter seemed to bring with him into the room an atmosphere of doom and desolation and despair, of charnel houses and winding sheets and spectral voices wailing in the wind. There was a murky gloom about Ambrose Tennyson's aspect, as if he had just been reading a bad notice in a weekly review, and Monty, eyeing him, came shrewdly to the conclusion that Miss Blossom must have fulfilled her promise of having that word with him of which she had spoken so feelingly.

He was not mistaken. The lady belonging to the school of thought which holds that we should not let the sun go down on our wrath, the interview had taken place that same night shortly before the hour of retiring to rest, and it had sent Ambrose to bed in a condition of sandbagged pessimism which still prevailed in all its pristine intensity. Red hair and meekness are two things which seldom go together, and Lottie Blossom specialized in the former. The scene began and finished on the upper deck, and the interested listener who bet another interested listener two dollars that Ambrose would not be able to get a word in within the space of ten minutes by the smoking-room clock came very near to winning his wager. A musical-comedy training, followed by a post-graduate course in Hollywood studios, had taught Miss Blossom to talk first, talk quick and keep on talking. By the time she had had her say only broken fragments remained of what had once been a sturdy and promising young engagement.

These things put their stamp on a man, and one look at his brother was sufficient to send Reggie sliding from the room, muttering something about seeing Monty later. Ambrose was thus enabled to secure the latter's undivided attention. He approached the bed and stood for a moment glaring down at its occupant with the unlovable air of a First Murderer out of Shakespeare.

It was not merely the fact that his heart was broken that caused Ambrose Tennyson to look like this. Other circumstances had contributed to his moroseness. It irked him to be used by Mr Llewellyn as a messenger boy: he resented having been compelled for even a few moments to breathe air tainted by the presence of his brother Reginald: and he thought the idea of Monty acting on the films the most idiotic he had ever heard.

His manner, accordingly, as he delivered his message, was curt, even abrupt. He came to the point without preamble, wishing to get the thing over and done with, so that he might return to the promenade deck and resume his day-dreams about taking a running jump over the vessel's side – a policy which he considered, and perhaps rightly, would make Miss Blossom feel pretty silly.

'You know Llewellyn?' he said.

Monty admitted to knowing Mr Llewellyn, though only slightly. Just, he explained, in the way of asking him to spell things, if Ambrose knew what he meant. The impression he conveyed was that if he happened not to have his pocket dictionary handy, he used Ivor Llewellyn.

'He wants you to go into the pictures,' said Ambrose scowling heavily.

A slight confusion occurred here. Monty interpreted the announcement as an invitation from the president of the Superba-Llewellyn to accompany him to some motion-picture performance which was to be held on board the ship, and he spoke for a while in appreciative vein of the marvels of modern ocean travel – all these liners, he meant to say, with their ballrooms and swimming-baths and cinema palaces and what not.

Lavish, said Monty, not mincing his words, absolutely lavish. He predicted a not distant future when vessels plying between Southampton and New York would offer their patrons a polo field, a full-size golf course and a few hundred acres of rough shooting.

This caused Ambrose to grind his teeth a little. The panegyric had cut into his valuable time. Every minute spent in this state-room meant a minute when he was not on the promenade deck contemplating suicide.

'Not "to" the pictures,' he said, wishing that when Monty had fallen into the fountain that bump-supper night at Oxford he had not been idiot enough to pull him out. ' "Into" the pictures. He wants you to act for him.'

Monty could make nothing of this. He stared, perplexed.

'Act?'

'Act.'

'What – act?'

'Yes, act.'

'You don't mean,' said Monty, clutching at the word which seemed to provide a sort of shadowy clue to what his companion was driving at, 'act?'

Ambrose Tennyson clenched his fists and groaned a silent groan. Better balanced men than he had found Monty Bodkin in what might be called his goggling mood a little trying.

'Oh, for heaven's sake! You have the most infernal habit,' he said, 'when anyone says the simplest thing to you, of letting your lower jaw drop and looking like a half-witted sheep staring over a fence. Don't do it. I'm not quite myself just now, and it makes me want to hit you with something. Listen. Ivor Llewellyn, in his capacity of president of the Superba-Llewellyn Motion Picture Corporation of Llewellyn City, Southern California, produces motion pictures. In order to produce these motion pictures he requires actors to act in them. He wants to know if you will be one of those actors.'

Monty brightened. He had seen daylight.

'He wants me to act?'

'That's right – act. He sent me to ask if you would accept a contract. What shall I tell him?'

'I see. Oh, ah, yes. Yes,' said Monty coyly. 'H'm. Ha.'

'And what the devil, precisely,' inquired Ambrose, 'does *that* mean?'

He was saying to himself that he must be strong, that he must have self-control and ride himself on the curb. Juries, he knew, looked askance at men who strangled even the half-witted in their beds.

Monty's coyness was now positively painful to the eye.

'But I've never acted in my life. Except once at my old kindergarten.'

'Well, do you propose to begin now? Or not? For goodness sake let me have something definite. He is waiting for me to report.'

'I don't see how I can.'

'Right. That's all I wanted to know.'

'I can't understand why he wants me to.'

'Nor can I. But apparently he does. Well, I'll go and tell him you thank him for the offer but have other views.'

'Yes, I like that. Other views. That's good.'

'Right.'

The door slammed. Monty, finding himself alone, left his bed without delay and, hurrying to the mirror, stood peering into it with a questioning, what-is-it-master-likes-so-much expression on his face. He was consumed with curiosity as to what there could be about his personal appearance that had caused Ivor Llewellyn, presumably a hard man to please in the matter of faces, to single him out from the crowd and make him so extraordinarily flattering an offer.

He sifted the evidence thoroughly – examining his reflection full face, side face, three-quarter face and over the left shoulder, smiling genially, tenderly, cynically, and bitterly; and finally frowning, first with menace and then with reproach. He also registered surprise, dismay, joy, horror, loathing, and renunciation.

But when the returns were all in, he still had to confess himself baffled. No matter how much he smiled and frowned, he was totally unable to see what Mr Llewellyn had seen. Where the president of the Superba-Llewellyn apparently beheld one of those faces that launch a thousand ships, all he could detect was just the same old regulation, workaday set of features

which he had been carrying around the West End of London
for years – without, it is true, exciting actual hostility or mob
violence, but certainly not knocking the public in any sense cold.

He had given the thing up as one of those insoluble mysteries
and was wondering whether, now that he was out of bed, he
might not as well stay out and get dressed, when there was a
loud cry without, a forceful bang upon the door, and Miss
Lotus Blossom came sailing over the threshold in the confident
manner of one on whom the freedom of some city is about to
be bestowed.

Monty's absence from the life of the ship on the preceding
day had not passed unnoticed by Lottie Blossom, and she had
decided that as soon as she was up and about this morning it
would be only neighbourly if she called and made inquiries. By
this she meant that she would go and hammer on his door and
shout 'Bring out your dead!' through the keyhole. She was a
kind-hearted girl.

That she had not done so earlier was due to the fact that she
was a leisurely riser when making an ocean voyage. At Hollywood she could, if her art demanded it, be on the set made up
at 6 a.m., but on board ship she preferred to take her breakfast
in bed and linger over it. It was only now, accordingly, that she
found herself able to pay the proposed visit.

Having bathed, she fed her alligator – who, if she could not
get a human finger, liked the yolk of a hard-boiled egg of a
morning – and dressed herself in a white and green sports suit
topped off with a leopard-skin cape and a coal-heaver hat in
scarlet felt. Then she tied a pink ribbon round the alligator's
neck, tucked it under her arm and set forth on her errand of
mercy.

As she came out of her state-room Ambrose came out of
Monty's.

'Oo, look!' she cried. 'Hello, Ambrose.'

'Good morning,' said the novelist. His voice was cold and
hard and proud and aloof. It had shaken him to see her there,
but he did not betray his emotion by any weak simperings. He
bore himself like a man who has purged all weakness from his
soul. 'Good morning,' he said, and stalked off towards Mr
Llewellyn's room without another word – about as dignified

an exit, he flattered himself, as man had ever made. By speaking thus, and stalking in that manner, he had, he rather fancied, made it pretty clear to Miss Blossom that there went a man in whose iron bosom regret and remorse had no existence.

As for Lottie, a tender smile played over her face, the smile of a mother who watches her child in a tantrum. She followed him with loving eyes till he had disappeared; then, turning to Monty's door, smote it a hearty buffet, issued her demand for corpses and went in.

The sight of her sent Monty leaping between the sheets again as if he had been shot out of a gun. No nymph surprised while bathing could have been quicker off the mark.

Lottie Blossom did not share his modest confusion.

'Hello, beautiful,' she said. 'Were you doing your daily dozen?'

'No, I – er –'

Monty was finding it difficult to play the host. A courteous ease of manner was beyond him. It seemed only too plain that his visitor was planning for the duration of the voyage to treat his state-room as a sort of annex to her own, and the prospect filled him with tremors and alarms. For though, as Albert Peasemarch had pointed out, it was not likely that a pure, sweet English girl would come wandering into his bedchamber, there was always the hideous possibility of such an occurrence. As he watched his guest seat herself with effortless grace on the foot of the bed, the thought of Gertrude was bulking very largely in his mind.

He was also wishing that if Miss Blossom found it necessary to invade his privacy, she would not bring her alligator with her.

Lottie Blossom was all cheerfulness and affability. The sombre mood which had caused her to go 'Oomph, oomph' in this state-room two days before had been a mere thing of the moment. She was now in excellent fettle – as radiant and happy as only a redhaired girl who enjoys emotional quarrelling can be after a thoroughly invigorating turn-up. Life, to be really life for her, had to consist of a series of devastating rows and terrific reconciliations. Anything milder she considered insipid. Lotus Blossom had been born a Murphy of Hoboken, and all the Hoboken Murphys were like that.

'Well, kid,' she said, 'how's tricks?' She placed the alligator lovingly on the coverlet and gazed about her like a returned exile surveying his boyhood home. 'Seems ages since I was last in here. And yet everything in the dear old place comes back to me. How's the Horror on the Bathroom Wall? Still there?'

'Still there,' Monty assured her.

She struck a philosophical note.

'Funny to think that if somebody like Sinclair Lewis had written that, he'd have got about a dollar a word for it. Whereas I get nothing. Ah, well, that's how it goes.'

Monty, with a silent nod, expressed his agreement. That, his nod said, was how it went.

'I say,' he said, changing the subject and turning to one that was very near his heart, 'is that bally animal safe?'

'You mean my alligator?'

'Yes.'

Miss Blossom seemed surprised.

'Why, sure. Who's going to hurt him?'

'I mean,' said Monty, perceiving that she had missed the gist, 'doesn't he gnaw one to the bone, or anything?'

'Not,' said Miss Blossom, 'if you don't tease him. I wouldn't wiggle my toes if I were you. He's apt to snap at moving objects.'

A great calm fell on Monty's toes.

'Well,' said Miss Blossom, returning to her original theme, 'how's tricks? You weren't feeling so good yesterday, were you? Is this your first trip across?'

Monty, about to nod, refrained, fearing lest the movement might come under the head of those that the alligator was accustomed to snap at.

'Yes,' he said.

'Then I don't wonder that storm upset you. Personally, I enjoyed it. I always feel that if there's a storm you're getting your money's worth. Talking of storms, I met Ambrose outside.'

'Yes. He had been in here.'

'How did you think he was looking?'

'A bit on the mouldy side, what?'

120

'Me, too.' Miss Blossom smiled tenderly. 'Poor clam,' she said, with a loving quaver in her voice. 'I've broken our engagement, you know.'

'Oh, yes?'

'Yes, sir. That's what I meant about storms. One broke loose on the top deck that first night out. Some breeze!'

'Oh, yes.'

'Yes, sir. We went to the mat all right.'

'And the engagement's broken?'

'Well, call it cracked. I'm going to make it up today.'

'That's good. He seemed to me as if he was brooding on it a bit.'

'Yes, he's taken it pretty hard. Still, it's all for his own good. He'll be much happier in the long run if he gets it into his bean that he can't pull a James Cagney on me every time he's a mite upset. Just imagine! Flying off the handle that way because I kissed his brother Reggie! Why shouldn't I kiss Reggie?'

'Quite.'

'I think a girl's right to put a stick of dynamite underneath the loved one every now and then, when he gets above himself, don't you?'

'Oh, rather.'

'Her dignity demands it.'

'Definitely.'

'This makes the third time I've done it. Broken the engagement, I mean. The first was forty-three seconds after I'd said I would marry him.'

'Forty-three seconds?'

'Forty-three seconds. I guess that's a record. European, anyway. Yessir, forty-three seconds after I'd said I'd marry him I broke the engagement because he took a swing at Wilfred.'

'Your little brother?'

'My little alligator. I held Wilfred up to his face and said: "Kiss papa," and Ambrose gave a short horrible gurgle and knocked him out of my hands. Imagine! Might have cracked him.'

She spoke indignantly, as one confident of the sympathy of her audience, but Monty found himself entirely pro-Ambrose. He considered that in the scene thus vividly described the novelist had acted with great courage and spirit, and wished, as Wilfred, yawning broadly, nestled against his right foot, that he was man enough to do the same. This alligator was, no doubt, of great value to his guest in her professional capacity, but meeting it socially, as it were, like this was preying upon his spirits.

He was also wondering how much longer Miss Blossom intended to remain.

'It took him a week to square himself that time. The other time was more kind of serious, because it really looked as if it was going to be the finish. It was when we'd got to discussing what we were going to do after we were married. He wanted to live in London, and me, my career being in good old Dottyville-on-the-Pacific, naturally I wanted to go there. Well, sir, we argued back and forth and didn't get nowheres. Ambrose is about as pig-headed as they come, and there aren't many mules that couldn't pick up hints from me once I've made up my mind to a thing, so there we were, and in the end I got mad and said: "Oh, hell, let's call it all off," and we did. And then suddenly along comes Ikey Llewellyn with this offer of his and everything was hotsy-totsy.'

Miss Blossom fell to powdering her nose. Monty coughed. He looked at her like a hostess collecting eyes at the end of a dinner-party. Had it been simply a matter of enjoying listening to her, he would have been well content to prolong this interview, for he found her conversation replete with interest. But that fear of his would not be stilled, that haunting fear that Albert Peasemarch might prove to have been an unreliable judge of form where pure, sweet English girls were concerned.

'Er – well –' he said.

'That time,' resumed Miss Blossom, studying her nose in her mirror and giving it a final touch, 'things did look kind of serious. Yessir. But what's happened now is nothing. In about half an hour he'll be folding me in his arms and saying can I ever forgive him, and I'll be saying: "Oh, Ambrose!" and he'll be saying that it isn't only the thought of having hurt me that hurts him, though that hurts him a lot, but that why he's really hurt is because he knows it hurts me to feel that he has hurt himself by hurting me. I have to laugh when I think of him out in that corridor just now. He's a scream, that boy, and I love him to bits. You never saw anything so haughty. "Good morning," he said, and he just drew himself up and gave me one look and irised out. What nuts men are! There ought to be a law.'

Monty coughed again.

'Quite,' he said. 'And now, as I expect you've all sorts of things to do this morning –'

'Oh, that's all right.'

'Engagements here and engagements there –'

'No, I've no dates.'

Monty was reluctantly compelled to make himself plainer.

'Don't you think,' he suggested deferentially, 'that it might be as well if you were pushing along now, what?'

'Pushing along?'

'Beetling off,' explained Monty.

Lottie Blossom looked at him, surprised. This attitude was new to her. Men, as a sex, were inclined rather to court her society than to endeavour to deprive themselves of it. Indeed, in the case of Spaniards at Biarritz it had sometimes seemed to her that it would be necessary to keep them off with a stick.

'But we're just beginning to take our hair down and have a real good gossip. Am I boring you, neighbour Bodkin?'

'No, no.'

'Then what's biting you?'

Monty picked at the coverlet.

'Well ... it's like this ... it occurred to me ... it crossed my mind ... as a possibility, don't you know ... that – er – Gertrude –'

'Who's Gertrude?'

'My fiancée ... It struck me that Gertrude might possibly take it into her head to look in here to see if I was awake... In which event –'

'I didn't know you were engaged.'

'I am. To be absolutely frank, yes, I am.'

'Would that be the girl I met in here that first day?'

'Yes.'

'Seemed a nice girl.'

'Oh, rather. She is.'

'Gertrude, did you say?'

'That's right. Gertrude.'

Miss Blossom's eyebrows contracted thoughtfully.

'Gertrude? I'm not sure I like the name Gertrude much. Of course, there's Gertrude Lawrence –'

'Quite,' said Monty. 'But it isn't Gertrude Lawrence I want to stress so much, if you see what I mean, at this juncture, as Gertrude Butterwick.'

Miss Blossom laughed that hearty laugh of hers.

'Is that her name? Butterwick?'

'Yes.'

'What a scream!'

'I don't like it much myself,' agreed Monty. 'It always reminds me of J. G. Butterwick, her father, of Butterwick, Price & Mandelbaum, Export and Import Merchants. But that isn't the point. The point is –'

'You think she'd be sore if she found me in here?'

'I don't think she'd be any too pleased. She wasn't last time. In fact, I don't mind telling you that you took quite a bit of explaining away.'

Miss Blossom pursed her lips. She seemed to disapprove.

'Got one of those low minds, has she, this Miss Buttersplosh?'

'Not at all,' said Monty warmly. 'Far from it. She's got about as high a mind as she can stick. And her name isn't Butter-splosh. It's Butter-wick.'

'Just as bad,' said Miss Blossom critically.

'It's not half as bad. There's no comparison. And, anyway, we aren't talking about her name, we're talking about what she would think if she saw you sitting here, practically on my toes. It would give her a fit. You see, there are wheels within wheels. Reggie Tennyson, like a silly ass, went and gave her the impression that I was a fairly mere butterfly. And that, coming right on top of that tattoo mark on my chest –'

'What tattoo mark would that be?'

'Oh, it's a long story. Boiling it down, I was once engaged to a girl called Sue Brown and I had her name tattooed on my chest with a heart round it –'

'Golly!' said Miss Blossom, much intrigued. 'Let's look.'

Monty was sitting with his back against the head of the bed, so was unable to recoil far. But he recoiled as far as he could.

'No, dash it!'

'Ah, come on.'

'No, really.'

'What's the matter with you? Chests are nothing among friends. You can't shock me. I once played the love interest in *Bozo the Ape Man*.'

'I dare say, but –'

'Come on. Do.'

'No, I'm dashed if I will.'

'Oh, very well. Keep your old chest, then.'

Hurt and disappointed, Miss Blossom gathered up the alligator, adjusted the pink ribbon about its neck and left the room. It was as she closed Monty's door and started to go to her own in order to restore Wilfred to his wickerwork basket that Gertrude came along the passage.

It had been Gertrude's intention to knock on Monty's door and tell him that he ought to get up and enjoy the lovely sunshine. She abandoned this project. Having stared for a moment, she turned sharply and went on deck again.

It seemed to Monty from time to time during the remainder of that day of blue skies and soft breezes that the girl he loved was a little rummy in her manner. Nothing that you could put your hand on exactly, but rummy. She fell into sudden silences. Every now and then, glancing up, he would find her gaze on him in a rather thoughtful way. Or not so much thoughtful, perhaps, as ... well, rummy. It weighed upon him a little.

By night-time, however, the slight sense of depression induced by this rumminess had left him. By nature resilient, he soon found it vanishing under the influence of the excellent dinner set before him by the authorities who had composed the evening's menu.

These kindly men, believing that there is nothing like a bite to eat for picking a fellow up, had provided five kinds of soup, six kinds of fish, and in addition to these preliminaries such attractive items as chicken hot-pot, roast veal, ox tail, pork cutlets, mutton chops, sausages, steak, haunch of venison, sirloin of beef, rissoles, calf's liver, brawn, York ham, Virginia ham, Bradenham ham, salmi of duck and boar's head, followed by eight varieties of pudding, a wide choice of cheese and ice-creams and fruit to fill up the chinks. Monty did not take them all, but he took enough of them to send him to the boat deck greatly refreshed and in a mood of extreme sentimentality. He felt like a loving python.

The atmospheric conditions on the boat deck were of a nature to encourage these emotions. It was a still, warm night of stars and moonshine, and if only his cigarettes had held out Monty might have remained where he was indefinitely, prob-ably even going to the length of trying to compose poetry.

Opening his case, however, at the end of the first hour or so and finding it empty, he decided to go to his state-room and stock up. If Gertrude had been with him on the boat deck, he would, of course, have had no need for cigarettes: but Ger-trude had pleaded a bridge engagement with Jane Passenger and a couple of her team mates. So Monty went below, and he was in the act of opening the door of his state-room when he was checked by an exclamation of shocked reproof and turned to perceive Albert Peasemarch.

The steward was looking his most Victorian.

'You can't go in there, sir,' he said.

Monty stared at the man. He was at a loss. Every time they met, it seemed to him, this vassal sprang something new and cryptic on him.

'What do you mean?'

Albert Peasemarch appeared astonished by the question.

'Didn't the young lady apprize you, sir?'

'Do what?'

'Inform you of what had transpired? Not the young lady next door, I don't mean. The other young lady, Miss Butter-wick. Didn't she tell you that she had changed state-rooms with you and that you are now in B 36?'

Monty leaned weakly against the wall. As on a previous occasion, the steward had become two stewards and was flicker-ing at the rims.

'Yes, sir, that's what she's gone and done. Changed state-rooms with you. Quite a general post it's been with you this

126

voyage, hasn't it, sir,' said Albert Peasemarch sympathetically. 'I expect it's becoming a case of you dunno where you are, as the song says. First your gentleman friend shifts you, and now the lady shifts you. Pretty soon you'll be having to be keeping a daily memo, to remind you which actually is your current shed.'

He chuckled at the quaint conceit, considered it for a moment, then, feeling that it was much too clever to be said only once, repeated it.

'Pretty soon you'll have to be keeping a daily memo. to remind you which actually is your current shed. But don't think, sir,' said Albert Peasemarch, striking a graver note, for he could be serious as well as witty, 'that I approve of all this chopping and changing. I ventured to observe to the young lady that it was all highly irregular and shouldn't ought to be done without the cognizance and permission of the purser, but she just replied: "Damn your eyes, steward," or words to that effect, "you do what you're told and let's have less back-chat about it," so I shifted you, as requested. But I naturally assumed that the young lady would have apprized you.'

'Steward,' said Monty, speaking in a low, croaking voice.

'Sir?'

'Peasemarch ... Do you happen to know, Peasemarch, if Miss Butterwick has – has gone into the bathroom yet?'

'Oh, yes, sir,' said Albert Peasemarch brightly. 'She went in first thing.'

'And –?'

'Oh, yes, sir, she saw that undeliable writing. Well, she could hardly have missed it, could she? She seemed highly interested. She stood looking at it for a while, and then she turns to me and says: "Coo, steward! What's all this?" And I replied: "That is writing, miss, done in lipstick." And she said "Oh!"'

Monty clutched at the wall. It seemed the only solid thing in a disintegrating world.

'Oh?'

'Yes, sir, that's what the young lady said – "Oh!" She then dismissed me and closed the door. Some little time later, she pressed the bell for the tabby – the stewardess, sir, and gave her a note to take to your state-room – B 36, in case you've forgotten, sir – that's on the deck immediately above this one, this being the C deck – and there no doubt you'll find it.'

Monty left him. He had had sufficient of Albert Peasemarch's society for the time being. The steward had the air of a man who was about to point out that all this was just another example of the inscrutable workings of Fate – as no doubt it was. For, as Monty realized, if Gertrude Butterwick had never been born – if, indeed, she had been born without arms or with one leg shorter than the other, she would never have been selected to accompany the All England Ladies' Hockey Team to America: in which case, she would not have been on board the liner *Atlantic* and would not have been in a position to think things over and come to the conclusion that a Monty Bodkin next door to Miss Lotus Blossom was a Monty Bodkin who would be much more happily situated on Deck B.

Nothing could be truer than all this, but Monty did not wish to stand there and listen to Albert Peasemarch expounding it.

With leaden feet he stumbled to State-room B 36. Its air was still faintly scented with his favourite perfume, that affected by Gertrude Butterwick, but he did no sentimental sniffing. His whole attention was absorbed by two objects that lay upon the dressing-table.

One was an envelope with his name on it in the handwriting he knew so well. The other was a brown plush Mickey Mouse with pink coral eyes.

It beamed up at him with a wide-smiling cheerfulness which in the circumstances he found tasteless and intolerable.

# Chapter 14

Fully as tasteless and intolerable to Monty's mind was the way
in which, on the morning following these cataclysmic events,
all Nature smiled. Nothing could have been fairer or brighter
than the weather next day. There was no rain, no fog, not even
a fresh north-easterly breeze. Heedless of the fact that it contained a young man for whom life no longer held any meaning,
the sun came pouring into State-room B 36, and dancing
merrily on the ceiling, as if everything had been for the best in
the best of all possible worlds.

At a few minutes after nine there was a shuffling of carpet-
slippered feet in the passage and Reggie Tennyson entered.

The sight of his old friend did nothing to alleviate Monty's
gloom. His views on congenial society at the moment were
exactly opposite to those expressed by Julius Caesar. He did
not want men about him that were fat; sleek-headed men and
such as sleep o' nights. And while Reggie was not fat, he had
plainly enjoyed an excellent night's rest and was in capital
spirits. As he walked in he was smiling as broadly as the Mickey
Mouse. And that animal's unceasing joviality had been jarring
on Monty ever since he had woken up.

His 'What ho', accordingly, lacked spontaneity and heartiness. He was just settling down to breakfast, and had hoped
to be alone with his grief and kippers. And if solitude were to
be denied him, he would have preferred some such visitor as
Ambrose. Yond Ambrose had a lean and hungry look, and
that was the sort of thing Monty required this morning. He felt
scarcely capable of coping with Reggie.

Still, one has to be civil. He prepared to make conversation.

'You're up early,' he said glumly.

Reggie leaned against the foot of the bed, draping his
dressing-gown around him.

'You bet I'm up early,' he replied with a sort of Boy Scoutful exuberance which turned the kipper to ashes in Monty's mouth. 'I've better things to do than frowst in bed on a morning like this. What a morning! I don't know when I've known such a morning. The sun is shining –'

'I know, I know,' said Monty peevishly. 'I've seen it.'

Reggie's effervescence diminished a little. He seemed wounded. He looked for a moment rather like Albert Pease-march in one of his hurt moods.

'Well, all right,' he said. 'There's nothing to get stuffy about. It's not my fault it's shining, is it? I wasn't consulted. I merely mentioned the fact to explain why I'm up and doing with a heart for any fate at a gosh-awful hour like this. I'm going to find Mabel Spence and play shuffleboard with her. Have you met Mabel, Monty?'

'Just to speak to.'

'What a ripper!'

'I dare say.'

'What do you mean, you dare say?' said Reggie warmly. 'I'm telling you. She's the sweetest girl on earth. Gosh, I wish I was Ambrose.'

'Why?'

'Because he's going to Hollywood, where she lives, whereas I am headed for Montreal – curse the place and may worms attack its maple trees – and shall probably never see her again after the voyage ends. Still, no use,' said Reggie bravely, 'worrying about that. The thing to do is to gather rosebuds while ye may. And, talking of rosebuds, old boy, do you re-member a tie you bought in the Burlington Arcade and came to lunch in at the Drones one day? About a week before the Two Thousand Guineas, it would have been. Throw your mind back. It had a sort of pink roses effect on a dove-grey back-ground, and it is exactly what I need to add the finishing touch to the costume in which I propose to flash upon Mabel this morning. You haven't brought it with you, by any chance? If so, I'll borrow it.'

'Look in the left-hand top drawer,' said Monty wearily. He swallowed a moody forkful of kipper. He was ill attuned to talk of ties.

'Got it,' said Reggie, having looked.

He returned to the foot of the bed. The momentary gloom caused by the thought of parting from Mabel Spence had disappeared. He was smiling again, as if at some thought or memory which amused him.

'Tell me, Monty,' he said, 'what on earth are you doing up here? The way you whizz about this ship is enough to make a chap's head swim. I do think, as an old friend, you might have told me you had moved. I plunged into what I thought was your state-room just now and gave the sleeping figure in the bed a hearty wallop –'

Monty uttered a broken cry.

'– and it tore off its whiskers and it was Gertrude. An embarrassing moment for all concerned.'

'You didn't?'

'I certainly did. What's the idea? Why the switch?'

'Didn't she tell you?'

'I didn't wait to be told anything. I reddened and withdrew.'

Monty groaned.

'Gertrude suddenly made up her mind to change state-rooms after dinner last night. She left a note for me here explaining why she had done it. That blighted Blossom girl came into my room yesterday morning soon after you had left, and apparently Gertrude was passing along the corridor and saw her coming out and going into her own cabin. From this she seems to have drawn two conclusions – one, that the Blossom and I were on pretty matey terms, and secondly that we were next door to one another. So she decided to change. She didn't say a word about it to me, so my chances of heading her off were nil. Abetted by Albert Peasemarch, she simply went ahead and did it.'

Reggie had listened to this narrative with the natural concern of a big-hearted young man for a friend in trouble. His nimble mind leaped without hesitation to what was plainly the nub of the tragedy.

'But, gosh! If Gertrude's in that room, she'll see that writing on the wall.'

Monty groaned again.

'She has seen it. Naturally, it was the first thing her eye lit on when she checked in.'

'Did she touch on that in her note?'

Monty waved a sombre fork at the dressing-table.

'Look. That Mickey Mouse. I gave it her the first day of the voyage. I found it here when I came in last night.'

'She had sent it back?'

'Sent it back.'

'Gadzooks! The one hundred per cent raspberry.'

'Yes.'

' 'Odsblood,' said Reggie, pondering.

There was a pause. Monty finished his kipper.

'She saw Lottie coming out of your state-room, did she?'

'Yes. So she tells me in her note. But, dash it, she didn't say a word about it all the time I was with her yesterday afternoon and evening. If she had, I could have explained that the woman simply sat and talked about Ambrose and what a silly ass he was and how much she loved him and that not a word passed between us that could not have been broadcast in the B.B.C.'s Children's Hour. And now, of course, it's too late to do any explaining, because she's seen that writing and thinks I'm a sort of secret Mormon elder.'

Reggie nodded understandingly.

'Yes. One can follow her mental processes, of course. First, she finds that tattoo thing on your chest. You square yourself over that, but it leaves her a bit shaken. Then – foolishly, I admit, though with the best motives – I tell her – By the way, how did you square yourself over that? All that stuff of mine about you being such a lad?'

'I told her you were the biggest liar in London.'

'Good.'

'That nobody ever believed a word you said.'

'Very sound.'

'And that you were always doing that sort of thing, because you thought it funny. I said you had a distorted mind.'

'Admirable,' said Reggie. 'Most judicious. The best move you could have made. I see now why her manner to me has been a bit cold of late.'

'Has it?'

'Very cold. In fact, the only time it has really approached warmth since the first day out was just now in that state-room. There was a sort of hummock in the bed,' said Reggie, living over a scene which was plainly green in his memory, 'and I said to myself: "This is where I give Monty a laughable surprise," and I spat on my hand and hauled off and let it go. As I say, most embarrassing. Well, what you have told me makes the procedure absurdly simple. I can put you straight with her in a second. I will go to her at once and tell her that it was I who wrote that writing on the wall.'

The tray on Monty's lap heaved and rattled. For the first time he began to regard the dancing of the sunbeams on the ceiling as something other than an offensive piece of gate-crashing. He could meet the smiling eye of the Mickey Mouse without wincing.

'Reggie! Would you do that?'

'Of course. The only plan.'

'But will she believe you?'

'Of course she'll believe me. It all fits in perfectly. You seem to have made me out such a bally hound that she will be ready to believe anything to my detriment and discredit.'

'I'm sorry about that.'

'Don't apologize. Very strategic.'

'But where would you have got lipstick?'

'Lipstick can be borrowed.'

Monty's last doubts as to the feasibility of the scheme were removed. He gazed upon Reggie emotionally. He saw how wrong he had been in hastily taking him for a pest and an excrescence when he had entered the room. A sort of modern Sydney Carton was what Reggie seemed to him now.

He could not, however, repress a certain qualm as he considered this thing that his friend was about to do for him.

'I'm afraid she'll be pretty peeved with you.'

'Peeved? Gertrude? My first cousin? A girl I've seen spanked by a nurse with a hair-brush? You don't suppose I care what old pie-faced Gertrude thinks of me, do you? Good heavens, no. One laughs lightly and snaps the fingers. Don't you worry about me.'

Powerful emotions were wrestling with one another in

Monty's bosom. In addition to relief there was the agony of hearing the girl he loved described as 'old pie-faced Gertrude', sheer wonder at the realization that there could exist a man who did not value her good opinion, and a burning resentment against a nurse capable of perpetrating the hideous outrage specified. But relief was the most powerful.

'Thanks,' he said.

It was with difficulty that he could utter even that simple word.

'Well,' said Reggie, 'that seems to clean you up nicely as far as the writing on the wall is concerned. As regards your playing kiss-in-the-ring with Lottie Blossom in your state-room —'

'We weren't playing kiss-in-the-ring!'

'Well, postman's knock, or whatever it was.'

'I told you we were simply talking about Ambrose.'

'It sounds a little thin to me,' said Reggie critically. 'Still, if that's your story, you are no doubt wise to stick to it. All I'm saying is that with regard to Lottie you must use your own efforts to put things right. But I can certainly square you over the writing, and I will do so without delay. I'll see Gertrude immediately, and after that I'm going to throw out a drag-net for Mabel Spence. In which connection, would you say — suede shoes, white flannel bags, the tie and a Trinity Hall blazer, or suede shoes, white flannel bags, the tie and neat blue jacket?'

Monty reflected.

'Neat blue jacket, if you ask me.'

'Right,' said Reggie.

Mabel Spence, meanwhile, all unaware of the treat in store for her, was in Ivor Llewellyn's state-room, hearing from that agitated man's lips the story of the breakdown of yesterday's negotiations. Mr Llewellyn was still in bed, and the salmon-pink of his pyjama jacket seemed to take on a deeper hue in contrast to the apprehensive pallor of the face above it.

'The guy said he had other views!'

The motion-picture magnate's voice shook as he spoke these sinister words, and Mabel Spence also seemed to find them ominous. She gave a little whistle and with a thoughtful tight-

134

ness about her lips took a cigarette from the box beside the bed, a simple action which somehow had the effect of stirring Mr Llewellyn to extreme irritability.

'I wish you wouldn't use my cigarettes. Haven't you got any of your own?'

'All right, old Southern Hospitality. I'll put it back . . . Other views, eh?'

'That's what he said.'

'I don't like that.'

'You and me both.'

'It looks to me as if he wasn't going to play ball. Tell me exactly what happened.'

Mr Llewellyn hitched himself up against the pillows.

'I sent young Tennyson to him with a blank contract. See what I mean? Money wasn't to be any object, see? All I wanted to know was would he come and act for the S.-L., because if so he could fill in the figures just as it suited him. And back comes Tennyson and says the guy thanks me, but he has other views.'

Mabel Spence shook her head.

'I don't like it.'

The remark seemed to infuriate her brother-in-law as much as her helping herself to his cigarettes had done.

'Where's the sense in standing there saying you don't like it? Of course you don't like it. *I* don't like it. You don't see me dancing about and clapping my hands, do you? I'm not singing, am I? I'm not calling for three rousing cheers, am I?'

Mabel continued to ponder. She was completely puzzled. If she had been Monty Bodkin, she would have said that the thing was inexplicable. What she did say was that it beat her.

'Sure. And it beat me,' said Mr Llewellyn, 'till Tennyson went on and told me something else. Do you know what he told me? He said this guy Bodkin is next door to a millionaire. See what that means? It means he just does this spying work for the kick he gets out of it. Like a ghoul or something. The money end don't mean nothing to him. All he wants is to watch people suffer. How can you fix a man like that?'

He brooded for a moment. He seemed to be feeling that it was just his luck that the only Customs spy he had ever fallen

135

foul of should be one who combined large private means with a fiendish disposition.

'Well, this lets me out. I know when I'm licked. I'm going to declare that necklace of Grayce's and pay the duty.'

'I wouldn't.'

'I don't give a darn what you would do. I'm going to.'

'Oh, well, suit yourself.'

'You're right. I'll suit myself.'

'I was only thinking,' said Mabel pensively, 'of the wireless I had from Grayce last night.'

Something of Mr Llewellyn's sturdy resolution left him. His face, which emotion had made almost a match for the pyjama jacket, lost some of its colour. As Monty Bodkin had done on another occasion, he moistened his lips with the tip of the tongue.

'Wireless? From Grayce?'

'Yes.'

'Let's see it.'

'It's in my state-room.'

'What did she say?'

'I can't remember the exact words. Something about "tell you that if you didn't come through she knew what she was going to do about it".'

'She knew,' murmured Mr Llewellyn, like a man in a trance, 'what she was going to do about it.'

Mabel Spence eyed him with a certain commiseration.

'Honestly, Ikey,' she said, 'I'd go ahead with the thing. I wouldn't take chances with Grayce. You know what she's like. Impulsive. And don't forget she's actually in Paris, so all she's got to do if she wants a Paris divorce is to put on her hat and call a taxi.'

Mr Llewellyn was not forgetting this.

'And even if this fellow Bodkin won't sit in, why worry? Suppose he does know you're planning to put something over. Suppose he does tip off his pals on shore to keep their eyes skinned when you show up at the Customs sheds. What of it? There won't be anything doing till they start to examine your baggage, and by that time George will be a mile away with the stuff.'

136

Mr Llewellyn refused to be comforted. It was probably the fact that his wife's brother George was to be a principal in the affair that prejudiced him against what he had come to label in his mind the Hat Sequence, but prejudiced he undoubtedly was. Instead of the happy smile, Mabel's optimism produced only the bitter sneer.

'You think a smart guy like that won't get to thinking things when he sees George and me knocking each other's hats off and changing them like a couple of fellows in vaudeville? The second he sees it he'll know that there's funny business going on.'

'He won't see it. He won't be there.'

'Won't be there? He'll be tagging along a yard behind me from the minute we get ashore.'

'No, he won't. We'll hold him on board till you've got off and met George.'

'Yes? And how are you going to do that?'

'Easy. Reggie Tennyson can get him out of the way somehow. They're friends. Reggie can take him off somewhere to talk about something. You leave it to me. I'll fix it.'

Mr Llewellyn, as we have seen, could never be really fond of his sister-in-law, but he had to admit that there was something about her personality that inspired confidence. His breathing became easier.

'I won't tell Reggie why he's got to do it, of course. I'll just say I want him to.'

'And that'll be enough?'

'Sure.'

'Say, you two seem to be getting along pretty well together.'

'Yes. I like Reggie. And I'm sorry for him. Poor boy, his family are sending him to work in an office in Montreal, and he's all broken up about it. He says, if he's got to work at all, he'd prefer it to be somewhere out in the great open spaces where men are men and, more particularly, women are women – like Hollywood.'

Mr Llewellyn's eyes narrowed warily. A suspicious expression came into them. He smelt a rat. He saw it floating in the air.

'Oh?' he said. 'He does, does he?'

'Yes. And I was wondering,' said Mabel, 'if you couldn't find him something to do at Llewellyn City, Ikey?'

All that was visible of Ivor Llewellyn above the bedclothes shook as with a palsy, and a ripple among the blankets showed that the invisible part of him was shaking, too. Often as he had been through discussions of this kind, he was never able to remain quite calm when they came up. When an opportunity of doing something at Llewellyn City for a relative or a friend of a relative or a relative by marriage or a friend of a relative by marriage was offered to him, it always made him feel as if his interior organs were being stirred up with a pole. On these occasions it was his practice to bark like a sea-lion asking for fish, and he did so now.

'Ha!' he cried. 'I was wondering when that was coming. I was just waiting for that.'

'Reggie could be very useful to you.'

'How? There's already a fellow sweeps out my office.'

'You often use English sequences in your pictures. He could keep you straight on them. Couldn't you, Reggie?' said Mabel, addressing the vision in shining flannel trousers and neat blue jacket which had just sauntered in without, as Mr Llewellyn sourly noted, bothering to knock. People who wished to enter Ivor Llewellyn's presence on the S.-L. lot at Llewellyn City had to wait anything from one to two hours in an ante-room, and this was not the first time the motion-picture magnate had found himself irked by the less formal conditions prevailing on shipboard.

'What ho!' said Reggie cheerily. 'What ho, what ho, and again what ho. Good morning, Mabel, and you, Llewellyn. You're both looking extraordinarily well and attractive. I like those pink pyjamas, Llewellyn. Every man his own sunset. I've been scouring the ship for you, young M. Spence, and they told me you were in here. How do you react to the idea of a spot of shuffleboard?'

'I'd love it.'

'I'd love it, too. Extraordinary, have you ever realized, how similar our tastes are? Twin souls is about what it tots up at, if you ask me. Ah, cigarettes?' said Reggie, observing the box by the bedside. He helped himself and began to smoke with a

138

nod of appreciation. 'You buy good cigarettes, Llewellyn,' he said genially. 'I like them. Did I,' he went on, 'hear you ask me some question as I came in? The words "Couldn't you, Reggie?" seem to be floating in the memory. Couldn't I what?'

'Help Ikey.'

'I am always pleased to help Ikey, when and if feasible. How?'

'We were discussing the possibility of your working for the Superba-Llewellyn. I know how you hate the prospect of this Montreal job of yours.'

'I loathe it. It would make me feel like a bird in a gilded cage. What an admirable idea!' said Reggie, rewarding Mr Llewellyn with an approving smile. 'A really first-class notion. My dear fellow, I shall be delighted to work for the Superba-Llewellyn. It was like your kind heart to suggest it. In what capacity would you propose?'

'I was saying that you could put him right on his English sequences. You know all about English Society life.'

'I invented it.'

'You hear that, Ikey? Now you won't have any more people fox-hunting in July.'

'By Jove, no. No, from today, my dear Llewellyn, you may be quite easy in your mind about your English sequences. Leave them entirely to me. And now,' said Reggie, taking another cigarette, 'about terms. My brother Ambrose tells me that you are paying him fifteen hundred dollars a week. I should be perfectly satisfied to start with that. No doubt you will let me have a line in writing at your convenience. No hurry. Any time that suits you, my dear Llewellyn.'

Mr Llewellyn found speech. Until this moment the emotion which any reference to that fox-hunting in July thing always caused him had held him dumb. It was a sore subject with him. One of the features of his super-film, *Glorious Devon*, it had been the occasion of much indignation in the English Press and of such a choking and spluttering and outraged what-whatting among purple-faced Masters of Hounds in the Shires as had threatened to produce an epidemic of apoplexy. This Mr Llewellyn could have borne with fortitude. But it had also resulted in the complete failure of the picture throughout the island kingdom, and that had cut him to the quick.

'Get out of here!' he cried.

Reggie was surprised. Not quite the note, he considered.

'Get out of here?'

'Yes, get out of here. You and your English sequences!'

'Ikey!'

'And you,' boomed Mr Llewellyn, turning his batteries on his sister-in-law, 'you stop saying "Ikey!". So you want that I should hire more loafers to pick my pockets, do you? It's not enough, your brother George and your Uncle Wilmot and your cousin Egbert and your cousin Genevieve?'

Here Mr Llewellyn had to pause for an instant in order to grasp at the receding skirts of his self-control. He was greatly affected by those concluding words. There had always been something about that weekly three hundred and fifty dollars paid out to his wife's cousin Egbert's sister Genevieve which for some odd reason afflicted him more than all his other grievances put together. A spectacled child with a mouth that hung open like a letter-box, Genevieve was so manifestly worth a maximum of thirty cents per annum to any employer.

'You want, do you,' he resumed, thrusting the image of the adenoid-ridden girl from his mental vision with a powerful effort, 'not just that I should support your whole damned family, but when there isn't any more family I'm to go out and find strangers to give my money away to, because maybe if I didn't I might have a couple of dollars I could call my own? I'm to fill up Llewellyn City till there isn't standing room with English dudes what except eat and sleep they've never done a thing in their lives but hold hands with my wife's sister on promenade decks?'

'Boat decks,' corrected Mabel.

'I'm to buy a pack of bloodhounds, am I, and set them to smelling after fresh young guys who if I hadn't bloodhounds I might overlook? I'm to buy a pack of St Bernards, am I, and train them to go out and drag them in?'

Reggie turned to Mabel, eyebrows raised. Mr Llewellyn's words, to which he had been listening with great interest, seemed to him to point to but one conclusion.

'I believe the deal's off,' he said.

'I'm to buy a pack of fox-hounds, am I –'

140

Reggie checked him with a gesture.

'Llewellyn, my dear fellow, please,' he said, a little stiffly. 'We are not interested in your kennel plans. Do I understand that you do *not* wish me to assist you with your English sequences?'

'I guess that's what he's hinting at,' said Mabel.

Reggie clicked his tongue regretfully.

'You're missing a good thing, Llewellyn. Better think again.'

Mr Llewellyn resumed, in another vein of imagery.

'I'm the United States Sub-Treasury, am I, that I should waste good money on loafers like him?'

This struck Mabel as unfair discrimination.

'You're paying George a thousand,' she argued.

Mr Llewellyn quivered.

'Don't talk to me about George.'

'And Genevieve –'

Mr Llewellyn quivered again, more noticeably.

'And don't,' he begged, 'talk to me about Genevieve.'

'And Reggie's brother Ambrose fifteen hundred. If you can afford to pay Reggie's brother Ambrose fifteen hundred dollars a week, I shouldn't have thought you were so particular about loosening up.'

Mr Llewellyn stared, genuinely astonished. He had been about to inquire of his sister-in-law if she had by some error of judgement mistaken him for Rockefeller, Pierpont Morgan, Death Valley Scotty or one of these Indian Maharajahs, but this remark diverted him.

'Ambrose Tennyson? What do you mean? He's cheap at fifteen hundred a week.'

'You think so?'

'Of course I think so.'

'What's he ever done?'

'He's a great writer.'

'Have you read his books?'

'No. When do I ever get time to read? But everyone else has. Even your brother George. Matter of fact, it was George that told me I ought to get him for the S.-L.'

'George must be crazy.'

Reggie felt compelled to intervene. Except when the latter

was chasing him along corridors and threatening to wring his neck, he was fond of Ambrose, and this sort of talk, he felt, was calculated to do him harm in his chosen profession. Subversive.

'I wouldn't say that,' he urged. 'Ambrose turns out pretty good stuff.'

'What do you mean, pretty good stuff?' said Mr Llewellyn indignantly. 'He's famous. He's one of the big noises.'

Mabel sniffed.

'Who told you that?'

'You did, for one,' said Mr Llewellyn triumphantly. He enjoyed the experience, which came his way but rarely, of being able to bathe his sister-in-law in confusion.

'Me?'

'Yes, you. At dinner one night at my house, when that English playwright that I hired was shooting off his head about books and all that. The fellow with the horn-rimmed glasses. He was saying that Tennyson was all wet, and you came right back at him and said Tennyson was swell and it was only a few smart Alecks said he wasn't. You said people would be reading Tennyson when this guy with the glasses wasn't even a number in the telephone book, and he sort of sniggered and said: "Oh, come, dear lady!" and ate a banana. And I happened to be talking to George next day and I asked him if this Tennyson was really such a hot number and George said he was a smacko and when I was in London I should certainly ought to get after him.'

A choking sound proceeded from Mabel Spence.

'Ikey!' she moaned.

She was staring at him with something of awe in her gaze, the awe with which we look at an object which is the only one of its kind.

'Ikey! Tell me it ain't so!'

'Hey?'

'It can't be. It's too good to be. You haven't gone and signed Reggie's brother up, thinking he was the Tennyson?'

Mr Llewellyn blinked. He was beginning to feel uneasy. A suspicion was growing with him that, in some way which he did not at present understand, he had been gypped. Then, on

142

top of this uneasiness, came a consoling thought. Ambrose's contract was not yet signed.

'Isn't he?'

'You poor fish, Tennyson's been dead forty years.'

'Dead?'

'Certainly. George was just stringing you. You ought to know by this time what a kidder he is. It's a wonder he didn't advise you to sign up Dante.'

'Who,' asked Mr Llewellyn, 'is Dante?'

'He's dead, too.'

Mr Llewellyn, as we say, could understand by no means all of this, but one thing was clear to him, that his brother-in-law George, not content with drawing from the coffers of the firm a thousand dollars a week more than he was worth, had been trying to fill the Superba-Llewellyn lot up with corpses: and for a moment all he felt was a very justifiable resentment against George. Overlooking the fact that corpses would probably be just as good at treatment and dialogue as most of the living authors already employed by him, he objected to George's indulgence in his celebrated sense of fun and expressed himself to that effect in a few well-chosen words.

Then bewilderment returned.

'Well, who's this guy Ambrose Tennyson?'

'Just Reggie's brother.'

'Is that all?'

'Yes, that about lets him out.'

'Isn't he an author?'

'Of a sort.'

'Not a smacko?'

'No, not a smacko.'

Mr Llewellyn bounded at the bell and placed a thumb on it.

'Sir?' said Albert Peasemarch.

'Fetch Mr Tennyson.'

'Mr Tennyson is already present, sir,' said Albert Peasemarch, with an indulgent smile.

'Mr Ambrose Tennyson.'

'Oh, Mr Ambrose Tennyson? Oh, yes, sir. Pardon me, sir. Yes, sir. Very good, sir,' said Albert Peasemarch.

The Ambrose Tennyson who entered the state-room some

few minutes later was a very different person from the morose misogynist whose manner and deportment had so depressed the passengers of R.M.S. *Atlantic* during the last two days. A fervent reconciliation with Lotus Blossom on the boat deck just before lunch on the previous afternoon had completely restored him to his customary buoyancy and good humour. He came in now like a one-man procession of revellers in an old-fashioned comic opera, radiating cheeriness and goodwill.

There is no actual rule about it, of course, and the programme is subject to change without notice, but Nature, in supplying the world with young English novelists, seems to prefer that they shall fall into one of two definite classes – the cocktails-and-cynicism or the heartiness-and-beer. It was to the latter division that Reggie's brother Ambrose belonged. He was large and muscular, with keen eyes, a jutting chin, a high colour and hands like hams, and was apt, when on holiday, to dash off and go climbing the Pyrenees – and, what is more, to sing while he did it.

He was looking as if with the smallest encouragement he would burst into song now, and Mabel Spence, seeing him, was pierced by a pang of remorse. She regretted the impulsive candour which had led her to open her brother-in-law's eyes to the inside facts on the Tennyson situation.

Reggie, also, was disturbed. He had listened to the recent exchanges in silence, dazed by the rapidity with which events had developed. This effervescent bird before him was, he knew, walking into a spot, and he eyed him pityingly, feeling that somebody – himself, if he could only think what to say – ought to prepare the poor blighter for what lay before him.

There was, however, little opportunity for anyone to do much in the way of preparing Ambrose Tennyson's mind. Mr Llewellyn had begun to speak almost before he was inside the room.

'Hey, you!' he barked.

The kindliest critic could not have pretended that his manner was anything but abrupt, and Ambrose was a good deal taken aback. Indeed, he looked for an instant like a man who has run into a lamp-post. But he was in a mood of sunny benevolence towards all men and decided to overlook the brusquerie.

'Good morning, Mr Llewellyn,' he said cheerily. 'I hear you

want to see me. About Bodkin again, I suppose? Mr Llewellyn,' he explained to Reggie, beaming upon his worried junior, 'has got it into his head for some reason that Monty Bodkin would make a good picture actor.'

This amazing statement succeeded in diverting Reggie's mind from its fraternal solicitude.

'What!' he cried. 'Monty?'

'Yes,' said Ambrose, laughing heartily. 'Can you imagine? He wants to make poor old Monty a star.'

'Well, I'm dashed.'

'I shouldn't think Monty has ever acted in his life, has he?'

'Not that I know of.'

'Oh, yes, now I come to remember, he told me he had once – at his first kindergarten.'

'I'll bet he was a flop.'

'I expect so. Extraordinary, isn't it?'

'It's inexplicable.'

Mr Llewellyn broke in on this brotherly duologue. He would have done so earlier, but had had a little difficulty with his vocal cords. Ambrose's ebullient gaiety was affecting him like some sort of skin complaint, causing him to tingle all over.

'Stop that babbling!' he shouted. 'It's got nothing to do with Bodkin. Listen, you! Keep that trap of yours shut for half a minute, if you know how, and attend to me.'

Ambrose stared at him, astonished. It was not thus that the other had been wont to address him in previous interviews. Hitherto, he had found the president of the Superba-Llewellyn quiet and respectful.

'I hear you're not the right Tennyson.'

Ambrose's bewilderment increased. He looked at Reggie, as if wondering if anyone could suppose him to occupy that position.

'I'm afraid I don't quite understand.'

'I'm talking English, ain't I?'

Ambrose's manner lost something of its bonhomie. His tone became a little acid.

'You are – of a kind. But I still don't understand you.'

'Why have you been keeping it under your hat all this time that you aren't the right Tennyson?'

'You keep using that peculiar expression. If you will kindly explain what you mean by "the right Tennyson", I may be able to answer you.'

'You know what I mean. The Tennyson who wrote books.'

Ambrose eyed Mr Llewellyn frostily. He was now definitely stiff. He might have been back at the Admiralty, rebuking a subordinate for allowing the veiled adventuress to steal the naval plans.

'I was under the impression,' he said, an Oxford chill creeping into his voice, 'that I was the Tennyson who wrote books. I know of nobody else of my name who does literary work. Of course, there was a not uncelebrated poet called Tennyson, but I presume you did not suppose –'

The time had come, Reggie felt, to break the news.

'Yes, he did, old boy. That's precisely what he did suppose. Misled by his brother-in-law George, who appears to be a little ball of fun and the life and soul of Hollywood, he got the wires crossed. He took you for the genuine half-a-league, half-a-league, half-a-league onward bloke.'

'You don't mean that?'

'I do.'

'Not really?'

'Positively.'

Ambrose's good humour was completely restored. Any passing annoyance that he may have felt at the oddness of Ivor Llewellyn's manner, disappeared. He threw his head back and laughed a loud, jolly laugh that went rumbling about the stateroom like thunder.

Its effect was to remove the last traces of Mr Llewellyn's reserve. The face above the pink pyjamas turned purple. Mr Llewellyn's eyes did not actually start out of his head, but it was rather a near thing. He spoke in a thick, strangled voice.

'You think it funny, do you?'

Ambrose was trying to restrain his chuckles. It was unkind, he felt, to laugh.

'You must admit,' he gurgled apologetically, 'that it is a little.'

'Okay,' said Mr Llewellyn. 'Well, snicker at this one. You're fired. As soon as we hit New York, you can take the next boat back to England or jump off the dock and drown yourself or do anything you darn please. What you aren't going to do is come to Llewellyn City and have a good time on my money.'

Ambrose had ceased to chuckle. Reggie, watching the smile fade from his face, wished there was something he could do by way of showing brotherly sympathy, but could think of nothing. Sorrowfully, he helped himself to another of Mr Llewellyn's cigarettes.

'What!'

'That's what.'

'But – but you engaged me.'

'When?'

'Our contract –'

'When did I ever sign any contract?'

'But, damn it –'

'All right, all right.'

'You can't let me down like this.'

'Watch me.'

'I'll bring an action.'

'Sure,' said Mr Llewellyn. 'Come up and sue me some time.'

Ambrose's fresh complexion had lost its colour. He was staring, wide-eyed. Reggie, too, was much disturbed.

'Crikey, Ikey,' he said with emotion. 'This is pretty raw.'

Mr Llewellyn turned like a bull on a picador.

'Who asked you to butt in?'

'It is not a question,' said Reggie with quiet dignity, 'of who *asked* me to butt in. The point does not arise. One is scarcely called upon to feel that one requires a formal invitation to induce one to give it as one's opinion that one ... now I've forgotten what I was going to say.'

'Good,' said Mr Llewellyn.

Ambrose choked.

'But you don't understand, Mr Llewellyn.'

'Eh?'

'On the strength of your promise to employ me to write scenarios I gave up my position. I resigned from the Admiralty.'

'Well, go back to the Admiralty.'

'But ... I can't.'

It was precisely this fact that had caused Reggie to feel so disturbed. Right from the start he had spotted this snag and recognized it for the Class A snag it was.

Reggie's views on jobs were peculiar, but definite. There were some men -- he himself was one of them – who, he considered, had no need for a job. A fair knowledge of racing form, a natural gift for bridge and poker, an ability to borrow money with an easy charm which made the operation a positive pleasure to the victim – these endowments, he held, were all that a chap like himself required, and it was with a deep sense of injury that he had allowed his loved ones to jockey him into the loathsome commercial enterprise to which he was now on his way. A little patience on their part, a little of the purse-strings to help him over a bad patch, and he could have carried on in such perfect comfort. For Reggie Tennyson was one of those young men whom the ravens feed.

But – and this was the point – the ravens do not feed the Ambroses of this world. The Ambroses need their steady job. And if they lose it they find it dashed hard to get another.

'Reflect, Llewellyn!' said Reggie. 'Consider! You cannot do this thing.'

Mabel Spence stepped into the arena. She was aghast now that those careless words of hers, spoken merely with a sister-in-law's natural desire to lower a brother-in-law's self-esteem, should have precipitated this appalling disaster. Ambrose Tennyson's haggard face was a silent reproach. She was rather vague as to what the Admiralty was, but she gathered that it was the source from which Ambrose drew his means of livelihood, and those means of livelihood, it was clear, she had caused him to lose.

'Reggie's quite right, Ikey.'

'Now, don't *you* begin,' urged Mr Llewellyn.

'You can't do this.'

'Is that so?'

'You know perfectly well that, even if you hadn't signed the contract, there was a verbal agreement.'

'To hell with verbal agreements.'

'And why do you want to do it? Where's the sense in ditching Mr Tennyson like this? He may not be Shakespeare, but I'll bet he writes well enough for the Superba-Llewellyn.'

'Shrewdly spoken, girl,' said Reggie approvingly. 'Ambrose will do the Superba-Llewellyn proud.'

'Not the Superba-Llewellyn, he won't,' corrected the president of that organization. 'I want no piece of him.'

'But what is he going to do?'

'Don't ask me. I'm not interested.'

'Why not at least give him a trial?'

'I won't give him a trial.'

'He might be just the man you want.'

'He isn't.'

Reggie crushed out his cigarette and took another. His face was cold and stern.

'Llewellyn,' he said, 'your behaviour is inexplicable.'

'Will you stop horning in!'

'No, Llewellyn, I will not stop horning in. Your behaviour, I say, is inexplicable. You don't seem to know the first thing about running your business.'

'Is that so?'

'Don't interrupt, Llewellyn. You do not, I repeat, appear to know the first thing about running your business. You tumble over yourself trying to secure the services of a chap like Monty Bodkin who – excellent egg though he is in other respects – has never acted in his life and couldn't play the pin in *Pinafore*, and in the same breath, as it were, you decline those of an Ambrose Tennyson, who is a recognized comer in the writing world. About myself I will say nothing, beyond observing that when you were offered the chance of getting hold of a really knowledgeable bird to put you straight on your English sequences you failed to catch the bus – thereby placing yourself in a position where you will no doubt find yourself flooding the world with screen dramas in which Ascot occurs in mid-winter and the Derby is portrayed as a greyhound race taking place on Plumstead Marshes towards the end of October. That's the position you've gone and placed yourself in, Llewellyn,' said Reggie. 'Silly idiot,' he added, summing it all up.

'Yes,' resumed Mabel. 'Listen to me, Ikey –'

The greatest generals are those who know when to make, and

are not ashamed to make, a strategic retreat. Reggie by himself Mr Llewellyn might have endured. Mabel by herself he might have faced undaunted. But Reggie supplemented by Mabel broke his spirit. There was a sort of earthquake among the bedclothes, the leap and rush of a flying pink-pyjamaed form, and the next moment he was in the bathroom, with the door locked. The sound of a gushing tap told that he was protecting his ears from further assaults.

Mabel did her best. Reggie did his best.

'Ikey!' cried Mabel, pounding on the bathroom door,

Ikey!' cried Reggie, doing the same.

As suddenly as they had begun, they ceased. It was only too plain that the man was entrenched beyond their reach, Reggie turned to commiserate with his stricken brother.

'Ambrose, old boy –'

He stopped. Ambrose Tennyson was no longer among those present.

# Chapter 15

That neither Reggie Tennyson nor Mabel Spence should have observed Ambrose's departure affords striking proof of the whole-heartedness with which they had addressed themselves to the task of trying to secure Mr Llewellyn's attention. For it had been the reverse of noiseless.

At the moment when the novelist decided to remove himself from the state-room, Albert Peasemarch had been resting easily against the door with one large red ear in close juxtaposition to the woodwork, absorbed in the drama within. Doors on ocean liners open inward, and the sudden opening of that of State-room C 31 caught him unprepared. Abruptly deprived of support, he fell into the room rather in the manner of a dead body tumbling out of a cupboard in a mystery play and, colliding with Ambrose, clasped him in a close embrace, so that for an instant the thing resembled the meeting after long separation of a couple of Parisian boulevardiers of the old school.

Then Ambrose, with a muttered 'Grrrh!', hurled Albert Peasemarch from him, and Albert, with a muttered 'Coo!', reeled across the passage and gave himself a nasty bump. Ambrose hurried off with long, agitated strides, and Albert was left rubbing that sensitive part of his person which came immediately at the conclusion of his short white jacket.

Presently, as he stood there adjusting his faculties, Reggie and Mabel came out and, like Ambrose, disappeared down the corridor, and he gathered that the curtain had been run down and the entertainment was over.

With the gradual lessening of the pain, his equanimity returned. He realized that he had been privileged to listen in on a performance of outstanding human interest, and there came upon him an insistent desire to find a confidant to whom he could relate the history of these remarkable happenings.

Nobby Clark, the steward who shared his labours on this section of the C deck, was the obvious choice, but at the moment he was unfortunately not on cordial terms with Mr Clark. The latter had taken exception to him jogging his elbow when he was shaving that morning in the Glory Hole and further exception to his attempt to shift the onus on to an inscrutable Fate, and had expressed himself in a manner which had wounded Albert Peasemarch's sensitive nature very deeply and which could not readily be overlooked.

Casting about in his mind for a substitute, Albert remembered that he had not yet removed the breakfast-tray from Miss Lotus Blossom's state-room.

'Quite an argle-bargle in Shed 31 just now, miss,' he said genially, walking in a few moments later. 'Surprised me, I must confess. Heated remarks. Raised voices. And how I came to happen to be, as it were, present was like this. I was going about my duties, when the bell rang –'

Lottie Blossom, her costume completed, was sitting before the mirror putting those last touches to her face which make all the difference. She wanted to look her best, for she was about to go on deck and meet Ambrose. She interrupted Albert Peasemarch.

'This isn't one of your longer stories, is it?' she asked courteously, but with a certain restiveness.

'Oh, no, miss. And in any case I'm sure you will be highly interested, it having to do with Mr Ambrose Tennyson and you being betrothed to him.'

'Who told you that?'

'Bless your heart, miss,' said Albert Peasemarch paternally, "it's all over the ship. As to who actually was my specific informant, there you rather have me. I fancy it was my coworker, a man of the name of Clark, and he had it from someone who had met someone who had happened to be passing while you and Mr Tennyson were in conversation on the boat deck.'

'Nosey devils, you stewards.'

'We generally manage to apprize ourselves of what's going on,' said Albert, acknowledging the compliment with a slight bow. 'I always say it's like the serfs and scullions in a medeevial

152

castle taking an interest in the doings of the haughty nobles, because, as I believe I have observed to you, or if it wasn't you it was someone else, a steward during a voyage gets to look upon himself as a feudal retainer. I think it was Clark who gave me the information, but I am unable to veridify the supposition by actual personal inquiry, because after the manner in which he addressed me in the Glory Hole this morning I am not speaking to Nobby Clark.'

A pang of envy for this favoured child of Fortune shot through Miss Blossom.

'The lucky stiff!' she said. 'Well, get on with it. And keep it crisp, because I'm raring to go. What about Mr Tennyson?'

'He was the cause of the imbrolligo.'

'The what?'

'A technical term,' explained Albert Peasemarch indulgently, 'meaning argle-bargle. Mr Tennyson was the cause of this dust-up in Mr Llewellyn's shed.'

'Oh, Mr Llewellyn was mixed up in it, was he?'

'He certainly was, miss.'

'What happened? Did Mr Tennyson start trouble with Mr Llewellyn?'

'To put it that way would be giving a wrong idea of the facts, miss. It wasn't so much a case of Mr Tennyson starting trouble with Mr Llewellyn as Mr Llewellyn starting trouble with Mr Tennyson. It appears that Mr Llewellyn took umbrage because Mr Tennyson wasn't the right Mr Tennyson, and told him off proper. And then Mr Tennyson junior and Miss Spence, who were also present, joined in –'

'How do you mean – the right Mr Tennyson?'

'The great Mr Tennyson, miss. I don't know if you are familiar with the works of the great Mr Tennyson? He wrote "The Boy Stood on the Burning Deck".'

Lottie Blossom's eyes widened.

'You don't mean Ikey thought Ambrose was that guy?'

'Yes, miss. Misled, it seems, by his brother-in-law George.'

'Well, of all the saps! That must have handed Ambrose a laugh.'

'Yes, miss; I heard him laugh.'

'Where were you during all this?'

'Well, I happened to be passing –'

'I get you. So Ambrose laughed, did he?'

'Yes, miss, very hearty, and Mr Llewellyn didn't like it. Very upset, he sounded. He said it made Mr Tennyson laugh, did it? Ho, well, Mr Tennyson could laugh at this one, he said, and with that he said that Mr Tennyson wasn't going to come to Llewellyn City and enjoy himself on his money. "You're fired," he said.'

'What!'

'Yes, miss. Those were his very words. "You're fired," he said. A heated imbrolligo then ensued, with a lot of back-chat and people shouting "Ikey!" and then the door flew open, precipitating me . . .'

Albert Peasemarch ceased. He found that he was playing to empty benches. Something prismatic had shot past him, and he was alone in the state-room. Ruefully reflecting that there never was a woman yet who knew how to listen, he gathered up the breakfast-tray, ate the slice of cold bacon which lay on it, and departed.

Lottie Blossom came out on to the promenade deck, to find it in the state of mixed torpor and activity which always prevails on promenade decks on fine mornings. There was a long line of semi-conscious figures in chairs, swathed in rugs and looking like fish laid out on a slab, and before their glassy gaze the athletes paraded up and down, rejoicing in their virility, shouting to one another 'What a morning!' and pointing out that twice more round would make a mile.

Here and there were groups which fell into neither division. A little too active for the fish brigade and a little too limp for the athletes, they leaned on the rail and stared at the sea or just stood about and looked at their watches, to ascertain how soon they might expect soup.

Ambrose was not to be seen, but presently Lottie's keen eye detected Reggie. He was brooding apart; between his lips one of the cigarettes with which he had filled his case before leaving Mr Llewellyn's state-room. Grim though the recent proceedings had been, they had had one bright spot in them. They had enabled Reggie to stock up with cigarettes.

'Listen,' said Lottie, wasting no words on formal greetings, 'what's all this about Ambrose and Ikey?'

Reggie removed the cigarette from his lips, contriving to lend to that simple action a solemn sadness which set the seal on Lottie's apprehensions. She abandoned the faint hope which she had been trying to cherish that Albert Peasemarch in order to make a good story might have exaggerated the facts.

'A pretty sticky situation,' said Reggie gravely. 'Did he tell you?'

'No, I had it from the Boy Orator – that steward guy. He seems to have been in a ringside seat. Is it true what he says about Ikey firing Ambrose?'

'Quite.'

'But he can't go back on a contract.'

'There isn't any contract.'

'What!'

'No. Apparently it had to be signed at the New York office.'

'Well, there must have been a letter or something?'

'I gathered not.'

'You mean Ambrose hadn't a line in writing?'

'Not a syllable.'

Amazement held Lottie Blossom dumb for an instant. Then she raged desperately.

'What chumps men are! Why couldn't the poor fish have consulted me? I could have told him. Fancy selling up the farm and starting off for Hollywood on the strength of Ikey Llewellyn's word! Ikey's word! What a laugh that is. Why, if Ikey had an only child and he promised her a doll on her birthday, the first thing she would do, if she was a sensible kid, would be to go to her lawyer and have a contract drawn up and signed, with penalty clauses. Oh hell, oh hell, oh hell!' said Miss Blossom, for she was much stirred. 'Do you know what this means, Reggie?'

'Means?'

'To me. Ambrose and I can't get married now.'

'Oh, come,' said Reggie, for his meditations on the deck had shown him that the situation, though sticky, was not so sticky as he had at first supposed. 'He may be broke, having given up his job at the Admiralty and all that, but you've enough for two, what?'

'I've enough for twenty. But what good is that? Ambrose won't live on my money. He wouldn't marry me on a bet now.'

'But, dash it, it's no different than marrying an heiress.'

'He wouldn't marry an heiress.'

'What!' cried Reggie, who would have married a dozen, had the law permitted it. 'Why not?'

'Because he's a darned ivory-domed, pig-headed son of an army mule,' cried Miss Blossom, the hot blood of the Hoboken Murphys boiling in her veins. 'Because he isn't human. Because he's like some actor in a play, doing the noble thing with one eye counting the house and the other on the gallery. No, he isn't,' she went on, with one of those swift transitions which made her character so interesting and which on the Superba-Llewellyn lot had so often sent overwrought directors groping blindly for the canteen to pull themselves together with frosted malted milk. 'He isn't anything of the kind. I admire his high principles. I think they're swell. It's a pity there aren't more men with his wonderful sense of honour and self-respect. I'm not going to have you saying a word against Ambrose. He's the finest man in the world, so if you want to sneer and jeer at him for refusing to live on my money, shoot ahead. Only remember that a cauliflower ear goes with it.'

'Quite,' said Reggie, somewhat dazed. 'Oh, definitely.'

A pause followed, during which a girl with a sniff and no chin came up and asked Miss Blossom to write her name and some little sentiment in her autograph album. With the air of a female member of the Committee of Public Safety signing a death warrant during the Reign of Terror, she did so. The interruption served to break the thread of her thoughts. Alone with Reggie once more, she looked at him in a bewildered way, like an awakened somnambulist.

'Where were we?'

Reggie coughed.

'We were talking about Ambrose. And I was saying that I thought it simply magnificent, this stand he was taking about refusing to marry you and live on your money.'

'Were you?'

'I was.' Reggie spoke with a good deal of emphasis. He wanted no misapprehensions on this point. 'It's terrific. Great. Splendid. One feels a thrill of pride.'

'Yes,' said Lottie doubtfully. 'He's right, I suppose. Only where do I get off?'

'There's that, of course.'

'It seems kind of tough on me.'

'It does.'

'We'd have been so happy.'

'Yes. Still, there it is.'

'If you ask me,' said Lottie, suddenly coming out of a brooding silence, 'I think the man's crazy. He ought to have his head examined. Why would he be living on my money? He could be writing his books.'

Reggie, though still nervous about his personal safety, felt compelled to put her straight on the matter of Ambrose's books.

'My dear old shipmate,' he said, 'Ambrose – splendid fellow though he is – high-principled, crammed to the gills with honour and self-respect – isn't a frightfully hot writer. I don't suppose he makes enough out of a novel to keep a midget in doughnuts for a week. Not a really healthy midget.'

'What! Is he a bust?'

'With the pen, yes. But,' added Reggie carefully, 'full of honour and self-respect. His principles, too, are very high. Very high indeed. I've always said so.'

Lottie Blossom stared disconsolately at the ocean.

'Well, then?' she said bleakly.

'Seems a bit of a mix-up,' agreed Reggie. 'The only word of good cheer that I can drop –'

'What?'

'Well, you know Llewellyn better than I do. Is he, perhaps, one of those fellows who say things in the heat of the moment which they subsequently regret? How does his bark compare with his bite? What, in other words, would you quote as the odds against a sudden gush of remorse? Do you suppose there's a chance that when he thinks all this over quietly in his bath – he was about to take a bath when I left him – his heart will melt –'

'He hasn't a heart.'

'I see.'

'I'd like to wring his neck.'

'But he hasn't a neck, either.'

They fell into a moody silence again, musing on Ivor Llewellyn. The man seemed armed at all points.

'Well, then,' said Reggie, 'there's just one thing. An outside chance, as you might say . . .'

'What? What?'

'I'm not saying it's going to lead to anything, mind you. . .'

'Go on. What?'

'Well, brooding just now, I suddenly remembered something – to wit, that this Llewellyn, for some distorted reason known only to himself, is extraordinarily anxious to induce Monty Bodkin to come and act for him.'

'Bodkin? The fellow next door to me?'

'He isn't next door to you now. He's in B 36. But that's the chap.'

Lottie Blossom rubbed her chin. She seemed perplexed.

'Bodkin? Bodkin? Well, I thought I knew the whole muster-roll of our hams, from Baby Leroy downwards, but I never heard of him as an actor.'

'He isn't an actor. Nevertheless, Llewellyn seems bent on making him one. I had this from Ambrose, and Mabel Spence confirms it. Any time Monty cares to say the word, Llewellyn will sign a contract. I suppose the fact of the matter is the man's got ants in the pantry.'

Lottie saw deeper into the thing. Her perplexity vanished.

'No, I see what's happened. Ikey gets that way sometimes. All these big bugs in Hollywood do now and then. They get the idea that they are sort of wonder-men who can just look around and find talent where nobody else would suspect it. It makes them feel good. But what about it?'

'Well, apparently Monty turned him down. And what I was thinking was that if he could be induced to reconsider, he might make it a condition of his signing the contract that Ambrose was taken on, too, in some capacity. As far as I can figure it out, Llewellyn is so keen to get Monty that he would agree to anything. It seems to me that Monty is the bird to work on.'

Lottie Blossom's eyes gleamed with a new hope.

'You're dead right. Where did you say he was now?'

'B 36. My cousin Gertrude, with whom he is walking out, apparently didn't like him being next door to you, so she shifted him.'

'She suspects me of being the menace in the treatment?'

'To some extent, I gather.'

'That's right, too. I remember. Brother Bodkin said as much last time we were having one of our get-togethers.'

'All right, then,' said Reggie, 'I'll push along, shall I, and see Monty and try to talk him into this acting wheeze?'

Lottie Blossom shook her head.

'Not you. I'm the one to handle this. We're great buddies, this Bodkin and me. We've had two visits already, and got along together like a couple of Warner brothers. Would he be up yet?'

'Not if I know him.'

'Then I'll go right along to his state-room. What you need in a thing like this,' said Miss Blossom, 'is the woman's touch.'

The woman's touch, administered with a brisk knuckle on his door a few minutes later, found Monty, clad in a bathrobe, reading for the seventh time the note which he had received from Gertrude Butterwick shortly after Reggie had left him on his errand of mercy. State-room B 36 possessing no bathroom, he was about to go down the passage for his tub. But before doing so he could not resist the urge to read that note once more.

His heart warmed to Reggie as he read. A true friend, he felt. To have produced such a communication from Gertrude, Reggie must have stepped on the gas without reserve. For the letter breathed in its every line of love and of remorse for suspicions which the writer now saw so clearly to have been unworthy. It ended with the statement that if Monty happened to be in the library at about twelve o'clock he would receive a warm welcome.

It was in order to render himself fit for this encounter that he had shaved almost to the bone and laid out his grey suit with the thin blue stripes and was now preparing to make for the bathroom. The only small cloud on his happiness was the recollection that he had lent Reggie that tie with the pink roses on it. It was the one tie which in this supreme moment he would have selected to set off the grey suit.

To say that he was glad to see Miss Blossom would be an exaggeration. But he bore her intrusion without open dismay. The reflection that at any moment he could terminate the interview by bounding past her and finding refuge in the bathroom served to fortify him. For even Lottie Blossom, he considered, specialist though she was at barging in where she was not wanted, would find it dashed difficult to come and hob-nob with a fellow who was in his bath with the door locked.

He hullo-hullo-hulloed, therefore, with something approaching geniality. He was not glad to see her, but he knew that the strategic railways in his rear were in good working order.

'Looking for somebody?' he asked civilly.

'I'm looking for you,' said Miss Blossom, and was about to speak further when her eye fell on the Mickey Mouse as it beamed at her from the dressing-table: and so powerful was its spell that she broke off with a sharp, emotional gulp, her mission completely forgotten. She had never seen anything which made a more immediate appeal to all that was best and deepest in her.

'Of all the cute . . .' Words failed her. She stood staring, open-mouthed. You sometimes see people looking like that at the Winged Victory in the Louvre. 'Say, give me that!' she cried hungrily.

Monty did his best not to be severe, for he was sorry for the girl. He saw that she loved the Mickey Mouse, which, ever since Gertrude's note had arrived, he had been loving himself. But he was very firm.

'No.'

'Ah, come on.'

'I'm sorry. No. That mouse belongs to my fiancée.'

'To Gertrude – ha, ha – Butterwick?'

Monty stiffened.

'I wish,' he said coldly, 'that in mentioning my fiancée's name you would not shove in that bally "ha, ha" before the "Butterwick". It is uncalled-for and offensive, and –'

'How much do you want for it?'

160

'Want for what?' said Monty, annoyed, for no man likes to be interrupted just as he is getting to the nub of a rather stately rebuke.

'The mouse, chump. State your terms. What price the mouse?'

Monty decided that all this rot must cease.

'I have already apprized you,' he said, drawing on Albert Peasemarch for the telling verb, 'that this mouse is the property of my fiancée, Miss Gertrude Butterwick ... not Miss Gertrude – ha, ha – Butterwick, but Miss Gertrude Butterwick pure and simple. A nice thing it would be if I went about the place giving away or selling her Mickey Mice – and to you of all people.'

'Why me of all people?'

'Because,' said Monty, feeling that the moment had arrived for absolute frankness and that now was the chance of a lifetime to warn this vermilion-haired menace to his happiness off the grass once and for all, 'I don't mind telling you that your habit of haunting my state-room like a family spectre has caused Gertrude considerable alarm and despondency. The fact that the poor child is not able to pass my door without seeing you come popping out of it is making her as sick as mud. She chafes, and I don't blame her for chafing. I have no wish to be unkind, nothing is further from my intention than to tick you off, but you must see for yourself that it is not the sort of thing a girl likes. A fat chance I should have of ever leading her to the altar if she saw you swanking about in possession of that mouse. Dismiss absolutely the idea of getting your hooks on it. It can't be done.'

Miss Blossom seemed impressed by this eloquence. She registered resignation, and while she was doing so Monty suddenly remembered the words which had been lurking at the back of his mind, waiting to be spoken, from the moment when she had made her entrance. Only the fact that she had suddenly gone off at a tangent and begun talking about this Mickey Mouse had prevented him speaking them directly he saw her.

'To what,' he said, 'am I indebted for the honour of this visit?'

Like one waking from a dream, Lottie Blossom removed her fascinated gaze from the mouse, and with a little shake of the shoulders seemed to dismiss it from her thoughts. She was reproaching herself for having allowed it to divert her from the main business in hand.

'I've come for a conference,' she said.

'A –?'

'Conference. We're strong on those at Hollywood. All God's chillun got conferences out there. I remember once trying to get Ikey on the phone, and his secretary would have none of it. "Sorry, Miss Blossom," she said. "Quate impossible. Mr Llewellyn is greatly conferencing just now." And talking of Ikey brings me nicely to the point. I've come about that business. You know.'

'I don't know.'

'That business he sent Ambrose to take up with you. About your signing a contract to act for the S.-L.'

Nothing had been further from Monty's intention than to smile at any point during this interview. He had planned to conduct it throughout with the utmost austerity, preserving from start to finish what Miss Blossom would have called a 'dead pan' and what he himself had been mentally labelling the frozen face. But at these words he was unable to check a faint, gratified simper. Or, perhaps, more a smirk. His lips involuntarily parted and for an instant he smirked.

It was, he meant to say, beyond a question extraordinarily flattering, this persistence. He shot a sidelong glance at the mirror, but it told him nothing that it had not told him before. There was the old Bodkin face, as far as he could see, just buzzing along in the old familiar way. He was utterly unable to detect in it any hidden magic. And yet this Ivor Llewellyn, who met hundreds of people every day without giving them a second look, was not merely desirous of securing this face, but positively clamouring for it.

A solid respect for Ivor Llewellyn's intuition began to burgeon within Monty Bodkin. It was the fashion to laugh at these motion-picture magnates – everybody was very funny and satirical about them – but you couldn't get away from it, they had a *flair*. They *knew*.

'Oh, ah, yes,' he said.

'Well, what about it?'

162

'You mean, am I going to sign a contract?'

'Yes.'

'No. Emphatically no.'

'Ah, come on.'

'No, I couldn't.'

'Why not?'

'I simply couldn't, dash it.'

Lottie Blossom stretched out an appealing hand. Her intention of attaching herself to the lapel of his bathrobe and winsomely twisting it was so plain that Monty backed a step. He had had the lapels of his garments twisted by girls before, always with unfortunate results.

'I simply couldn't,' he repeated.

'Why not? Is it that you have your pride, that there are some things to which a Bodkin cannot stoop? Ever hear the one about the mother who was walking with her child past the Brown Derby and a bunch of fellows came out in make-up? The kid points and says: "Look, mamma. Movie actors!" And the mother says: "Hush, dear – you don't know what *you* may come to some day." Is that it?'

'No, no.'

'Well, then?'

'No, I simply couldn't act. I'd feel such a chump.'

'Don't you feel that already?'

'Yes, but not that sort of chump.'

'Haven't you ever done any acting?'

'Only once. It was at a kind of jamboree at my first kindergarten, when I was about five. I played the Spirit of Modern Learning. I wore white reach-me-downs, I remember, and carried a torch, and I came on and said: "I am the Spirit of Modern Learning." At least, I didn't, because I blew up in my lines, but that was the idea.'

This segment of autobiography seemed to depress Miss Blossom a little.

'Nothing further?'

'No.'

'That is the whole sum of your experience?'

'Yes.'

'Oh? Well,' said Miss Blossom thoughtfully, 'I've known

163

people come to the screen with a better record, I admit. George
Arliss, for one. Still, you never can tell in the movies. After all,
it's mostly a case of having a map that photographs well and
getting a good cameraman and director. I was no Bernhardt
when I broke in. All I'd done was be in musical comedy.'

'Oh, were you in musical comedy?'

'Sure. I used to sing in the chorus, till they found out where
the noise was coming from. And then I went to Hollywood
and had my photograph taken and found I was swell. It might
be the same with you. Why not take a chance? You would like
Hollywood, you know. Everybody does. Girdled by the ever-
lasting hills, bathed in eternal sunshine. Honest, it kind of gets
you. What I mean, there's something going on there all the
time. Malibu. Catalina. Aqua Caliente. And if you aren't getting divorced yourself, there's always one of your friends is,
and that gives you something to chat about in the long evenings. And it isn't half such a crazy place as they make out. I
know two-three people in Hollywood that are part sane.'

'Oh, I expect I'd enjoy it all right.'

'Well, come along, kid, where Opportunity beckons. You
might be a whale of a hit. You never know. There's plenty of
room at the top. And if you can't get to the top, you can
always sit at the bottom and make excuses. And think of the
money. Don't you like money?'

'Yes, I like money.'

'Me, too, bless its heart. What great stuff it is, isn't it? Don't
you love to hear it crackling? Do you know, I still keep a little
wad tucked away in my stockings, same as I used to in the old
merry-merry days. Every week I would put my thirty bucks
next to the skin you love to touch, and I do it to this day. It
sort of seems to give me a cosy feeling. Yes, sir, there's six
fives in my stocking at this very moment. Look, if you don't
believe me,' said Miss Blossom, beginning to undrape a shapely
leg.

This was precisely the note which Monty wanted to dis-
courage. The chariest maid, he felt, is prodigal enough if she
unmask her beauty to the moon. With a certain feverish haste,
he assured his companion that her word by itself was sufficient
to carry conviction.

164

'Well, then, coming back to it, if you're fond of money –'

'But, you see, I've such a frightful lot of my own already.'

'You have?'

'Yes. Hundreds of thousands of quids.'

Lottie Blossom's animation died away.

'Oh?' she said, discouraged. 'That's different. Got the stuff already, have you? I didn't know that. I knew you were a friend of Reggie's and I thought that all you prominent young London clubmen were down to your last bean, like him. If you're one of these well-to-do millionaires, I can see why you might not want to come to Hollywood. It's a pleasant enough spot, but I don't say I'd hang around there myself if somebody gave me the United States Mint. Kayo, chief. I see the thing's cold.'

'I'm sorry.'

'Not half so sorry as I am. I was hoping you would be able to swing things for Ambrose.'

'How do you mean?'

'Well, you see, poor old Ambrose is in bad. That contract of his with the Superba-Llewellyn has fallen through.'

'Good Lord! You don't mean that?'

'Yes, sir. Ikey has just found out he didn't write "The Boy Stood on the Burning Deck".'

'But why should he?' asked Monty, mystified.

'Because that was the Tennyson Ikey thought he was getting – the big shot, the fellow you hear his name everywhere.'

'Tennyson didn't write "The Boy Stood on the Burning Deck".'

'He did, too.'

'The Tennyson we used to have to turn into Latin verse at school, do you mean?'

'I don't know what you turned him into at school, but there's one sure thing, you didn't turn Ambrose, and that's what Ikey is beefing about.'

'Shakespeare wrote "The Boy Stood on the Burning Deck".'

'He did not any such thing. Tennyson did. And what does it matter, anyway? The point is that there's a right Tennyson and a wrong Tennyson, and Ambrose turns out to be the wrong one. So Ikey refuses to come through with that contract and all that fifteen-hundred-a-week thing has gone west.'

'Well, I'm dashed.'

'So am I. And I was hoping that you would be nice about coming and acting for Ikey, so that then you could have made him put in a clause that if you went Ambrose must go too. And I can't see why you won't, even if you have got all this money. You would have lots of fun at Hollywood.'

Monty shivered.

'I wouldn't act if I was starving. The mere thought of it makes me tremble like a leaf.'

'Oh, you give me hay fever... Well?'

The remark was addressed to Albert Peasemarch, who had just entered. One of the fascinations of travelling on R.M.S. *Atlantic* was that there was never any stint of Albert Pease-march's society.

'I came to bring Mr Bodkin his sponge, miss, which he inadvertently left in the state-room he vacatuated last night,' said the steward. 'No doubt you missed the sponge, sir?'

'Thanks. Yes. I spotted I was a sponge short.'

'Say, listen, buddy,' said Miss Blossom, 'didn't you tell me Tennyson wrote "The Boy Stood on the Burning Deck"?'

'Quite right, miss.'

'Mr Bodkin says he didn't.'

Albert Peasemarch smiled a pitying smile.

'Mr Bodkin, miss, so I understand from the ties in his drawer, was educated at Eton. That's where he's handicapped in these matters. Eton, as you may have heard, is one of our English public schools, and the English public-school system,' said Albert, warming to a subject to which he had given a good deal of thought, 'isn't at all what an educational system should be. It lacks practicality and inspiration. If you ask me, they don't learn the little perishers nothing. The whole essence of the English public school system with its hidebound insistence on –'

'All right.'

'Miss?'

'That'll be all.'

'Very good, miss,' said Albert Peasemarch, wounded, but still feudal.

'Well, listen,' said Lottie, turning to Monty with the air of one who has successfully put a green baize cloth over a canary, 'if you won't sign up with Ikey, you can at least string him along and make him think you're going to and get him to take Ambrose on again. Go and talk to him after you've had your bath.'

Albert Peasemarch had a word to say about this.

'I shouldn't, sir,' he advised, in a serious, friendly tone. 'I wouldn't recommend anyone to go and talk to Mr Llewellyn at the present juncture.'

'You wouldn't?'

'No, sir. Not anyone that didn't want to get his head bit off. Let me tell you a little experience of my own, sir. I was in his shed not so long ago, and purely because I happened absent-mindedly to sing a couple of bars of the "Yeoman's Wedding Song" – '

'Eh?'

'It's a number I'm rendering at the second-class concert to-night,' explained Albert. 'You often find on these trips that the voluntary talent isn't enough to fill out a programme, and then the purser tells Jimmy the One to tell off a member of the corps of stewards to render a number. Usually it's me and my "Yeoman's Wedding Song", it being well and favourably known to all on this boat. Well, having this 'Yeoman's Wedding Song" to brush up, as it were, for this second-class concert and being somewhat distray, as the French say, on account of it, I inadvertently sang the bit where it goes "Ding dong, ding dong, ding dong, I hurry along" in Mr Llewellyn's shed while removing of his breakfast-tray. Sir, he turned on me like a tiger of the jungle. Quite an animal snarl he emitted, if I may say so. I really wouldn't advocate anyone having anything in the nature of social intercourse with Mr Llewellyn for a long time to come.'

'Hear that?' said Monty, well pleased.

Miss Blossom was regarding the steward with a lowering gaze.

'You would come sticking your oar in, wouldn't you?'

Albert Peasemarch bridled, like a sensitive serf unjustly rebuked by a chatelaine.

'I was merely recommending Mr Bodkin here to allow Mr Llwellyn to simmer down to some extent before –'

'Of all the pests –'

'You see,' said Monty. 'If he's feeling like that, what's the sense of my going and talking to him? What could I hope to effect? The whole project, therefore, becomes null and void, and now, if you will excuse me, I think I'll be dashing off and having my bath. I have an urgent appointment in the library pretty soon.'

When the spirit of a man of sensibility has been exercised by a distressing scene with a member of the opposite sex there are few things that more swiftly restore him to composure than a plunge into cold, stinging sea-water. Monty, having carefully shot the bolt of the bathroom door, for one never knew, revelled ecstatically in his tub. It is true that he howled sharply as he got in and felt the first icy touch on his spine, but after that he became all that was gay and debonair. He sang freely as he splashed about, employing for that purpose, perhaps by way of a courteous tribute to Albert Peasemarch, as much as he could remember of the 'Yeoman's Wedding Song'.

It was not that he was callous. Nobody could have been sorrier for poor old Ambrose. A dashed shame, he considered, that things had gone into a tail spin for him like that. But remembering what had been in Gertrude's note and reflecting that in about two ticks he would be up in the library gazing into her eyes, he found it impossible not to be happy.

It was with a certain wariness that he returned to the stateroom. To his relief, Miss Blossom had removed herself. Only Albert Peasemarch met the eye. The steward was reading the news-sheet which ocean liners provide for their passengers each morning.

'I see,' he said, rising politely as Monty entered, 'where gas explosion occurs in London street, sir, slaying four.'

'Oh, yes?' said Monty, reaching for his trousers and sliding gaily into them. He knew that it was too bad of him not to feel more grieved about this unfortunate quartette, but he simply could not pump up a decent concern. He was young, the sun was shining, and at noon Gertrude would be in the library.

168

Four hundred could have been slain in a London street without spoiling his morning.

'And well-dressed woman absent-mindedly has bonny baby in Chicago street-car. Or, rather,' said Albert Peasemarch, correcting himself after a closer scrutiny of the text, 'leaves. And that's odd, too, sir, when you come to think of it. Shows what women are like.'

'It does,' agreed Monty, putting on the only shirt in the world worthy of being present at the forthcoming meeting in the library.

'The fact of the matter is, sir, women haven't got the heads men have got. I believe it's something to do with the bone structure.'

'True,' said Monty. He adjusted his tie and looked at it critically in the mirror. A little sigh escaped him. It was not a bad tie. He would go further, it was a jolly good tie. But it was not the tie with the pink roses on the dove-grey background.

'Take my old mother,' proceeded Albert Peasemarch, with that touch of affectionate reproach which comes to a thoughtful man when he contemplates the shortcomings of the opposite sex. 'Always losing and forgetting things, she is. She could never keep her spectacles by her for two minutes on end. Many a rare hunt I've had for them when I was a young chap. She'd have lost those spectacles if she'd been alone on an iceberg.'

'Eh?'

'My mother, sir.'

'On an iceberg?'

'Yes, sir.'

'When was your mother ever on an iceberg?'

Albert Peasemarch perceived that his remarks had not secured his overlord's undivided attention.

'My mother was never on an iceberg, sir. I'm simply saying that if she had been she'd have lost her spectacles. And it's just the same with all women, on account of the bone structure of their heads. As I say, they're always losing things and forgetting things.'

'I expect you're right.'

'I know I'm right, sir. Why, that young lady in here just now, your Miss Blossom –'

169

'I wish you wouldn't call her my Miss Blossom.'

'No, sir. Very good, sir. But what I was about to say was that she'd got half-way down the corridor without remembering to take her plaything with her. I had to run after her and give it to her. "Hi, miss," I said, "you omitted to fetch away your mouse." And she said: "Oh, thank you, steward, so I did." ... Sir?'

Monty had not spoken. What had proceeded from his lips had been a mere animal wail. He raked the dressing-table with starting eyes, hoping against hope that he had not heard his companion aright.

But there was no mistake. That broad, friendly smile was not there to greet him. Desolation reigned on the dressing-table. The Mickey Mouse had gone.

# Chapter 16

Monty supported himself with a hand on the dressing-table and stared at Albert Peasemarch. His jaw was drooping and his complexion had shaded away to about the colour of the underside of a fish. His demeanour occasioned the steward some little concern. He had often seen passengers look like this, but never when the vessel was riding, as now, upon an even keel. As far as appearance went, Monty might have been one of the victims of that gas explosion in the London street. Even such a man so faint, so spiritless, so dead, so dull in look, so woebegone, drew Priam's curtain in the dead of night and would have told him half his Troy was burnt – or so it seemed to Albert Peasemarch.

'Sir?' he said, bewildered.

Monty found himself unable to speak. For the past few moments he had merely been making a sort of low, gulping sound, reminding the steward of a cat belonging to his mother which had always gulped like that when about to be sick.

'You gug –?'

'Sir?'

'You gug – gug –?'

'Sir?'

'You gug – gave –?'

'Yes, sir. I gave the lady her mouse.'

Another long, silent stare played about Albert Peasemarch like a death-ray. Then Monty shook from tie to socks as with an ague, and for an instant it seemed as if words like molten lava were about to gush from him. But they remained unspoken. His was not an extensive vocabulary, and he found it impossible to think of anything which would really do justice to his feelings regarding Albert. Shakespeare might have managed it. So might Rabelais. Monty could not. Of all the nouns and adjectives which presented themselves for his inspec-

171

tion there was not one that he did not recognize as paltry and inadequate. So, being in no mood to accept the second best, he remained silent. Still silent, he put on his coat, brushed his hair and under his companion's wondering gaze tottered out of the room.

As he dragged his stumbling feet along the corridor, he was musing on Albert Peasemarch and the grave social problem which such men as Albert Peasemarch presented. You could not murder them. You could not even have them shut up in asylums. Yet, left to run around loose, what a gangrene in the body politic they were. He seemed to picture the world as a vast cauldron of soup, with good men like himself for ever standing on the brink and for ever being shoved into it by the Albert Peasemarches.

And at the end of the voyage, mark you, he would have to tip the fellow...

Deep in his sombre thoughts, he ran into Reggie Tennyson.

'Oh, there you are,' said Reggie.

Monty might have replied that what the other saw before him was not really the Bodkin he knew but merely the shell or husk of that Bodkin after Albert Peasemarch had done with it. But he was not equal to metaphysical flights. He said yes, there he was.

'I was just coming to see you.'

'Were you?'

'I wanted to hear if Lottie had talked you into the scheme of going to Hollywood. Have you seen her?'

'I've seen her.'

'And did she?'

'No.'

Reggie nodded.

'I had an idea she wouldn't. Rummy, this going-to-Hollywood business. I'd give anything to buzz off there. So would Ambrose. Whereas you, with everybody begging you on bended knee to give the place a trial, will have none of it. Ironical. Still there it is. Have you seen Gertrude?'

'Not yet.'

'I squared you all right.'

'I know. I had a note from her.'

'Everything in good shape now?'

'Oh, yes.'

Reggie was a little piqued. A man may say to himself that he desires no thanks, that he is only too delighted and so forth, but he does like a certain measure of recognition of his acts of kindness.

'You don't seem overpleased,' he said frigidly.

'Reggie,' said Monty, 'the most awful thing has happened. The Blossom has got away with Gertrude's mouse.'

'Mouse?'

'Yes.'

'White mouse?'

'Mickey Mouse. You remember that Mickey Mouse I gave her and she sent back . . .'

'Ah, yes.' Reggie shook his head rather censoriously. 'You shouldn't have given Gertrude's mouse to Lottie, old man.'

Monty raised his eyes to the ceiling, as if pleading with heaven not to allow him to be pushed too far.

'I didn't give it to her.'

'But she's got it?'

'Yes.'

'Tell me the story in your own words,' said Reggie. 'So far, it sounds goofy to me.'

But when the tale had been told he had no comfort to offer. It seemed to him that his friend was in a spot, and he said so.

'Your best plan is to get that mouse back,' he suggested.

'Yes,' said Monty. This had occurred to him independently.

'If Gertrude sees it in Lottie's possession –'

'Yes,' said Monty.

'She'll –'

'Yes,' said Monty.

Reggie clicked his tongue impatiently.

'You'll have to do something better than go about looking like a frog and saying "Yes", my lad. I'd get in touch with her immediately, if I were you.'

'But I've got to meet Gertrude in the library.'

'Well, directly you've pushed her off. What are you going to say to Gertrude, by the way, if she asks you for the thing?'

'I don't know.'

'You don't know much, do you? Listen. This is what you say. No,' said Reggie, after a moment's thought, 'that's no good. How about this? No, that's no good, either. I'll tell you what to do. Go off in a corner somewhere and think of something.'

And with these helpful words Reggie Tennyson took his departure. He had suddenly remembered that, what with one thing and another, he had not yet had that game of shuffleboard with Mabel Spence.

Monty tottered off to the library.

The library was empty. Gertrude had not yet arrived at the tryst, and even the most hardened indoor knitters and picture-postcard writers had been shamed into the open by the glorious sunshine. Sinking into a chair and clutching his head with both hands in order to assist thought, Monty gave himself up to a supreme effort to formulate a plan of action.

The mouse – how to recover it?

It would be no easy task. That much was certain. If ever Monty had seen love at first sight, it was when Lotus Blossom had come into his state-room and focused that mouse. She had unmistakably yearned for it. And now that Fate, aided by its old crony Albert Peasemarch, had enabled her to secure it, would she lightly let it go?

Monty feared not. Her whole attitude had been so patently that of a girl from whose grasp it was going to be exceedingly difficult to prise this particular mouse, once she had frozen on to it. Still ...

Yes, it might be done. The woman presumably had a conscience and had been taught, either at her mother's knee or elsewhere, the fundamentals of an ethical system. If he could get in touch with her and point out to her that in accepting at Albert Peasemarch's hands a Mickey Mouse which she was perfectly well aware it was not in his power to bestow she had been guilty of something approaching very close to grand larceny, she might consent to disgorge. Much, of course, depended on the extent to which life in Hollywood had warped her sense of right and wrong. If it had warped it a good deal, all was lost. If, on the other hand, it had not warped it very much, surely an appeal to her better feelings ...

A voice broke in upon his thoughts, just as he seemed to be beginning to get somewhere.

'Hullo, Monty.'

He looked up, distrait.

'Oh, hullo,' he said.

If anybody had told Monty Bodkin – say, while he shaved that morning – that a time would come, and that ere yonder sun had set, when he would not be glad to see Gertrude Butterwick, he would have placed the speaker in the mental class to which Albert Peasemarch belonged. Yet now he felt no responsive thrill as his eyes met hers. She represented merely an obstacle between himself and the task that lay before him, the task of getting hold of Lottie Blossom and somehow choking that mouse out of her. He wanted to think, not to have to talk, even to the divinest of her sex.

Gertrude's gaze was melting. Remorse had softened her up. A child could have taken a hockey ball from her.

'What a lovely morning!'

'Yes.'

'Did you get my note?'

'Yes.'

A look of anxiety came into Gertrude's shining eyes. In the dreams she had dreamed of this lovers' meeting she had not budgeted for a rigid Monty, a smileless Monty, a Monty who looked as if he had been stuffed by some good taxidermist. She had been expecting something that beamed and prattled and rather leaped about a bit. Could it be, she asked herself, that the Bodkins never forgave?

'Monty,' she faltered, 'you aren't cross?'

'Cross?'

'You seem so funny.'

Monty came out of his reverie with a start. He pulled himself together. Preoccupation, he realized, was causing him to squander a golden moment. Whatever might happen subsequently, the present was the present.

'I'm awfully sorry,' he said. 'I was thinking of something. Sort of musing, don't you know.'

'You aren't cross?'

'No, I'm not cross.'

'You looked cross.'

'Well, I wasn't cross.'

'I was afraid you might be cross because I thought such

horrid things about you. Can you ever forgive me, darling?'

'Forgive you?'

'I seem to do nothing but make a fool of myself.'

'No, no.'

'Well, I'm glad you're not cross.'

'No, I'm not cross at all.'

'Monty!'

'Gertrude!'

It was not for some moments that a reporter, had one been lurking in the vicinity with his note-book, would have overheard any conversation worthy of being recorded. Each party to the scene seemed to feel instinctively that it was one that called for business rather than dialogue. But presently, the first emotional transports over, Monty straightened his tie and Gertrude patted her hair, and conversation was resumed.

Gertrude, opening it, began to speak of Reginald Tennyson, throwing out the opinion that he ought to be skinned. Alive, she specified. And, she added, for she was not a girl who believed in spoiling the ship for a ha'porth of tar, dipped in boiling oil. It was her view that that would teach him.

Monty was conscious of a pang. Indeed, his heart ached for his friend. Lightly though Reggie had talked about not valuing Gertrude's good opinion, he could not bring himself to believe that he could possibly really feel like that. To himself a world in which Gertrude Butterwick was going about saying that he ought to be skinned alive and dipped in boiling oil would have been a desert, and he could not imagine how anyone could hold a different view.

'Oh, Reggie's all right,' he said awkwardly.

'All right?' Gertrude's voice was that of one who is thunderstruck. 'After the way he has behaved?'

'Oh, well.'

'What do you mean – "Oh, well"?'

'I mean, see jewness savvay,' said Monty, once more availing himself of Albert Peasemarch's non-copyright material. 'I mean to say, I suppose he was rather an ass, but young blood, don't you know, if you know what I mean.'

'I certainly don't know what you mean. There's no excuse for him whatsoever. He might have ruined both our lives. I can't imagine a man being so idiotic. For quite a long while, when he came and told me that it was he who had written that stuff on the wall, I couldn't believe him. Jane Passenger was so certain that it had been done by a woman.'

Monty passed a finger round his collar. A perfect fit, made to measure by the finest hosier in London, it seemed to be too tight.

'You shouldn't listen to Jane Passenger.'

'Well, I thought it was a woman's handwriting myself. And then I remembered.'

'Eh?'

'I suddenly remembered that when we were children together Reggie used to write things on walls. Things like –'

'Yes, yes,' said Monty hurriedly. 'I know what you mean.'

'Things like "Death to Blenkinsop".'

Monty blinked.

' "Death to –"?'

'We had a butler called Blenkinsop in those days, and he reported Reggie to father for stealing jam, and father beat Reggie, and Reggie went out and wrote "Death to Harold Blenkinsop" on all the walls in white chalk. Blenkinsop was very annoyed about it. He said it would weaken his authority with the lower domestics, especially as he had always been most careful to keep it from them that his name was Harold. Well, when I remembered that, I knew that Reggie was telling the truth this morning.'

A silent vote of thanks to H. Blenkinsop, in whatever quiet haven he might be passing the evening of his life, floated out from Monty's soul. But for that sterling butler's admirably austere attitude towards the stealing of jam . . .

'I suppose, really,' said Gertrude, more charitably, 'he must be mad. But don't let's waste time talking of Reggie. I can only stay a minute, because Jane wants all the team to show up in the gymnasium before lunch. She saw Angela Prosser, our inside left, take three helpings of pudding at dinner last night, and she's scared of our getting out of condition on board. When are you going to give me back my mouse?'

There were probably moments when Damocles forgot about

the sword which hung over his head. Certainly, during these last few rapturous minutes, the thought of the peril menacing him had been completely purged from Monty's mind. It now returned in full measure, and he quivered from stem to stern like some vessel buffeted by the storm.

'Mer-mouse?' he said, in a low, hoarse voice.

'My Mickey Mouse. I wish you would go down and get it now. I shan't feel that everything is really all right again till I have it.'

'Oh, ah,' said Monty. 'Oh, ah, yes.'

'Yes,' she said.

'Well, I'll tell you,' he said.

And then, for the second time in four days, he received inspiration, thereby putting himself in a class of his own as far as the Bodkins were concerned – his nearest competitor being that Sir Hilary Bodkin, *temp.* Queen Anne, who, according to family tradition handed down over the years from father to son, got an idea just before the Battle of Blenheim and another in the following spring.

'Well, I'll tell you,' he said. 'I'm frightfully sorry, but as a matter of fact that mouse is off the active list for the moment.'

'You haven't lost it?'

'Not lost it, no. But as a matter of fact when you sent it back to me I'm afraid I was so peeved that I sort of gave it a bit of a kick ... as a matter of fact I hoofed it across the state-room ... and as a matter of fact one of its legs came off.'

'I'll sew it on again.'

'It's being sewn on again. By the stewardess. A slow worker. A very slow worker. I doubt if she will be able to put it back into circulation for some time to come ... some little time ... As a matter of fact –'

'Oh, well, so long as you know where it is.'

'I know where it is,' said Monty.

Gertrude, reluctant to leave but obedient to the call of duty, went off to do bending and stretching exercises with her comrades of the All England Hockey Team, and Monty remained seated in his chair, immobile except for what had the appearance of an occasional attack of St Vitus's dance.

For some twenty minutes he sat thus; then suddenly he shot up like a young Hindu fakir with a sensitive skin making acquaintance with his first bed of spikes. He had just realized that he was wasting precious time. Every moment was of importance. The slightest delay in getting together with Lottie Blossom might be fatal. He hurried from the room and began to search the more likely spots of the vessel for her. Ten minutes later he found her on the boat deck. She was playing quoits with the ship's doctor.

This practice of ships' doctors of always grabbing the prettiest girl on board and carrying her off to play quoits or deck-tennis is one of the most disturbing phenomena of ocean travel, and it is one that has caused many a young man to chew the lower lip and scowl with drawn brows. But few young men had ever chewed and scowled with more rancour than did Monty. Hovering about, standing now on this leg, now on that, he found his resentment against this frivolous pill-slinger who was preventing the girl from getting into conference with him growing more and more intense as the minutes went by.

There were a thousand things the fellow ought to have been doing – looking at people's tongues, extracting people's appendices, bottling the mixture as before or even just sitting in his cabin with his text-books, brushing up his medical knowledge. Instead of which, there he stood, laughing all over his fat face, bunging quoits at a wooden peg with Lottie Blossom.

A pretty state of things, felt Monty with justifiable bitterness.

The only policy that suggested itself to him was to walk past them very quickly with a sharp cough and a meaning glance and then to walk very quickly back again with another sharp cough and another meaning glance. And he had done this perhaps half a dozen times when he perceived that the treatment was beginning to take effect. Halfway through the seventh lap he saw Lottie stir as if mildly surprised. The eighth had her plainly wavering. And as he turned to begin lap nine she was staring at him with undisguised interest.

So was the doctor. Quoit in hand, he eyed Monty keenly, and a close observer would have noticed on his face a look of professional interest. Always alert for significant symptoms in the passengers under his charge, he thought that he detected in this young man marked indications of a paranoiac diathesis.

And then, just as it seemed that solid results were about to be obtained, from the direction of the gymnasium, her face flushed with healthy exercise, came Gertrude Butterwick.

'Monty,' she called, and Monty spun round as if the word had been a gimlet inserted in his person. He had forgotten that the gymnasium was on the boat deck.

'Oh, hullo, darling,' he said. 'Finished already?'

'Already?' said Gertrude. 'Why, it's nearly lunch-time. Come for a walk. There's something I hadn't time to say to you down in the library.'

With a cold glance at Miss Blossom, she led him away and they descended the steps to the promenade deck.

'Monty,' said Gertrude.

'Hullo?'

She seemed to hesitate.

'Monty, will you think me an awful idiot if I ask you something?'

'I should say not.'

'But you haven't heard what it is. I was going to ask if you would promise me something.'

'Anything.'

'Well, it's about that Blossom girl. Oh, I know,' said Gertrude, as Monty began to fling his arms heavenwards, 'that there's absolutely nothing between you. But oh, Monty darling, will you promise me never to speak to her again?'

Monty moved to the rail and leaned limply against it. He had not foreseen this complication.

'What!'

'Yes.'

'Not to speak to her?'

'No.'

'But –'

A slight, a very slight chill crept into Gertrude's manner.

'Why,' she said, 'do you want to so much?'

'No, no. Positively not. Only –'

'Only what?'

'Well, you know what she's like.'

'I do. That's why I don't want you to speak to her.'

Monty dabbed at his forehead.

'I mean, she's a bit inclined rather to thrust her society on a fellow somewhat, if you know what I mean. What I'm driving at is suppose she speaks to *me*?'

'In that case, you simply bow and say quietly: "I should prefer to hold no sort of communication with you, Miss Blossom." '

'Who, me?' said Monty, appalled.

'And walk away. She's a very dangerous woman.'

'But, dash it, she's engaged to Ambrose.'

'So she says.'

'But she is. It's a well-known fact.'

'Well, even if she is, what difference does that make? A girl like that would never be content with one man. I expect she's flirting with half the men on the ship. Look at the way she was going on with that doctor up there.'

Monty felt compelled to challenge this statement.

'No, I say, dash it! All she was doing was playing quoits with the chap – and pretty blamelessly, it seemed to me.'

The chill in Gertrude's manner deepened.

'You certainly stick up for your friends.'

Monty sawed the air once more.

'She isn't a friend. Just an acquaintance – if that.'

'Well, that's the way I want her to stay,' said Gertrude. 'The if-thatter the better. So you will promise not to speak to her again, won't you?'

It was not immediately that Monty replied. When he did, it was with an odd, grating sound in his voice.

'Right ho.'

'Splendid.'

The note of a bugle floated through the air.

'Lunch!' said Gertrude happily. 'Come along.'

To a young man who wishes to communicate with a young woman and has promised his betrothed not to speak to her our modern civilization, for all the unpleasant things which have been said about it from time to time, undeniably offers certain advantages which earlier ages would have had to do without.

Had Monty Bodkin been a trilobite wallowing in the primeval slime, he would not have been able to establish contact with Lottie Blossom at all. Had he been Cro-Magnon Man, he would have been confined to expressing himself by means of painting paleolithic bisons on the wall of a cave, and everybody knows how unsatisfactory that is. Living in the twentieth century, he had pencils, envelopes and paper at his disposal, and he intended to make use of them.

Immediately after lunch, avoiding the ship's public rooms for fear of encountering Gertrude, he withdrew to his stateroom, taking a plentiful supply of stationery with him, and at three-fifteen summer-time the Bodkin-Blossom correspondence broke out with extraordinary virulence.

In affairs of this kind it is always the first letter that is the most difficult to write, because it sets the tone. Withheld from beginning 'Miss Blossom, your behaviour is inexplicable' owing to the fact that, Mr Llewellyn having failed him, 'inexplicable' was a word which he still did not know how to spell, Monty very wisely fell back on the third person.

'Mr Bodkin presents his compliments to Miss Blossom and Mr Bodkin would be glad if Miss Blossom would return Mr Bodkin's Mickey Mouse which Miss Blossom was given by that ass Albert Peasemarch at Miss Blossom's earliest convenience.'

He read this through and was satisfied with it. It seemed to him both lucid and dignified. He had never seen a diplomatic note from the ambassadorial representatives of one great power to another, but he imagined that such a note would have been worded in very much the same style – civil and restrained, but getting crisply down to brass tacks.

He pressed the bell and requested his bedroom steward to send Albert Peasemarch to him.

In every exchange of diplomatic notes a messenger is essential, and Monty felt very strongly that Albert Peasemarch, having been directly responsible for the whole trouble, was the ideal choice. A glance at the boat deck had shown him that Lottie Blossom was up there again playing quoits, and that meant that there would be a good deal of sweating about and climbing stairs to be done by the intermediary. The thought of

182

Albert Peasemarch sweating about and climbing stairs made a powerful appeal to him.

Presently there was a faint sound of the 'Yeoman's Wedding Song' without, and Albert appeared.

'What ho, Peasemarch.'

'Good afternoon, sir.'

'I want you,' said Monty, 'to take this note to Miss Blossom and bring back an answer. You will find her on the boat deck.'

There was already a look of disapproval on the steward's face, for Monty's summons had broken in upon him at a moment when he had been hoping to enjoy a quiet lie down and a pipe. At these words it became intensified. He drew his lips together in that duenna-like way with which Monty was so familiar. It was plain that the moral aspect of the matter was troubling him.

'Is this wise, sir?' he said gravely.

'Eh?'

'I am, of course, aware,' proceeded Albert Peasemarch, with a dignified humility which became him well, 'that it is not my place to offer criticism or censure, but if I may take the liberty of saying so, I have become respectfully attached to you in the course of the voyage, sir, and I have your best interests at heart. And I say – Is this wise? If you insist upon me taking this letter to Miss Blossom, I will, of course, do so, being always willing to oblige, but I say again – Is it wise?'

'Peasemarch,' said Monty, 'you're an ass.'

'No, sir, begging your pardon, sir, I am nothing of the kind. I've seen more of life than what you have, if you will excuse me saying so, sir, and I know what I'm talking about. My uncle Sidney, who was a travelling salesman for a Portsmouth firm, used to say to me: "Never put anything in writing, Albert," and you'll find there's no better rule in life. It was the salvation of my uncle Sidney. Oh, I know how it is with you, sir. Don't think I don't understand. This Miss Blossom is what I might call a fam fatarl, and in spite of being engaged to a pure, sweet English girl, if you'll excuse me mentioning it, you've gone and fallen beneath her spell –'

'Listen,' said Monty. 'You just pop off as requested with that note and look slippy about it.'

'Very good, sir,' said Albert Peasemarch with a sigh. 'If you insist.'

The somewhat lengthy interval which separated the steward's departure and return Monty occupied in pacing the floor. Owing to limitations of space, the pacing is never very good in liner state-rooms, but he did the best he could and was still going well when the door opened.

'The lady gave me a letter, sir,' said Albert Peasemarch, speaking in a voice which disapproval, the heat of the day and unaccustomed exercise rendered thick and unmusical.

'Did she say anything?'

'No, sir. She laughed.'

Monty did not like the sound of this. He could imagine that laugh. No doubt one of those mocking, tinkling ones which in certain circumstances can churn a man up as if an egg whisk had been introduced into his vitals. It was in no sanguine spirit that he opened the envelope, and it was as well that he had not been optimistic, for the tone of the communication was in no sense encouraging.

'Miss Blossom presents her compliments to Mr Bodkin and declines to return any Mickey Mice except on certain conditions. Miss Blossom says: Come on up and have a talk about it.'

Albert Peasemarch mopped a heated brow.

'Will that be all, sir?'

'All?' Monty stared. 'We've only just begun.'

'You aren't going to ask me to climb all those steps again?'

'I jolly well am.'

'I ought to be practising my "Yeoman's Wedding Song", sir.'

'Well, practise it as you climb the steps.'

The steward would have spoken further, but Monty, deep now in literary composition, waved him down with an imperious hand. Frowning, he read what he had written. He did not see how he could improve on it. Unless ... His pencil hovered over the paper.

'*You* don't know how to spell "inexplicable", do you?' he asked.

'No, sir.'

Monty decided not to add the sentence he had been contemplating.

He read the thing again, and crossed out one of the 't's' in the word 'conditions'.

'Mr Bodkin presents his compliments to Miss Blossom and begs to inform her that how on earth can he come up and have a talk about it when he has promised his fiancée not to speak to her again? The whole point of this writing notes business is that Mr Bodkin is not allowed to speak to Miss Blossom.

'Mr Bodkin is at a loss to understand what Miss Blossom means about conditions. Mr Bodkin would like to point out to Miss Blossom that this is a straight, clean-cut issue of returning a Mickey Mouse which belongs to Miss Butterwick and does jolly well not belong to Miss Blossom.'

There was a still longer interval this time, but eventually a sound of puffing heralded Albert Peasemarch's return. He handed Monty an envelope and with a courteous word of apology sat down on the bed and began to massage a corn which was paining him.

Monty opened the envelope, read its contents and stood spellbound. The revelation of the depths to which women can sink is always a stunning one.

'Miss Blossom presents her compliments to Mr Bodkin and he knows very well what she means by conditions. If he wants his mouse, he must go to Ikey Llewellyn and sign up with him and get him to consent to overlook the fact that poor old Ambrose did not write "The Boy Stood on the Burning Deck" and give him a contract.

'Miss Blossom asks Mr Bodkin to sort out all these He's and Him's to see that she has got them right and in conclusion informs Mr Bodkin that unless he kicks in she is going to parade the promenade deck tomorrow with that Mickey Mouse and when Miss Butterwick (ha, ha) comes up and says: Where the heck did you get that mouse? she, Miss Blossom, is going to say: Why, tee-hee, Mr Bodkin gave it to me with warm personal regards. And if that doesn't make Miss Buttersplosh kick Mr Bodkin in the slats and hand him his hat, Miss Blossom will be vastly surprised.

'P.S. Think on your feet, boy!'

Monty came out of his trance. He was breathing hard. He

185

had decided to stand no more nonsense. There are times when a man has to forget his chivalry and talk turkey to the other sex. His ancestor, the Sieur Pharamond, had realized this when, returning home from the Crusades rather earlier than had been expected, he found his wife in her boudoir singing close harmony with three troubadours.

There must, he saw, be no more of that polished third-person stuff. What the situation demanded was good, sinewy prose, straight to the button. He dashed off a single, searing line and handed it to Albert Peasemarch.

It ran:

'Do you know what you are?'

Miss Blossom replied:

'Yessir. I'm the girl that's got your Mickey Mouse.'

Impatient with this frivolity, Monty became sterner:

'You're a thief!'

Five minutes later Albert Peasemarch limped back to G.H.Q. with the following:

'My God! Not that?'

Monty declined to abate by so much as a jot or tittle the gravity of the charge:

'Yes, you are. A bally thief.'

To which Miss Blossom, in philosophic vein:

'Oh, well, I've got a nice day for it.'

Monty then delivered an ultimatum:

'Return that mouse by bearer, or I go to the purser.'

But when Albert Peasemarch returned, panting like the hart when wearied in the chase, there was no Mickey Mouse in his hand. He bore nothing but a sheet of paper on which was written a single ribald word. And Monty, reading it, frowned darkly.

'All right!' he said, between clenched teeth. 'All jolly right!'

186

# Chapter 17

It was as the ship's clocks were pointing to four and busy stewards were bustling about preparing tea and cake for famished passengers who had not touched food since half-past two that Reggie Tennyson, roving the vessel in search of Monty, observed him coming out of the purser's office.

Reggie's was not an unsympathetic nature. It is true that he had left Monty somewhat abruptly at a moment when the latter would have been glad of his advice and comfort, but that was because he wanted to play shuffleboard with Mabel Spence. He had by no means failed to give his friend's hard case a good deal of thought, and after lunch and another game of shuffleboard he went to look for him, anxious to ascertain how things were coming along.

For some considerable time his quest had been unsuccessful, but at four o'clock his efforts were rewarded. Happening, as has been said, to pass the purser's office, he caught sight of Monty emerging.

Monty was not alone. The ship's doctor was with him. The ship's doctor had placed an arm about his shoulder and there was a kindly, solicitous expression on his face.

'There is nothing to be alarmed about,' he was saying. 'You just go to your state-room and lie down. I'll send a steward along with something which I would like you to take in a little water every two hours.'

And with these words the ship's doctor administered a cheery little pat on the shoulder and made off, in his bearing the unmistakable look which ship's doctors always wear when they are going back to play quoits with the prettiest girl on board.

Reggie hailed Monty with a friendly 'Hoy!' and the latter turned, blinking. He seemed a little dazed.

'What,' inquired Reggie, 'was all that? Have you gone and got leprosy or something?'

'Come on up to the smoking-room,' said Monty feverishly. 'I want a drink.'

'But the medico told you to go to your state-room and lie down.'

'Blast the medico and curse the state-room,' said Monty, with that same odd feverishness.

Reggie decided to postpone any attempt at reasoning with his friend. Whatever scourge he had got, it was plain that he had no intention of lying down and taking things in a little water every two hours. His whole mind was manifestly intent on reaching the smoking-room and getting a snootful. And as the heat of the afternoon was making Reggie feel that he, too, could do with a spot of refreshment, he suspended his remarks and followed, wondering but silent.

It was only after Monty had had one quick and another rather slower that he seemed to return to this world from whatever misty empyrean it was in which his soul had been wandering. He looked at Reggie as if he were seeing him for the first time, and as his eye was now bright and unclouded and as intelligent as it ever was, the latter considered that he might go on where they had left off.

'What,' he asked, 'was all that?'

A shudder shook Monty.

'Reggie,' he said, 'I've made a bit of an ass of myself.'

'How?'

'I'll tell you. Where's that steward?'

'What do you want the steward for?'

'What do you think I want the steward for?'

With a replenished glass at his side, Monty became calmer. He still had that shaken look and one could see that he had passed through some experience which had tested him to the utmost, but his voice, if toneless, was level.

'I've just had the dickens of a time, Reggie, old man.'

'With Lottie Blossom?'

'With the purser and the doctor and the ship's detective. Did you know ships had detectives? I didn't. But they have. Big chaps with moustaches. Have you ever seen a sergeant-major? Well, that'll give you some idea.'

He fell into that trancelike silence again, and it was only by placing the lighted end of his cigarette gently on the back of his hand that Reggie was enabled to secure his attention once more.

'Ouch!' cried Monty.

'Carry on, old boy,' said Reggie. 'You have our ear. You were talking about pursers and doctors and ship's detectives.'

'So I was. Yes. I see now, of course,' said Monty, 'that I ought never to have gone.'

'Gone where?'

'To the purser. But when the Blossom took that attitude, there seemed no other course.'

'What attitude?'

'I'm telling you. A beastly, low-down, sneering, jeering –'

'You've been chatting with her, then?'

'No, I haven't. We corresponded per Peasemarch.'

'Oh, you wrote to her?'

'And she wrote to me. And Peasemarch flitted to and fro, singing the "Yeoman's Wedding Song".'

'Doing what?'

'Nothing, nothing. What I'm driving at is that I wrote to her demanding the immediate return of the Mickey Mouse, and she wrote back – per, as I say, Peasemarch – informing me that unless I went to old Llewellyn and signed on with him and got him to give Ambrose a contract she was going to flaunt the mouse openly and tell Gertrude that I had given it to her.'

Reggie looked grave.

'I hadn't thought of that. Yes, I see, that's the line she would take. Holding you up, what? Strategic, beyond a doubt, though a thoroughly dirty trick, of course. Still, women are women.'

'No, they aren't. Not all of them.'

'Perhaps you're right,' said Reggie pacifically. 'What did you do then?'

'I let her have it straight. I said I would go to the purser.' Monty gave a little shiver. 'I've just been,' he said.

'What happened?'

Monty endeavoured to restore his composure with a sip at his glass. It was evident that it hurt him to dwell upon what had occurred.

'It was an unfortunate move, old man. I thought the whole

thing was going to be perfectly plain and straightforward, but it wasn't.'

'What happened?'

'I'm telling you. I went in and said: "Could I have a word," and the purser said yes, I could have a word, so I sat down and said: "I must ask you to treat this as entirely confidential," and he said: "Treat what as entirely confidential?" and I said: "What I am about to tell you. Entirely confidential is what I must ask you to treat what I am about to tell you as," and he said: "Right ho," or words to that effect, and I said: "Purser, I've been robbed!"'

'That stirred him up?'

'Quite a bit. He touched a bell, seeming distraught. As a matter of fact, he clutched it.'

'The bell?'

'His hair. I wish you would listen. I tell you he clutched his hair. And when he had clutched his hair, he said something about there being notices posted all over the ship, imploring people not to play cards with strangers, and in spite of that he had never known a single voyage finish without someone coming to him and complaining that they had been rooked by sharpers. And I said I hadn't been rooked by any sharpers, I'd been robbed. And he clutched his hair again and said did I mean that I had had valuables stolen from me? and I said: "Yes, absolutely." And at this juncture old William the Walrus came in – in response, no doubt, to the bell.'

'This W. Walrus being who?'

'That's what I wondered for a moment, but the purser said: "This is the ship's detective," and something about tell him my story and: "My God this sort of thing doesn't do the Line any good, people being robbed as soon as they set foot on board," so I said: "Good afternoon, detective, I've been robbed." And the detective said: "You don't say that, sir?" And I said: "You silly ass, I've just said it." I was a bit overwrought at the moment, you understand?'

'Quite.'

Monty sipped and resumed.

'Well, then the purser and the Walrus started greatly conferencing. The purser said had the Walrus noticed any gangs on board? And the Walrus said: "No, not what you would call gangs." And the purser said that that was rummy, because these big robberies were usually the work of some gang of international crooks. And then they conferenced a bit more, and then the Walrus said that the first thing to do was to get a full description of the lost valuables, and he hauled out a note-book and said: "Perhaps, Mr Bodkin, you will just give me a complete list of the missing jewellery." And it was at that moment, old man, that I began to see that I had made a bit of an ass of myself. You know how it is.'

Reggie nodded. He knew how it was.

'It was only then that it suddenly occurred to me that it might seem a little odd, a chap sending out SOS's and calling in ship's detectives because he had lost a brown plush Mickey Mouse. And they did think it odd, too, because no sooner had I sprung the news than the purser gave a sort of gulp and the Walrus gave a sort of gulp and they looked at one another, and then the purser went out and came back in a minute or two with the doctor, and the doctor asked me a lot of questions about: "Did I feel dizzy?" and: "Were there floating spots in front of my eyes?" and: "Had I as a child ever been dropped on my head?" and: "Did I hear voices and imagine that people were following me about?" and the upshot of the whole thing was that he led me out in a foul, fatherly sort of way – very kind and gentle, if you know what I mean, and told me to lie down and keep out of the hot sun and take something which he would send me, in a little water every two hours.'

Reggie Tennyson was a clear, keen thinker. He could read between the lines.

'They thought you were off your rocker.'

'That's the way it looked to me.'

'H'm ... *Were* you ever dropped on your head as a child?'

'Not that I know of.'

'I was just wondering.'

Reggie pondered.

'Most unpleasant,' he said.

'Most,' agreed Monty.

'And when all the smoke's blown away you're still minus the mouse.'

191

'Yes.'

'And Lottie isn't just bluffing? She'll do what she said?'

'Yes.'

Reggie pondered again.

'It looks to me as if the only thing you can do is meet her conditions.'

'What, become a movie actor?'

'That's about how it seems to pan out.'

A febrile spasm shook Monty.

'I won't become a bally movie actor. The mere thought of it gives me the pip. I hate acting. I've always dodged even amateur theatricals. Many's the time I've had an invitation to go and stay for a couple of weeks at some house and wanted to go and found out at the eleventh hour that they were doing A Pantomime Rehearsal or something in aid of the local Church Organ Fund and backed out like a rabbit. It's a regular what-d'you-call-it with me.'

'How do you mean, a what-d'you-call-it?'

'I can't remember the name. One of those ob things.'

'Obsession?'

'That's right. It's a regular obsession.'

'Curious,' mused Reggie. 'I like acting myself. Did I ever tell you –?'

'Yes.'

'When?'

'Oh, some time or other. And, anyway, we're talking about this mouse of mine.'

'Yes,' said Reggie, called to order, 'that's true. So we are. Well, if you won't become a movie actor, it seems to me that we come back to the original problem. How are you to secure the mouse?'

'Can you suggest anything?'

'Well, it crossed my mind – No, that wouldn't work.'

'What were you going to say?'

Reggie shook his head.

'No, dismiss the idea.'

'How the devil,' demanded Monty, not without a certain show of reason, 'can I dismiss it if I don't know what it is? What crossed your mind?'

'Well, it was just that it occurred to me that usually when anyone has something that you want to get hold of, you can buy it back, and I was wondering if this mouse binge couldn't be put on a commercial basis.'

Monty started.

'Gosh!'

'But in this case, I'm afraid ... what's that extraordinarily clever thing you're always saying?'

Monty was unable to help him out. His manner seemed to suggest that the field of identification was too wide.

'I remember. Wheels within wheels. In this case, I'm afraid, there are wheels within wheels. It wouldn't be any use offering Lottie money. What she wants is to get Ambrose a job. Because his principles are so high that unless he gets one he won't marry her. She would scorn your gold.'

Monty was not to be discouraged so readily. He thought the idea good. The notion of making a cash transaction of the thing appealed to him. It had not occurred to him before.

'How much gold do you think she would scorn?' he asked anxiously. 'Two thousand quid?'

Reggie started. It gave him a shock to hear a sum like that mentioned in such a matter-of-fact way. He had known Monty so long and was so accustomed to him that his amazing oofiness had a tendency to slip from the mind.

'Two thousand quid? You wouldn't give that?'

'Of course I'd give that. Still, I suppose, as you say,' said Monty, the first gush of enthusiasm ebbing, 'there's no use talking about it, blast it.'

A strange light had come into Reginald Tennyson's eyes. His nose twitched. He borrowed a cigarette with ill-concealed excitement.

'Ah, but wait,' he said. 'Wait! This situation is beginning to develop. I see possibilities in it. Let me get this clear. You seriously assert that that Mickey Mouse is worth two thousand pounds to you?'

'Of course it is.'

'You would really hand over that colossal sum to the person who restored it to you?'

'On the nail. Why, dash it, I gave Percy Pilbeam a thousand

to take me on as a skilled assistant in his Private Inquiry Agency, didn't I? This is a much more vital issue.'

Reggie drew a deep breath.

'All right,' he said. 'Make out the cheque to R. Tennyson.'

Monty's brain was not at its brightest.

'Have *you* got the mouse?'

'Of course I haven't, ass.'

'Then why did you say you had?'

'I didn't say I had. But I'm going to get it.'

Reggie leaned forward. Already, at an earlier point in the conversation, he had looked about him and ascertained that the smoking-room, as generally at this hour, was empty but for themselves; nevertheless, he lowered his voice. So much so that all Monty could hear was a confused buzzing sound in which he seemed to detect the words 'Mabel Spence'.

'Speak up,' he urged a little petulantly.

Reggie became more audible.

'It's this way, old boy. I don't mind telling you that I am at a man's cross-roads. You know Mabel Spence?'

'Of course.'

'I love her.'

'Well, get on.'

Reggie seemed a little wounded. However, he decided to continue without comment.

'I love Mabel, and in about forty-eight hours she will be on her way to Hollywood and I shall be headed for Montreal. And what I have been asking myself is: "Shall I follow her to Hollywood or shall I carry on and go to Montreal, as planned?" The catch to the latter scheme being that I shall probably pine myself into a decline without her: the catch to the former scheme being that I should arrive in Hollywood with about five quid in my pocket and no job in sight. And two minutes ago,' said Reggie frankly, 'I would have laid a hundred to eight against the Golden West. Because, however much you're in love, you've got to eat, what?'

Monty said he supposed so. In his present distraught state, he could not imagine ever eating again himself, but he presumed some people liked doing it.

'But what you tell me,' said Reggie, 'alters the entire lay-out.

194

With a couple of thousand tucked into my stocking, I can go West without a tremor. Lottie Blossom told me once that you could get a room for eight dollars a week in Hollywood and a second-hand car for five and, if you played your cards right, live entirely on the appetizers at other people's cocktail-parties. Why, dash it, I could make two thousand pounds last about twenty years.'

Monty was interested not so much in his companion's living arrangements for the next two decades as in the method by which he was proposing to place himself in a position to undertake the visit to California. He returned to the main point at issue.

'But, Reggie, you can't really get that mouse, can you?'

'Of course.'

'How?'

'Easy. It must be in Lottie's state-room.'

'You mean you would go and look for it?'

'Certainly. Pie. Take me about ten minutes.'

This was not the first time that Monty Bodkin had found himself in the role of the capitalist who hires underlings to do sinister work for him. Not so many weeks had elapsed since in the smoking-room of Blandings Castle he had engaged Percy Pilbeam, that nasty little private investigator, to purloin the manuscript of the Hon. Galahad Threepwood's celebrated Memoirs. It was not, therefore, because the idea was new and strange to him that he now bit thoughtfully at his lower lip. It was because he was fond of Reggie and was experiencing much the same emotions as would have been his had the latter informed him of his intention of entering a tiger's cage.

'Suppose she catches you?' he said, quailing at the vision which the words conjured up.

'Ah!' said Reggie. 'That thought occurred to me, too. That's the thing we've got to give a little attention to. Lottie, roused, might be quite on the violent side. Yes, yes, we must not ignore that aspect of the matter. I'll tell you what, I'll just go and take a turn up and down the deck and bend the brain to it.'

There had been moments earlier that afternoon when Monty had chafed at the slowness of Albert Peasemarch's movements, but the steward, for all that he was scant of breath and handicapped by a tender corn, seemed to him to have been sheet-lightning itself in comparison with Reggie. Hours, he felt, must have elapsed before the familiar form once more appeared in the doorway of the smoking-room.

But Reggie speedily cleared himself of any suspicion of having wasted his time. It was not day-dreams or idle conversations with fellow-passengers that had delayed him.

'It's all right,' he said. 'I've been talking to Lottie. Everything's fixed.'

Monty was at a loss.

'What did you want to talk to her for?'

'Strategy, my dear chap,' said Reggie with modest pride. 'I said I had come from you, acting as your agent. I said that you had told me all and had empowered me to offer her a hundred quid for the mouse.'

Monty became more fogged than ever. His friend's complacent manner, which seemed to suggest that he imagined himself to have accomplished a brilliant diplomatic coup, bewildered him.

'But what on earth was the good of that? I suppose she laughed herself sick?'

'She seemed amused, certainly. She explained, what I had already told you was the case, that money was no object. What she wanted, she said, and what she was jolly well going to get, was a job for Ambrose. I affected to reason with the girl, and in the end – what I was working up to, of course, in my snaky way – I said: "Well, listen, will you meet Monty tonight and talk it over?" And she said she would, at ten o'clock on the dot.'

'But, dash it –'

'So you are to meet her then.'

'Yes, but, dash it –'

Reggie held up a hand.

'All right. I know what's on your mind. You're thinking of the risk of Gertrude seeing you chatting with Lottie. Is that it?'

Monty said that that was precisely it.

'Don't worry. You don't suppose I forgot that, do you? I have eliminated all risk. The tryst is arranged for the second-class promenade deck. Don't forget the hour, because we shall be working to schedule. Ten o'clock to the tick.'

'Second-class promenade deck,' said Monty musing. 'Yes, that ought to be all right.'

'Of course it will be all right. How can there be any chance of Gertrude seeing you? First-class passengers don't go strolling all over the second-class. There can't be a hitch. At ten o'clock you will meet Lottie on the second-class promenade deck, she having told Ambrose that she is turning in early owing to a headache, and you will detain her there for a quarter of an hour or so, talking any sort of rot you like so long as it isn't bad enough to make your audience walk out on you. By the end of that period I shall have thoroughly scoured her state-room and got the mouse. I mean to say, we know the thing must be there, and there aren't so many spots in a state-room where a fairly sizeable Mickey Mouse could be, so there you are. See any flaws in that continuity?'

'Not a flaw.'

'Nor do I. Because there aren't any. It's money for jam. Tell me once again, for I like hearing the sound of the words, you'll really slip me –?'

'Two thousand quid?'

'Two thousand quid,' murmured Reggie, rolling the syllables round his tongue.

'Yes, you shall have it.'

'Don't say "it", old boy. Keep saying "two thousand quid". It's like wonderful music. Do you realize that if I arrive in Hollywood with two thousand quid in my pocket there is nothing that I will not be able to accomplish?'

'No?'

'Literally nothing. I shall expect to own the place within the year. Two thousand quid! You couldn't sing it, could you? I should like to hear it sung.'

# Chapter 18

With the possible exception of a certain brand of cigarette – one puff of which, one gathers from the advertisements, will make a week-old corpse spring from its bier and dance the Carioca – there is nothing that so braces a girl up as a reconciliation with the man she loves. As Gertrude Butterwick tripped to her state-room after dinner that night to fetch a forgotten handkerchief, she came as near to floating on air as was within the scope of one who, owing to years of developing her physique with hockey and other outdoor sports, weighed a hundred and thirty-three pounds in her step-ins. An afternoon of roseate dreams, topped off by a warm salt-water bath and a substantial meal, had put her in the pink. Her step was jaunty. Her eyes sparkled. She seemed full of yeast.

Markedly different was the demeanour of Albert Peasemarch, whom she found in the state-room tidying up for the night. The steward was breathing heavily, and there was on his face an anxious, careworn look, as if he had just glanced out of a port-hole and seen his mother searching for her spectacles on an iceberg.

His gloom was so pronounced that Gertrude felt compelled to inquire into it. His appearance quite shocked her. Hitherto, she had always known the steward, if not actually as a ray of sunshine, certainly as cheerful and respectfully vivacious. It was as if a new and strange Albert Peasemarch now stood before her, a Peasemarch into whose soul the iron had entered.

'Is anything the matter?' she asked.

Albert Peasemarch heaved a heavy sigh.

'Nothing that you can cure, miss,' he replied, picking up a shoe from the floor, breathing on it, and placing it in a cupboard.

'You seem to be in trouble.'

'I am in trouble, miss.'

'You're sure I can't do anything?'

'Nothing, miss. It's just Fate,' said Albert Peasemarch, and walked sombrely into the bathroom to fold towels.

Gertrude lingered uncertainly in the doorway. She had secured the handkerchief for which she had come, but she was feeling that to go away and leave this sufferer alone with his grief would be inhuman. It was obvious that pain and anguish were racking Albert Peasemarch's brow, and nobody who had studied the works of the poet Scott at school could fail to be aware that in such circumstances a woman's duty was clear. Always kind-hearted, Gertrude Butterwick was tonight more than ever in the mood to play the role of ministering angel.

As she stood hesitating the steward uttered a sudden loud moan. There was no mistaking the note of agony. Gertrude decided to remain and, though he had said that there was nothing that she could do, at least to offer first aid.

'What did you say?' she asked as he emerged.

'When, miss?'

'I thought I heard you say something.'

'In there in the bathroom?'

'Yes.'

'Merely that I was the Bandollero, miss,' said Albert Pease-march, still with that same inspissated gloom.

Gertrude was perplexed. The word seemed somehow vaguely familiar, but she could not identify it.

'The Bandollero?'

'Yes, miss.'

'What's a Bandollero?'

'There, miss, you have me. I've an idea it's a sort of Spanish brigand or bandit.'

Enlightenment flooded upon Gertrude.

'Oh, you mean the Bandolero? You were singing that song, "The Bandolero". I didn't recognize it. It's a favourite song of Mr Bodkin's. I know it well.'

Albert Peasemarch's face twisted with uncontrollable emotion.

'I wish I did,' he said mournfully. 'I keep forgetting the second verse.'

Gertrude's perplexity returned.

'But does that worry you?'

'Yes, miss.'

'I mean, why not just hum it?'

'Humming is no good, miss. It would not satisfy the public's demands. I've got to sing it.'

'In public, do you mean?'

'Yes, miss. Tonight, at the second-class concert. This very night, as near ten o'clock as may be, I shall be standing up on that platform in the second-class saloon, going through with it. And where am I going to get off if I can't even pronounce the word, let alone remember verse two? You say it's not Bandollero . . .'

'No, I know it's not Bandollero.'

'But how are we to know whether it's Bandol-*ero* or Bandol-*airo*?'

'Try it both ways.'

Albert Peasemarch heaved another of his heavy sighs.

'Have you ever considered the extraordinary workings of Fate, miss? Makes you think a bit, that does. Why am I in this position, faced with singing "The Bandoll" – or rather – "lero" or "lairo" at the second-class concert tonight? Purely and simply because a gentleman named J. G. Garges took it into his head to travel on this boat.'

'I don't understand.'

'It's intricket,' agreed Albert Peasemarch with a sort of moody satisfaction. 'And yet at the same time, if you follow me, it's not intricket at all, but quite simple. If Mr J. G. Garges wasn't on board, I wouldn't be in the position what I am. And when you consider all the various things – the chain of circumstances, as you might call it – that had to happen to get him on board at this particular time . . . well, it just makes you realize what helpless prawns we all are in the clutches of a remorseless –'

'Who is Mr Garges?'

'One of the second-class passengers, miss. Beyond that I know nothing, him being merely a name to me. But here he is, travelling in the second cabin of this boat, and I want you to look at how Fate has brought that about, miss. Take a simple

200

aspect of the matter. J. G. Garges must have had croup or measles or such-like during his infancy as a child. ... You concede that, miss?'

'Yes, I suppose so.'

'Good. Well, then. Suppose he had succumbed? Would he be on board this boat now? No. Well, would he, miss?'

'I don't see how he could, quite.'

'Exactly. Or make it even simpler. Suppose, as might quite well have happened, he'd of become during his lifetime a sufferer from asthma or bronchitis or some other complaint which touches you in the wind. How about it then? Would he be in a position to be singing the "Yeoman's Wedding Song" at the second-class concert tonight? No. You'll hardly dispute that, miss?'

'No.'

'Of course he wouldn't. And why? Because he'd never of been able so much as to contemplate undertaking that line where you have to stow away all the breath you've room for and just hang on, hoping for the best. Are you familiar with the "Yeoman's Wedding Song", miss? It goes like this.'

Fixing Gertrude with an eye that reminded her of a fish she had once seen in an aquarium, Albert Peasemarch drew in great quantities of air, inflated his chest and sang in an odd, rumbling voice, like thunder over the hills, these words:

> 'Ding dong, ding dong,
> Ding dong, I hurry along,
> For it is my wedding morning;
> And the bride so gay in bry-ut array
> For the day
> Is herself ador-OR-or-or-or-or-or-ning.'

He paused and seemed, as it were, to come to the surface. He gasped a little, like some strong swimmer in his agony.

'You see what I mean, miss?'

Gertrude saw. An asthmatic Garges could certainly never have managed that last line. To her inflamed fancy it had appeared to go on for about ten minutes.

'But I still don't understand,' she said. 'Why do you object to Mr Garges singing that song?'

Albert Peasemarch's brow darkened. It was plain that he was suffering from an intolerable sense of injustice.

'Because it's my song, miss. My special particular song, rendered by me at two out of every three ship's concerts ever since I took office on this boat. It's come to be a regular item in the programme – Solo: "The Yeoman's Wedding Song" – A. E. Peasemarch. My mother looks forward to my giving her the programme at the end of each trip. She pastes them in an album. Well, when I tell you that the purser himself once said to me – in a joking spirit, no doubt, and nothing derogatory really intended – "If you'd *do* more hurrying along, Peasemarch, and less singing about it," he said, "I'd be better pleased," he said, well, you can see how in a manner of speaking me and my "Yeoman's Wedding Song" have sort of grown into quite a legend.'

'I see.'

'So when Jimmy the One sent for me this morning and told me off to render a number at the second-class concert, the voluntary talent having proved to be short again, as usual, I said: "Yes, sir, very good, sir. The old 'Y.W.S.', of course, sir?" and he said he was afraid so, and everything was comfortable and settled. And then, round about ar-parse four it would have been, he sends for me again and you could have knocked me down with a feather, because he told me the "Yeoman's Wedding Song" was off, as far as me rendering it was concerned, on account of a passenger of the name of J. G. Garges having expressed a desire to sing it. And he hands me this blooming "Bandolero" and says, "Get that off your chest, cocky." And when I protested and said you couldn't ask an artist to change his act at the eleventh hour like that, he threatened to dock me a day's pay. So here I am, faced with this "Bandolero" and only about an hour to go. Can you wonder, miss, that I'm all of a twitter?'

Gertrude's gentle heart was touched. It ached for the man. Hers had been till now the easy, sheltered life of the normal English girl, and she had come but rarely into contact with tragedy.

'What a shame!'

'Thank you, miss. It's kind of you to sympathize. I can do

with a bit of sympathy, I don't mind telling you. When I start voicing my grievance in the Glory Hole, all they do is throw things at me.'

'But I wouldn't worry,' urged Gertrude. 'I'm sure you will be a tremendous success. "The Bandolero" is a splendid song. I always like hearing Mr Bodkin sing it. It has such a swing.'

'It has got a swing,' admitted Albert Peasemarch.

For a moment the cloud wrack lowering on his brow seemed about to lift. But only for a moment. Then his eyes, which had shown signs of brightening, glazed over again.

'But how about the words? Have you considered that, miss? Suppose I forget my words?'

'Then I should just go on singing: "I am the Bandolero, yes, yes, oh yes, I am, I am the Bandolero", or something like that. Nobody will notice anything wrong. They won't expect a Spanish song to make sense. They'll think it's atmosphere.'

Albeart Peasemarch started. It was plain that his companion had opened up a new line of thought.

'I am the band, I am the band,' he crooned tentatively.

'That's right. Mr Bodkin often does that. And *caramba*, of course.'

'Miss?'

'*Caramba.* It's a Spanish word. Another is *mañana*. If you find yourself drying up, I should go on repeating those. I remember Mr Bodkin singing "The Bandolero" at our village concert last Christmas, and the second verse was practically all *caramba* and *mañana*. He never went better in his life.'

Albert Peasemarch drew in a breath as deep as any that had ever assisted him through the "Yeoman's Wedding Song".

'Miss,' he said, his eyes doglike, 'you've put a new heart into me.'

'I'm so glad. I expect you'll be the hit of the evening.'

'I've a good quick ear for music and can generally get the hang of a chune, but it's the words I'm always shaky on. Coo! I remember the first six times I sang the "Y.W.S." I used to get it wrong regular. I used to sing: "And the *day* so gay in bright array", which spoiled the sense.'

He paused. He hesitated. His fingers twiddled.

'I wonder, miss ... Mark you, I think I'll be all right now, what with all these *carambas* and all, but I wonder, miss ... I wouldn't for the world take a lib., and no doubt you've a hundred things to do ... but I was wondering if by any chance –'

'You would like me to come and help with the applause?'

'That's the very words I was trying to say, miss.'

'Why, of course I will. When did you say you would be going on?'

'I'm billed for ten o'clock precisely, miss.'

'I'll be there.'

Words failed Albert Peasemarch. He could but gaze adoringly.

In a self-centred world it is never easy for those in travail to realize that other people have their troubles, too, and if anybody had informed Albert Peasemarch at this difficult moment in his career as a vocalist that his was not the severest attack of stage fright on board the R.M.S. *Atlantic*, he would have been amazed and incredulous. He might have said 'Coo!' or he might have said *'Caramba!'* but he would not have believed the statement. Yet such was undoubtedly the case.

The ordeal of waiting for ten o'clock, which we have seen afflicting the steward's nervous system so sorely, had not left Monty Bodkin unaffected. At twenty minutes to the hour, he, too, was all of a twitter. Seated at a table in the smoking-room, he gazed before him with unseeing eyes. From time to time he shuffled his feet, and from time to time he plucked at his tie. There was whisky and soda before him, but such was his preoccupation that he had scarcely touched it.

What was worrying Monty was the very same haunting fear which had racked Albert Peasemarch. He was afraid that he was going to blow up in his words.

When Reggie Tennyson had told him that all he had got to do was to hold Lottie Blossom in conversation for the space of a quarter of an hour on the second-class promenade deck while he, Reggie, thoroughly scoured her state-room, the task had seemed a simple one. He had accepted it without a tremor. Only now, when he contemplated the possibility of failure, did he wonder what words he could select so magical as to keep a girl of Lottie's impatient temperament hanging about on a draughty deck for a full fifteen minutes. It seemed to him in this dark hour of self-distrust an assignment at which the most silver-tongued orator might well boggle.

His case, of course, was far more delicate than that of Albert Peasemarch. The latter, thanks to Gertrude's kindly counsel, had the consolation of knowing that, if the worst occurred and he found himself unequal to the situation, he could always fill in with a few 'mañanas'. No such pleasant thought came to cheer Monty. Yes, to put it in a nutshell, he had no 'mañanas'. Not only had he got to make sense, he had got to be interesting. And not merely interesting – absorbing, gripping, spellbinding.

As he sat there, quailing at the prospect before him, a solid body suddenly lowered itself into the chair opposite, and he perceived that his solitude had been invaded by Mr Ivor Llewellyn.

'Join you?' said Mr Llewellyn.

'Oh, right ho,' said Monty, though far from cordially.

'Just want a little chat,' said Mr Llewellyn.

If there is one quality more than another which a man must have who wishes to become president of a large motion-picture corporation, it is tenacity, that sturdy bulldog spirit which refuses to admit defeat. This Ivor Llewellyn possessed in large measure.

Many men in his position, up against an obdurate Customs spy who had flatly declined an invitation to play ball, would have been completely discouraged. Their attitude would have been that of Albert Peasemarch caught in the toils of a remorseless Fate – bitter, resentful, but supine. They would have told themselves that it was futile to go on struggling.

And that is what for a whole afternoon and evening Ivor Llewellyn had told himself.

But dinner had wrought a wondrous change in his outlook. It had made him his old thrustful self again. He had had vermicelli soup, turbot and boiled potatoes, two whacks at the chicken hot-pot, a slice of boar's head, a specially ordered soufflé, Scotch woodcock, and about a pint of ice-cream, and had finished with coffee and brandy in the lounge. A man of spirit cannot fill himself up like this without something happening. With Mr Llewellyn what had happened was the dawning of hope. The thought came to him as he sat in the lounge, stuffed virtually to the brim, that the reason for Monty's refusal to join the Superba-Llewellyn might quite conceivably be that the ambassador sent to sound him had bungled his end of the negotiations.

The more he examined this theory, the more plausible did it seem. Apart from being the wrong Tennyson, Ambrose, he considered, lacked charm. He remembered now that, when despatched to place the Superba-Llewellyn offer before Monty, the fellow had been wearing an unpleasant, sullen, brooding look. He must, on starting to parley with Monty, have been too curt or too obscure or too something. It was the old, old story, felt Mr Llewellyn – no cooperation. What was needed was a personal appeal from himself. That would put everything right. He had now come to make it.

He could hardly have selected a worse moment. Already all of a twitter, Monty, resenting his intrusion, had become keenly exasperated. As he had told Ambrose, except for asking him how to spell things he scarcely knew Mr Llewellyn, and at a time like this he would have preferred to dispense with the society of his dearest friend. He wanted to be alone, to meditate without interruption on what the dickens he was going to say to Lottie Blossom that would keep her rooted to the spot for a quarter of an hour.

Chafing, he took out a cigarette and lit it.

'Beautiful!' said Mr Llewellyn.

'Eh?'

'Beautiful!' repeated Mr Llewellyn, nodding his head in a sort of ecstasy, as if someone had shown him the Mona Lisa. 'The way you lit that cigarette. Graceful... Easy... Deb-whatever-the-word-is. Like Leslie Howard.'

It was not Ivor Llewellyn's habit to flatter those whom he was hoping to employ, his customary mode of procedure being a series of earnest attempts to create in them an inferiority complex which would come in handy when the discussion of terms began. But this was a special case. Here, clearly, was one of those rare occasions when nothing would serve but the old oil, and that in the most liberal doses.

'I dare say,' he proceeded, continuing the policy of applying the salve, 'you're thinking that it isn't anything to make a song and dance about – simply lighting a cigarette. But let me tell you that it's just those little things that you can tell if a fellow's got real screen sense. You have. Yessir. There!' exclaimed Mr Llewellyn with a fresh burst of enthusiasm. 'The way you took that drink of whisky. Swell! Like Ronald Colman.'

Satisfied that he had made a good beginning and that the leaven must shortly start to work, he paused to allow these eulogies to sink in. He gazed admiringly across the table at his gifted young companion, and when, doing so, he encountered a glare which might have made another man wilt, was in no way disconcerted. He seemed to relish it. Even for that peevish glare he had a good word to say.

'Clark Gable makes his eyes act that way,' he said, 'but not so good.'

Monty was beginning to experience some of the emotions which one may suppose a bashful goldfish to feel. He seemed unable to perform the simplest action without exciting criticism. The fact that this criticism so far had been uniformly favourable made it no better. His nose had begun to tickle, but he refrained from scratching it as he would have done in happier circumstances, feeling that should he do so Mr Llewellyn would immediately compare his technique to that of Schnozzle Durante or such other artist as might suggest himself to his lively imagination.

A generous wrath began to surge within him. He had had enough, he told himself, of all this rot. First Ambrose, then Lotus Blossom, and now Ivor Llewellyn... It was absolute dashed persecution.

'Look here,' he said heatedly, 'if all this is leading up to your asking me to become a bally motion-picture actor, you might just as well cheese it instanter. I won't do it.'

Mr Llewellyn's heart sank a little, but he persevered. Even in the face of this obduracy he could not really bring himself to believe that there existed a man capable of spurning the chance to join the Superba-Llewellyn.

'Now listen,' he began.

'I won't listen,' cried Monty shrilly. 'I'm sick of the whole dashed business. From morning till night, dash it, I do nothing but comb people who want me to become a motion-picture actor out of my hair. I told Ambrose Tennyson I wouldn't do it. I told Lotus Blossom I wouldn't do it. And now, just when I want to devote my whole mind to thinking about – to thinking, up you come and I've got to stop thinking and tell you I won't do it. I'm fed up, I tell you.'

'Don't you want,' asked Mr Llewellyn, a quaver in his voice, 'to see your name up in lights?'

'No.'

'Don't you want a million girls writing in for your autograph?'

'No.'

Optimist though the chicken hot-pot had made him, Mr Llewellyn was unable to disguise it from himself that he was not gaining ground.

'Don't you want to meet Louella Parsons?'

'No.'

'Wouldn't you like to act opposite Jean Harlow?'

'No. I wouldn't like to act opposite Cleopatra.'

A sudden idea flashed upon Mr Llewellyn. He thought he saw where the trouble lay.

'I've got it now,' he exclaimed. 'Now I see the whole thing. It's the idea of acting you don't like. Well, come and do something else. How would you feel about being a production expert?'

'What's the sense of asking me to be a production expert? I wouldn't know enough.'

'It ain't possible not to know enough to be a production expert,' said Mr Llewellyn, and was about to drive home this profound truth by adding that his wife's brother George was one when Monty, who had just looked at his watch, uttered a sharp cry and leaped from his seat. So absorbing had been the other's conversation that he had not remarked the passage of time. The hands of the watch stood perilously near the hour of ten.

'I've got to rush,' he said. 'Good night.'

'Hey, wait.'

'I can't wait.'

'Well, listen,' said Mr Llewellyn, perceiving that no words of his could hold this wild thing. 'Just chew it over, will you?

Think about it when you've got a minute, and if you ever do feel like playing ball with me, let me know and we'll get together.'

Despite his agitation, Monty could not help being a little touched. Rather charming, he felt, that this tough man of affairs, who might have been expected after years of struggle with ruthless competitors to become hardened and blasé, should so have preserved the heart of a child as to yearn to play ball with people. He paused and regarded Mr Llewellyn with a kindlier eye.

'Oh, rather,' he said. 'I will.'

'That's good.'

'I wouldn't be a bit surprised if I didn't want to play ball one of these days.'

'Fine,' said Mr Llewellyn. 'Think over the production expert idea.'

'We'll take it up later, what? – when I've more time. For the moment,' said Monty, 'pip-pip. I must be pushing.'

He left the smoking-room and set a course for the other end of the vessel. And such was the speed with which he leaped from point to point that a mere minute sufficed to put him on the dimly-lit promenade deck of the second-class. Looking about him and finding it empty, he was well content. Lottie Blossom had not yet arrived at the tryst.

He lit a cigarette and began to muse again upon the coming interview. But once more his thoughts were diverted before he could really get the machinery going properly. Strains of music fell upon his ear.

There appeared to be a binge of some sort in progress hard by. A piano was tinkling, and a moment later there burst into song a voice in its essentials not unlike that of the ship's fog-horn. The painful affair continued for some little time. Then the voice ceased, and tumultuous applause broke out from an unseen audience.

But though the song was ended, the melody lingered on. This was due to the fact that Monty was humming it under his breath. For this was a song he knew, a song which he himself had frequently rendered, a song which evoked tender memories – none other, in fact, than 'The Bandolero'.

His bosom swelled with emotion. From the days of his freshman year at the university he had always been a Bandolero addict – one of the major problems confronting his little circle of friends being that of how to keep him from singing it – but recently the number had become inextricably associated in his mind with the thought of Gertrude Butterwick.

Twice, at village revels, he had sung it to her accompaniment, and these two occasions, together with the rehearsals which had preceded them, were green in his memory. Today, when he heard 'The Bandolero' or thought about 'The Bandolero' or sang a snatch of 'The Bandolero' in his bath, her sweet face seemed to float before him.

It seemed to be floating before him now. In fact, it was. She had just emerged from a doorway in front of him and was standing gazing at him in manifest surprise. And the recollection that in about another two ticks Lottie Blossom would come bounding out of the night, turning their little twosome into a party of three, filled him with so sick a horror that he staggered back as if the girl he loved had hit him over the head with a hockey-stick.

Gertrude was the first to recover. It is not customary for the haughty nobles of the first-class to invade the second-class premises of an ocean liner, and for a moment she had been quite as astonished to see Monty as he was to see her. But a solution had now occurred to her.

'Why, hullo, Monty, darling,' she said. 'Did you come to hear it, too?'

'Eh?'

'Albert Peasemarch's song.'

No drowning man, about to sink for the third time, ever clutched at a lifebelt more eagerly than did Monty at this life-saving suggestion.

'Yes,' he said. 'That's right. Albert Peasemarch's song.'

Gertrude laughed indulgently.

'Poor dear, he was so nervous. He asked me to come and applaud.'

All those old bitter anti-Peasemarch thoughts which had turned Monty Bodkin's blood to flame after the man's bone-headed behaviour in the matter of the Mickey Mouse came surging back to him now, as he heard Gertrude speak those words. So that was why she was here! Because Albert Peasemarch had asked her to come and applaud his loathsome singing!

The thing made Monty feel physically unwell. It was not only the sickening vanity of the fellow – come and applaud him, forsooth! – why couldn't he be content like a true artist to give of his best and care nothing for the world's applause or censure? – it was something deeper than that. We all have a grain of superstition in us, and it had begun to seem to Monty that there was something eerie and uncanny in the way this Peasemarch kept cropping up in his path. It was like one of those Family Curses. Where the What-d'you-call-'ems had their Headless Monk and the Thingummybobs their Spectral Hound, he had Albert Peasemarch.

In a blinding flash of mental illumination Monty saw Albert Peasemarch for the first time for what he really was – not a mere steward but the official Bodkin Hoodoo.

'You've just missed him,' said Gertrude. 'He finished a moment ago. He went quite well. In fact, very well. But nobody sings "The Bandolero" like you, Monty.'

It was a graceful compliment, and one which in happier circumstances Monty would have appreciated to the full. But such was his agony of mind at this moment that he scarcely heard it. He was gazing about him like Macbeth expecting the ghost of Banquo to appear. Ten o'clock to the tick, Reggie had said when outlining the arrangements for the Bodkin-Blossom conference, and it was already some minutes past ten o'clock to the tick. At any moment now, Lotus Blossom, red hair and all, might be expected to loom up through the darkness.

And then what?

'I say,' he asked feverishly, 'what do you make the time?'

'Why?'

'Oh, I don't know. I was just wondering if my watch was right.'

'What do you make it?'

'Five past ten.'

Gertrude consulted the dainty timepiece on her wrist.

'I think you're fast. I make it five to.'

A snort of relief escaped Monty.

'Let's buzz off,' he urged.

'Oh, why? It's such fun being here.'

'Fun?'

'It's like being on another ship.'

'I hate it.'

'Why?'

'It's – er – it's so dark.'

'I like it dark. Besides, I must see Peasemarch.'

'What on earth for?'

'To congratulate him. He did go quite well, and he was feeling terribly nervous, because they made him change his song at the last moment. I expect he's relieved it's all over. I think he would be hurt if I didn't tell him how good he was.'

'That's right,' he said. 'Of course. Quite. Yes. You're absolutely correct. Wait here. I'll go and fetch him.'

'There's no need to fetch him.'

'Yes, there is, definitely. I mean to say, he may be returning to the first-class by devious routes. You know, via passages and water-tight compartments and what not.'

'I never thought of that. All right. But don't fetch him. Tell him to go to my state-room and get me a wrap, and then come back here.'

'Right ho.'

'Or shall I come with you?'

'No,' said Monty. 'No. No. Don't you bother. In fact, no.'

It was some minutes before he returned. When he did so, his demeanour had undergone a marked change for the better. His brow was smooth and he no longer mopped it. He had the air of a man who has passed through the furnace and now prepares to relax in cooler surroundings.

'Jolly,' he said, 'it is out here. Like being on another ship.'

'That's what I said.'

'Yes. And you were absolutely right.'

'You don't mind it being dark?'

'I prefer it being dark.'

'Did you see Peasemarch?'

'Oh, yes. He was just finishing a beer which a few friends and admirers had stood him.'

'I suppose he was pleased his song was such a success?'

'Oh, most. I gather that he intends to add "The Bandolero" to his repertoire. Up till now, it appears, he has more or less concentrated on the "Yeoman's Wedding Song".'

'Yes. Did you ask him to bring me a wrap?'

'Yes. I gave him instructions to that effect, which will no doubt bear fruit anon.'

He did not add, for a man likes to have his little secrets, that he had also instructed Albert Peasemarch, before executing this commission, to proceed to the junction of the first and second-class decks and to hold that post, as Horatius did his bridge, against the invasion of Lottie Blossom. It was this strategic move that had caused the fever in his soul to abate. Everything, he felt, was all right now. The steward, as we have seen, was not in his opinion one of the world's great master-minds, but he could be relied on not to bungle a simple, straightforward job like that.

He drew in a deep breath of Western Ocean air, feeling like a general at the end of a successful campaign. He kissed Gertrude fondly, not once but many times.

It went well. There was no question of that. She plainly appreciated it. But she seemed unable to give herself up entirely to the ecstasy of the moment. There was in her manner a reserve, and in her voice when she spoke just that slight flatness which tells of a mind not wholly at ease.

'Monty,' she said.

'Hullo?'

There was a pause.

'Monty, you remember what we were talking about before lunch?'

'Eh?'

'About your not speaking to Miss Blossom.'

'Oh, ah, yes.'

'You haven't, have you?'

Monty's chest swelled. Had he had on a stiff-bosomed shirt and not one of the more modern soft *piqué*, that shirt would have crackled. No chest swells so elastically as that of the man with a clear conscience.

'Absolutely not.'

'I'm so glad.'

'I haven't so much as seen her.'

That slight flatness returned to Gertrude's voice.

'I see. You mean you would have spoken to her, if you had?'

'No, no. Not so, quite. I doubt if I would even have bowed.'

'Oh, you would have bowed.'

'No.'

'I wouldn't mind you bowing.'

'Well, perhaps I might have bowed – coldly.'

'No more.'

'Not an inch more.'

'I'm so glad. She's not a nice girl.'

'No.'

'I suppose it's living in Hollywood that makes her like that.'

'I shouldn't wonder.'

'Or having red hair.'

'That, too, possibly.'

'But you haven't spoken to her?'

'Not a syllable.'

'I'm so glad . . . Monty!'

'Gertrude!'

'No, don't. There's someone coming.'

A white-jacketed figure was approaching through the darkness. A certain heaviness of breathing and an occasional reference to 'The Bandolero' removed any doubts as to its identity.

'Peasemarch?' said Gertrude.

'Ah, there you are, miss,' said the steward gently; 'I've brought your wrap, miss.'

'Thank you so much.'

'Whether it's the right wrap or the wrong wrap, I couldn't say, but I found it hanging in your wardrobe. It is fleecy in its nature, and blue.'

'That's the one I wanted. How clever of you. Thank you ever so much. I'm so glad your song went so well, Peasemarch.'

'Thank you, miss. Yes, I fancy I knocked them. The applause was unstinted. It's a good number, miss. As you pointed out yourself, it has lots of swing. I intend to render it frequently in the future.'

'So Mr Bodkin was telling me.'

214

The steward peered in the uncertain light.

'Oh, is that Mr Bodkin standing beside you, miss? I was unable to identify him for the moment. I've a message for you, sir,' said Albert Peasemarch affably. 'I met Miss Blossom, as you instructed me, and headed her back, informing her that you would not be able to meet her here as per your existing arrangement, and she told me to tell you that it was quite all right and would you come to her state-room any time between eleven p.m. and midnight.'

# Chapter 19

Sidling along passages, tiptoeing down stairs, starting at the sight of stewards and wincing guiltily away from stewardesses and such of his fellow-passengers as he encountered *en route*, Reggie Tennyson, who had left the main lounge at ten precisely, arrived outside the door of Lottie Blossom's state-room at three and a half minutes past. His heart was beating rapidly and felt as if it had become dangerously enlarged. His spine had begun to crawl about under his dinner jacket like a snake. It was so long since he had breathed that he had almost forgotten how to. Like Monty Bodkin facing the task of keeping Miss Blossom engaged in conversation; like Albert Peasemarch cowering before the nameless perils of 'The Bandolero'; Reginald Tennyson, contemplating the ordeal before him, was suffering from a bad attack of stage fright.

It had been his intention, when setting out upon his journey, to make it in an easy and nonchalant manner, like a carefree young fellow enjoying an after-dinner saunter with no particular object in view. But with every step he took the portrayal had grown less convincing, until now, as he halted and looked furtively up and down the quiet corridor with the low, sinister creaking of the woodwork adding to his mental discomfort, he seemed to have changed his conception of the part completely. What he was giving at this moment was a perfect representation of one of those men who are always getting arrested by the police for loitering with intent. A policeman, had one been present, might have been uncertain as to whether Reggie was meditating murder, arson, robbery from the person with violence, or the purchase of chocolates after eight p.m., but he would have known it was something pretty bad.

For perhaps forty seconds the young man stood motionless except for his darting, swivelling eyes. Then, just as it had begun to seem that he might continue to do so indefinitely, a thought appeared suddenly to float into his mind, a thought that gave him energy and courage and brought back elasticity to the limbs. His face stiffened, his backbone followed its example, his shoulders ceased to sag, and his lips might have been seen to move silently. It was as though some inner voice had whispered in his ear the words 'Two thousand quid!' and he had been saying: 'I know, I know. I hadn't forgotten.' With a swift, nervous twitch of the wrist he turned the handle and went in.

Considering that the proprietress of this state-room had once been very dear to him; that he had, indeed, on one occasion actually gone to the length of asking her to be his wife; it might have been supposed that a certain sentimentality would have gripped Reggie Tennyson as he now gazed upon the intimacies of her sleeping-apartment, causing him to pick up a hair-brush and press it to his lips with a tender little sigh, or fondle for an instant an orange stick or an eyebrow tweezer.

This, however, was not the case. His emotions were identical with those of Desmond Carruthers, the hero of the book which he had taken out of the ship's library that morning, when entering the Hindu temple to steal the great sapphire which formed the eye of the idol therein. Desmond had confined his thoughts strictly to business, and so did Reggie. His whole attention was riveted upon the cabin-trunk which stood in the corner. And when, investigating it, he found that it was locked, he felt much as Desmond Carruthers had done on discovering that between himself and the idol some canny priest had placed a couple of large cobras. Just the same hollow feeling that comes to a man when he perceives that the laugh is on him.

For a space he stood baffled.

He was not baffled, however, for long. Reason told him that where there are cabin-trunks there must be keys, and intuition led him to the dressing-table. The keys were in the first drawer he examined, and he had snatched them up and was about to slink back to the trunk when his eye fell on a photograph which stood in a silver frame against the mirror – a full-face photograph of his brother Ambrose smoking a pipe.

Novelists of the virile school ought to be prohibited by law from having themselves photographed with pipes in their mouths. It is not fair on those of the public who suddenly catch sight of them. It makes them look so strong and stern that the observer cannot but sustain a nasty shock. Reggie did. There was something horrible to him in the forceful way Ambrose was chewing that pipe. The thought that this rugged man was at large about the ship and might quite possibly pop in and catch him here chilled Reggie Tennyson, and for an instant he was incapable of movement.

Then that inner voice whispered: 'Two thousand quid!' in his ear again, and he shook off the momentary weakness. He returned to the trunk, found the key that fitted the lock and, pulling its jaws apart, began to search it with feverish haste.

He might just as well have spared himself the trouble and nervous strain. The briefest exploration was sufficient to tell him that wherever the Mickey Mouse might be it was not in Lottie Blossom's cabin-trunk. The very nature of a Mickey Mouse makes it easy for a seeker after it to detect whether it is or is not present in any given spot. It is not like a Maharajah's ruby or a secret treaty, which might get shoved away under a camisole and escape the eye. A Mickey Mouse has bulk. If you open a drawer and do not find it immediately, it is not in that drawer. It is merely a waste of time to go on routing about among négligées and step-ins.

Nevertheless, for several anguished minutes Reggie continued so to rout about. A man with as much at stake as he had does not readily give in and admit defeat. That inner voice – whose conversation, if it had a fault, was perhaps a little on the monotonous side – kept whispering: 'Two thousand quid!' and the words were a spur that drove him on. If he had been one of those Customs inspectors who had been figuring so largely of late in Mr Ivor Llewellyn's nightmares, he could not have routed about more sedulously.

It seemed to him absolutely incredible that this trunk should not deliver the goods and supply the happy ending. In what other place in the whole bally room, he reasoned, could that Mickey Mouse possibly be?

He had already examined the drawers of the dressing-table.

It was not in one of them. He had searched the wardrobe. It was not there. He had felt behind the life-saving apparatus on top of the wardrobe. Not there, either. And a single glance about the apartment had been enough to assure him that the thing had not been left lying on a chair or thrown carelessly upon the bed. It positively must be somewhere in this ghastly trunk, he told himself, and with twitching fingers he groped among handkerchiefs, scarves, belts, woollen jumpers, silk jumpers, green jumpers, red jumpers, rummy things with ribbons on them, rummy things without ribbons on them and what his knowledge of the facts of life told him was knee-length underwear.

It was no good. He had to give it up. Reluctantly, with many a longing, lingering look behind, he closed the trunk, replaced the keys in their drawer, tried to avoid the eye of Ambrose's photograph, failed to do so, shuddered, and then, standing in the middle of the room, began to revolve slowly on his axis, his gaze fixed on the carpet as if in the hope that it might harbour trap-doors and secret oubliettes.

And suddenly, as he did so, there came into his face a new animation and ardour. He had seen something. There were no trap-doors or secret oubliettes, but there was, tucked away at the side of the bed so that it had up till now escaped his notice, a wickerwork basket – smallish, but not too small; just the sort of wickerwork basket, in fact, in which an ingenious girl with a brown plush Mickey Mouse to hide might quite well have hidden it.

'Yoicks!' cried the inner voice, for once varying its formula.

'Tally-ho!' replied Reggie Tennyson.

'Two thousand quid!' said the inner voice, returning to the old programme.

'Absolutely!' said Reggie.

Brimming over with sunny optimism, he bounded forward. He reached the wickerwork basket. He stooped over it. He lifted the lid and plunged his hand in.

The time was now precisely fifteen minutes past ten.

Lottie Blossom had taken coffee with Ambrose in the lounge at the conclusion of dinner and had sat there with him for an hour or more, endeavouring to lighten his gloom with guarded remarks – they had to be guarded – to the effect that all was not yet lost and that a way might still be found out of the unfortunate position in which they were placed. In this fashion she passed the time until a glance at her watch showed her that it was ten o'clock, the hour at which she had arranged to meet Monty on the second-class promenade deck and talk things over.

As she was quite determined not to part with the fateful mouse until he had fulfilled her already stated conditions, it seemed to her a mere waste of time to talk to Monty; but she had given her promise, so at one minute past ten she placed a hand to her forehead, registered distress with practised skill, and informed Ambrose that she had a headache and proposed now to withdraw to her state-room and go to bed.

This naturally gashed Ambrose like a knife, and the process of soothing his anxiety and allaying his fears and convincing him that the malady, though painful, was not dangerous occupied another five minutes. It was not till ten-seven that she was able to get away. When she did, she moved quickly, and reached the junction of the first- and second-class decks in one minute and thirty-six seconds. And there, as had already been indicated, she found Albert Peasemarch straddling, like Apollyon, right across the way.

Her interview with Albert was brief. It was not the steward's wish that it should be so, for he could have spoken – and, indeed, endeavoured to speak – at considerable length of his triumphs on the concert platform. But years of experience in the studios of Hollywood had made Lotus Blossom a past-mistress of the art of throttling down people who tried to tell her how good they were. By twelve minutes past ten Albert Peasemarch had delivered Monty's message and vanished into the night. Miss Blossom then turned and started to go down to her state-room.

She was annoyed, and not without reason. It irked her to have to immure herself in a state-room at this early hour, for she was a girl who liked the night life of cities and of ships, and always got brighter and brighter and happier and happier up till about four-thirty in the morning. But she had left herself no alternative. The very artistry with which she had played the role of a fragile invalid with shooting pains across the temples made it impossible for her to return to the lounge and its lights and music. Were she to do so, Ambrose would inevitably suppose that she was being brave and enduring silent tortures in order to entertain him and keep him from being lonely, and his chivalrous soul would revolt at the idea. He would fuss like a shepherd with a sick lamb and probably make her go to bed anyway, so that was out.

No, there was nothing for it but the state-room at what – she looked at her watch as she turned into the corridor and saw that it was just fourteen minutes past ten – was virtually the shank of the afternoon. Muttering an observation which she had once heard from the lips of a director as she walked off the set at the height of his activities, she approached the door. And as her fingers touched the handle she jerked them away as if it had been red-hot.

From inside the room there had suddenly rent the air a sharp, agonized scream.

She did not hesitate. Lottie Blossom may have had her faults – Gertrude Butterwick could have pointed out dozens – but lack of courage was not one of them. She had jumped about six inches on hearing that scream, it is true, but most girls in her position would have jumped twelve. Returning to terra firma, she acted swiftly. She was not armed, and the fact that somebody had just been murdered in her state-room argued that there must be a murderer in there as well as a corpse, but she pulled open the door without an instant's vacillation.

Her eyes rested on her old friend Reginald Tennyson. He was doing a sort of Astaire pom-pom dance round the room with the little finger of his right hand in his mouth.

A girl who has been led to suppose that there is a fiend in human shape in her sleeping-quarters and discovers instead a young man with whom she has frequently dined and supped and trodden the measure is apt to experience a certain difficulty in finding words with which to express her astonishment. Nor is this difficulty diminished if she notes that he is dancing about the floor sucking his finger. Lottie Blossom, accordingly, in the first moments of this unexpected meeting merely stood in the doorway with her mouth open.

Nor was Reggie more conversational. He had stopped gyrating on observing her, but he did not speak. Often, while making his way to this state-room tonight, he had speculated as to what he should say if by some mischance its owner happened to come in and catch him. Now that this had actually occurred, he said nothing. His finger was giving him considerable pain, and he went on sucking it in silence.

It was Lottie, after all, who was first to find words.

'Why, Reg-GEE!' she said.

Reginald Tennyson withdrew his finger from his mouth. He would have had every excuse for looking guilty and shamefaced, but he did not look guilty and shamefaced. His demeanour was that of a man who seethes with righteous indignation, a man who has been badly treated and legitimately resents it.

'What the devil,' he enquired emotionally, 'have you got in that basket?'

Lottie began to see daylight. Amusement took the place of surprise. She had a simple, wholesome mind, easily entertained by clean, simple comedy, and the reactions of those who opened her little wickerwork basket always diverted her.

'That,' she said, 'is Wilfred, my alligator.'

'Your *what*?'

'Alligator. Don't you know what an alligator is? Oh, well, you will another time '

The clearing up of the mystery did nothing to soothe Reggie.

'Alligator? What on earth is the idea of having the place alive with alligators? What's the bally thing doing in a civilized state-room?'

Lottie Blossom was anxious to get on to the main enquiry or probe, but she perceived that it would be impossible to rivet her guest's attention until this point had been explained to his satisfaction.

'It's just a Press stunt. My Press agent thought it would help the general composition. He wavered at one time between it and a mongoose, and then he wavered between it and my being at heart a simple little home body who was never so happy as when among her books, but in the end he cast his vote on the

222

alligator ticket, and I'm glad he did, because an alligator is certainly value for money. Yessir, believe it or not. It's publicity
of the right sort, and nobody who has not had personal experience of travelling around with an alligator in a little wickerwork basket, can have any conception of the amount of quiet
fun there is to be got out of it. What happened? Did Wilfred
snap at you?'

'He merely nearly took my bally arm off.'

'You shouldn't have teased him.'

'I did not tease him.'

'Then I guess he mistook you for a fly.'

'The animal must be non compos. Do I look like a fly?'

Lottie Blossom had been smiling in the pleased, jolly way in
which she always smiled when conversing with those who had
recently lifted the lid of Wilfred's wickerwork basket. The smile
now faded from her lips, leaving them tight and compressed.

'Shall I tell you what you look like?'

'What?'

'You look,' said Miss Blossom quietly, but none the less
formidably, 'like a man who's going to tell me what he's doing
in my state-room.'

From the very beginning of this interview, Reggie had been
uneasily aware that sooner or later he would be called upon to
throw light on that very point. Now that the moment had
arrived, his uneasiness was not lessened. He was conscious of
being in a distinctly equivocal position and, like most men
who are conscious of being in distinctly equivocal positions, he
fell back on bluster.

'Never mind that! We're not talking about that. We're talking about this damned man-eating crocodile of yours. Look
what it's done to my finger. If that's not a nasty sore place, I've
never seen one. Crocodiles, forsooth!' said Reggie with bitterness, for it was a subject on which he felt strongly.

Lottie Blossom corrected him.

'We *are* talking about that. We're talking about that right
now. What are you doing in my state-room, you blot on the
escutcheon? You'd best come clean, young by golly Reggie
Tennyson, or we'll have to see what we're going to do about it.'

Reggie coughed. Still sucking the little finger of his right hand, he passed the forefinger of his left round the inside of his collar. He coughed once more.

'Well?'

Reggie made up his mind. If he had thought bluster would be any good, he would have gone on trying it, but a single glance at his hostess was enough to convince him that it would be no good at all. There was about Lottie Blossom now none of that geniality which had made her in happier days so agreeable a companion at the dinner-table. Her air was that of a girl stonily resolved to get down to brass tacks and have no more evading of issues. He noted the glitter in her eyes, the prominence of her out-thrust chin, the ominous pressing together of her strong front teeth. By an odd sort of optical illusion, due no doubt to the craven panic induced by these phenomena, it seemed to him that her hair had suddenly grown redder.

He decided on absolute frankness.

'Listen, Lottie.'

'Well?'

'I'll tell you everything.'

'You better had.'

'I came here to look for that mouse of Monty's.'

'Ah!'

'The one you pinched from him, you know. He wanted me to get it back.'

Lottie Blossom was smiling again now, but it was a grim smile, not one that in any way softened the menace of her aspect. The revelation had occasioned her no surprise. Her mind was capable of drawing conclusions from evidence submitted to it, and she had long since begun to suspect the hidden hand of Monty Bodkin.

'Ah,' she said. 'And did you find it?'

'No.'

'No luck, eh?'

'No.'

'I see. Well, you've found it now.'

From beneath the wrap which she carried over her arm she drew the Mickey Mouse.

'Good gosh!'

'Well, you didn't think I'd be such a chump as to leave it

lying about in my state-room, with young thugs like you prowling around, did you?'

Reggie was gaping at the mouse with undisguised emotion.
Indeed his eyes were rolling in his head.

'Lottie!' he cried. 'Give me that mouse!'

Lottie Blossom stared at him amazedly. Long and intimate
acquaintance with Reginald Tennyson had left her in no doubt
that he was a young man abundantly possessed of crust, but
she had never supposed that he had as much crust as this.

'Do what? *Give* it to you?'

'Yes.'

'Black out on that laugh,' advised Lottie. 'You'll never be
able to top it. Give you this mouse! Yes, that's good. What do
you think I am?'

Reggie swung his arm in a wide, passionate gesture.

'A pal!' he cried. 'Lottie, old bird, you don't know what it
means to me if I get it.'

'Reggie, old caterpillar, you don't know what it means to me
if I keep it.'

'But Lottie, have a heart! I'll tell you the whole thing. I'm in
love.'

'I've never known you when you weren't.'

'But this time it's the real thing, the real registered A1 at
Lloyd's stuff.'

'Who is she?'

'Mabel Spence.'

'A good sort,' said Lottie cordially. 'I've always liked Mabel.
Have you fixed it up?'

'No. And why?'

'Because she's got too much sense.'

Reggie sawed the air wildly.

'She hasn't got too much sense. At least, I hope she hasn't.
But I can't move an inch in the matter unless I get that mouse.
I haven't a bean in the world. My only chance of getting a
good square pop at Mabel is to secure that mouse and hand it
over to Monty. If I do, he says he'll slip me two thousand
quid...'

'What!'

'Yes. And if I had that I should be able to go to Hollywood

225

and pursue Mabel with my addresses. Whereas without it I shall have to tool off to Montreal to that foul office job and stay mouldering there for the rest of my life.'

The fire had faded from Lottie Blossom's eyes. Her lips had lost their tautness. They unmistakably quivered. If the Hoboken Murphys had hair-trigger tempers, they also possessed hair-trigger hearts.

'Oh, Reggie!'

'You see what I'm driving at now?'

'Sure.'

'Then how about it?'

Lottie Blossom shook her flaming head remorsefully.

'I can't.'

'Lottie!'

'It's no good saying "Lottie!" I can't do it. If Bodkin has been wising you up on this mouse sequence, you know how things are with me. I want to get Ambrose his job, and that mouse is the only shot in my locker. And it's no good looking at me like that, either. I've as much right to want to marry Ambrose as you have to want to marry Mabel, haven't I? And he won't marry me unless he gets a job. So I've got to hold Bodkin up.'

'I suppose you know it's practically blackmail?'

'It *is* blackmail,' she assured him. 'And if it's any comfort to you and him to know it, I hate and despise myself for doing it. But I'd a darned sight rather hate and despise myself than lose my Ammie. Oh, Reggie, you know there's almost nothing in this world I wouldn't do for you, my pet. I've always felt towards you like a mother with an idiot child. But you're asking just the one thing I can't do. I can't give you this mouse – I can't, I can't. You must see that?'

Reggie nodded. He knew when he was licked.

'Oh, all right.'

'Don't look like that, Reggie darling. I can't bear it. Oh, why can't you persuade this fool of a Bodkin to sign up with Ikey Llewellyn? If only he would, everything would be jake. He could get Ikey to take Ambrose back as soon as look at you.'

'Not a chance, I'm afraid. Monty swears nothing will induce him to become an actor. He told me it's a regular obthingummy with him.'

'He makes me tired.'

'Me, too. Still, there it is. Well,' said Reggie, 'I think I'll be pushing along. Thanks for a pleasant evening.'

Thoughtfully sucking his finger and directing as he went a cold look at the wickerwork basket, he moved to the door. The door closed. Lottie let him go. There was nothing that she could do or say.

She sat down on the bed. Normally, had she found herself alone in her state-room, she would have lifted the lid of the wickerwork basket and chirruped to its occupant just to show him that he was among friends and had not been forgotten, but with her emotions lacerated by the recent harrowing scene she was in no mood for chirruping to alligators. She sat staring before her, and it is probable that she would have given way to the tears which, when her emotions were lacerated, were never far from the surface, had not her meditations been interrupted by a knock on the door.

She rose. Her eyes, which had begun to swim, dried and became hard. She had an idea that this might be Albert Peasemarch, come ostensibly to brush bits of fluff off the carpet and set the place to rights, but in reality to enjoy one of those long, cosy talks to which he was so addicted. And she was just in the vein to bite the fat head off any steward who came babbling to her now.

'Come in,' she called.

The door opened. It was not Albert Peasemarch who stood on the threshold, but Ambrose Tennyson.

There was a bottle in Ambrose Tennyson's hand and another sticking out of his pocket, for a man in love who has seen the adored object totter from his presence with a hand to her forehead and her lips drawn together in almost unendurable pain does not just go on sitting in an armchair smoking his cigar – he hastens to the ship's doctor in quest of headache remedies. Ambrose Tennyson had done so the moment Lottie had parted from him in the lounge. While she had taken the high road and gone off to the second-class promenade deck, he had taken the low road that led to the dispensary somewhere down in the bowels of the ship.

There had been a certain delay after that, for the doctor had had to be fetched. During the day ships' doctors play quoits with the prettiest girl on board. After dinner, they gather up the prettiest girl on board – or, if she is not available, the second prettiest – and settle down to a little backgammon. Eventually, however, he had appeared, and Ambrose had secured two highly recommended mixtures. He had now come to deliver them.

'Well,' he said, 'how are you feeling?'

The unexpected sight of the man she loved had had an odd effect on Lottie Blossom. Seeing him instead of the Albert Peasemarch for whose entry she had been bracing herself, she had come, as it were, temporarily unstuck. A sudden yearning tenderness had flooded over her, bringing a lump to her throat and into her eyes those tears which had so nearly been there before. She broke down completely.

'Oomph,' she sobbed. 'Oomph.'

It has been pointed out earlier in this narrative that to a man in whose presence a girl is going oomph there is but one course open – namely to administer gentle pats to the subject's head or shoulder. But this naturally applies only to comparative strangers of the male sex. If the onlooker is a man who loves this oomphing girl and is loved by her, something of a far more emphatic nature is called for. It is for him to embrace, to fondle, to kiss the tears away, to drop on his knees at her side and murmur broken words.

Ambrose Tennyson did none of these things. He stood there motionless, a bottle in his hand and another sticking out of his pocket. On his face there was a cold, set look.

'I have brought you some stuff,' he said in a dull voice. 'For your headache.'

Although she had by no means had her cry out, Lottie Blossom sat up and dried her eyes. She was astonished. That Ambrose could have watched her weep without so much as stepping forward and taking her hand in his was so amazing that her tears stopped as if a tap had been turned.

'Ammie!' she exclaimed.

Ambrose's manner continued aloof and polished.

'I would have come earlier,' he said, 'but the doctor kept me waiting.'

He paused. His face was expressionless.

'And when I did get here,' he said, 'I heard you talking to some man and assumed that you would not wish to be interrupted.'

He placed the bottles on the dressing-table and turned to the door. He found Lottie standing between him and it. There was nothing tearful about her now. She was brisk and decisive.

'Half a minute, Ambrose. Just one minute, if you please.'

Ambrose's cold veneer seemed to crack. His face worked. He looked very unlike that photograph in the silver frame. If he had had a pipe in his mouth now, it would have dropped out.

'You told me you had a headache!'

'I know –'

'And you left me and you slipped off here –'

'Listen, Ammie,' said Lottie. 'If you'll give me half a chance, I'm going to explain that. For the love of Peter let's not have another battle. Heaven knows a good turn-up is meat and drink to me, as a rule. But not now. Sit down and I'll put you straight about this business.'

# Chapter 20

It was not immediately after he had withdrawn from Lottie
Blossom's presence that Reggie Tennyson sought out his principal and employer to make his report of what had occurred.
In the first numbing shock of a great disappointment, when all
the castles he has been building in the air have come tumbling
about his ears and his soul seems to have been tied in knots
and passed through a wringer, a man's instinct is for solitude.
Reggie wanted to be alone to lick his wounds – and not merely
figuratively, at that. Owing to that slowness in the uptake which
rendered Wilfred the alligator unable to distinguish between
an Old Etonian and a fly, the skin on his little finger still needed
attention.

He first sought refuge in the drawing-room. But he did not
stay there long. It was empty, which was to the good, but it was
also stuffy. It had that queer, elusive aroma peculiar to draw-
ing-rooms on ocean liners, as if it were just on the point of
smelling most unpleasant, but never quite beginning. Finding
that this was merely increasing his depression, Reggie went out
and took to the open deck.

It was the right move. The soft night air refreshed and
strengthened him. He still would have preferred to brood apart,
but he now found himself able to contemplate without actual
physical nausea the thought of sitting talking to Monty, and
some twenty minutes after he had left Lottie's state-room he
went down to the B deck to do so.

He had just reached Monty's door, when it opened with a
sharp abruptness as if somebody with an overflowing soul had
jerked at the handle, and his brother Ambrose came out. Ambrose's face was drawn and his eyes haggard. He looked dazedly at Reggie for an instant, then passed on without speaking.
And Reggie, having stared after him till he was out of sight,

230

went on into the state-room. And the first thing he beheld as he crossed the threshold sent him rocking back on his heels as if alligators had snapped at him.

Monty Bodkin was seated on the bed. In his hand was the Mickey Mouse. He was absently screwing its head on and off.

'Oh, hullo, Reggie,' he said dully. He screwed off the head of the Mickey Mouse, screwed it on again, and began to screw it off once more.

Reggie Tennyson was in the grip of that feeling that some-times comes to one in dreams, the feeling that things are not making sense. Before him sat Monty Bodkin, and there, in Monty's possession, if a fellow could trust his eyesight, was the Mickey Mouse in person, the mouse of fate, the identical mouse there had been all this fuss about. Yet Monty was looking like a lump of putty, his manner listless, his *tout ensemble* devoid of sparkle. There was only one word that described the position of affairs adequately – the word 'inexplicable'.

'What ... what ...?' he ejaculated feebly, pointing a shaking finger.

Monty continued to look like a lump of putty.

'Oh, yes,' he said, 'I've got it back. Ambrose just brought it.'

Reggie collapsed into a chair. He held firmly to the side of it. This seemed somehow to help a little.

'Ambrose?'

'Yes.'

'You say *Ambrose* restored this mouse?'

'Yes. Apparently the Blossom told him that she had got it and was holding me up with it, and Ambrose put the presi-dential veto on the scheme. He would have none of it. He told her it wasn't playing the game to hold chaps up with Mickey Mice, and he made her give it to him, and then he brought it to me.'

Reggie's grip on the chair tightened. Reason had been tot-tering on its throne already, and this amazing piece of informa-tion nearly unseated it.

'You don't seriously mean that?'

'Yes.'

'He told her it wasn't playing the game?'

'Yes.'

'And by the sheer force of his personality made her yield up the mouse?'

Reggie drew a deep breath. He was feeling about his brother Ambrose as he had never felt before. In a tolerant sort of way he had always liked the chap, but he had never admired him particularly. Certainly he had never even begun to regard him as a bally superman. Yet, if he had really, as stated, succeeded in altering the trend of Lottie Blossom's mind when it had congealed into a determination to do dirty work at the cross-roads, it was in the superman class that he must beyond a question be placed. No argument about that, whatever. He stepped straight into it, like Napoleon and Sir Stafford Cripps and the rest of the boys.

'Coo!' said Reggie, like a thunderstruck Albert Peasemarch.

'It was pretty decent of old Ambrose,' said Monty with the first sign of feeling that he had shown. 'You can't say it wasn't a square sort of thing to do. Lots of chaps would have just sat back and let the thing go on and sucked profit from it. But not old Ambrose.'

'Sound bloke,' agreed Reggie.

'He would have none of it. He made her disgorge. I thought it was pretty decent of him, and I told him so.'

There was a pause. Monty screwed on the head of the Mickey Mouse, screwed it off once more, and began to screw it on again.

'But, dash it . . .' said Reggie.

'Well?'

'What about you?'

'Me?'

'Yes. Why aren't you as bucked as dammit? What are you sitting there looking like that for, if you've got the thing back? Why no ringing cheers? Why no spring dances?'

Monty laughed a short, bitter, barking laugh.

'Oh, me? I've nothing to cheer about. Getting this mouse back doesn't make any difference to me. Everything's off.'

'Off?' The word shot from Reggie Tennyson's lips in a sharp gasp, as if he had received a blow in some tender spot. 'Everything's off?' His eyes dilated. If the expression meant what he

232

supposed it to mean, it was the end of all things. Bim went his two thousand quid, and as for his dreams of becoming a well-known and popular member of Hollywood's young married set, he might as well abandon them right away. 'Everything's off?' he quavered pallidly, clutching for support at his chair. 'Not you and Gertrude?'

'Yes.'

'But why?'

Monty screwed off the head of the Mickey Mouse, screwed it on again, and began to screw it off once more.

'I'll tell you,' he said. 'When you fixed up that bally clever scheme of yours for my meeting the Blossom on the second-class promenade deck, you omitted to take into your calculations the fact that there was a second-class concert on tonight. You didn't know that Albert Peasemarch was singing at that concert and that he was going to ask Gertrude to come along and ginger up the applause . . .'

'My gosh! And Gertrude turned up?'

'She did.'

'And found you with Lottie?'

'No. I got hold of Albert Peasemarch and told him to go and head Lottie off. So he went and did it, and shortly afterwards came gambolling up to me, as I stood talking to Gertrude, and saluted in a sailorly manner and said that it was all right – that he had seen Miss Blossom and told her that I couldn't get together with her then and that she had said that she quite understood and would I come to her state-room round about eleven.'

'What!'

'Yes.'

'My sainted aunt!'

'Yes.'

'What a dashed infernal idiot!'

'A trifle shortish on *savoir faire*, yes,' agreed Monty. 'The effect of these few words on Gertrude was a bit noticeable. You occasionally read in the paper about gas explosions in London streets which slay four. The whole thing was rather along those lines. I won't tell you exactly what she said, because I would prefer, if you don't mind, not to dwell upon it.

But you can take it from me that everything is off – finally, definitely, and absolutely.'

Silence fell upon the state-room. Reggie sat clinging to the side of his chair. Monty screwed on the head of the Mickey Mouse, screwed it off again, and began to screw it on once more.

'I'm sorry,' said Reggie at length.

'Thanks,' said Monty. 'Yes, it is a bit of a nuisance.'

'Quite. Well, I think,' said Reggie rising, 'I'll go and stroll for a while on the boat deck.'

He had been gone some few minutes when there was a knock on the door. Mabel Spence entered.

'Hope I didn't disturb you,' said Mabel. 'I'm looking for Reggie Tennyson.'

'Just left,' said Monty. 'Boat deck.'

'Right,' said Mabel.


It was pleasant on the boat deck, or would have been to any man whose life was not wrecked and whose hopes were not lying in ruins. A soft breeze was blowing and quiet stars shone down from a cloudless sky. Reggie hardly felt the breeze, scarcely saw the stars. He clutched the rail as a short while before he had clutched his chair. Solid wood to grasp at is what a man needs at these moments.

It was thus that Mabel Spence found him. The sound of her footsteps made him turn. He released the rail and stood staring at her.

It is never easy to see clearly on boat decks at night, but love sharpens the eyesight and despite the velvet blackness that enshrouded her Reggie was able to detect that Mabel Spence was looking like a million dollars. A hardy girl, who believed in fresh air and its health-giving effect on the skin, she wore no wrap. Her neck and arms gleamed whitely under the stars. And the realization that all this loveliness would shortly be popping off to Southern California while he stayed languishing in Montreal came home to Reggie with such poignant bitterness that the deck seemed to quake under his feet like a morass and he could not check a hollow groan.

Mabel appeared concerned.

'Something the matter?'

'Nothing, nothing.'

'You can't be feeling seasick on a night like this.'

'I'm not feeling seasick. It's just –'

'What?'

'Oh, I don't know.'

'Love?'

Reggie clutched the rail again.

'Eh?'

Mabel Spence was a girl who had no use for circumlocution. She never beat about the bush. When there was a matter of urgency on the agenda paper, she lost no time in getting down to it in that quietly efficient way which, though it had never appealed to her brother-in-law Ivor Llewellyn, was considered by most of those who knew her to be one of her attractions.

'I've just been talking to Lottie Blossom. She said you had told her you were in love with me.'

Reggie tried to speak, but found that his vocal cords were not working.

'And I came hunting after you to find out if it was official. Is it?'

'Eh?'

'Is it true?'

The foolishness of the question annoyed Reggie so much that he found his power of speech miraculously restored. Too damn silly, he felt, her asking a thing like that when for days he had been going out of his way to make it so abundantly clear what his feelings were towards her. An intelligent girl like herself, he meant to say, was surely aware that a fellow does not look at her as he had been looking, squeeze her hand as he had been squeezing it and kiss her on dark decks as he had been kissing her on dark decks, unless he means something by it.

'Of course it's true. You know that.'

'Do I?'

'Well, you ought to. Haven't I been goggling at you for days?'

'Yes, you have goggled.'

'And squeezed your hand?'

'Yes, and squeezed my hand.'

'And kissed you?'

'Yes, you've done that, too.'

'Well, then.'

'But I know what you city slickers are like. You think nothing of trifling with the affections of the poor working girl.'

Reggie bumped back against the rail, aghast.

'What!'

'You heard.'

'You don't imagine –?'

'Well?'

'You don't imagine that I'm one of those butterflies, do you, that my cousin Gertrude talks about?'

'Does your cousin Gertrude talk about butterflies?'

'Yes. And she's right off them. They flit and sip. But I'm not like that. I love you like the dickens.'

'Well, that's fine.'

'I've loved you ever since you nearly twisted my neck off that first day.'

'Great.'

'I started in worshipping you at that precise moment.'

'Swell.'

'And day by day in every way it's been getting worse and worse ever since.'

'Don't you mean better and better?'

'No, I don't mean better and better. I mean worse and worse. And why? Because it's all hopeless. Hopeless,' repeated Reggie, thumping the rail. 'Abso-bally-hopeless.'

Mabel Spence laid a gentle hand upon his arm.

'Hopeless?' she said. 'Why? If what's worrying you is that you think I don't love you, dismiss the foolish notion. I'm crazy about you.'

'You are?'

'Dippy.'

'Would you marry me if I asked you?'

'I'm going to marry you even if you don't ask me,' said Mabel.

She spoke with a happy gaiety which to many people – Reggie's uncle John, for one; Mr Ivor Llewellyn, for another

236

– would have seemed quite unintelligible. The world, indeed, was full of those who could not have imagined anyone talking in that cheery, light-hearted way about marrying Reginald Tennyson.

The effect of her words on Reggie was to make him plunge like a horse, as if he were about to dash his head against the rail. He was profoundly moved.

'But you aren't, dash it. That's the whole point. Can't you understand? I haven't a bean in the world. I can't go about the place marrying people.'

'But –'

'I know. You've enough for two, what?'

'Plenty.'

'And it wouldn't be any different from marrying an heiress, and all that. I know, I know. But it can't be done.'

'Reggie!'

'It can't be done.'

'Reggie, darling!'

'No, don't tempt me. It can't be done, I tell you. I won't live on your money. I never thought that high-mindedness of Ambrose's was catching, but so it has proved. I've gone down with it now.'

'What do you mean?'

'I'm telling you. Watching Ambrose prancing about the ship exuding honour at every pore has made me a changed man. If you had come to me as short a while ago as yesterday and asked me, "Do the Tennysons play the game?" my reply would have been, "Some do and some don't," but now I am compelled to answer, "Yes, blast it, every single bally one of them." I love you, young Mabel, I love you like nobody's business, but I'm positively dashed if I'm going to go through life helping myself out of your little earnings. And that's that, if I die of a broken heart.'

Mabel sighed.

'That's that, is it?'

'Definitely that.'

'You couldn't be just a little less noble?'

'Not a fraction.'

'I see. Well, I respect you, of course.'

'And a fat lot of good that is! I don't want to be respected. I want to be married. I want to sit opposite you at breakfast, pushing my cup up for more coffee –'

'– While I tell you the cute thing little Reggie said to his nurse.'

'Exactly. Now that you have brought the point up, I don't mind admitting that there was some sketchy notion of some such contingency floating at the back of my mind.'

'But you still feel you've got to be noble?'

'I'm sorry, old girl, I must. It's like getting religion.'

'I see.'

There was a silence. Reggie drew Mabel Spence to him and placed an arm about her waist. He nearly cracked a rib, but brought no comfort either to himself or her.

'The thing that makes me froth so frightfully at the mouth,' he said moodily, breaking the long pause, 'is that everything so nearly came right this morning. Those English sequences of old Pop Llewellyn's, you remember. If he had given me a contract to look after those, I should now be in a position to marry at the drop of the handkerchief. And he was within an ace of doing so when that Ambrose business sent him shooting off the deep end.'

'Would you say within an ace?'

'Well, perhaps not quite within an ace, but I think we could have talked him into it. Doesn't it make you sick to think that there is that ghastly brother-in-law of yours, that Llewellyn, perfectly able, if he cared to, to solve all our troubles, and we can't get him into the frame of mind. Or can we? Would it be any good working on him, do you think?'

'Working on him?'

'You know. Clustering round him. Doing him little acts of kindness. Trying to fascinate the old son of a bachelor.'

'Not the least.'

'I suppose not. Though how about putting him under some obligation? Saving his life, I mean, or something like that ... Rescuing him from a runaway horse –'

'Reggie!'

Mabel Spence's voice rang out sharply. So did Reggie's. In her excitement, she had clutched at his arm, and those dainty

238

fingers, trained to steely strength by years of osteopathy, seemed to bite into his flesh like pincers.

'I'm sorry,' said Mabel, relaxing her grip, 'I'm sorry. But that sudden flash of intelligence of yours startled me. Reggie, do you know what you've said? A mouthful, no less. That's exactly what we are going to do.'

'Rescue Llewellyn from a runaway horse?' In spite of a naturally optimistic disposition and an inherent willingness to try anything once, Reggie seemed dubious. 'Not so dashed easy on board an ocean liner, what?'

'No, no, I mean there is something you can do for Ikey that will make him give you anything you care to ask for. Let's find him and put it up to him right away. He'll probably be in his state-room.'

'Yes, but what –?'

'I'll explain as we go.'

'Short of murder, of course?'

'Oh, come along.'

'Yes, but –'

Mabel extended a clutching hand.

'Do you want me to pinch your arm again?'

'No.'

'Then get a move on.'

Mr Llewellyn was not in his state-room, its only occupant at the moment of their arrival being Albert Peasemarch. Albert Peasemarch seemed delighted to see them, and at once made it plain that he would be glad to tell them all about his recent triumphs. But Mabel's way with people who tried to tell her of their triumphs was as short as Lottie Blossom's. Scarcely had the steward begun to touch upon second-class concerts and Bandoleros, when he found himself thrown for a loss. A brief 'Yes, yes' and a courteous word to the effect that at some later date he must be sure to tell her all about it, for she was dying to hear, and Mabel had sent him off in quest of her brother-in-law. And presently Mr Llewellyn appeared, looking agitated. All nervous conspirators look agitated when they have just been informed that a fellow-conspirator wishes to see them immediately upon urgent business.

As he observed Reggie, his agitation became tinged with other emotions. He halted in the doorway, staring offensively.

Mabel ignored the stare.

'Come on in, Ikey,' she said, in that admirably brisk way of hers. 'Don't stand there looking like a statue of the Motion Picture Industry Enlightening the World. Take a look up and down the passage and make sure that that steward isn't listening, then step along in and shut the door.'

Mr Llewellyn did as he was directed, but with an ill grace. His air was still that of a man who would shortly require Reggie to be fully explained to him.

'Now, listen, Ikey. I've just been telling Reggie about that necklace of Grayce's that you're going to smuggle through the Customs.'

A banshee-like howl broke from the motion-picture magnate's lips, causing Reggie to wince and frown disapprovingly.

'Don't sing, Llewellyn. Not now. If you must, later.'

'You – you've told him?'

Reggie shot his cuffs.

'Yes, Llewellyn, she has told me. I know all, my dear Llewellyn. I am abreast of the whole position of affairs – the necklace, your spiritual agony at the prospect of having to smuggle same and, in short, everything. And in return for certain concessions on your part I have agreed to take the entire assignment off your hands.'

'What!'

'I say in return for certain concessions on your part I am willing to take the entire assignment off your hands. *I* will smuggle that necklace. So perk up, Llewellyn. Clap your hands and jump round in circles and let us see that jolly smile of yours of which everyone speaks so highly.'

There was nothing in the look which Mr Llewellyn was directing at Reggie now to awaken the critical spirit in the latter. It was entirely free from that pop-eyed dislike which the young man had found so offensive in the early stages of this conference. It was, indeed, very much the sort of look the wounded soldier must have directed at Sir Philip Sidney.

'You don't mean that?'

'I do mean that, Llewellyn. In return for certain –'

'What we were talking about this morning, Ikey,' said Mabel. 'Reggie wants a contract to superintend your English sequences.'

'For three years.'

'Five years. At a salary of –'

'Seven hundred and fifty –'

'A thousand.'

'Of course, yes. How right you are. Much nicer sum.'

'Rounder.'

'Exactly. Easier to remember. Pencil in as the salary, therefore, Llewellyn, a weekly one thousand dollars.'

'And none of your options.'

'What,' asked Reggie, 'are options?'

'Never mind,' said Mabel. 'There aren't going to be any in your contract. I know Ikey's options.'

In spite of the gratitude and relief surging so freely within him, Mr Llewellyn could not but offer a feeble resistance to this unholy condition. Whatever soul a motion-picture magnate possesses always revolts against the heretical suggestion of a contract without options.

'No options?' he said wistfully, for he loved the little things.

'Nary a one,' said Mabel.

For a moment Ivor Llewellyn hesitated. But, as he did so, there rose before his eyes a vision. It was the vision of a man who wore a peaked cap and chewed gum, and this man was standing on the dock at New York examining his baggage. And in that baggage there was nothing, absolutely nothing, to bring the frown of censure to the brow of the most exacting Customs inspector. He hesitated no longer.

'Very well,' he said resignedly.

'And now,' said Mabel, 'here's a fountain-pen and here's a sheet of paper. I think we'll have a few brief lines in writing.'

The business deal concluded, the door closed behind them, and Mr Llewellyn left alone to get into his pink pyjamas with the prospect before him of the first peaceful night's rest he had enjoyed since the voyage began, it was Mabel's view that another visit to the boat deck would be agreeable.

To this, however, Reggie, though he yielded to none in his

affection for the boat deck, was compelled to demur. His conscience would not permit him to accept the programme as put forward. Tonight he had ceased to be the careless, self-centred young man thinking only of his personal enjoyment. Purged in the holocaust of a mighty love, Reggie Tennyson had become an altruist.

'You pop up there,' he said, 'and I'll join you in a minute. I have a slight spot of work to do.'

'Work?'

'Diplomatic work. A couple of young hearts to knit together. Poor old Monty Bodkin, largely owing to me, though I acted throughout with the best intentions, has had a bust-up with my cousin Gertrude –'

'The one who doesn't like butterflies?'

'That's the baby. Largely owing to me, though, as I say, my intentions were admirable, she has got it in to her nut that Monty is a butterfly. Before sauntering on boat decks, I must correct this view. Can't leave poor old Monty wallowing in the soup, what?'

'Not even till tomorrow?'

'Not even till tomorrow,' said Reggie firmly. 'I couldn't be easy in my mind and give of my best on that boat deck if I didn't perform this act of kindness. The fact of the matter is, all this happy ending stuff has left me so full of sweetness and light that I want to go spreading it.'

'Well, don't be long.'

'Expect me in five minutes. Unless I have difficulty in locating Gertrude. But no doubt I shall find her in the lounge. I've noticed that the tendency of the female is rather to flock there at this hour.'

His intuition had not led him astray. Gertrude was in the lounge. She was sitting in a corner with Miss Passenger, the captain of the All England Ladies' Hockey Team, and Miss Purdue, the vice-captain.

She eyed him coldly as he approached, for, as has been indicated, she was not pleased with Reggie. Not to put too fine a point upon it, she thought Reggie a mess.

'Well?' she said haughtily.

A man who has recently had a Lottie Blossom saying that

word to him from between clenched teeth is scarcely likely to quail before the 'Well?' of a mere female cousin.

'Step out of the frame, Mona Lisa,' said Reggie briskly. 'I want a couple of words with you.'

And attaching himself to her hand, he scooped her from her seat and drew her apart.

'Now then, young G.,' he said sternly, 'what's all this rot about you and Monty?'

Gertrude stiffened.

'I don't want to talk about it.'

Reggie clicked his tongue impatiently.

'What you want to talk about and what you're going to talk about are two very different things. And, anyway, you don't have to talk – all you've got to do is just drink in what I'm going to say. Gertrude, you're an ass. You're all wrong, you unhappy chump. If ever a girl misjudged a bloke, you have misjudged poor old Monty.'

'I –'

'Don't talk,' said Reggie. 'Listen.' He spoke urgently. Not for a moment did he forget that time was of the essence. By now, Mabel Spence would be up on the boat deck, leaning on the rail in the starlight. If ever a man proposed to make it snappy, it was Reginald Tennyson. 'That's all you've got to do – listen. Here are the facts *in re* Monty. Let them sink in.'

Nobody could have given a clearer exposition of the position of affairs than he proceeded to do. Although, as has been said, he was in a hurry; although, as he spoke, the vision of Mabel Spence alone on the boat deck kept rising before him; he did not scamp his tale. Conscientiously omitting nothing, he took her step by step through all that had occurred.

'So there you are,' he concluded. 'You'll find Monty in his state-room. If he has not yet disrobed, go in and fling yourself on his neck. If he has already retired to rest, shout "Bung-o!" through the keyhole and tell him it's all right and will he meet you on the boat deck first thing tomorrow for the big recon-ciliation. And now –'

Gertrude Butterwick laughed a low, hard, bitter, sneering laugh.

'Oh?' she said.

'What the hell do you mean, "Oh?"' demanded Reggie with pardonable annoyance. This interview, to which in the prospect he had mentally allowed five minutes, had already occupied nearer ten, and Mabel Spence was still gazing at the stars in solitude. It was the last moment when he wanted cousins saying 'Oh?' to him.

Gertrude laughed again.

'It's a splendid story,' she said. 'I particularly liked that bit about Miss Blossom stealing the mouse. I wouldn't have thought you and Monty were so clever.'

Reggie gaped. Incredulity was a thing for which he had not budgeted.

'You aren't suggesting I'm lying, are you?'

'Well, don't you usually?'

'But, good gosh, all this is true to the last drop.'

'Oh?'

'You mean you don't believe it?'

'Is it likely that I would believe anything you told me, after all I've found out about you? Good night. I'm going to bed.'

'Yes, but half a second –'

'Good night!'

Gertrude swept haughtily from the lounge. In the corner where she had been sitting, Miss Purdue looked at Miss Passenger, eyebrows raised.

'Butterwick seems off her oats,' said Miss Purdue.

Miss Passenger sighed.

'Butterwick is in love. And the man has let her down, poor girl.'

'He has?'

'With a thud. Poor old Butterwick!'

'Poor old Butterwick!' echoed Miss Purdue. 'Too bad. Have another gasper and tell me all about it.'

# Chapter 21

Unless delayed by such Acts of God as typhoons and water-spouts or slowed up *en route* by mutiny on the high seas and piracy, the R.M.S. *Atlantic* was what is technically known in transatlantic shipping circles as a four-day boat. That is to say, she did the voyage in six days and a bit. On the present occasion, having sailed from England at noon on a Wednesday, she was expected to dock in New York shortly after lunch on the following Tuesday, and she did not disappoint her public. She came steaming up the bay well on time.

Everything during the concluding stages of the trip had worked out according to plan. The first-class concert (No. 6, Solo: 'The Bandolero' – A. E. Peasemarch) had been performed. The final dinner had been eaten. The morning papers had come aboard, reassuring citizens who had been absent for some time from their native shores that American womanhood had not abandoned the fine old custom of hitting its husband over the head with hammers and that sugar daddies were still being surprised in love-nests. The port officials had appeared and issued landing tickets in the rather grudging way that characterizes the port officials of New York; as if they had reluctantly decided to stretch a point for once, but wished it to be understood that this sort of thing must not occur again. And now the voyagers had disembarked and were in the Customs shed, waiting for their baggage to be examined.

As far as the permanent staff of a transatlantic liner is concerned, joy is always the prevailing sentiment when the vessel arrives at journey's end. The captain is happy because he is at last freed from the haunting fear that this time he may have taken the wrong turning and fetched up in Africa. The purser is happy because he will now be able to get away for a little from the society of people like Monty Bodkin. The doctor is congratulating himself on having come through one more orgy of quoits-playing and backgammon-playing without committing himself to anything definite. The crew like the idea of a few days' rest and repose, and the stewards are pleased for the same reason – while those of their number who are bigamists have long since got over the pang of parting from their wives and children in Southampton and are looking forward with bright affection to meeting once more their wives and children in New York.

Coming to the passengers, however, we find mixed emotions, varying according to the circumstances of the individual. In the crowd which was thronging the Customs sheds today there were hearts that were light and also hearts that were heavy.

Ambrose Tennyson's, for example, was heavy. He had derived no enjoyment from the sight of New York's celebrated skyline, and did not think much of the Customs sheds. Reggie Tennyson, on the other hand, though still exercised in his mind about Monty's broken romance, felt at the top of his form. He had kissed Mabel Spence almost incessantly all the way up the bay and had told her he thought her high buildings were wonderful.

Another of the debonair brigade was Ivor Llewellyn. He had not felt blither since the time when he had stolen three stars and a Czecho-Slovakian director from the Ne-Plus-Ultra-Zizzbaum in a single morning. Able, now that the weight of that necklace was off his mind, to devote the whole force of his powerful intellect exclusively to his brother-in-law George and the sock in the waistcoat which he was going to give the latter when he slapped him on the back, he had administered that sock precisely in the manner of which he had dreamed, causing George to double up like a pocket-rule and nearly swallow his bridge-work. He was now talking to the reporters about Ideals and the Future of the Screen.

Turning to Monty Bodkin, we find gloom once more. The skyline of New York had left Monty as cold as it had left Ambrose. It had seemed to him in his black despondency just a skyline, if that, and all he had thought about the Statue of Liberty was that it reminded him of a frightful girl in the Hippodrome chorus named Bella something, with whom he had

246

once got landed at a theatrical luncheon party. Moodily clutching the Mickey Mouse which Albert Peasemarch had done up for him overnight in a neat brown paper parcel, he opened his trunks for inspection, his nervous system in no way soothed by the fact that, their names both beginning with a B, he had found himself standing practically cheek by jowl with Gertrude Butterwick.

For one fleeting instant he had caught her eye. It had stared through him, coldly and proudly. He had been relieved when some fellow-travellers named Burgess, Bostock and Billington-Todd had insinuated themselves and their trunks between them, hiding her from his view.

Nor was Gertrude herself in serener mood. This close proximity to the man she had once loved had put the last touch but one to the depression and anguish which had been weighing on her since she got out of bed that morning. The final touch was now being applied by Albert Peasemarch, who for some ten minutes had been frolicking about her like a white-jacketed grasshopper.

For Albert Peasemarch was a man who took his duties conscientiously. He was not one of those stewards who pocket their tip on the last morning and are never seen again. When the vessel docked, he sought out his clients and became helpful. He had been helping Gertrude now, as we say, for some ten minutes, and her gentle soul had begun rather to resemble that of a female rogue elephant. There are times when one is in the vein for airy conversation with stewards, and times when one is not. Gertrude yearned to be able to look round and find that Albert Peasemarch was not there.

And quite suddenly the miracle happened. Albert disappeared. One moment, he had been deep in an anecdote about a dog belonging to a friend of his in Southampton; the next he had gone. The solitude she had so greatly desired was hers.

But not for long. The sigh of relief had scarcely passed her lips when he was back again.

'You will excuse me running off like that, miss,' he said, with gentlemanly apology, reappearing like a rabbit out of a conjuror's hat. 'I was beckoned for.'

'Please don't stay if you're busy,' urged Gertrude.

Albert Peasemarch smiled a chivalrous smile.

'Never too busy to be of assistance and help to a lady, miss,' he said gallantly. 'It was simply that out of the tail of my eye I happened to observe Mr Bodkin beckoning to me. That was why I ran off. I have a message from Mr Bodkin, miss. Mr Bodkin presents his comps, and could he have the privilege of a word with you?'

Gertrude quivered. Her face flushed and her eyes grew hard, as if she had had a goal disallowed in an important match.

'No!'

'No, miss?'

'No!'

'You do not desire to speak with Mr Bodkin?'

'No!'

'Very good, miss. I will nip back and convey the information.'

'Ass!'

'Sir?'

'Not you,' said Reggie Tennyson, for it was he who had spoken. He had come up from the direction of the 'T' section, taking them in the rear. 'I was addressing Miss Butterwick.'

'Very good, sir,' said Albert Peasemarch, and disappeared.

Reggie was regarding Gertrude with a cousinly sternness.

'Ass!' he repeated. 'Why won't you speak to Monty?'

'Because I do not wish to.'

'Fool! Chump! Cloth-head!' said Reggie.

There are doubtless girls in the world who will stand quite a lot of this sort of thing from their first cousins, but Gertrude Butterwick was not one of them. Her face, already flushed, grew pinker.

'Don't talk to me like that!' she cried.

'I shall talk to you,' said Reggie, with unabated sternness but taking the precaution of stepping behind a large cabin-trunk, 'just like that. I come here, hoping to discover that you have thought things over and changed your mind, and the first thing I hear is you telling stewards that you do not wish to speak to poor old Monty. You make me sick, young Gertrude.'

'Oh, go away.'

'I will not go away. Do you mean to tell me that, having had two days to brood on it and sift the evidence and weigh this

248

against that, you still refuse to believe that I was telling you the truth that night? Why, good gosh, look how the thing hangs together. It's like what we used to have to swot up at school about the inevitableness of Greek tragedy. One thing leading to another, I mean to say. Lottie Blossom steals the mouse from Monty... In order to lure her from her state-room while I search it, he arranges a tryst with her on the second-class promenade deck...'

'I know, I know.'

'Well, then?'

'I don't believe a word of it.'

Reggie Tennyson expelled a deep breath.

'Young Gertrude,' he said, 'your sex protects you. I will not, therefore, give you the biff in the eye for which you are asking with every word you utter. But I'll tell you what I will do. I'll fetch Ambrose. Perhaps you will listen to him.'

'I won't.'

'You think you won't,' corrected Reggie, 'but I'll bet you will. Wait here. Don't stir a step.'

'I shall not wait here.'

'Yes, you jolly well will,' said Reggie, 'because you haven't had your luggage examined yet. So sucks to you, young Gertrude.'

For some moments after he had gone, Gertrude remained heaving gently, and staring with unseeing eyes at the back of Mr Billington-Todd, who was having a little trouble with his inspector about a box of cigars. The recent unpleasant scene seemed to have put the clock back. Once more, she seemed to be a child – raging, as she had so often raged in those distant days when they had shared a mutual nursery, because Reggie had worsted her in cousinly debate. Like lightning flashes athwart a stormy sky, there flickered through her mind all the bitter, clever things she would have said if only she had thought of them.

As one waking from a trance, she became aware of her friend Miss Passenger at her side. On Miss Passenger's face was a grave, kindly, solicitous look; in her muscular hand a brown paper parcel.

'Well, Butterwick.'

'Oh, hullo, Jane.'

There was no welcoming ring in Gertrude's voice. She liked Miss Passenger as a woman and respected her as a captain and a dashing outside-right, but she did not desire her company now. She feared . . .

'That young man of yours, Butterwick . . .'

That was what Gertrude had feared, that Miss Passenger was about to twist the knife in her heart by talking of Monty. Ever since she had been so unguarded as to make the captain of the All England Ladies' Hockey Team a confidante in the matter of her wrecked romance, the latter had shown an unwelcome disposition to turn the conversation to that topic when they found themselves alone together.

'Oh, Jane!'

'I've just been talking to him. I was coming along to see how you were getting on, and as I passed he called out to me. He says you won't speak to him.'

'I won't.'

Miss Passenger sighed. For all her rugged exterior, she was at heart a sentimentalist, and both as a private individual and as a hockey captain she mourned over this sundering of two young lives. As an individual, she had been devoted to Gertrude for many years – right back, indeed, to the days of cocoa-parties in the dormitory at the dear old school – and hated to see her unhappy. As a hockey captain, she feared lest blighted love might put her off her game.

It would not be the first time in Miss Passenger's experience that that had happened. She had not forgotten that county match when, with the score at one all and three minutes to go, her goalkeeper, who had recently severed relations with the man of her choice, suddenly burst into tears during a hot rally in the goalmouth, and, covering her face with her hands, let a sitter go past her into the net.

'You're making a mistake, Butterwick.'

'Oh, Jane!'

'Well, you are.'

'I don't want to talk about it.'

Miss Passenger sighed again.

'Just as you please,' she said regretfully. 'Anyway, what I was going to say was that your Bodkin gave me this parcel to give to you. I gather that it contains a Mickey Mouse of yours.'

Not even the information that the brown paper parcel contained mice in the flesh could have made Gertrude start back with greater aversion.

'I don't want it!'

'It isn't my Mickey Mouse. It's Mr Bodkin's. Give it back to him.'

'He's left.'

'Then run after him.'

'No, I'm dashed if I do,' said Miss Passenger. She was amiable, but there are limits. 'I'm not going to chivvy young men about Customs sheds. Life's too short.'

'You don't think I intend to keep this mouse, do you?'

'I don't see what else you can do.'

Gertrude bit her lip.

'Would you like it, Jane?'

'No,' said Miss Passenger, with decision. 'No, Butterwick, I would not.'

Through the crowd came Albert Peasemarch, looking helpful.

'Peasemarch!' cried Gertrude.

'Miss?'

'Would you like a mouse?'

'No, miss.'

'Then do you know what hotel Mr Bodkin is going to?'

'The Piazza, miss. I recommended it. A nice, up-to-date hotel, possessing all the comforts of home and within easy reach of all the theatres and places of public amusement.'

'Thank you.'

'Thank *you*, miss. Anything further I can do for you?'

'No, thank you.'

'Very good, miss,' said Albert Peasemarch, and went off to be helpful elsewhere.

'Jane,' said Gertrude, 'I shan't be coming to your hotel with the rest of the team. I'm going to the Piazza.'

'Eh? Why?'

Gertrude's teeth came together with an unpleasant clicking sound.

'Because,' she said, 'Mr Bodkin is there, and I intend to

return this Mickey Mouse to him if I have to make him swallow it.'

For the third time since this interview had begun Miss Passenger was unable to check a sigh.

'Don't be a chump, Butterwick.'

'I'm not a chump.'

'You are, old chap, honestly you are. I know how you're feeling. You're sore, and you have every right to be sore. But why not let bygones be bygones? We women always regret it if we don't make allowances and forgive. I never told you, but I was once engaged to a dear, good fellow, about as smart an inside-right as you ever saw, and I broke it off because one afternoon when we were playing in a mixed game down in the country he kept trying to go through on his own instead of flicking the ball out to me on the wing. A selfish hound, I remember I called him, and I gave him back the ring. Next day, of course, I was sorry, but like an ass I was too proud to say-so, and we parted, and a couple of months later he married a girl who played left-back for Girton. So I appeal to you, old man, be sensible. Don't cancel this fixture. Forgive Bodkin!'

'No!'

'You must!'

'I won't.'

'Butterwick, you're one of my oldest pals, but I tell you straight you're behaving like a mug.'

'I'm not behaving like a mug!'

'You flatter yourself,' said the voice of Reggie Tennyson at her elbow. 'You're behaving like the worst young mug that ever broke biscuit. Gertrude,' said Reggie, 'I've brought Ambrose to have a little talk with you.'

# Chapter 22

While these conversations were in progress in Section B of the Customs sheds, in the street outside into which the voyager steps as he comes off the White Star pier Lottie Blossom was standing waiting for Ambrose.

The mind of the New York Customs inspector being the unpleasant, suspicious thing it is, a motion picture star returning to her native land from a visit to Europe usually finds the clearing of her baggage a rather lengthy process. But today Lottie had got through quickly. The official told off to examine her belongings had begun by examining the little wicker-work basket which she was carrying, and after that had seemed unable to put any real heart and thoroughness into his work. His sense of duty was strong enough to make him ask her to unlock her trunks, but his whole attitude when going through them had been that of a man who has had his lesson and feels that prudence is best. Perfunctory about sums it up.

This, taken in conjunction with the fact that she perceived herself to be an object of frank admiration to the group of stevedores and gentlemen of leisure standing by, should have made her happy, for she hated hanging about Customs sheds and was a girl who enjoyed admiration, even from the humblest. Nevertheless, she chafed as she stood there. A frown was on her face, and from time to time she spurned the sidewalk irritably. She was getting tired of waiting for Ambrose.

She was, indeed, on the point of giving him up and hailing a cab to take her to the Hotel Piazza, where she always stayed when in New York, when Mabel Spence came out into the street.

'Oh, there you are, Lottie,' said Mabel. 'I've a message for you from Ambrose Tennyson. He says not to wait.'

'He does, does he?' said Lottie. 'I wonder what he thinks

253

I've been doing this last ten minutes, the poor fish! What's keeping him?'

'He and Reggie are wrestling with the Butterwick girl –'

'Who's winning?'

'In prayer,' explained Mabel. 'I only had a hurried word with Reggie before he jumped back into the ring, but it seems they're trying to get Miss Butterwick to forgive Mr Bodkin.'

'What's Mr Bodkin done?'

'Well, you ought to know. It's about you that all the trouble is.'

Amazement shone from Lottie Blossom's fine eyes. She stared like a girl with a spotless conscience who is completely bewildered.

'Me?'

'That's what Reggie told me.'

'Why, I never so much as touched the man.'

'As pure as the driven snow, are you?'

'Purer. I may have sauntered into his state-room once or twice to pass the time of day, but jiminy Christmas –'

'Well, all right,' said Mabel. 'You don't have to convince me. I'm just an innocent bystander. But that's how the scenario is, and Reggie seems all worked up about it. He's fond of Mr Bodkin. So, anyway, it's no use your pounding the pavement out here. They may be hours. Where are you off to?'

'The Piazza.'

'Then I can't offer you a lift. I'm headed for the Bar building. I've got to see a lawyer.'

'A what?'

'Lawyer. A man skilled in the law. I want legal advice.'

'What for? Has Reggie backed out already, and are you bringing an action for breach?'

Mabel's eyes lost their efficient brightness for an instant and became soft and dreamy.

'Reggie's a precious little pink-and-white lamb –'

'Ugh!' said Lottie, revolted.

'– and he's just as crazy about me as I am about him. No, what I'm seeing lawyers about is this contract of his. I've got that letter, of course, but –'

'Contract? What are you talking about?'

254

'Hasn't Reggie told you? Ikey's signed him up for five years to superintend his English sequences, and all we've got so far to hold him to it is a few lines I made him scribble on a bit of paper. And, knowing what Ikey is, I want a regular legal contract drawn up, with as many seals stuck on it as there's room for. I wouldn't put it past Ikey to have written that letter in vanishing ink. Hi, taxi,' said Mabel.

It was not often that Lottie Blossom permitted those with whom she was conversing to utter without interruption speeches as long as the one to which she had just been listening, but the astounding nature of the information which Mabel's words had conveyed had made interruption impossible. She could only gape. Not until her companion had stepped into the cab and closed the door was she able to utter.

'Wait!' she cried, recovering speech and the power of movement simultaneously. She leaped forward and clutched the edge of the window. 'What did you say? Ikey has given Reggie a contract?'

'Yes. As a superintendent of English sequences.'

'But–'

'I really must be getting along,' said Mabel. 'I may have to spend the rest of the afternoon with these people. You know what lawyers are like.'

Gently but firmly detaching Lottie's fingers, she instructed the driver to snap into it, and he did so. The cab rolled off, and Lottie was left to ponder over this extraordinary occurrence alone.

Her mind was in a whirl. If this news was true, strange things must have been happening to Ivor Llewellyn. It was obvious that no balanced person would employ Reggie. Nobody but a Santa Claus would even contemplate it. The only explanation, therefore, that offered itself was that Mr Llewellyn must suddenly have turned into a Santa Claus. He must have been overcome by one of those curious fits of universal benevolence hitherto confined to characters in the novels of Charles Dickens. Yet why? It was not Christmas-time. He could not have been hearing carol-singers.

But wait. Yes, it came back to her now. Once, in the days when she had been in the chorus in musical comedy, she had heard in the dressing-room a fantastic tale of a prominent theatrical manager who, emerging from an automobile accident with an egg-shaped lump on his head, had become a changed man, even to the extent of deliberately refraining from chiselling an author out of his share of the movie rights. That was what must have happened to Ivor Llewellyn, something on those lines. Perhaps he had bumped his head against the bureau while groping for a dropped collar-stud.

She thrilled with joyous excitement. If Ivor Llewellyn had bumped himself badly enough to make him give five-year contracts to Reggie, he was clearly in a mental condition to do the same by Ambrose. This, she felt, was a good thing and must be pushed along. Without delay she must repair to the offices of the Superba-Llewellyn on Seventh Avenue, whither the man always went like a homing pigeon the moment he stepped off the boat, and strike while the iron is hot – slip it across him, in other words, before he had time to come out from under the influence.

There was, however, as it happened, no necessity for her to make the journey to Seventh Avenue, for at this moment the man she was seeking came out into the street, attended by a porter with suit-cases, and passed her by with a jaunty wave of the hand which had doubled up his brother-in-law George. With this wave of the hand, as if feeling in his benevolence that there must be no stint, Mr Llewellyn threw in a genial smile and a 'Hello, there, Lottie!' – a smile so genial, in fact, and a 'Hello, there, Lottie!' so gay and cordial that she had no hesitation in making one of her tigrine leaps and seizing him by the lapel of his coat. She was convinced. Once a ten-minute egg, Ivor Llewellyn had become a Cheeryble brother.

'Hey, Ikey!' she cried, beaming up at him with all the confidence of a favourite child about to ask a fond father for chocolate. 'Listen, Ikey, what's all this I hear?'

'Eh?'

'From Mabel. Mabel's been telling me about your deal with Reggie Tennyson.'

The joviality faded from Mr Llewellyn's face, as if it had been wiped off with a squeegee. Abruptly, he looked tense, anxious, alarmed, like a fly inspecting a piece of fly-paper.

'What did she tell you?'

'She said you had given him a five-year contract.'

Mr Llewellyn's tension relaxed.

'Oh? Yes, that's right.'

'Well, then, what about Ambrose?'

'What do you mean?'

'You know what I mean. If you're giving five-year contracts to the Tennyson family, why leave Ambrose out of the distribution?'

Mr Llewellyn's face darkened. Her words had touched an exposed nerve. It may seem to some a venial fault not to have written 'The Boy Stood on the Burning Deck', but Ivor Llewellyn could not bring himself to forgive Ambrose Tennyson for not having done so. At least, he could not forgive him for not being the right Tennyson. The whole subject of the rightness and wrongness of Tennysons was one on which the president of the Superba-Llewellyn would not be able to think calmly for a long time to come.

'Pshaw!' he cried, stirred to his depths.

'Eh?'

'I've no use for that fellow.'

'Ikey!'

'I wouldn't have him on the lot,' said Mr Llewellyn with deep emotion, 'not if you paid me.'

He detached her fingers – it seemed to Lottie that everybody was detaching her fingers this afternoon – and with a nimbleness which would have surprised anybody who did not know how nimble even the stoutest motion-picture magnate can be when evading people who are asking favours of him, shot into a taxi and was carried off.

It was at this moment that Monty Bodkin came out into the street.

In the parts round about the entrance to the White Star pier New York is admittedly not at its best – indeed, it is to be wondered at that some committee of patriotic citizens has not put up one of those signs, so popular in the rural districts, which urge the visitor not to judge the town by the 'deepo'. Nevertheless, this rather raffish district has a quality which other, showier portions of the city lack.

257

Technically, the Customs sheds are American soil and should excite all sorts of emotions in the bosom of one who is arriving for the first time in the United States. But in actual fact it is only when such a person comes out through the door at the bottom of that toboggan slide where they shoot down the light baggage that he says to himself: 'At last!' Then, and then only, does he really feel that he is in America and that a new life is beginning for him.

To Monty, as he stood in the doorway, this feeling came particularly vividly. Even more than the ordinary immigrant, he was starting afresh, with the future a blank scroll before him. In returning that Mickey Mouse to Gertrude Butterwick, it was as if he had written 'Finis' to a definite phase of his life. The act had been symbolic. He had not actually said 'Good-bye to all that,' but that was what it had amounted to.

He was in a new world, with no plans. He might do anything. He might seek solace in one of those round-the-globe cruises. He might visit the Rocky Mountains and shoot bears. He might bury himself in some distant South Seas island and grow or catch copra – according to whether (a fact which he had never been quite able to grasp) it was a vegetable or some kind of fish. Or he might go into a monastery. It was all uncertain.

Meanwhile, he sniffed New York and thought it smelt funny.

And as he stood there sniffing there was a sudden rush and whir and he found himself blinking under the bright gaze of Lottie Blossom.

'Hey!' she was saying, plainly in the grip of some very strong emotion. She attached herself to the lapel of his coat. 'Hey, listen!'

The sight of Monty had affected Lottie profoundly. In all the swirl of recent events she had never forgotten that, however abruptly Ivor Llewellyn might turn off the milk of human kindness in his bosom, there was one man who could make him turn it on again. And it was this man who stood before her. On the authority of both Reggie and Ambrose she had it that Ivor Llewellyn yearned to secure this bimbo Bodkin's artistic services and would agree to anything in order to obtain his signature to a contract. Undeterred, therefore, by her recent failure to get results by holding the lapel of Mr Llewellyn's coat, she now attached herself to Monty's.

'Hey, listen!' she cried. 'You've got to do it! You've just got to, see?'

There had been a time, only a few brief days since, when Monty Bodkin's immediate reaction to the discovery that Lottie Blossom was adhering to his coat would have been an attempt to brush her off. But now he made no move to do so. He remained listless and inert. It mattered little, he reflected with infinite sadness, if he was festooned from head to foot with Lottie Blossoms.

'Do what?' he said.

'Go to Ikey Llewellyn and make him give Ambrose his job back. If you have a spark of common decency in you, you can't refuse. Look what Ammie is doing for you at this very moment.'

'Eh?'

'I said: "Look –"'

'I know. And I said: "Eh?" I mean, what is he doing?'

'Squaring you with your Buttersplosh.'

Monty stiffened.

'The name is Butterwick.'

'Well, Butterwick, then. At this very moment Ambrose is in those Customs sheds, working like a beaver trying to make things hotsy-totsy for you with the Butterwick beasel.'

Again Monty stiffened.

'I would prefer that you did not call Miss Butterwick a weasel.'

'Beasel.'

'Beasel or weasel, I see little difference. And a fat chance, I fear, there is of any hotsy-totsiness resulting from anything Ambrose can do, though I appreciate the kind thought. All is over. She . . .' His voice shook. 'She wouldn't speak to me.'

'Oh, that'll be all right. Ambrose will fix that.'

Monty shook his head.

'No. The situation is beyond human fixing. The bird has been definitely given. Still, as I say, it is decent of old Ambrose to have a pop.'

'Ammie is wonderful in that way.'

'Yes.'

'What a pal!'

'The whitest man I know,' agreed Monty moodily.

'There's nothing he wouldn't do for a friend.'

'I suppose not, no.'

'Well, then,' said Miss Blossom insinuatingly, tightening her grasp on the coat lapel, 'won't you do this little thing for him? Won't you go and sign up with Ikey and tell him that before you put pen to dotted line Ambrose must have his contract, too? Oh, I know how you feel about it. You hate the idea of becoming a motion picture actor. But have you considered that you'll probably be so lousy that they'll pay to get rid of you at the end of the first week? I mean, it isn't as if you would have to go *on* acting –'

'As a matter of fact,' said Monty, 'that part of it is all right. Llewellyn says I can be a production expert.'

'Well, ısn't that great!'

'The only thing is, I was rather thinking of going into a monastery.'

'I wouldn't.'

'Perhaps you're right.'

'And listen,' said Miss Blossom urgently. 'I don't believe you're hep yet to the real vital issue. It's this way. If Ammie doesn't get a job, he and I can't be married.'

'Eh? Why not?'

'Well, it seems he doesn't make a whole lot out of writing his books, so it would be a case of me supporting the home, and he balks at the notion of being one of these Hollywood husbands, living on the little woman's salary and working out his keep by brushing the dog and doing odd jobs around the house. And I don't blame him. But it certainly puts the bee on anything in the shape of wedded bliss. So he must get this job. He must. You will go to Ikey, won't you?'

Monty was gaping at her, aghast. He had never dreamed that the happiness of two lives depended on his falling in with Mr Llewellyn's wishes – hung, as it were, upon his whim.

'You don't mean that?'

'Don't mean what?'

'When I said "You don't mean that?" I didn't mean you

didn't mean it; I meant ... well, what I mean to say is, this item of news has come as rather a sock on the jaw. I hadn't an idea things were like that.'

'They are. Ambrose is as proud as the devil.'

'How perfectly foul for you! Why, of course I'll go to Llewellyn.'

'You will?'

'Certainly. I've absolutely nothing on at the moment – I mean to say, no plans or anything. As a matter of fact, I was just thinking when you came up how footloose I was. Until the day before yesterday I was more or less employed at a detective agency – the Argus – I don't know if you have heard of it – telegraphic address, Pilgus, Piccy, London – but that was only because there were wheels within wheels. I had to have a job in order to marry Gertrude. But when Gertrude gave me the bird on that second-class promenade deck, there didn't seem any point in carrying on, so I sent the agency chap a wireless, resigning my portfolio. Which leaves me absolutely free. I had been thinking, as I say, of going into a monastery, and I had also turned over in my mind South Sea islands and Rocky Mountains and what not, but I can just as well go to Hollywood and become a production expert.'

'I could kiss you!'

'Do, if you like. Nothing matters now. I'll secure a cab, shall I, and go off and see this Llewellyn? Where do I find him?'

'He'll be at his office.'

'Well, as soon as I've clocked in at my hotel –'

'What hotel were you going to?'

'The Piazza. Albert Peasemarch speaks well of it.'

'How funny! I'm going to the Piazza, too. I'll tell you what let's do. I'll drop you at Ikey's and go on and engage you a room... Or do you millionaires like suites?'

'A suite, I think.'

'A suite, then. And I'll wait in it till you come.'

'Right ho.'

Lottie released Monty's coat and stepped back, eyeing him adoringly.

'Brother Bodkin, you're an angel!'

'Oh, not at all.'

'Yes, you are. You've saved my life. And Ambrose's, too. And I'm sure you won't regret it. I'll bet you love Hollywood. What I mean, suppose this beasel –'

'Not beasel.'

'Suppose this Buttersplosh –'

'– wick.'

'Suppose this Butterwick of yours *has* handed you your hat, what of it? Think of all the hundreds of girls you'll meet in Hollywood!'

Monty shook his head.

'They will mean nothing to me. I shall always remain true to Gertrude.'

'Well, there,' said Miss Blossom, 'you must use your own judgement. I'm only saying that if you do feel like forgetting the dead past, you'll find all the facilities in Hollywood. Hi, taxi! The Piazza.'

Ivor Llewellyn, meanwhile, a cigar in his mouth, contentment in his heart, and his hat on the side of his head, had reached the ornate premises of the corporation of which he was the honoured president. His interview with Lottie Blossom had left him ruffled, but it did not take him long to recover his spirits. There is a bracing quality about the streets of New York, and only a very dejected man can fail to be cheered and uplifted by a drive through them in an open taxi on a fine summer afternoon. Lottie and her importunities faded from Mr Llewellyn's mind, and while still several blocks from his destination he had begun to hum extracts from the musical scores of old S.-L. feature films. He was still humming as he got out and paid off the cab, and it was with a theme song on his lips that he entered the dear, familiar office. Ivor Llewellyn's heart was in Southern California, but he loved his New York office, too.

The sort of miniature civic welcome which motion-picture corporations give returning presidents occupied a certain amount of time, but presently the last Yes-man had withdrawn and he was alone with his thoughts again.

He could have desired no pleasanter company. At any moment now, he reflected, Reggie Tennyson would be calling to report and the whole unpleasant affair of Grayce's infernal necklace could be written off as finished. It was with a grunt of satisfaction that, reaching for the telephone on his desk some minutes later, he learned that a gentleman waited without, desirous of seeing him.

'Send him right in,' he said, and leaned back in his chair, assembling on his face a smile of welcome.

The next moment, the smile had disappeared. It was not Reggie Tennyson who stood before him, but the spy, Bodkin. Mr Llewellyn tilted his chair forward again, cocked his cigar at a militant angle, and looked at this Bodkin.

The difference between the way in which a motion-picture magnate looks at a Customs spy when he is on an ocean liner and has his wife's fifty-thousand-dollar necklace in his state-room and the way in which he looks at him when he is in his office on shore and knows that the necklace is on shore, too, is subtle but well-defined. In Mr Llewellyn's case, more well-defined than subtle. He directed at Monty a glare so grim and hostile that even he was able to notice it. Preoccupied though he was with his broken heart, Monty perceived that something had wrought a change in the president of the Superba-Llewellyn. This was not the effervescent, chummy man who had buttonholed him in the smoking-room of the R.M.S. *Atlantic* and complimented him so cordially on his technique in the difficult arts of cigarette-lighting and whisky-drinking. The person before him looked like the bad brother of that man.

He felt a little damped.

'Er – hullo,' he said tentatively.

Mr Llewellyn said: 'Well?'

'I – er – thought I'd look in,' said Monty.

Mr Llewellyn said 'Well?' again.

'So – er – here I am,' said Monty.

'And what the hell,' inquired Mr Llewellyn, 'do you want here?'

The question could have been more cordially worded. Even off-hand, Monty was able to think of several ways in which the speaker could have lent to it a greater suavity and polish. But the main thing was that it had been asked, for it placed him in a position to get down to cases without further delay.

'I've been thinking it over,' he said, 'and I'll sign that contract.'

Mr Llewellyn switched his cigar across his face, starting in the left hand-corner and finishing in the right-hand corner.

'Oh, yes?' he said. 'Well, I've been thinking it over, and you won't sign any contracts in *my* office.'

'Well, where would you like me to sign it?' asked Monty agreeably.

Mr Llewellyn's cigar travelled back across his face, clipping a fraction of a second off its previous time.

'Listen,' he said, 'you can forget about contracts.'

'Forget about them?'

'There ain't going to be any contracts,' said Mr Llewellyn, making his meaning clearer.

Monty was at a loss.

'I thought you said on the boat –'

'Never mind what I said on the boat.'

'I thought you wanted me to be a production expert.'

'Well, I don't.'

'You don't want me to be a production expert?'

'I don't want you to be a dish-washer in the commissary – not the Superba-Llewellyn commissary.'

Monty thought this over. He rubbed his nose. Sombre meditation had left his mind in rather a clouded state, but he was beginning to gather that the other was not in the market for his services.

'Oh?' he said.

'No,' said Mr Llewellyn.

Monty scratched his chin.

'I see.'

'I'm glad you see.'

Monty rubbed his nose, scratched his chin and fingered his left ear.

'Well, right ho,' he said.

Mr Llewellyn did not speak, merely looked at Monty as if he had been a beetle in the salad and sent his cigar off on another exercise gallop.

'Well, right ho,' said Monty. 'And how about Ambrose?'

'Huh?'

'Ambrose Tennyson.'

'What about him?'

'Will you give him a job?'

'Sure.'

'That's fine.'

'He can go up to the top of the Empire State Building and jump off,' said Mr Llewellyn. 'I'll pay him for his time.'

'You mean you don't want Ambrose, either?'

'I mean just that.'

'I see.'

Monty rubbed his nose, scratched his chin, fingered his left ear and rubbed the toe of one shoe against the heel of the other.

'Well, in that case – er – pip-pip.'

'You'll find your way out,' said Mr Llewellyn. 'The door's just behind you. You turn the handle.'

The mechanics of getting out of the office of the president of the Superba-Llewellyn proved to be just as simple and uncomplicated as its proprietor had stated, and Monty, though feeling as if strong men had been hitting him on the head with sand-bags, had no difficulty in making his departure. After he had gone, Mr Llewellyn left his chair and began to strut up and down the room, satisfaction in every ripple of his chins. He felt as if he had just ground a rattlesnake under his heel, and nothing tones up the system like a brisk spell of rattlesnake-grinding.

He was still strutting when Mabel Spence was announced, and not even the fact that Mabel had brought with her and proceeded immediately to submit to his attention a heavily sealed contract, drawn up by one partner in New York's hardest boiled legal firm and inspected and approved by two other partners, was able to take the sparkle out of his eyes and the elasticity from his bearing. Given a choice, he would have preferred not to be compelled to commit himself so irrevocably to becoming Reginald Tennyson's employer, but he had long since resigned himself to the fact that he was not given a choice. Reggie, he recognized, was the pill that went with the jam. Calmly, if not actually with a merry bonhomie, he attached his signature to the document.

'Thanks,' said Mabel, when the four witnesses on whose collaboration she had insisted had withdrawn. 'Well, that fixes Reggie all right. For though you're a better man than most, Gunga Din, I'll defy you to wriggle out of this one.'

'Who wants to wriggle out of it?' demanded Mr Llewellyn, with some indignation.

'Oh, well, you never know. All I'm saying is that it's nice to feel you can't. If ever you need good lawyers, Ikey, these are the people to go to. Most thorough and conscientious. You would have laughed at the way they kept thinking up penalty clauses. They didn't seem able to stop. The way they had it by the time they were through, I believe Reggie'll be able to soak you for substantial damages if you don't give him a good night kiss and tuck him up in bed. Swell,' said Mabel, placing the document in her vanity-bag with a light-hearted gaiety which Mr Llewellyn could not bring himself to share. 'Well, Ikey, what's the news? Seen Reggie yet?'

'No,' said Mr Llewellyn querulously. 'And I can't think why. He ought to have been here half an hour ago.'

'Oh, I know. Of course. He stopped to talk to his cousin, Miss Butterwick.'

'What for? He'd no business –'

'Well, it doesn't matter, anyway. He got the necklace through.'

'How do you know?'

'I was with him when his baggage was examined, and they let it by without a murmur.'

'Where did he put the thing?'

'He wouldn't tell me. Very secretive he was.'

'Well, I wish –'

His remark was interrupted by the ringing of the telephone. He took up the receiver.

'Is that Reggie?' said Mabel.

Mr Llewellyn nodded briefly. He was listening intently. And, as he listened, his eyes slowly protruded from his face and his complexion took on that purple tinge which always made it so pretty to look at in times of great emotion. Presently he began to splutter incoherently.

'What on earth is the matter, Ikey?' asked Mabel Spence in

266

some alarm. She was not fond of her brother-in-law, but when he showed signs of being about to perish of apoplexy in her presence she became concerned.

Mr Llewellyn replaced the receiver and sagged back in his chair. He breathed stertorously.

'That was your Reggie!'

'Bless his heart!'

'Blast his kidneys,' corrected Mr Llewellyn. He spoke thickly: 'Do you know what he's done?'

'Something clever?'

Mr Llewellyn quivered. His cigar, which during these moments had been clinging to his lower lip by a thread, relaxed its hold and fell into his lap.

'Clever! Yes, darned clever. He says he thought and thought of the best way of getting that necklace through the Customs, and in the end he decided to put it in a brown plush Mickey Mouse belonging to that fellow Bodkin. And Bodkin's got it now!'

# Chapter 23

The fury which had burned in Gertrude Butterwick's bosom in the Customs sheds was still burning briskly when she arrived at the Hotel Piazza, engaged a room, and went up to it and took off her hat. Placid by nature, she was disturbed as a rule only by venal and prejudiced hockey referees who said she was off-side when she was nowhere near offside; but the mildest girl may be excused for breathing flame through the nostrils under the provocation which she had received.

The calm crust of Montague Bodkin in returning that Mickey Mouse to her after what had occurred, and dashing away before she could hurl it scornfully back at him, afflicted her like a physical pain. She accepted ice-water at the bell-boy's hands because he seemed to wish it, but her thoughts were not with ice-water. She had ascertained at the desk the number of Monty's suite, and she was telling herself that as soon as this uniformed child had made himself scarce she would step down there – it was only on the next floor – and deliver that mouse as it should be delivered. The one look which she proposed to give Monty as she placed it in his hands would, in her opinion, be quite sufficient to put him where he belonged and indicate even to his weak mind his standing in the estimation of G. Butterwick, of the All England Ladies' Hockey team.

Directly the bell-boy had died away in the distance, accordingly, she took the Mickey Mouse and set out. And presently she was knocking at the door which she had been told was his.

In spite of herself, the sound of footsteps from within caused her heart to beat a little more quickly. And she was telling herself that she must be strong and resolute, when the door opened and she found herself face to face with Lottie Blossom.

'Hello, there,' said Lottie, in the friendliest possible manner, as if Gertrude had been a welcome guest whom she had long been expecting. 'Come on in.'

And such was the compelling power of her personality that Gertrude went on in.

'Take a chair.'

Gertrude took a chair. She was still incapable of speech. For all that Monty was nothing to her, it was as if that smouldering fire within her had blazed up into a searing flame. The sight of this woman at her ease in Monty's suite, behaving absolutely like a hostess, did not surprise her. It merely confirmed all the existing evidence. Nevertheless, it was agony. She clutched the Mickey Mouse and suffered.

'Bodkin's out,' said Lottie. 'He's gone to see Ikey Llewellyn about a contract for Ambrose. He'll be tickled pink when he comes back and finds you here. I'm tickled, too, if you don't mind me saying so. Brother Bodkin is not one of my intimate circle, of course, but he's a good sort and Reggie's told me how worked up he got about your giving him the air the way you did. So I'm glad you've thought it over and decided to forget those cruel words. Hell's bells,' said Lottie warmly, 'where's the sense in having fights with the man you love? I've had them with Ambrose, but I'm never going to have any more. I'm cured. They're a barrel of fun at the time, but they're not worth it. When you've come as near as I have to losing the adored object, you begin to think. By the beard of Sam Goldwyn, I'll say you do. An hour ago it looked as if there wasn't a chance on earth of me and Ambrose setting up house, and I could have howled like a dog. I kept thinking how mean I'd been to him at times, and I suppose that's what you've been feeling about Brother Bodkin.' She broke off. An eager light had come into her eyes. 'Say, you wouldn't consider parting with that mouse, would you?'

At length, Gertrude was able to speak.

'I came to give it back.'

'To Bodkin?' Lottie nodded resignedly. 'Then I guess there's no chance. He won't let it go. Anyways, he wouldn't before. He told you about me swiping it, I suppose?'

Gertrude started. Up to the present, she had scarcely heard what her companion had been saying, but here was something that really struck home.

'What!'

'Yes, I swiped it. Didn't you know? Ambrose made me give it back to him.'

'What!'

'Well, when I say "swiped it", what actually happened was that that steward guy Peasemarch thought it was mine and slipped it to me and I held on to it. I told Bodkin that unless he went to Ikey and got Ambrose a contract I was going to kid you into thinking he had given it to me. And if that wasn't a dirty trick, you tell me one. I can see it now, but at the time it seemed a peach of an idea. It wasn't till Ambrose talked to me like a Pilgrim Father that I realized what a hound I was being.'

Gertrude choked. Strange tinglings were in progress up and down her spine. Cumulative evidence was doing its work. 'What I tell you three times,' said the Bellman in *The Hunting of the Snark*, 'is true;' and this was the third time she had heard the story of the mouse. Reggie had told it. Ambrose had told it. And now here was Lotus Blossom adding her testimony.

'Do you mean . . . do you mean it's all true?'

Lottie seemed surprised.

'What's true?'

'What everybody has been telling me ... Reggie ... and Ambrose.'

'I don't know about Reggie,' said Lottie, 'but whatever my Ammie has been telling you you can take as gospel. But what do you mean, is it all true?' asked Lottie, puzzled. 'Didn't you know it was true?'

'I didn't believe it.'

'Then what an extraordinary little sap you must be, if you'll excuse me saying so. Naturally, I took it for granted, when I found you scratching at the door, that you had seen the light and had come to tell Brother Bodkin the fight was off. Do you mean to say you simply came to start another round?'

'I was going to give him back his mouse.'

'To show him that all was over?'

'Yes,' said Gertrude in a small voice.

Lottie Blossom drew in her breath, amazed.

'Well, in the friendliest spirit, Buttersplosh, you make me sick. Of all the cuckoos! So you seriously thought there was funny work going on between this Bodkin of yours and me?'

'I don't think so now.'

'I should hope you darned well didn't by golly think so now. Bodkin! That's a laugh. Why, I wouldn't touch Bodkin if you served him up to me on an individual skewer with Bearnaise sauce. He could go automobiling with me for weeks on end and never once have to get out and walk. And why? Because there's only one man for me – my Ammie. Gosh, how I love that bimbo!'

'No more than I love Monty,' said Gertrude. She was close to tears, but she spoke with spirit. While rejoicing that this girl was after all no rival, she had not at all liked her saying that she would not find any appeal in Monty, even if served up with Bearnaise sauce on an individual skewer.

'Well, that's fine,' said Lottie. 'I'd tell him so, if I were you.'

'I'm going to. But – do you think he will ever forgive me?'

'For your unworthy suspicions? Oh, sure. Men are swell that way. You can treat them like dogs, but they'll always be there with their hair in a braid when it comes to the slow fade-out on the embrace. I'd run at him and kiss him, if I were you.'

'I will.'

'Make a flying tackle and utter some such words as "Oh, Monty, darling!"'

'I will.'

'Then get on your toes,' said Lottie Blossom, 'because this'll be him.'

The bell had rung as she spoke. She went to the door and opened it. Gertrude relaxed her tension. For it was not Monty who entered, but Ambrose Tennyson and his brother Reggie.

Reggie was looking keen and intent, the man with much on his mind and no time to waste.

'Where's Monty?' he asked. 'Oh, hullo, young G. You here?'

'Sure,' said Lottie. 'She's waiting for Mr Bodkin. Everything's jake.'

'Scales fallen from her eyes at last?'

'That's right.'

'About time, the silly young juggins,' said Reggie, with cousinly sternness. He dismissed Gertrude and returned to the main issue. 'Where's Monty?'

'Over at Ikey's. He's fixing up your contract, Ammie.'

'What!'

'Yes. I wrestled with him in prayer, and he went off to arrange things. By this time it's probably all settled.'

Ambrose Tennyson swelled like a balloon.

'Lottie!'

He could say no more. He clasped Miss Blossom to his waistcoat. Reggie tut-tutted.

'Yes, yes, yes,' said Reggie, not peevishly, but with a business man's impatience of the softer emotions. 'But when's he coming back? It is imperative that I see him.'

'What do you want to see him about?'

'I want to see him, and that without delay, about a certain ... Good Lord! There it is all the time, staring me in the face. Gertrude,' said Reggie crisply, 'kindly slip me over the Mickey Mouse you're dandling on your knee.'

His conduct during the voyage and in particular his most offensive attitude in the Customs sheds had left Gertrude Butterwick almost totally devoid of that warm affection towards Reggie which one likes to see in a girl towards her near relatives. These words did nothing to restore it.

'I won't!' she cried.

Reggie's foot tapped the carpet.

'Gertrude, I require that mouse.'

'Well, you're not going to get it.'

'What on earth do you want it for?' asked Ambrose with that slight brusqueness so often noticeable in an elder brother when addressing his junior.

Reggie's manner became guarded. He looked like a young ambassador being requested to reveal secrets of state.

'I can't tell you that. My lips are sealed. But there are wheels within wheels, and I must have it.'

Gertrude's mouth tightened. So did her grip on the object in dispute.

'This is Monty's mouse,' she said, 'and I'm going to give it back to him. Then he'll give it back to me.'

'And then I can have it?' asked Reggie, as one willing to accept a compromise.

'No!'

'Tchah!' said Reggie. It was not an expression he often used, but it seemed to him that the situation called for it. And as he spoke the door-bell rang.

Lottie Blossom had advised Gertrude Butterwick to run at Monty, when he appeared, and kiss him, and this was what she did the moment the door opened. Though she would have preferred the sacred scene to have taken place in private, she did not scamp her work because of the presence of an audience. She kissed Monty and broke into a torrent of remorseless eloquence. At the same time, Reggie asked Monty if he could have that mouse, and Ambrose and Lottie asked him if he had brought his negotiations with Mr Llewellyn to a satisfactory conclusion. All this confused Monty, and he had been quite considerably confused already.

It was Lottie who was the first to perceive that the subject was gasping for air.

'Lay off him, can't you,' she urged. 'One at a time, darn it. All right, Buttersplosh,' she said, for she was a fair-minded girl and recognized Love's prior claim, 'you have the floor. Only keep it snappy.'

'Monty, darling,' said Gertrude, bending tenderly over the chair into which he had sunk, 'I understand everything.'

'Oh, ah?' said Monty mistily.

'Miss Blossom has told me.'

'Oh?' said Monty.

'I love you.'

'Ah?' said Monty.

Reggie advanced.

'Right,' he said briskly. 'She loves you. That's that. Now, Monty, old man, shifting to the subject of Mickey Mice ...'

'What about Ambrose's contract?' asked Lottie.

A spasm of pain passed over Monty's face.

'Has he signed it?'

'No.'

'What!'

'No. He says he won't.'

'Won't?'

Lottie gazed at Ambrose. Ambrose gazed at Lottie. Their eyes were round with consternation.

'But, good heavens!' cried Ambrose, 'I thought –'

'But, sweet suffering soup-spoons!' cried Lottie. 'You told me –'

'I know.'

'You said you would tell Ikey you would sign up with him –'

'I know. But he doesn't want me either.'

'What!'

'I am not at liberty,' said Reggie, resuming his remarks, 'to disclose why I require this Mickey Mouse, my lips being sealed, but –'

'He doesn't want you, either?'

'No.'

'I don't understand,' said Gertrude. 'Were you going to sign a contract to go to Hollywood?'

'I was, yes.'

'But, Monty, darling, how could you have gone to Hollywood? You're working for Mr Pilbeam and his Inquiry Agency.'

Again, that spasm of pain passed over Monty's face.

'No longer. I've resigned.'

'Resigned?'

'Yes. I sent Pilbeam a wireless after you gave me the bird that night.'

'Monty!'

Ambrose, Lottie, and Reggie spoke.

'But Llewellyn definitely told me –'

'But Ikey was running around in circles, begging people to persuade you –'

'This Mickey Mouse –'

'But, Monty,' gasped Getrude, 'do you mean to say you are out of a job again?'

'Yes.'

'But if you haven't a job we can't get married. Father won't let us.'

Reggie rapped the table.

'Gertrude!'

'Well, what do *you* want?'

'I want you,' said Reggie, controlling himself with an effort, 'to stop talking rot. You are cluttering up the debate with frivolous issues and taking Monty's mind off the things that really matter. Your father won't let you get married? I never heard such bilge. Do you seriously expect us to believe that in these enlightened days a girl gives a hoot for what her father says?'

'I can't marry without father's consent.'

'So!' Reggie's voice was withering. 'So you will allow Monty's happiness to depend on the whim of my pop-eyed uncle John!'

'Don't call father your pop-eyed uncle John!'

'I certainly shall. He *is* my pop-eyed uncle John. If he's not,' said Reggie, reasoning keenly, 'whose pop-eyed uncle John is he? Except Ambrose's.'

'What are you talking about?' asked Ambrose, roused by the sound of his name from the dark reverie into which he had been plunged.

Reggie turned to him as if glad to be able to converse with a reasonable being.

'Well, I appeal to you, old man. Here's this ghastly young Gertrude saying that she won't marry Monty unless uncle John gives his consent. Is that loony, or is it loony?'

'It would kill father if I married without his consent.'

'Rot!'

'It's not rot. Father's got a weak heart.'

'Utter rot!'

'It's not utter rot.'

'It is utter rot, and if there were not ladies present I would characterize it even more strongly. Weak heart forsooth! The old blister's got both the face and the physique of a carthorse.'

'Father has not got a face like a carthorse.'

'Pardon me –'

'Listen,' said Lottie Blossom. 'I don't want to horn in on a family argument, and I'd love to know what your father really looks like, but there's someone ringing at the door, and I move that we postpone the discussion till we've found out who it is.'

Ambrose was nearest the door. He opened it in a distrait manner, for he was back in his reverie again.

Mabel Spence entered, followed by Ivor Llewellyn.

# Chapter 24

In the demeanour of Mr Llewellyn, as he came tripping into
the room, there was no trace of that mental and physical col-
lapse which he had exhibited at the telephone. It had been but
a passing weakness, and it was over. Presidents of large motion-
picture corporations are tough and resilient. They recuperate
quickly. You might make Ivor Llewellyn turn purple, but you
could not quench his gallant spirit. He was a man who knew
how to take it as well as dish it out. Through years of arduous
training he had acquired the ability to assimilate the blows of
Fate and then rise on stepping-stones of his dead self and by
his genius turn disaster into victory.

This was what he had come to do now. A hasty conference
with Mabel, and his plans were formed, his schemes perfected.
The fact that they would involve a complete reversal of his
policy of grinding rattlesnakes beneath his heel and that the
first thing he would have to do would be to conciliate these
rattlesnakes and fraternize with them, did not trouble him. No
motion-picture magnate is ever troubled by the *volte-face*.

'Hello, there, Mr Bodkin,' he boomed benignantly, firing the
first gun of his campaign.

So engulfed was Monty at the moment in his personal Slough
of Despond that only some very novel and surprising happening could have jerked him out of it. This change for the cheerier
in Mr Llewellyn's manner did so. He stared, amazed.

'Oh, hullo,' he said.

'Say, listen, Mr Bodkin, I've an explanation to make to you.'
Mr Llewellyn paused. His attention seemed to have been mo-
mentarily diverted. 'Say, that's cunning,' he said, pointing.
'That mouse. Yours?'

'It belongs to Miss Butterwick.'

'I don't think I've had the pleasure of meeting Miss Butterwick.'

276

'Oh, sorry. Miss Butterwick, my fiancée, Mr Llewellyn.'

'How do you do?'

'How do you do?' said Gertrude.

'Both the Mr Tennysons I know, and of course Lottie. Well, well,' said Mr Llewellyn genially, 'looks like we were all friends here, eh? Ha, ha.'

'Ha, ha,' said Monty.

'Ha, ha,' said Gertrude.

Lottie, Ambrose, and Reggie did not say 'Ha, ha,' but Mr Llewellyn appeared satisfied with the 'Ha, ha's' he had got. He seemed to feel that he had now placed matters on a chummy basis all round. He beamed a little more, and then allowed his smile to fade out, leaving behind it a grave, concerned look.

'Say, listen, Mr Bodkin. I was saying I had an explanation to make to you. It's this way. After you'd left my office, my sister-in-law here blew in and I told her of our little conversation, and what she said made me look at the thing from a new angle. Listening to her, it suddenly occurred to me that you might have thought I was serious when I handed you that line of talk. And I felt mighty bad about it. Got all worked up, didn't I, Mabel?'

'Yes,' said Mabel Spence. Not as a rule a 'yes-girl', she knew that there were times when 'yessing' was essential.

'I'll say I was worked up,' proceeded Mr Llewellyn. 'The last thing in the world I expected was that you'd take all that stuff seriously. I thought you'd have been on to it right away that I was just kidding. Sure! Ribbing, we call it over here. When you've been on this side a little longer, you'll get used to our American kidding. Well, gee!' said Mr Llewellyn, in honest surprise, 'the idea that you'd really think I'd switched right around and didn't want you with the S.-L. never so much as crossed my mind till Mabel made me see it. No, sir, I don't blow hot and cold that way. You can't make money in my business if you don't know your own mind better than that. When I come to a decision, that decision stays come to.'

Monty was aware of a constriction at the heart. He gulped. He was not a young man of swift perceptions, but there was

277

that in the other's words which had caused him to tremble with a sudden hope.

'Then you –'

'Eh?'

'Then you *do* want me to come to Hollywood?'

'Why, sure,' said Mr Llewellyn heartily.

'And Ambrose?' said Lottie Blossom.

'Why, sure,' said Mr Llewellyn, his heartiness undiminished.

'You'll sign a contract?'

'Why, sure. Certainly I will. Any time the boys care to look in at my office. Can't do it here, of course,' said Mr Llewellyn, chuckling amusedly at the quaint idea of signing contracts in hotel sitting-rooms.

Mabel Spence corrected this view.

'Yes, you can,' she said reassuringly, opening her vanity-bag. 'I've Reggie's contract here. Reggie and I can be copying it out while you go on talking, and then you'll be able to sign it before you leave, and everything will be fine.'

Mr Llewellyn ceased to chuckle. He had not intended while he was in this room to allow his cheeriness to go out of high, but at this suggestion a keen observer would have noted a distinct indication in his manner of something not unlike pain.

'That's right, too,' he said.

He spoke not in his former ringing tone, but slowly and huskily, as if something sharp had become embedded in his windpipe. At the same time, he gave his sister-in-law one of those looks which men give a relation by marriage whom they consider to have been deficient in tact.

Mabel Spence did not seem to have observed the look.

'Sure,' she said brightly. 'It only means altering a line or two. You want Mr Bodkin as a production expert and Mr Tennyson as a writer. Watch out for that, Reggie, when you come to the places.'

'Quite,' said Reggie, 'Production expert ... Writer. I get you.'

'Then the only other thing,' said Mabel, 'is terms. I mean, the penalty clauses and all that we can just copy out as they stand.'

'Yes,' said Reggie.

'Yes,' said Ambrose.

278

'Yes,' said Mr Llewellyn. He still seemed to be troubled by that substance in his windpipe.

'I would suggest –'

'Say, listen –'

'Well, no need to argue about Ambrose,' Reggie pointed out. 'We're all straight there, what? He gets fifteen hundred, as per previous arrangement.'

'Of course. And Mr Bodkin –?'

'How about a thousand? Nice round sum, you remember we agreed.'

'Say, listen,' said Mr Llewellyn, with a quaver in his voice, 'a thousand's a lot of money. I only pay my wife's cousin Genevieve three hundred and fifty, and she's a very valuable girl ... And there's a depression on ... And things don't look any too good in the picture business ...'

'Oh, make it a thousand,' said Reggie, impatient of hair-splitting. 'You're willing to take a thousand, Monty?'

'Yes.' Monty, like Mr Llewellyn, was not quite normal about the windpipe. 'Yes, I'll take a thousand.'

'Right. Then everything's settled. Let's get at it.'

The two scribes withdrew to the writing-table, and their departure from the centre of things brought about a lull in the conversation. The realization that, owing to the officiousness of his sister-in-law, a girl whom he had never liked, he would have to sign these contracts before getting the mouse, instead of getting the mouse and then refusing to sign any contracts whatsoever, had induced in Mr Llewellyn a quiet, pensive mood. And as none of the others seemed to have anything to say that called for immediate utterance, silence fell – a silence broken only by a scratching of pens to which Mr Llewellyn tried not to listen.

Reggie and Mabel were both quick writers. It was not long before they were able to rise with their task completed and place the results before the party of the first part.

'Here's a pen,' said Mabel.

'And here's where you sign,' said Reggie. 'Where my thumb is.'

'But don't sign the thumb,' said Mabel. 'Ha, ha.'

'Ha, ha,' said Reggie.

They were both delightfully jolly and breezy about the whole thing, and their gaiety seemed to burn into Ivor Llewellyn's soul like vitriol. His suffering as he affixed his signature was indeed so manifest that Mabel Spence's heart was touched. She determined that sunshine should now enter his life in compensation for the rain which had been falling into it.

'That certainly is a cute mouse, Miss Butterwick,' she said, and Mr Llewellyn shook with emotion and made a blot. 'You wouldn't part with it, would you?'

'Good Lord, no!' cried Monty, shocked.

'Oh, I couldn't,' said Gertrude.

Mabel nodded.

'I was afraid not,' she said. 'I was hoping we could get that mouse for Josephine, Ikey.'

'Oh, yeah?' said Mr Llewellyn guardedly. This was the first he had heard of Josephine.

'Ikey,' explained Mabel, 'has a little crippled niece, and she had set her heart on a Mickey Mouse.'

Gertrude stirred uneasily. Monty stirred uneasily. Mr Llewellyn stirred hopefully. He did not like Mabel, but he liked her work. He gazed at her with a sudden sharp admiration. That 'crippled'. Exactly the touch the treatment needed to make it box-office.

'Crippled?' said Monty.

'Crip-pippled?' said Gertrude.

'She was run over by a car last year.'

'A Rolls-Royce,' said Mr Llewellyn, who liked to do things well.

'And she has been on her back ever since. Ah, well,' said Mabel, with a sigh, 'I must go and hunt round the stores. Though I'm afraid they won't have just the right thing. It's so difficult to get exactly the kind she wants. You know how fanciful children are when they are ill and suffering –'

'She has golden hair,' said Mr Llewellyn.

'Monty,' said Reggie, who knew that his employer liked Service and Cooperation, 'are you going to be such a low-down hound as to withhold that mouse from this poor blighted child?'

'And blue eyes,' said Mr Llewellyn.

'Monty!' cried Gertrude appealingly.

'Absolutely,' said Monty.

'Of course she must have it, poor little thing,' said Gertrude. 'I wouldn't dream of keeping it.'

'Well spoken, my young hockey-knocker,' said Reggie cordially, if perhaps a little patronizingly.

'You're sure?' said Mabel.

'Of course, of course,' said Gertrude, who had been eyeing Reggie in a rather unpleasant manner. 'Here it is, Mr Llewellyn.'

It was plainly something of a wrench for her to part with the precious object, and a really nice-minded man might have accepted it with a certain show of reluctance and hesitation. Mr Llewellyn snatched at it like a monkey jumping for a coconut. The next moment, he was backing towards the door, as if fearful of second thoughts.

At the door, he seemed to realize that he had fallen a little short of polish and courtesy.

'Well, say . . .' he began.

It is probable that he was meditating a stately speech of thanks. But the words would not come. He stood for an instant, beaming uncertainly. Then he was gone. And as the door closed behind him, the telephone rang.

Reggie went to answer it.

'Hullo? . . . Right. Send him up. Albert Peasemarch below,' he said, 'demanding audience.'

Monty smote his brow.

'Good Lord! I never tipped him! and I was in his stateroom half the voyage.'

In the interval which elapsed between the announcing of Albert Peasemarch and the appearance of Albert Peasemarch in the flesh, an informal debate took place in the sitting-room concerning the ethics of the thing. Lottie Blossom was anti-Peasemarch. She maintained that if this line of behaviour was to be allowed to continue and develop – if, that was to say, stewards of ocean liners were to be permitted to pursue forgetful clients to New York hotels, it would not be long before they started hunting them all over America with dogs. Reggie, more charitable, said that justice was justice and Monty ought to have slipped the fellow something. Monty was busy trying to secure two fives for a ten.

On Albert Peasemarch's face, when he finally entered, there was the old, familiar look of respectful reproach. He gazed at Monty as at an erring son.

'Sir,' he said.

'I know, I know.'

'It was not a right thing for you to have gone and done, sir –'

All idea of trying to get two fives for his ten had now left Monty. Looking into those reproachful eyes, hearing that reproachful voice, he burned with shame and remorse. It was with the ten in his hand that he now bounded upon Albert Peasemarch.

'I know, I know,' he said. 'You're quite right. It beats me how I came to forget. I had a lot on my mind. Here you are.'

At the sight of the bill, Albert Peasemarch's austerity seemed momentarily to melt.

'Thank you, sir.'

'Not at all.'

'Very generous of you, sir.'

'Not a bit.'

'I am much obliged for the gift and the kind thought behind it,' said Albert Peasemarch. He folded the bill and slipped it into his sock. 'I wasn't expecting this, and it's made it difficult for me to speak as I ought to speak. Nevertheless, sir, I feel constrained to do so. As I was saying, sir, it was not a right thing for you to have gone and done. A thing's either right, or it's not right, and if it's not right it's a man's duty, especially if he feels as kindly disposed towards the bloke in question as I, if I may say so, do towards you, wishing you well and hoping to see you prosperous and successful –'

There were very few people in the world capable of damming Albert Peasemarch when in full flood, but most fortunately one of these happened to be in the room at this moment.

'Hoy!' said Lottie Blossom.

'Miss?'

Lottie was severe.

'What's the idea, you poor fish,' she demanded warmly, 'coming butting in here on a pleasant gathering of friends and shooting your head off? What do you think this is? Some sort of a hall you've hired? Or Commencement Day, with you delivering the valedictory address?'

'I fail to follow you, miss.'

'Well, let's put it this way. Who let you loose? What are you here for? Why the speech? And when do you propose to give us some idea of what you're talking about?'

Her manner pained Albert Peasemarch.

'Mr Bodkin knows what I'm talking about, miss.'

'Do you?' asked Lottie, turning to Monty.

'No,' said Monty. 'I was just wondering.'

'Come, come, sir,' said Albert Peasemarch. 'Look in your heart, sir.'

'Look in my –?'

'Examine your conscience. We all know,' said Albert Peasemarch, dropping easily into his stride once more, 'that there are things a gentleman does not want mentioned in the presence of others, but that is very different from saying you don't know what I'm talking about. Look in your heart, sir. Read its message. Think, sir . . . Reflect –'

'Steward,' said Lottie.

'Miss?'

'Mr Llewellyn has just given Mr Tennyson a five-year contract to go to Hollywood and write scenarios for him, and Mr Tennyson and I are getting married almost immediately.'

'I'm delighted, miss.'

'You should be. Because it's the one thing that's stopping me giving you a sock on the side of the head which you would remember for the rest of your life. If I wasn't feeling so happy, you'd be on your way to the hospital right now. Now, listen, steward. Will you tell us – get this, steward – in a few simple words – mark that clause – what it is that you are trying to get off that fat chest of yours?'

Albert Peasemarch, always a Bayard of courtesy towards the opposite sex, inclined his head.

'Certainly, miss, if Mr Bodkin has no objection.'

'I'd enjoy it,' said Monty.

'Then, miss, I am alluding to Mr Bodkin's questionable action in endeavouring to smuggle a valuable pearl necklace through the New York Customs without paying duty on it as prescribed by law.'

'What!'

'Yes, miss.'

'Is that true?' said Lottie.

'Certainly not,' said Monty. 'The man's loony.'

'Then perhaps,' said Albert Peasemarch, with quiet triumph, 'you will explain, sir, what it was doing inside of that Mickey Mouse what you gave me to wrap up into a brown paper parcel last night.'

'What!'

'That is what I said, sir – What? Last night,' said Albert Peasemarch, addressing the company at large, 'Mr Bodkin here rang his bell for his steward and sent him to request me to come to his state-room, and when I came Mr Bodkin said, "Peasemarch," and I said, "Sir?" and Mr Bodkin said, "Peasemarch, I have here a plush Mickey Mouse what I'd be obliged if you would wrap up into a brown paper parcel," and I said, "Certainly, sir," and I took it away to wrap it, and I hadn't hardly started doing so when I says to myself, "Hullo!" I said, "there's something inside of this mouse," and investigation proved that my surmise was correct, for I unscrewed the animal's head and there was this valuable pearl necklace to which I've been alluding. "Ho!" I said to myself. I was astonished, sir,' said Albert Peasemarch, looking at Monty like a governess. 'Astonished and grieved.'

'But, dash it –'

'Yes, sir,' repeated Albert Peasemarch firmly. 'Astonished and grieved.'

'But, dash it, I know nothing –'

Reggie felt compelled to intervene.

'The matter is – what's that expression of yours? – the matter is susceptible of a ready explanation, old man. This necklace belongs to old Llewellyn. In return for certain concessions I agreed to smuggle it through for him. Watching you screwing off and screwing on the head of that mouse that night we chatted in your state-room gave me the idea for –'

'And that,' said Mabel, 'is why Ikey wanted the mouse so badly just now.'

Albert Peasemarch seemed uninterested in these exchanges.

'Yes, sir,' he resumed, 'I said to myself, "Ho!" and I was astonished and grieved, because smuggling is contrary to the law and I wouldn't have thought it of you, sir. So I said to myself –'

'Never mind what you said to yourself,' interposed Lottie. 'What did you do with the thing?'

'There is a strict rule, which every member of the corps of stewards is enjoined to obey, miss, which says that all valuables found or discovered by them must be took at once to the purser and placed in his charge.'

'Gosh!' said Lottie.

She turned to the others, and read in their eyes that the word summed up their feelings, too.

Mabel was the first to speak.

'Poor old Ikey!'

Reggie endorsed this view.

'Quite. I don't say Pop Llewellyn is a man I would ever choose to go on a long walking tour with, but one feels a pang of pity.'

'He'll have to pay duty, after all,' said Mabel.

'Ikey can afford to pay duty,' argued Lottie.

'Sure. But Grayce told him not to. That's where the trouble is. I'm afraid this is going to stir Grayce up quite a little. You know what she's like.'

Lottie nodded. Mrs Ivor Llewellyn was no stranger to her.

'She's quite apt to rush off and get a Paris divorce.'

'That's true.'

'And another aspect of the matter,' Reggie pointed out, 'is that Pop Llewellyn on learning the news may quite easily explode. These men of full habit, as I dare say you know, frequently spin round and hand in their dinner pails under the influence of a sudden shock. They get what are called strokes. They clutch at their throats and keel over.'

'That's true,' said Lottie.

'So they do,' said Mabel.

'I should say,' said Reggie judiciously, 'that when Llewellyn discovers that he has given me a contract to superintend his English sequences and Ambrose a contract to write scenarios and Monty a contract to be a production expert – all at extremely high salaries – all for five years – and all for nothing, something in the nature of spontaneous combustion would supervene.'

'So I said to myself, "Ho!"' proceeded Albert Peasemarch, enabled by the silence that followed these remarks to secure the floor again. ' "Ho!" I said to myself. And then I thought for a bit and I said to myself, "H'm!" And then I thought for a bit more, and I said to myself, "Yes," I said. "I'll do it," I said to myself. "I wouldn't do it for everyone," I said to myself, "but I'll do it for Mr Bodkin, because he has always proved himself to be a pleasant, agreeable young gentleman, the sort of young gentleman a man likes to do a good turn for." So the upshot and outcome of it all was that I didn't take that necklace to the purser, as enjoined by the strict rule. I just slipped it into my pocket, and here it is.'

So saying, he produced from his trousers pocket a pencil, a ball of string, a piece of indiarubber, threepence in bronze, the necklace, a packet of chewing gum, two buttons and a small cough lozenge, and placed them on the table. He picked up the pencil, the ball of string, the piece of indiarubber, the threepence, the chewing gum, the buttons and the lozenge, and returned them to store.

It was some moments before any of those present were able to speak. Monty was the first to break the silence.

'Golly!' said Monty. 'I wish you could get the stuff over here.'

'What stuff, darling?' asked Gertrude.

'Champagne,' said Monty. 'To me, the situation seems to call for about six bottles of the best. I mean to say, you and I are fixed up, Ambrose and Miss Blossom are fixed up, Reggie and Miss Spence are fixed up, and I intend shortly to present Albert Peasemarch, ass though he is in many respects, with a purse of gold. But what mars the whole binge is that we've nothing to wash it down with but ginger ale. In America,' he explained to Gertrude, 'they have a foul thing called prohibition, which prevents –'

Lottie was staring at him, amazed that there should exist a man so ignorant of the facts of Life.

'You poor sap, they repealed prohibition ages ago.'

'They did?' Monty was stunned. 'Nobody told me.'

'Sure. If you go to that phone and call Room Service, you can get all the champagne you want.'

For a moment, Monty stood where he was, still dazed. Then he walked with a firm step to the telephone.

'Room Service!' he said.